Boston Public

D0422778

DEATH IN A FUNHOUSE MIRROR

Forge Books by Kate Flora

Chosen for Death
Death in a Funhouse Mirror

DEATH IN A
FUNHOUSE
MIRROR

Kate Flora

A TOM DOHERTY ASSOCIATES BOOK □ NEW YORK

Roslindale Branch Library
4238 Washington Street
Roslindale, MA 02131-2517

RO BR
FLORA
K

This is a work of fiction. All the characters and events portrayed in this novel are either fictitious or are used fictitiously.

DEATH IN A FUNHOUSE MIRROR

Copyright © 1995 by Kate Clark Flora

All rights reserved, including the right to reproduce this book, or portions thereof, in any form.

This book is printed on acid-free paper.

A Forge Book
Published by Tom Doherty Associates, Inc.
175 Fifth Avenue
New York, N.Y. 10010

Forge® is a registered trademark of Tom Doherty Associates, Inc.

Library of Congress Cataloging-in-Publication Data

Flora, Kate Clark.
    Death in a funhouse mirror / Kate Flora.
        p.   cm.
    "A Tom Doherty Associates book."
    ISBN 0-312-85600-8
    I. Title.
PS3556.L5838D4   1995   95-34739
813'.54—dc20   CIP

First Edition: November 1995

Printed in the United States of America

0 9 8 7 6 5 4 3 2 1

This book is for Karin Knudsen Rector and Pamela Boggs Franicevich, my first writing group, who have, together, given me seventy-five years of friendship and support.

ACKNOWLEDGMENTS

Thanks to all the people who helped me make this a better book: Former Concord Police Chief Carl Johnson, for detailed criticism, comma excision, and professional advice; my readers, Christy Bond, Christy Hawes, Professors Frances Miller and Richard Parker, Dr. Jacqueline Olds, Diane Englund, Jack Nevison, Nancy McJennett, Loretta Smith, Emily Cohen and A. Carman Clark, who were so generous with their time and advice; to Thea's mentor, Margaret Milne Moulton; to Robert Moll for the picture; to my friend Melinda Brooks for directing my reading on women and psychology—any errors are my own; to Bill Plauger, for helping me become more computer literate, and bailing me out when I am not; to my husband, Ken, and sons Jake and Max, for their patience; to the great guys at Gateway, who keep sending those cow boxes. And of course, to my agent, Carol McCleary, who believes that no means yes or at least, "Let's talk again tomorrow"; and my editor, Claire Eddy, who mothers me gently while pushing me to make it better.

CHAPTER 1

I LOOKED OVER the top of my book at Andre, asleep in his lounge chair, looking gorgeous and ridiculous in the tiny red bathing suit that had been the reason it took us from nine o'clock, when we woke up, until almost eleven to get from the bedroom out to the deck. It was the kind of suit I used to look at in stores and laugh, unable to imagine anybody wearing one. In fact, I had laughed when he came out of the bathroom wearing it, until he pointed out that my bikini bottom was even briefer. I disagreed, and we ended up standing in front of the mirror, hip to hip, comparing.

For us, getting that close is always dangerous. There are a lot of things we disagree about. He's a cop, a Maine state trooper, and I'm a consultant to independent schools. Sometimes I find him too rigid, too judgmental, or so distracted by his work—he's a homicide detective—that he's completely unavailable. He says I'm too impetuous, and too prim—an unlikely combination, if you ask me, but that's what he says—and I also have an incurable tendency to get wrapped up in my work. We don't live together. We don't even live in the same state, which may help us get along despite our differences, but when it comes to our physical relationship, we have no disagreements. So, even though we'd planned to have breakfast out on the deck and spend the morning reading, we'd gotten sidetracked.

Staring at that little bathing suit had naturally led to staring at his body. I'd always assumed those small, revealing suits were for slight men, or men with the exaggerated vee shapes of models. Andre isn't built like that. He has what I think of as a sturdy body. Not stocky, he doesn't have an ounce of fat, but he has a substantial presence, nice strong legs, and a comfortably hairy chest. It's okay with me. I like substantial men. I'm no peanut myself. If I were a frightened crime victim, Andre Lemieux is exactly the kind of cop I'd want to show up and protect me, strong and kind and comforting. If I were a bad guy, I'd sit up nights praying that he never came after me. There's something about the hard glare in his eyes, and a subdued anger that emanates from him, that tells you how much he hates the bad guys and makes you sure he'll get them in the end. I'd been on the receiving end of his inquisitorial technique when my sister Carrie was killed. I knew how tough he could be.

The "in the mirror" comparison eventually led to the conclusion that we had to take the suits off to compare them properly, and since we hadn't seen each other for three weeks, that naturally led to other things. We concluded with a frantic raid on the refrigerator instead of the genteel breakfast I'd envisioned, and now we were out on the deck of my new condo, where we could look past a patch of green lawn onto a delicious expanse of blue water, just like the real estate ad had promised.

Not that Andre was looking at anything. He'd arrived in the night, nearly comatose from exhaustion, announced that he'd finally arrested a suspect in his latest homicide and fallen asleep with his clothes on. Once we made it out to the deck, he hadn't even pretended he was going to read, just lay down in the chair, let me cover him with sunscreen, and asked to be turned in an hour. Andre the human steak.

I wasn't doing much better. My mind was so bleary from another frantic week of work that I had passed up the serious book I was reading and was dithering over a piece of bodice-buster trash. So far, the characters in the book had nothing on us. I kept losing my place and couldn't keep the players straight. All the women were bubbleheaded and gorgeous, even the ones who were supposed to be executives, and all the men were studly and smoldering. Their lives were so sexually supercharged no one could even buy a pair of socks without someone of the opposite sex staring intently at their trembling cleavage with knowing blue eyes. Their dialogue had been written by a third-grader. I stuck with it for a while, since my mother, who is no bubblehead, had suggested I'd like it, but familiarity bred contempt. I stuffed it under my chair and went around to the front to get the paper.

The headlines were the usual mix of financial scandals, the president's grandstanding in the international forum while the country went to hell, and the latest sensational murder. I often skip the front page, unless there's a story relating to education, but there was something about today's murder that caught my eye. A prominent woman psychologist, a so-called "founding mother" of the movement for introducing the woman's perspective into psychology, had been stabbed to death in Anson while she was out walking her dog. Gripping the paper, I dropped into my chair and read the story.

The woman, Helene Streeter, age fifty-three, had been on the staff of Bartlett Hill, a well-known private psychiatric hospital. Her husband, Clifford Paris, was head of the childrens' outpatient unit there. According to neighbors, it had been Ms. Streeter's custom to walk the family dog in the evenings after supper, often accompanied by Mr. Paris. When Ms. Streeter did not return from her walk, her husband had gone out looking for her. He had found her lying in the shadow of a hedge a few houses away. A trail of blood on the sidewalk indicated that she had crawled some distance before collapsing. She was rushed to Mt. Lucas Hospital, where she died from multiple stab wounds. A hunting knife, possibly the murder weapon, was found on the lawn of a house several blocks away.

The story continued, but I'd read enough. I folded up the paper with shaking ink-smudged fingers and stuffed it under a pot of geraniums so it wouldn't blow away. Most stories of violence and death occur under circumstances so remote from everyday life that they don't touch us. We read them, tut-tut about the state of things, and move on. This one was different. I hadn't seen much of them lately, but I knew Helene Streeter and I knew Clifford Paris. Knew them pretty well. Their daughter, Eve, had been my friend in college, and my roommate for a few years after college, when I was busy being a reporter and a social worker, and she was getting her master's degree in social work. We lived together until she moved to Arizona. Back then, Eve's relationship with her parents had been strained. They still treated her like a child and she still carried an adolescent chip on her shoulder so big it sometimes blocked her vision, but she went through the motions of a dutiful daughter, and that included dinner with her parents. I often went along as a buffer.

In some ways, Eve's estrangement was easy to understand. Like many psychiatrists' children, she had been extremely close to her parents as a child, sometimes, as she'd described it to me, to the exclusion of other children. That closeness had hampered her ability to make a comfortable social adjustment to her peers, and had also created an even greater distance to go when the time came to break away from her parents and become her own person. According to Eve, the struggles had been titanic. Her parents, so respected for their ability to help the troubled, had been completely baffled when it came to their own daughter's behavior. They'd reacted with an impossible combination of rules, restrictions and demands for dialogue to her every attempt to find her own identity. Even something as ordinary as a chaperoned boy-girl party had required a family meeting.

In self-defense, Eve resorted to deception, developing an

agreeable façade which appeared to conform to their wishes while doing exactly as she pleased. It was probably necessary to get her through adolescence, but having to lie made her angry, and the fact that they let her get away with it—these supposedly sensitive, insightful people—made her even angrier. Maybe they saw through it and let it go because it was the only way they could cope. I didn't know. I wasn't around then. By the time I met her, lying to them had become such a habit that she lied even when she didn't have to. After our first dinner with them, when I challenged her about some things that she'd said, Eve had responded, "It's terribly sad, Thea, but I've lied to them so long I'm not sure I'd know how to tell them the truth. Anyway, I don't even think of it as lying anymore. I just tell them what they want to hear and they're satisfied. They deal with so many serious problems every day. It's important to the stability of their world that things are all right with me."

It was so sad. Eve and her family sat around like people hiding behind cardboard cutouts of themselves, looking like the perfect family, and never told each other anything risky. Eve never told her mother, who specialized in treating abused women and children, that her boyfriend, Padraig, was abusive, and she never told her father, who knew a great deal about eating disorders, that she was bulimic. She just struggled along on her own and eventually she cured the bulimia herself and dumped Padraig. Dumping him had not been easy, since in his own perverse, possessive way, he'd loved Eve and didn't want to be discarded, and because Padraig, when he wasn't being abusive, was the most charming man on earth. He'd had hair the color of fire, a lilt in his voice that could woo statues off their pedestals and a passionate way of throwing himself at life that made you want to be swept along. But he'd had a dark side, too—moods of brooding intensity when he blamed everyone but himself for his failure to make it as an artist. Then he would take out his frustration on Eve.

Part of her reason for moving to Arizona was to get away from Padraig. As long as she was near him, she couldn't resist him. It was also to get away from her family. One day at lunch she'd said, "Lying to them is such an established pattern that I can't seem to stop. I hope by going away I can put enough distance between us that when I come back I can deal with them honestly. Maybe I'm deluding myself but that's what I hope." I'd helped her pack everything into the back of her little silver Accord and she'd driven away.

I could still see her face, peering out the window at me, bottom lip caught between her teeth, and little worry lines in her forehead. We were a strange pair. Me, Thea McKusick, tall, green eyed and serious, with my mop of impossibly long, curly hair, and Eve Paris, with her merry, adorable little face, cropped, string-straight hair, and small, strong body. Together we looked like the giant and the dwarf. Eve's bulimia hadn't been a reaction to anything wrong with her body. I guess that's often the case. She had an athletic build, but she was well proportioned and slim. It was just that Helene was so impossibly beautiful that anyone would have had trouble being her daughter. As Eve, one of whose strengths was her blunt self-awareness, once observed, "I can stick my finger down my throat until hell freezes over, and I'll never look like Helene." And now Helene was dead. I hoped Eve had had a chance to establish the kind of relationship with her parents that she wanted. I didn't know.

After Eve left to work on the reservation, I'd met David Kozak, gotten married, and immersed myself in a world of domestic bliss. A year later I read in the paper that Padraig had died in a car accident. I'd written her and sent her the clipping and she'd written back that his death was the loss of an important artistic talent. By the time she came back, David had been killed, and I'd dealt with my grief by becoming a workaholic. We'd had lunch a few times, dinner with her parents once, and spent one pleasant weekend on Cape Cod, but otherwise we hadn't seen each other much. Eve was working with cancer patients, and on the weekends she was doing a lot of cycling and kayaking. She seemed very happy.

It was a beautiful May Saturday. Brilliant sunshine. A fresh cool breeze. It was a day made to be enjoyed, but I couldn't stop thinking about what I'd read. I try to avoid thinking about death and dying. I'm not a depressed or morose person, I've just seen my share of death. It's been more than two and a half years since the car accident that killed David, and almost nine months since my sister Carrie was murdered. Hardly a day goes by when I don't think about them and miss them.

They say that with time a grieving process takes place and you get over things. I know that's true. Most of the time I'm fine. But sometimes, at a certain time of day, when the light slants a certain way, or when I hear a special song, catch a faint whiff of some man's cologne, or glimpse a tall, thin, dark-haired man walking toward me, I still expect to see David. Sometimes, when the phone rings and I hear a girlish, excited voice, I expect it to be Carrie. Then the disappointment, the loneliness, and the pain are just as real, immediate, and sharp as in those first awful days. So I had some idea of how it was going to be for Eve.

Andre put a warm hand on my shoulder. "Penny for your thoughts," he said.

"I was thinking about this," I answered, tugging out the paper and handing it to him. "I knew the woman—the victim. Her daughter is a friend of mine."

He scanned the article quickly and handed it back. "The mysterious stranger lurking in the bushes with a knife, huh? Statistically speaking, it's much more likely she was killed by someone she knew."

"But she knew everybody. And people loved her."

"Only one of them killed her, though, and I doubt that it was the butler."

"No," I said, "they didn't have a butler. A maid, but not a butler. Helene was an ardent feminist. In her world, it would have been the maid who did it. It isn't something we should joke about, though. Poor Eve."

"Eve is the daughter? Your friend?"

"Yes."

"Have you called her?"

"Called her?" It sounded dumb even to me. "Isn't it too soon?"

He shook his head. "She'll need people to talk to. Maybe not right away, but it will help her to know you're there. You understand what she's going through and you're sensible and compassionate. Go on. Go call." He made little motions with his hands, like someone shooing a flock of chickens.

"Don't you start telling me what to do," I said, but it was a pro forma complaint. We both had some expertise in this area and I knew he was right. I could be helpful. I also knew why I was hesitating. I might be able to help Eve, but not without cost to myself. Talking to Eve about her loss would make me think of my own.

His arched eyebrows rose quizzically, giving him a slightly elfin look I find very attractive. That was usually the prelude to a provocative remark, but this time all he said was, "You might bring some sandwiches on your way back out."

"Andre, you just had breakfast."

"I just had you, too, and I never get enough of that, either."

I groaned and went inside to call Eve.

there by two. Will you still be at your father's?"

"Yes, here in Anson. Thank you, Thea. I'll be looking for you." Eve hung the phone up quickly, as though she was afraid I'd change my mind.

I went back out to the deck to tell Andre. He was sitting sideways on the chaise, looking at the water, a pleasant, relaxed look on his face. When he saw me, his expression changed. I sat down beside him and put a hand on his thigh. "Something's wrong."

He shook his head. "It's nothing," and went back to looking at the sea.

"Doesn't look like nothing to me."

He turned around so that he was straddling the chair, facing me. "Okay, you asked," he said. His face was set and he wouldn't meet my eyes. A hard little knot of anxiety formed in my stomach. "I know what we've said about commitment. About not rushing things," he said. "And I understand your reasons. I know all about your defenses." He drew imaginary circles in the air. "The barbed wire here. The stone wall here. The moatful of crocodiles." He drew a fourth ring. "And other intangibles here. I know you're afraid to make another commitment after losing David. I respect that." There was a husky, intimate quality to his voice. He wasn't just talking, he was telling me something. "But three weeks is too long to be without you." He hesitated. "There were nights when I came back to my apartment and sat there alone in the dark and ached for you. For your hand on my shoulder. For you to ask how my day was. Just to look at you." He stopped talking and sat staring at my face. He was wearing his impassive policeman's face now, but his dark eyes were troubled. He didn't seem to know what to say next. He brushed a wayward strand of hair away from my face, his fingers lingering, caressing my cheek. "You are so lovely. Sometimes when I look at you, it takes my breath away."

That did it, of course. I forgot what I'd been about to tell him, forgot about Eve, forgot to be nervous about what he was going to say, and leaned forward into his arms. Having someone talk to me like that takes *my* breath away. I'm constantly being surprised by

CHAPTER 2

I LET THE phone ring eleven times at Eve's apartment, disconnected, and tried her parents' number. Eve answered on the fourth ring, her voice so strained it was almost unrecognizable. I knew how that was, how you had to keep talking to people while your throat was choked with tears, swallowing them and trying to keep going, even though you felt like screaming at everyone to go away and leave you alone. "Eve," I said, "it's Thea. I just heard about Helene. I'm so sorry. Is there any way I can help?"

"Thea? Is that really you?" She sounded like a child lost in a crowd who finally spots someone she knows. "Can you come and stay with me? Here? Today? Please say you'll come. I need you, Thea." She didn't sound anything like the spunky, matter-of-fact woman that I knew. She sounded sad and lost and very scared.

Reluctantly, I kissed all my plans good-bye. The long walk on the beach. An afternoon quickie with Andre. Cold dark beer and a delicious, unhealthy, greasy dinner at the local clam shack. Watching *Bull Durham* for the fourth time. And more Andre. Well, it was his fault, too, insisting that I call. I knew I had to go. I tried to keep the disappointment out of my voice. "Of course I'll come, Eve. As soon as I can." My watch said twelve. "I can be

Andre, by how good he is, and how good he makes me feel. How open and real he can be, despite his infuriating cop's ability to be completely opaque. It's something I never expected to have again.

I'd gone home with my husband, David, the first night we met, and never left again. We'd settled into a blissful happily-ever-after that suited us perfectly, but it only lasted two years, until the night David let an inebriated friend talk him into taking a joy ride in the friend's new car. The friend had wrapped David and the car around a tree, killed David and walked away with a few scratches and a broken arm. When he came to apologize after the funeral, I broke his nose and gave him two black eyes. It made me feel a little better, but for a long time I tried not to feel anything at all, to avoid being hurt again.

I was still prickly as a porcupine when I met Andre, unwilling to risk another relationship. From the start he had challenged my defenses, forcing me to be more honest with myself and more open with him. We had a good thing going—weekends and vacations together while retaining the freedom we both wanted for ourselves and our work. Now it sounded like he was looking for something more and I wasn't sure I was ready.

We ended up back in bed again. Afterwards, in the shower, I told him I had to leave. "I called Eve. She was very upset and Eve's pretty unflappable. She begged me to come and be with her. I told her I'd come this afternoon."

He made a face. "And since I insisted you call, I can't complain, can I? Can I at least come with you? I could answer the door, or help with the dishes. Or make coffee. I make great coffee."

"You'd be bored to death."

"I'd be with you. Besides, in my business, I'm used to being bored. At waiting patiently and watching. It's one of the things I'm good at." It was true, too.

"I didn't want to leave you anyway," I said. "Sure it isn't the lure of a crime scene, and not me, that's drawing you?" I was teasing, but a part of me was curious to see how he'd react to a crime that wasn't on his own patch. He gets as wrapped up in his work as I do.

He splashed water in my face. "Don't be silly," he said, "I'd follow you even if there was no crime."

We dressed quickly and without discussion, Andre in khaki slacks and a blue and white shirt, me in a dark flowered skirt and a white shirt. I pulled my hair back and fastened it with a barrette. We took my car. Andre drives the regulation unmarked Chevy washtub all the state police detectives drive. The State of Maine may think they're okay, but I think they have all the style of a marshmallow squashed by an elephant. I like something a bit more luxurious. I'm a confirmed Saab owner—the last one saved my life—especially since I got my new bright red one with all the fixings. I even have a car phone, which the salesman threw in for free, probably so he could keep me in the showroom and stare at my cleavage longer.

We stopped at a grocery store on the way, both knowing how it can be after a family death, and picked up the supplies Eve and her father might need. Coffee and cream. Coffee cake and dough-nuts. Bread and stuff to make sandwiches. Fresh fruit. And a chicken, for soup. After David died, I was so numb I couldn't even fix myself a meal. My partner, Suzanne, ignoring my protests, bul-lied her way in with a big pot of chicken soup and fed me like a toddler. Before that, I was skeptical about the therapeutic powers of chicken soup. After that, I was a true believer. In Suzanne and the soup.

Eve's parents' house was an imposing brick structure with mock gothic windows, a slate roof, and a round white-pillared portico over the door. It looked like it ought to be set among sev-eral acres of landscaped grounds, but in fact, while it was nicely landscaped, it was sandwiched on a small lot between two other equally imposing piles in radically different styles. One step more elegant than the current trend toward tract mansions, but still too crowded for me. Today the usually quiet, empty street was dotted with cars, and a uniformed officer was stationed by the front door.

I think cops have an instinctive recognition of one another, because he passed Andre with a nod and challenged me. I have a little trouble with authority figures. My back stiffened and my head went up but before I could respond Andre murmured, "Easy, Thea, he's just doing his job."

I substituted a smile for the snarl that was forming. "I'm Thea Kozak. Eve asked me to come." Before he could decide whether or not I was a suitable applicant, the door flew open and Eve hurled herself into my arms. I hugged her, and, keeping one arm tightly around her shoulders, led her back into the house. Andre came behind us with the groceries. I led her straight to the back of the house and into the kitchen. Andre put the bags down and shook her hand, and I put on the kettle for tea.

Eve climbed up on a stool, perching cross-legged on the top like a little imp. Her shiny black cap of hair was tousled, and she was wearing a black and white polka dot sleeveless minidress with a big collar over black bicycle shorts. Her eyes and nose were red, and she'd bitten her lips until they were raw. I took a Chapstick out of my bag and handed it to her. She took it with a smile. "You've been doing this as long as I can remember, Thea. Giving me Chapstick and making me tea. Sometimes I forget how nice it is to have a friend." She cast a quick glance at the door to the dining room. "I think this is the first normal moment I've had all day. The place is crawling with cops."

She looked at Andre, who was putting things in the refrigerator. "No offense, Detective. I'm just not used to it." She shook her head. "I just can't believe it. Helene dead. God! I got there, to the hospital, last night, just in time to see her die. I'm sorry. I guess I should ask, before I just blurt all this stuff out. It's pretty unpleasant. Do you mind?"

"Of course not, Eve. You can say whatever you want."

She tipped her head sideways, like a bright-eyed bird. "In front of him?"

"He's a homicide detective, Eve. He's spent a lot of time in situations like this. It won't make him uncomfortable. It depends on how you feel."

She shook her head, flipping her hair back away from her face, nibbled on a nail, a mass of nervous mannerisms. "Sorry. That wasn't a fair question. I guess I wanted you to read my mind, figure out what it is that I want. Don't mind me, I'm so muddled I couldn't think my way out of a paper bag today. Of course he can stay."

She stared past me toward the bright day outside with unfocused eyes. "I just can't stop thinking about it. She was butchered, Thea. I've never seen so much blood. It was like someone hated her. Wanted to destroy her. He must have stood there and slashed at her, again and again. She had those cuts . . . what do they call them . . . defensive cuts . . . all over her hands and arms. Two of her fingers were nearly cut off. But the Coffeys were home, and the Desjardins, and no one heard anything. No one helped her."

Her voice rose, shrill and strained, on the verge of losing control. "She was only a minute from home. Crawling along the sidewalk leaving a trail of her own blood. It's still out there, all over the sidewalk. Why wasn't Cliff out there with her? Maybe if there had been two of them, it wouldn't have happened." Behind me, the kettle added its own shrill cry to hers. She swayed on her perch and would have fallen if Andre hadn't braced her with his arm. She leaned against him wearily and closed her eyes.

"Do you want to go upstairs, Eve?" I asked. "To your old room?" She nodded. "You might lie down for a while. Andre could take you and I'll be up in a minute with the tea."

"Don't treat me like a child, Thea," she said.

I'd forgotten how touchy she could be. "I never suggested you were," I said. "Sometimes we *all* need taking care of." I gave Andre directions, still not sure whether she was going to cooperate, but she didn't object when he put an arm around her and steered her toward the door, her head resting against his shoulder.

I felt a momentary twinge, seeing him with his arm around another woman, then I stepped on it, hard, and squelched the thought. He probably did it all the time, comforting victims and their relatives.

I put some bread in the toaster, made a pot of tea, and fixed a tray with toast and jam, some fruit, and a sandwich for Andre. A small white dog crept out from under the table and stood by my feet, looking up at me sadly. I patted his head and scratched his ears. "Poor fellow," I said. "No one's paying any attention to you, are they?" I picked up the tray, but he whined and scratched at my foot. I gave him a piece of toast and headed for the stairs.

Ahead of me, I could see a group of men standing in the living room. Cliff Paris was with them. He broke away and met me at the foot of the stairs, resting a warm hand briefly on my shoulder. "Thea, I'm so grateful. It was good of you to come," he said, smiling with his eyes as well as his mouth. "Eve really needs you. She's taking this very hard." Just ordinary words, but it was part of Cliff Paris's magic that he could make a simple thank you seem like a heartfelt compliment. He had a magnetic sort of charm. A way of paying attention that made you feel what you said, the person you were, was the most interesting thing he'd ever experienced. His private patients were devoted to him. I'd found his style unsettling when I was younger, distrustful because it seemed like a highly perfected form of shrinkly caring yet mesmerized because everyone wants to feel as special as Cliff made me feel.

It didn't hurt that he looked like the shrink from central casting. Handsome in a rugged, outdoorsy way. Wavy, graying blond hair and a neatly trimmed beard. Sparkling, shrewd blue eyes surrounded by deeply etched lines that proclaimed him seasoned and experienced. His voice was melodic, caressing, a well-honed tool. Slim, athletic body. Elegant hands with long, tapered fingers. Today he wore carefully pressed designer jeans, a faded indigo cotton sweater, and boat shoes without socks, and his skin was drawn tight over his cheekbones and had a pale, dry cast that made him look years older.

"She was upset and I sent her up to rest. I'm just taking her some tea."

"Great," he said. "Good idea. She hasn't eaten anything all day. Said she couldn't. Who was that who went up with her?"

"My friend Andre Lemieux. He is down from Maine visiting me this weekend, so I brought him along."

He frowned. "You brought a house guest with you?"

I resented what that implied about my judgment. "It's not as incongruous as it sounds, Cliff. He's a homicide detective. He's used to this. He'll probably be better for her than I will."

"I see," was all he said. I had the impression that he didn't like my answer, but he turned away so quickly I couldn't tell and went back to the men in the living room. I couldn't tell whether he looked sad, either. The hair hid his face too well. Maybe that was why he had a beard—to protect his privacy. I went on upstairs with the tray.

Eve was in bed, under the covers, propped up with pillows. Her skin was almost as pale as the pillowcase, and with the big polka-dotted collar and her red nose, she looked like an unhappy clown. Andre was sitting beside her, holding her hand, talking softly. They both smiled when I came in. Eve pulled up her feet and I put the tray at the foot of the bed. I handed her some tea, set her toast on the bedside stand, and curled up at the foot of the bed beside the tray. "I made you a sandwich," I said, handing it to Andre. I took an apple from the tray and bit into it.

The room had the cold, static look that rarely used rooms acquire. Everything was too spare and neat, and the memorabilia saved from Eve's childhood—her horses and the elaborately dressed dolls—was dated and cloying.

Eve stared at her toast like it was something she didn't recognize. "Come on, Eve, you need to eat," I said. She picked it up obediently and started eating. "Cliff says you haven't eaten at all today."

"Cliff," she said bitterly, "has eaten like a horse today. It's obscene. You'd think nothing had happened. He stands down there, greeting everyone in his charming way, smiling that wan, subdued smile, showing only so many millimeters of teeth, the model of genteel bereavement. He's acting like it's an open house, and not the day after his wife's murder. Like her death doesn't matter. You should have seen him last night at the hospital. She'd just died. Not even cold. I was sitting there holding her hand . . ." She took a deep breath and let it out slowly, striving for control, but it didn't work. Her next words were half strangled by sobs. ". . . feeling eviscerated, with all this rage and sadness twirling around inside me, when he announced he st . . . st . . . stood up and announced he was going out walking with Rowan." Overwrought as she was, she spat out the word Rowan like it had an especially vile taste.

"Who is Rowan?" Andre said.

Eve was crying too hard to answer. I took her in my arms and held her tightly, rocking her like a baby. She cried a long time. When the sobs finally died away, she wasn't calm. She started talking, her voice becoming shrill and loud again, like it had downstairs in the kitchen. "She can't be dead, Thea. I'm not ready. I mean, I know sometimes I didn't even like her, I know I resented her for being beautiful and admired, but I always loved her." She clung to me frantically. "She was my mother. What will I do now? I need a mother. I need my mother back. Please! Please! Tell me she's not dead!"

I turned to Andre, who, true to his word, was waiting patiently. "Can you go down to the living room and get Cliff, please? He's the bearded one in blue," I said. "I think she needs a sedative. This isn't doing her any good."

Andre left. I heard his footsteps going down the stairs, and then footsteps coming back. Cliff appeared and stood in the doorway, watching. In my arms, Eve was tossing and moaning, crying for her mother. "I'm sorry, Thea," he said, "I thought you could handle it. I had no idea she was this bad. I'll be right back." He hurried out, the door banging behind him. Andre had followed him in quietly and was standing by the door, watchful and unobtrusive.

Suddenly Eve's raving stopped. "Rowan is my father's lover," she whispered. "That's why he killed my mother." Just as quickly as the clarity had come, it was gone and she was whimpering for her mother again. Cliff came back with a hypodermic, swabbed her bare arm with alcohol, and gave her a shot. She cried out as the needle went in, but almost immediately her body, which had been stiff in my arms, relaxed. I eased her back against the pillows and stood up. "Have a rest, Eve," I whispered.

"How long will she sleep?"

"An hour or two," Cliff said.

"I guess we should go then. When she wakes up, please tell her it's okay to call me anytime. Anytime. I'm sorry about Helene. I don't know what to say . . . I admired her so much. . . ."

Cliff wasn't listening. He stood beside the bed, his shoulders bowed, staring at the syringe in his hand. "Thank you," he said. "I think I'll sit with her a while. Would you tell the gentlemen downstairs?"

"Of course." I picked up the tray. Andre opened the door for me, and we went down to the kitchen together. I stopped in the living room to relay Cliff's message. One of the men, an attractive blond who was rather too delicate for me, said he was leaving and asked one of the others to tell Cliff he'd be back. The others said they'd wait.

I cleaned up the dishes while Andre made a pot of coffee. The smell brought two of the men into the kitchen. Recognizing Andre as one of the brotherhood, they accepted coffee and stopped to chat.

I decided that as long as he was occupied, I'd stay and make the soup. Eve's general demeanor, so unlike her, had upset me. Maybe some nice therapeutic cooking would help. Her revelation about her father, if true, was nothing short of astonishing. But it didn't seem possible. They hadn't been demonstrative, but Helene and Cliff always appeared to have a good relationship. She appreciated his advice and enjoyed his solicitous attentions; he seemed respectful and supportive of her political agenda. From all that Eve had told me, professionally they were both well established and admired. They entertained frequently and seemed to have lots of friends.

I got one of Helene's aprons and tied it on. If they had so many friends, I thought as I cut up the vegetables and threw them in on top of the chicken, why hadn't the phone been ringing? When Carrie died, the phone at my parents' house had screamed like a cat in heat, incessant and demanding. Just about everyone in the neighborhood appeared at the door, offering food and comfort. Where were the neighbors? Were they too intimidated by the policeman at the door? Except for the men in the living room, two of whom had turned out to be cops, this house was quiet. I threw in a bayleaf and a handful of salt, turned the flame to simmer, and put the lid on the pot. I chopped up some more vegetables to go in the finished soup, wiped down the counter, and went to see what the guys were up to.

In the breakfast alcove, where they were having coffee, I sat down beside Andre. He put an arm around me and pulled me close. "Thea Kozak, Detective Steve Meagher and Detective Dom Florio." We shook hands. I hadn't spent enough time around the police yet to recognize them. When Andre and I were together, we mostly kept to ourselves. If I'd seen Florio on the street, I would have assumed he was an accountant. He was tall, middle-aged, graying and unexceptional. His hair was receding and his eyes were hidden by glasses. A second look showed me that behind them were piercing, intelligent eyes. Meagher I would have taken for a bodybuilder. He was thick necked and muscular, with arms that bulged out of his short-sleeved shirt and a massive chest. He had gold chains around his neck and glossy dark hair cut short on top and long and wavy in the back. He would have been handsome if he hadn't looked chronically dissatisfied. I could tell they'd been telling war stories because the conversation died as soon as I joined them. "Don't let me disturb you guys," I said, "just pretend I'm a fly on the wall."

Meagher leaned forward with a predatory grin. "Honey," he said, "it would be hard not to notice you."

"Thea," I said.

He looked puzzled. "What?"

"My name is Thea, not Honey."

Andre gave me one of his looks, the one that says "put a lid on it, Thea, sometimes you have to compromise to get along with people." I ought to know that look. It has preceded many of our less harmonious discussions. I usually explain that I know how to keep my mouth shut when it advances my own interests, and he usually explains that it would be helpful if I'd occasionally consider doing it to advance his interests. Or just to make his life easier. Sometimes now I even cooperate, because I know he's right, but for sexist jerks like Meagher, I won't.

We don't really need to have the discussion anymore, we just give each other the looks. It's kind of like that old joke about the prison where there is only one joke book in the library and everyone reads it. The inmates are so familiar with them they don't bother to tell them anymore, they just refer to them by number and everyone laughs. One day at dinner, a new guy who's just read the book says a number and no one laughs. One old timer says to another, "Some people just don't know how to tell a joke." Andre and I are at the point where we just need to say the numbers.

Meagher didn't notice the exchange anyway. He'd given my face a quick once-over and settled his eyes on my chest like a hungry man staring at someone else's sandwich. We all chatted for a while, Meagher addressing all his remarks to my chest. Finally, he slid his coffee cup toward me. "Any more coffee, hon . . . Thea?"

Andre picked up the cup before I could answer. "I make the coffee on this team," he said. "The stuff she makes would take the enamel off your teeth. Black?" Meagher nodded. "You want some, Dom?"

Florio smiled. "I'm fine, thanks," he said. "I was just thinking about asking this young lady for the recipe for that soup. Sure smells good." He had a pleasant, engaging smile that was probably very effective getting nervous witnesses to trust him. I liked him. Like Andre, he had a patient, watchful quality. He struck me as someone who would listen and observe, think about what he'd learned, and come to understand the situation. Meagher, on the other hand, was impatient, the type to bull his way through things, pushing people and demanding answers. I didn't have to like Meagher to admit they probably made a good team.

Behind the Clark Kent glasses, Florio's quick blue eyes missed nothing. He'd caught the whole interplay between me and Andre, and I was willing to bet he could summarize my opinion of Meagher better than I could. Right now I was getting the full benefit of those assessing eyes. "How do you know Eve Paris?" he asked.

It was irrational since he was obviously a detective on the case, too, but I didn't want to talk about Eve in front of Meagher. "I have to check the soup," I said.

"Would you mind if I tagged along and asked you some questions?"

"Not at all." Florio followed me back to the stove and stayed there, lounging against the butcher block island, as comfortable as if he watched people cook every day of his life. I set a colander on top of a stockpot, dumped in the chicken and vegetables, and put the strained broth back on the stove, putting the burner on high to reduce it and make it richer. I flicked on the fan to pull the steam out of the kitchen. As I worked, I answered his questions about how I knew Eve, Helene and Cliff. While the chicken cooled, I put the carrots, celery and onions I'd cut up in a glass dish with some melted butter, and threw them into the microwave.

"You're going to put those in the soup?" he said. I nodded. "My grandmother would die if she saw you do that."

"So would my mother," I said, "but I've tried it both ways and I find the quick and dirty route usually tastes just as good." He didn't seem to find it strange that I'd come to comfort Eve and ended up in the kitchen. I often deny it, but I have a lot of my mother in me. If she were here, she'd be doing exactly the same thing, both because neither of us can bear to be still and because feeding people is an important part of social interaction. It was impossible not to cook in Helene's kitchen. It was the best room in the house. She'd redone it several years ago, pushing out the back wall and installing a huge greenhouse window extending about five feet back into the roof. Outside was a terrace surrounded by blooming azaleas, where Helene had planted masses of annuals in big terra cotta pots. Inside, there were acres of counters, a huge double sink, and fancy eurostyle appliances. A kitchen where things had to turn out right. It made me feel like Julia Child. I've always had an affinity for Julia. She's even taller than I am.

All those expensive renovations were absurd because Helene seldom cooked. She could cook. She was a fabulous cook, but she considered cooking political. If she cooked, she acknowledged she was the one with the obligation to care for the others. She believed that it was women's acceptance of the nurturing role that had led to them being devalued in a world which valued independence rather than interdependence. So Helene built her beautiful high-tech kitchen and then let the housekeeper cook. Even though the housekeeper was also a woman and not a very good cook.

Florio seemed puzzled when I told him what I knew about Helene and Cliff's lifestyle, staring at me quizzically as I stripped the meat off the bones. We must have looked very odd, Dom in his suit and I in my red oilcloth apron—portrait of a homicide detective at work. "Don't look at me like that," I said. "I'm just answering your questions. I'm not saying her behavior made sense. All I can tell you is that it made sense to her and I assume it made sense to Cliff. I never heard him complain. Of course, they presented a unified front to the world. I don't know what their relationship was in private." I turned down the heat under the pot, threw in the chicken, the vegetables, and several handfuls of noodles, tasted it and added more salt. It was almost dinner time. I couldn't speak for anyone else, but I was hungry. Andre was always hungry. I didn't know about Cliff. I was surprised that he hadn't come into the kitchen at all, at least to see what Florio and Meagher were up to.

The soup didn't seem like quite enough. I explored the refrigerator and the cupboards, and found the ingredients for my friend Fran's luscious, high-cholesterol muffins. I shifted into hyperspeed, trying to get the muffins in the oven so they'd be done when the soup was ready. Dom followed me around, passing me things as I needed them, asking his questions and listening carefully to my answers.

"How did Eve get along with her mother?"

"That's a loaded question."

"I don't think so," he said. "I just want your opinion. I'm going to ask other people the same questions I'm asking you. You know that."

"Right," I said, "I'm an expert informant in murder cases. Trained by old what's-his-name himself." He frowned at that, and I was sorry I'd said it. It wasn't that I didn't want to help, it's just that what the police saw as routine questions I saw as an invasion of privacy. A necessary invasion, I knew, but I still hated to be the one to answer them. It's not easy to share the details of a friend's personal life with a stranger. "I'm sorry. I'm not trying to be difficult. I'm just not very comfortable with this whole scene. Talking about Eve here in her own house, so soon after . . ." I said.

"The first few days are critical," he reminded me, so I tried to answer his questions.

"Anyway, Detective, it's not a short-answer question. And I can only speak for the past. I haven't seen much of Eve the last few years."

"You're not expected to produce the correct answer," he reminded me, "just information."

"It isn't easy to be the daughter of a beautiful woman," I said, "and Helene Streeter was beautiful. It isn't easy to be the daughter of two shrinks, and both of Eve's parents are . . . were . . . shrinks. It isn't easy to be the only child of two parents who feel obligated to produce a psychologically perfect specimen. And it isn't easy to be the daughter of a strident feminist. Eve and Helene had disagreements. Helene pressured Eve to confide in her; she wanted to know the details of Eve's life. When Eve was younger, Helene tried to run her life. She and Cliff both wanted to have a dialogue about everything. They discussed things to death, demanded confidences and intimacy when Eve needed privacy and independence. It was more complicated than I'm making it seem. I'm sure you realize that. They were also busy professionals and Eve was alone too much. It was sort of an all-or-nothing thing. Eve dealt with it by lying. She told them what they wanted to hear. Their relationship was no picnic, but whatever their differences, Eve loved her mother." I switched the oven to 425, got out a muffin tin, greased it, and dumped stuff into a bowl, stirring the blueberries in carefully so they wouldn't turn the muffins gray.

"What is that stuff?" he asked, looking over my shoulder.

"Clogged arteries and cardiac arrest," I said. "Is there any coffee left?" The uneasiness I'd been trying to avoid with my bustle wouldn't stay away any longer. I was upset by seeing Eve so distraught and disoriented. I didn't understand what she meant about her father and Rowan killing Helene, unless it was all just the product of hysteria. My attempts to distract myself by cooking weren't working. What was I doing here, determinedly cooking for no one in particular, in Helene's kitchen? I'd just swept in and taken over, in my usual "Thea will fix it" way, but I didn't belong here. I'd come because Eve was my friend, but she was asleep. She didn't need me right now and this wasn't even her house. I had no idea how Cliff felt about my being here, all I knew was that he hadn't been overjoyed to see Andre. Suddenly everything seemed too strange.

I burned my finger, hurrying to get the muffins into the oven, and the pain cut through my diversionary bustle and confusion like a plunge into cold water. I was still here because I didn't want Eve to wake up alone. I didn't want to leave until I saw that she was okay. The cooking was just something to do to pass the time.

"Rub this on it," Dom said, handing me a rubbery little green thing. "Aloe. It's good for burns."

"You don't miss much, do you?" I said.

"I hope not," he answered.

Cliff Paris came into the kitchen, carrying some empty glasses, looking lost and confused. "Something smells good, Mariah," he said. "Is that dinner?" He stopped and stared at me, his eyes narrowed with suspicion. "Thea? You're still here? I thought you left when Eve fell asleep. I was hoping that good smell meant dinner. Where's Mariah?"

I shrugged. "I don't know where Mariah is, Cliff. I don't even know who Mariah is."

"Of course you do," he said impatiently. "Mariah. Our housekeeper. Been with us for years. Excuse me." He stepped past me and toward the sink and tried to set down the glasses he was carrying. The first one teetered on the edge of the sink and fell in. The second missed the counter completely, shattering on the floor at his feet.

"But your housekeeper's name is Norah."

"I know that," he yelled, wheeling to face me. "I know that, dammit. Norah. Mariah. One of those gloomy Irish, wind-sighing-in-the-trees sort of names. What's the difference? Don't you be condescending to me in my own home. Why don't you leave? Eve and I don't need you." He took a step toward me, his hand raised in a fist. Dom stepped forward to intervene, but stopped when I shook my head. Suddenly Cliff's body sagged, like a puppet when the strings go slack. His hand dropped limply to his side. "What am I going to do without her?" he whispered. I put out my arms, and he came to me like a child seeking comfort, burying his head in my shoulder.

CHAPTER 3

IT WAS ONE of the strangest dinner parties I'd ever attended. The menu was perfectly ordinary—my chicken soup, which had come out just right this time, rich, oily and sustaining, Fran's blueberry muffins, steamy and fragrant, saved from being commonplace by just a hint of lemon rind, and a deceptively simple salad laced with peppercorns and mustard, all accompanied by a cool, buttery Chardonnay Cliff had produced. It was the company that was odd. The guests were Andre and the two homicide detectives; Cliff Paris, restored, after his brief lapse, to his normal, charming self; and Eve, pale and disoriented, stunned into silence by the responsibility of sitting in her mother's place. Around us, the mirrored walls gave us back multiple images of ourselves and brought me unwanted memories of other, happier meals in the room. Outside, the glorious day went on and on, an insistent reminder that summer was coming. It seemed impertinent. The sun should have known better than to shine so blatantly onto this house of grief.

Cliff made a few attempts at conversation, but after we got through the routine comments about the food, things lapsed into silence. No one wanted to talk about Helene, and no other subject

seemed appropriate. We sat in an awkward circle, the quiet punc-
tuated only by the tinkle of ice on glass, the rattle of silverware,
the quiet slurping of soup, with an occasional murmur when
someone asked for something to be passed. I thought, fleetingly,
of the beer and fried clams I was missing. Across the table, Andre
looked as uncomfortable as I felt, and weary as well. He'd had a
difficult three weeks and today hadn't been the relaxing day we'd
planned.

Finally, Eve broke the silence, tossing her soup spoon into her
bowl with a clatter. "This is ridiculous," she said. "If Helene were
here, she'd be laughing at us. She wouldn't have put up with this.
She would have chosen a topic and made us talk. She would have
sat here in this chair, tossed back her hair, and laughed at us. 'Nature abhors a vacuum,' she would have said, and then suggested a
topic." Eve planted her forearms on the table, clasped her hands
over her plate, and looked at us all expectantly.

"Delicious dinner, Thea," she said. "I think one of the best
gifts a person can have is a friend who makes soup. It's not the first
time you've rescued me with soup. I think I floated to my graduate
degree on a wave of your soup. Soup and common sense. But
we've already talked about soup. Let's talk about infidelity. Detective Florio, are you married?"

"Eve, don't," Cliff said. "You'll just get yourself upset again."

She tipped her head slightly sideways, reminding me again of a
bright little bird. "It's just conversation, Cliff," she said. "I'm not
going to get upset." She shifted her gaze back to Florio. "Detective?" There was a teasing note in her voice, but it wasn't playful
teasing, it was malicious teasing. You don't grow up with two parents skilled in dissecting every remark without learning the skill
yourself.

"Yes, I'm married."

"Is your wife faithful?"

"Eve," Cliff said, "intrusive personal questions are not appropriate table conversation."

"My mother would have . . ."

"Your mother would never have done anything like this!" he said.

"Helene had a tongue like a lancet," Eve said. "She might have been more subtle, but if she wanted to know something, she persisted until she got what she wanted."

"Eve, I wish you wouldn't . . . wouldn't try to intrude on the personal lives of complete strangers. It's just not appropriate . . ."

Eve cut him off. "Oh Cliff, you've been wishing I wouldn't do whatever it was I was doing since I was about nine. That's the last time I remember pleasing you." She shifted so her shoulder was toward her father. "Besides, these guys have been squatting here all day like a pair of toads, intruding on *our* personal lives, and I don't see them apologizing. Detective Florio, does the question bother you?"

He smiled neutrally. "It's not a conversation I'm used to having. But the answer to your question is I hope so."

She didn't like his answer. "Oh, come on, Detective, you mean when you and the other guys are sitting around some greasy spoon, talking about whatever crime of passion you're investigating, you never talk about yourselves, about how you'd react in the same situation?"

"Damn straight," Meagher said. "You see some guy who's nuts about a girl, and she's cheating on him seven ways to Sunday. He just can't take it, and he blows her away. You say to yourself, man, some bitch did that to me, I'd drop her like a hot potato. Trouble with some of these guys is, they just can't let go, you know what I mean? Like little kids on the playground. They've gotta have the last word. But when we look at our own lives, we know better. We don't think about killing people just because things don't go our way. That's one difference between the good guys and the bad guys."

"So you do talk about it," Eve said.

"You know we do, Ms. Paris," Meagher said. "Now let me ask you a question. Why do you want to talk about infidelity?"

"Oh, I was just making conversation," she said, sounding petulant, which was as unlike Eve as everything else I'd seen her do today.

"Right," Meagher said, "and I'm the Good Humor Man."

"Are you? I hadn't noticed."

"Does anyone want more to eat?" I asked. There were no takers and I got up to clear. Andre rose to help me. In the kitchen, we stacked the plates in the sink. "Since you make the coffee on our team," I said, "why don't you do that while I cut the cake. I'd hate to take the enamel off anyone's teeth."

"You know what that was about."

"I do. You were trying to stay nice while that lout was eyeballing my chest." I stopped bustling and hugged him. He still smelled faintly of soap. I thought of his broad hairy chest, hidden by that utterly respectable shirt, and how I'd rather be running my hands over it than serving coffee to two edgy homicide detectives and Eve and Cliff. "A nice man I wish I had someplace dark and private."

He arched his eyebrows. "Ma'am," he said, "you shouldn't be talking to me like that. I'm a policeman."

"So arrest me, mister," I said, holding out my hands to be cuffed.

"Later, honey," he said. "When we're alone. Then I'll let you play with my handcuffs."

"Ooh la la. I just love it when you call me honey." He was taking advantage of the fact that I had my hands full, and I was experiencing an urge to drag him down under the table and assault him. "Are you married, Detective Lemieux?"

"No. But I'm big on fidelity. Your friend Eve always like that?" he asked.

"No. Sometimes death brings out the worst in people, you know that."

"I sure do. Where'd the cake come from? Did you make that, too, while I was chatting with the workout boy?" Andre has an awful sweet tooth. He was pleased by the idea of cake.

"Distracting him while Dom gave me the third degree, right?

I found it in the refrigerator. You know how it is. Cakes are drawn to death like iron filings to a magnet."

"That's a pretty nasty simile."

"I never said I was nice. I said you were nice."

"Dom didn't give you a hard time, did he?"

"Florio? He's a hard man, that one. Didn't even flinch when I tore that chicken to shreds. Most men can't watch stuff like that."

"I expect he's seen worse."

I got out the cake and a cake knife, six small plates, coffee cups and silverware. It was an impressive cake. Didn't look home-made, though. Not too many people sit around their kitchens on Saturday mornings making perfect swirls in the fudge frosting, or shaving chocolate onto the whipped cream rosettes. I assumed a neighbor had dropped it off, but I didn't know. If so, it was almost the only sign of neighbors and friends. Maybe the psychiatric community believed in self-healing. I stuck everything on a tray and carried it into the dining room. I didn't know what had gone on, but Eve was sulking and Cliff looked angry. "Well, here we are," I said, imitating my mother's perky style and feeling like the exhausted hostess at an out-of-control birthday party, "is there anyone who doesn't want cake?"

"I don't," said Eve, "and it was supposed to be my birthday cake."

Why did she have to make everything so difficult, I thought unsympathetically. It was too late to take the damn thing back and stuff it in the trash. "I'm sorry, Eve. I didn't know. Do you mind if we eat it?" She shrugged. An ambiguous gesture. I blundered on, still trying to fix things. "I know we can't pretend this is a celebration, but maybe next week sometime we could go out. Just the two of us?" She just stared at the cake. "Do you want me to take it away?" I didn't know what she wanted. She'd already said she wanted a mind reader and I wasn't qualified for the job. She was unreadable today.

She shook herself like someone trying to wake up. "I'm sorry," she said. "I didn't mean to make a fuss. It's only a cake. We can eat it." I cut the cake and handed it out, while Andre served the coffee. Cliff sat and stared at his cake, but the two detectives ate theirs the same way they'd eaten dinner, like sensible men glad to get a good meal, recognizing that they wouldn't always be so lucky.

Cliff poured himself another glass of wine, drank most of it, and leaned back in his chair. "Are you still working for that education consultant, Thea?"

"Yes. In fact, I'm a partner now. Suzanne made me a partner last fall."

"There's still business, even with the current state of the economy?"

"Plenty of business, Cliff. We've been very busy this year."

He fingered his beard thoughtfully. "I'm not sure I understand exactly what it is that you do, though I'm sure you've told me. What sort of consulting is it?"

"We advise independent schools . . ."

"Which is another name for private schools?" he interrupted.

"Yes. Mostly we give them advice about marketing, about how to attract the students they want."

"I always thought they had no trouble getting students. I thought there was intense competition. That parents worried from the time their children were born about getting them into the right schools."

"That's true. The top schools don't have problems. But private schooling has gotten very expensive. Costs have grown a lot faster than inflation—like college tuition—and at the high school level, at least, there's been a shrinking pool of applicants. Even now that the population is growing again, schools still need advice, or at least we hope they want advice, about how to attract the applicants they want, or how to convince the desirable applicant, who may have two or three schools to choose from, to select our client's school." I sounded like I was reading from a brochure but Cliff seemed interested.

"I guess I've never really understood about consultants," he said. "How does it work? What is it, exactly, that you do?" He finished his wine, grabbed the bottle, and emptied it into his glass, staring sadly at the golden inch which was all that was left.

"If I tried to answer that question we'd be here all night. Let me just give you an example. Say a girls' school comes to us and says that they are having trouble attracting applicants. The number of applications and the number of acceptances are both falling, and the school can't figure out why, or what to do about it. Suzanne and I go in and talk to the administration about what they want. We talk to faculty, administrators, current students and alumnae about the school, and get an overview of the curriculum, the campus community, of how the members of that community perceive it. Then we look at two other groups—students who applied and were admitted, but chose not to attend, and students who are current or potential applicants—and find out how they perceive the school, and in the case of the students who chose not to attend, why they decided not to. We write up our findings and recommendations in a report and give it to the client."

"What's in your report?" Cliff said. He didn't seem to be merely making conversation, he seemed genuinely curious.

"You really want to know?" I was sure the others were bored to tears. I circled the table with my eyes. Except for Eve, who was chewing her lip and playing with the silverware, their expressions were politely interested. Yeah, right, I thought, nothing interests homicide cops like the details of a consultant's life. But Cliff wanted to hear more.

"Yes, Thea, I do."

"Okay. We describe the project, and how we conducted our research. Then we write up the results, depending on what we found. If the curriculum seems outdated or has the wrong focus, we might suggest changes in that. Or it might be that the school is actually a very dynamic, exciting place educationally, but it is perceived in the community as staid, dull and old-fashioned. Then we might recommend a PR campaign to change the school's image. Or we might find that the school is targeting the wrong applicant pool and suggest a new group to aim their marketing at. There are similarities, but each situation is also very different. Each school has its own character."

"Fascinating," he said. "Sounds like you enjoy your work. From the few headmasters that I've met, I have the impression that they'd be too hidebound, too traditional to try such a modern, sensible approach. You and your partner must be very good." He was charming me again, treating me to the full benefit of his attention. Once he got me going, I could have talked about my work all night, but Eve was playing with her cake, and the detectives' eyes were glazing over.

"Even the tweediest of them have to keep their beady eyes on the bottom line. Does anyone want more cake?" Florio shoved his plate my way. Meagher shook his head. He was probably watching his figure. I didn't even wait for Andre's response, I just reached for his plate.

The doorbell rang. Cliff got up and went to answer. I guess that meant the stalwart blue guardian of the front steps had left for the day. There were voices in the foyer and then Cliff came back in. "I hope you'll excuse me," he said. "A friend has stopped by and asked if I'd like to take a little walk. And I would like to do that." He didn't wait for a response, but turned to go.

"It's Rowan, isn't it?" Eve said. "I don't think you should go. I don't see how you can go out there at night anyway, after what happened."

"I'll be all right," he said.

"That's what Helene thought, too. But of course, you'll have Rowan to protect you, won't you."

"Don't be tiresome, Eve," he said. "I haven't complained about your friend being here. I don't see why you have to complain about mine."

"They aren't exactly comparable situations, are they?"

"I'm not going to argue about it," he said. He shrugged and turned away. There was a murmur of voices, and then the door shut behind them.

Eve glared at Meagher and Florio. "Bet you think we're a real fun family, don't you. I'm a bitch, and he doesn't give a damn. Isn't it time you went home? You do have homes, don't you? I mean, you've had all day. You must have finished going through her papers by now. I wish you would leave." She shoved her chair back, the legs scraping loudly across the hardwood floor, and stood up. "Shall we retire, Thea, and leave the men to their cigars?" I got up and followed her into the kitchen.

Eve was leaning against the counter, trying to stifle her sobs with a dirty dishtowel. "I'm sorry, Thea. I know I'm being a bitch but I can't seem to stop myself. They must think I'm awful!"

"Don't worry about them," I said. "They're used to people acting strange when they're upset. It goes with the territory. Being upset with the nosy strangers in your house I can understand, but what's this business between you and Cliff? I should think you'd be comforting each other."

"I wish," she said, "but he doesn't need me. He has Rowan."

"That's the third time he's come up. Who is this Rowan?"

She screwed up her face like she'd just tasted something bitter and nasty. "Rowan is Dr. Rowan Ansel, one of the up-and-coming residents my father is supervising. Though it's a toss-up which one is supervising the other. Cliff is supervising Rowan in the clinical setting, and Rowan is teaching Cliff the joys of manly love."

"You don't mean . . ." I began, feeling foolish for asking, and embarrassed about what I understood.

"Don't be naive, Thea. Cliff was experiencing a midlife crisis of sorts," she said. "Feeling very sad and depressed because his life was so settled and boring. He was so established, so married. He'd never climb mountains, or run the marathon, or drive across the country in a convertible sports car. Never be more than just one of the leading lights in the Boston psychiatric community. Not asked to be head of the society. You know, the whole midlife thing. He'd come as close to the pinnacle as he ever would and someone else was standing on top. He managed to maintain his public façade, but around us—me and Helene—he was irascible, depressed and sour. Then bang, along came Rowan, and led him down the primrose path. You probably saw him this afternoon. He was here—the effeminate blond in the purple sweater?"

"Helene knew about Rowan?"

"Of course. Cliff wasn't secretive about it. You know how they were, discussing everything to death. He was very open about the importance of exploring what he called the bisexual side of his nature. He was getting into all that male-bonding stuff. Went to a weekend retreat where they sat around in a sweat lodge and chanted, and beat on drums and danced, and worked themselves into a frenzy and then shared all their most intimate secrets. Such a lot of garbage. Women can do that over lunch."

"How did she react?"

"She didn't like it, but she thought he needed to get it out of his system. Pretty generous of her. They would never let me get anything out of my system, but then, neither of them was the product of the other, as I was their product. They were just a couple. She prided herself on her tolerance. But she didn't like it. Even though women's issues were very important to her, and she spent endless hours with her women friends thrashing out their precious theories, she was a rock-bottom heterosexual. She tried to be understanding, but deep down, she thought his male-bonding stuff was ridiculous and the bisexual stuff disgusting."

She shook her head. "Sometimes I wish I'd stayed in Arizona. I came back here thinking I was ready to be honest and open and truthful with them. At first I thought we were making some progress. But they'd changed. They were less accessible than ever. They were both too busy with their personal agendas to bother with me. Helene holding endless meetings with her colleagues, debating whether they should split away from Bartlett Hill and open their own clinic, staffed by women and treating only women, and in the next room, Cliff and his men's group, clutching their copies of *Iron John*."

"*Iron John?*"

"The bible of the men's movement."

"Well, at least they were concerned with issues, Eve. They could have been freebasing cocaine and listening to rap music."

"I'd almost have preferred that," she said. "They'd stopped being connected with regular life . . . things like friends and food and vacations and movies and fun. Especially fun. They'd both become so serious about their issues they couldn't think of anything else. They weren't even having sex anymore, as they both told me. Helene because she wouldn't sleep with a bisexual man. Too risky. Cliff because, as he put it, women had ceased to interest him. Can you imagine wanting to know that about your parents?"

"I know what you mean. I'm quite sure my parents have never had sex."

She threw the dishtowel onto the counter. "Let's clean this place up and get out of here. You don't mind dropping me at home, do you?"

"Not at all. You don't have your car?"

She glanced down at her funny clothes. "You don't seriously think I got up this morning and dressed like this? I came back here with Cliff last night. We came from the hospital in his car."

Together we loaded the dishwasher, put food away, and returned the kitchen to its pristine state. Eve started to put the cake in the refrigerator, hesitated, and then wrapped it in plastic. "You should take this, Thea. I don't want it, and Cliff doesn't do dessert. Bad for his figure."

"I don't usually do dessert either."

"No, but that gorgeous man of yours does."

"He's not mine, Eve."

"Oh, come on. I see how he looks at you," she said. I nodded. "You could do worse."

"Thanks. I know that."

"Right. Let's take the cake and run." We found Andre half-asleep in the living room, slumped in a corner of the couch. Meagher and Florio had left without saying good-bye.

There's something about a vulnerable man that brings out all my protective instincts. Andre certainly doesn't need protecting, but as he sometimes reminds me, everyone can use a little caring. I sat down beside him and nuzzled his neck. "Come on, sleepyhead, time to go home." He grabbed me in a bear hug and held me there, muttering something incomprehensible, but he's too well schooled in the necessity of instant response to linger in sleep, even on his days off. It didn't take him long to get to his feet.

The night was soft and damp, perfumed by drifts of scent from the flowers blooming everywhere. A perfect night. A night that invited a moonlight walk. And only a few hundred feet away, last night—which had been another night just like this—someone had stepped out of the shadows clutching a knife and slaughtered Helene. That thought, and the shadows all around me, gave me goose bumps. I practically ran down the walk to the car, shoved the key into the lock, and jumped in. Eve was right behind me, slamming her door and locking it behind her. Andre came more slowly, compelled by the policeman in him to survey the scene. The instant he was in the car, I started the engine and got out of there as fast as I could.

CHAPTER 4

ONCE AGAIN, IT was Andre who made the coffee. He brought a cup in to me where I was huddled in the bed, refusing to wake up. Or, more accurately, still trying to get to sleep. Awake, aware and alive, I'm great at handling difficult situations. Thea the calm and competent. I can handle the whole gamut, from tweedy, testy admissions directors who resent my presence to the shocked, emotionally labile children of recent murder victims who want to unload onto my shoulders. I can take it all in and still stay calm and wise. But every experience, every vivid, horrible image gets filed away, and the creative director in charge of my dreams uses it to full effect.

So while Andre had slept beside me, lost in leaden sleep, I had spent a miserable night watching intraskull slasher movies where the victims were people I knew. Grisly, full-color visions of Helene Streeter, her face dead white, eyes glazed with pain, trying to hold herself together as she crawled toward help. An androgynous, faceless figure with a dripping knife stood behind her, watching. A flash of white teeth in the darkness. A smile of satisfaction. Above her, floating against the blue-black sky, Eve perched on a stool, her small, black-capped head tipped sideways, watching curiously. Then the crunch of shoes on gravel, the murmur of voices in animated conversation as Cliff and Rowan strolled into the picture, arm in arm, and stayed to watch Helene's pathetic progress.

Helene, staring at Cliff and Rowan, speaking with an effort, pleading with them to help, and Cliff, smiling his irresistible smile, speaking in that warm, inviting voice. "It wouldn't be good for you, Helene. If you truly want to be a strong, independent woman, you have to help yourself. Anyway, I have my own personal agenda to pursue." He patted Rowan on the arm. "I really don't have the energy for your issues right now."

And Helene, propped up on the sidewalk, her body ripped open and her insides spilling out over her arm, trying to smile. "I know, Cliff. I understand. I just wish this once you could find some time for me." Footsteps as Cliff and Rowan walk off into the night. A thin snatch of laughter floating back.

Helene and Cliff had been among my heroes. Not good at childrearing, maybe, but otherwise admirable grownups. Real and accomplished and competent, yet genuinely interested in Eve and her friends and what we were doing. There had been a time in my impressionable youth when I thought I wanted to be a woman like Helene married to a man like Cliff. So of course I tried to step into the dream and help her, but it was a dream, and I was only the voiceless audience.

Then the dream changed. I was standing in my Uncle Henry's garage, wearing a bright red woolen jacket with a peaked little hood, an elfin figure, my breath coming out in clouds of steam, staring up at the six-point buck he'd shot. The deer hung from the rafters, innocent eyes vacant in death, proud antlers sprouting from its head, slender legs standing stiffly out, the belly a gaping red slash where he'd dressed it, and the graceful throat slit to let it bleed. He and my father were swapping hunting stories, while my brother Michael danced about, infected by their excitement, trying to get them to agree that he could have the antlers. And I, included at my own insistence in this sublimely male moment, disgraced myself by vomiting down the front of my new red jacket. Dad and Uncle Henry were solicitous and kind, but I felt them, and Michael, draw together in scorn for my female weakness.

The smell of vomit and the faintly metallic odor of blood were so vivid I awoke, afraid that I'd been sick. But except that I was drenched with sweat, I was fine. I got up and padded through the sleepy darkness to the kitchen, poured myself a stiff measure of bourbon, and took it out onto the deck, closing the slider quietly behind me. The cool wind off the water felt good. I lay back in the lounge chair and filled my lungs with salty air, letting the bourbon's sharp, sweet heat soothe me. Below me, the waves lapped the rocks like a cat giving itself a bath.

I've always been troubled by dreams. When I was small, I used to wake up screaming and scare my parents. It got better as I got older, though it never completely went away until I met David. Sleeping beside him with his arm pulling me tightly to his side, I felt a security I'd never felt before. In the two years we were together, I only had one dream bad enough to wake me up, and when I awoke, I couldn't remember what it had been about. It was the night before he was killed, and it may have been a premonition. I don't really believe in that stuff—signs and premonitions and omens—but a few times in my life, I've had these flashes where I knew what was going to happen before it happened, some sort of ESP, so while I would never expect it or depend on it, I'm not completely skeptical, either.

I heard the slider and then Andre came out. "You okay?"

"I had a dream that woke me up."

He didn't say anything, just sat down beside me and put an arm around me. He knows about my dreams. He took the glass from my hand and sniffed it curiously. I couldn't see his face in the dark, but I knew it would be troubled. He understands about my affinity for bourbon, but it worries him. He thinks drinking alone is dangerous. Too many of his colleagues have trouble with alcohol, and too much of the crime he sees results from it. He slid a warm hand down my bare arm. "You're all goose bumps," he said. "How long have you been out here?"

"Not long. The cool air felt good."

He stood up. "Come here. Let me warm you up."

"You never have any trouble doing that."

"I just meant . . ."

"I know what you meant," I said, getting up and going over to him. I buried my face in his chest, rubbing my cheek over the coarse, wiry hair, feeling the hardness of his muscles. "I miss your smell, when you're not here."

"I smell?"

"Don't be an idiot. I meant that combination of soap, shaving cream, and you that lingers on my pillow after you're gone. That kept me from changing the bed for two weeks, until there was so much grit between the sheets it was like sleeping in a sandbox and I gave up and washed you away."

"You have such a poetic way of talking."

"Well, you know how it is with wordsmiths; we toil all day long, beating the phrases into shape."

"Only it was uncomfortably close to 'I'm gonna wash that man right out of my hair . . .' Speaking of hair . . ." He reached over and pulled out the elastic that was holding it back. It fell onto my bare shoulders, tickling them with little wind-driven wisps. "There, that's better. Go stand over there by the railing." I stood by the railing, my hair floating on the wind, white nightgown billowing. "Wait there," he said. "I'll be right back." He disappeared inside, returning a minute later with the bedspread, which he spread out on the deck. He held out a hand. "Care to join me?"

He untied the ribbons that formed the shoulder straps of my nightgown, and watched, his eyes shining in the dark, as it drifted to the ground. I stepped out of it and into his arms. Later, over his shoulder, I saw a shooting star, and then, for an hour, we both slept heavily, until the chill of a rising fog drove us back inside. That hour was the only restful sleep I got. Back in bed, even with his comfortable warmth beside me, the dreams returned.

First it was the deer again, but this time as I watched, it grew Helene's head, and then her body, and it was her gaping bloody wound. Then the picture faded and became Eve again, but this time a corpulent, bloated Eve, bulging horribly in the bike shorts and tunic she'd worn today, perched on the stool like a dreadful toad, floating around the room like a witch from the *Wizard of Oz*, singing "Ding, dong, the witch is dead." And beside her, on a stool of his own, Padraig, his flaming hair long and dirty, his face dissipated and gaunt, floated with a cadaverous grin. Below them, Helene writhed and crawled, leaving a trail of blood on her impeccable kitchen floor.

I moaned and tried to wake up, but the unrestful sleep held me in its grip. The kitchen gradually faded out, the picture became black and white, and I was looking at a wooded path. Far ahead of me, on the path, someone was lying. I fought harder to wake up, because I knew this picture, knew what was up ahead on the path, but the reel kept running, the dream coming on, relentless, drawing me closer to the silent figure on the ground. "No. No. I won't look. Don't make me look." But you can't close your eyes in a dream. Then it was all right there in front of me. Carrie. My sweet little sister. Lying there battered on the ground, the earth beneath her dark with blood. Dead at twenty-one. And then the vile projectionist finally let up, sent the pictures spinning into oblivion, and I was just driving along in my car, windows down, listening to music.

Beside me, Andre stirred in his sleep, put an arm around me, and pulled me close. I moved my head across the pillow to his shoulder, finding, as I did so, that my pillow was wet with tears. After that I dozed, but never quite gave in to sleep, afraid that the dreams would come again.

Now, in the full glare of the sun, I was still in bed, exhausted and spacey, my head pounding, trying to drink the coffee. "Can I get some aspirin with this?" I asked.

"How about some brisk sea air and cool, refreshing orange juice?"

"What are either of those going to do for pain?"

"Take your mind off it," he suggested. I knew this agenda. It was bad to be someone who drank and woke with a headache and therefore it was necessary to work it out by exercising the flesh, pounding out the evil. A drill sergeant mentality. Only this wasn't a hangover. It was a grinding, lack-of-sleep headache.

"I do not have a hangover, you know." The sheet felt hot and damp and scratchy. I kicked it off, forgetting I was naked. He stared at my body with interest.

"Forget it, mister," I said, "that is the farthest thing from my mind right now."

"Don't mind me, ma'am," he said. "You know how it is with men and hormones. We're just slaves to our lust. If an attractive woman with a delightful body throws off her sheet right in front of me, what am I supposed to do?"

"You might try thinking about the British Empire. How about if we make a deal. I'll let you look if you bring me those aspirin?"

"Oh goody." He executed a joyous little caper that went so absurdly with his muscular body and serious face that it cracked me up, even though laughing hurt my head. "I'll be right back. Don't go away."

"Where would I go? I live here." But he was gone. I lay back against the pillows and massaged my temples. The light hurt my eyes and I hoped it wasn't the beginning of a migraine. I don't get them very often, but when I do, they can wipe me out for a day or two. He came back with two aspirin and a glass of water. "What shall we do today," I asked, "assuming that these work?"

He was standing at the window, looking out at the water, refusing to look at me. "I've got to get back," he said. "These were really stolen moments. I've still got people to talk to, and the paperwork, and court tomorrow. The arrest marks the end of one phase, but now we've got to make sure all the ducks are lined up so the guy doesn't just walk away. And I really don't want this one to walk." I didn't blame him. The guy they'd finally arrested had assaulted and strangled his twelve-year-old stepdaughter, though his wife—the child's mother—swore he hadn't done it. But the mother was spineless as a jellyfish, with a long history of not protecting her children, and the guy had abused the girl before.

"I thought we had the weekend," I said, aware of the sulky note in my voice. I didn't want him to go. I might feel lousy, and be bad company, but I still wanted him there. Besides, there was the stuff he'd hinted at yesterday, things we still hadn't had a chance to talk about.

"We've had much of the weekend. We didn't plan to spend most of yesterday with Eve. You know I'd stay if I could."

I did know that. No sense in arguing about it. He'd stay if he could, and I knew it. And I wanted him to stay, and he knew it. "Do you have to go right now?"

He checked his watch. "Soon. I have time for breakfast, if you feel like cooking again after yesterday."

"It was only six, Andre. I can do that with one hand tied behind my back. And it wasn't much of a meal."

"What else can you do with only one hand?"

"Depends on which hand." I'm not so good at verbal ping-pong when I have a headache. "What do you want for breakfast?"

"A caviar omelet. English muffins with loganberry jelly. Half a pound of bacon. Some melon. And you."

"That last item, at least, I know I have in the house. I'll have to check on the rest." I pulled on some underwear, running shorts, and the shirt he'd worn yesterday, and went into the kitchen, while he went and got the paper. The light wasn't hurting as much, so it didn't look like a migraine was looming. I got out the eggs, the caviar, an onion, and some sour cream. Pulled a pound of bacon out of the freezer and stuck it in the microwave to defrost. Found the English muffins and the butter. "How about cherry jam?" I asked. My cupboards tend to look like Old Mother Hubbard's, but knowing the way to Andre's heart is through his stomach, I'd shopped on Friday.

"Fine, dear." He peeked at me over the top of the paper. We were the very model of domestic bliss.

There's nothing I like better than a big breakfast, especially on Sunday. The first few meals we'd had together he'd cooked, including our first breakfast. He's a good cook because he likes to eat and lives alone. We both like to eat. If we didn't work so hard, and consequently often skip meals, and if we didn't pump iron, or, in my case, try to get to aerobics faithfully, we'd both be fat as hogs. We're both good-sized people—I'm 5'11" and he's a bit over 6'—and if we were fat as well, we could really take up some space.

I spread the bacon on a cookie sheet and stuck it in the oven. Beat the eggs and turned on the heat under the omelet pan. Stuck four muffin halves into the toaster, and chopped some onions. There was a honeydew melon on the counter. I sliced it open and sniffed it. Sweet, musky and ripe. "I'm getting close to blastoff point in here, can you set the table?" I called.

He came into the kitchen, but instead of getting things for the table, he grabbed me from behind. "Seven . . . six . . . five . . . four . . . three . . . two . . . one." He picked me up and swung me around. "We have liftoff!"

"At ease, trooper," I said. "Put me down." He set me back on my feet, his hands lingering briefly, and gathered what he needed to set the table. I melted some butter, poured in the eggs, and buttered the muffins. I stuck four more in the toaster, checked the bacon, and loosened the edges of the omelet. I stuck two melon quarters in bowls and shoved them across the counter. "These on the table. And the jam." I dumped some caviar and onions into the center of the eggs, folded in the sides, and moved the pan to a cool burner, forked the bacon onto some paper towels to drain, and stuck three muffins onto each plate. Then I cut the omelet in half, put half on each plate, and spooned some sour cream on top. "Ready."

The table was set with flowered placemats and he'd stuck my

cyclamen in the middle. The slider was open, and the fresh sea breeze was billowing the curtains toward us like ghosts. He noticed me watching them blow. "Just like your nightgown, last night," he said.

"I don't understand how you can be so romantic, doing what you do," I said.

"I have to be. How else could I stand it? My mind and body may belong to the state, but my soul belongs to me."

"Thought I had dibs on the body."

He grinned wickedly. "You're the perfect antidote to crime. You give me wit, warmth, and caring. . . ." He broke off abruptly and looked down at his plate. There was more he wanted to say, but he wasn't saying it. "Not bad."

"You haven't tasted it yet." He looked a thousand times better than he had on Friday night. His skin had color again, and without bags under his eyes, he no longer looked like a weary bloodhound.

"No, but to have one's wishes fulfilled, instantly like this, is enough. It doesn't matter how it tastes."

"To quote Suzanne, 'get real, mister,' I didn't make this food for show. Speaking of Suzanne, are you coming down for the dinner on Friday night or not until Saturday morning?"

He took a bite of omelet and stared at me, puzzled.

"Don't tell me it tastes bad."

He shook his head. "No. It's great. I just didn't understand what you meant about Friday, Saturday and Suzanne."

"The wedding."

"Wedding?" He sounded blank, as though the word wasn't in his vocabulary.

"Wedding. You know. Brides and grooms. White dresses and penguin suits. Pretty girls in flowery dresses. The organ plays *dum dum de dum*. The minister gets up and says, 'dearly beloved . . .' Is it coming to you now?"

He still looked puzzled, and a little annoyed. "I know what a wedding is, Thea. I mean, whose wedding? What does it have to do with us?"

"Suzanne and Paul. I'm the matron of honor. Sounds like the fat lady who sings the 'Star Spangled Banner,' doesn't it? Next Saturday. You are coming, aren't you?"

Suzanne was my partner. Small and blonde and very feminine. And a very tough customer. She could wrap a headmaster around her little finger and then slowly unwind him as she dazzled him with her understanding of independent schools and their problems. She was perfectly credentialed for the job. A girls' prep school, Wellesley, and graduate work at The Business School. She excelled at tennis, could discourse on the pitfalls of myriad golf courses, or the vagaries of sailing, and drink more than one glass of sherry in the afternoon without slurring her words. She was perfectly at ease when the headmaster with whom she was staying on a consulting job stumbled sleepily into the bathroom when she was emerging from the shower, and kept a section of her closet full of unusual handwoven garments to wear on such visits.

She was also my best friend. She'd comforted me when David died, brought me soup and done my laundry when I was sick, valued my work and boosted my confidence during the years we'd worked together, and honored me by inviting me to become her partner. She'd driven to Maine to rescue me when my investigation into Carrie's death landed me in the hospital, and believed in me when my whole family thought I was off the wall.

More than anything, Suzanne had wanted to settle down, get married, and have a family. After years on the relationship roller coaster, she'd met Paul at one of our client schools, and now they were about to embark on their happily-ever-after. Both of Paul's children were going to be in the wedding, and it looked like they had a good shot at a successful blended family.

I'd been looking forward to the wedding. I like my friends to be happy. And I'd been looking forward to being there with Andre, even though I wasn't ready for a commitment as serious as that with him. I was still afraid of that, afraid of getting as connected as I'd been with David. Andre has a dangerous job and I couldn't bear to lose someone again. But just because I wasn't ready to sign on the line didn't mean I didn't need him there. Going to a wedding alone, contrasting their happiness with your aloneness, despite anything Miss Manners might have to say about it being your job to focus on the bride and groom's happiness and not your own, can be seriously depressing. And right now Andre was wearing his impassive policeman's face, the one with all emotion locked out. From experience, I knew it wasn't just a look. He could be hard as a rock.

"You are coming, aren't you?" I repeated.

"I'm not sure." That was all he said. He stopped looking at me and concentrated on his breakfast, which disappeared with lightning speed. Only when everything was gone did he look up. "Is there more?"

I shoved my plate toward him. "You can have mine. I'm not hungry." He took it without argument, and started eating. I stared miserably at his bent bristly dark head. "You want to talk about it?"

He raised his eyes briefly to meet mine. "Not really. I'm just not sure I can go to a wedding with you. It's something I need to think about."

"That's not fair," I said. "Yesterday you hinted that you weren't satisfied with things the way they are. Today you say maybe you can't come to the wedding, something we've been planning for a long time. But you won't talk about it. That's no way to work on a relationship. Besides, it's just a social event. It's not such a big deal."

"If it isn't such a big deal," he said, "then it shouldn't matter whether I come or not. Anyway, talking about it won't make any difference. I'll say I want something more. You'll say you're not ready. Nothing will be changed. I hate wasting time on talking just for the sake of talk. My ex-wife was an expert at that. She'd give her opinion. I'd give mine. We'd do things her way. Sort of

looks like that's happening here. I'd just as soon pass, thank you."
He folded his arms and leaned back in his chair, body language
that said, as clearly as his words, that he was withdrawing. The
guy who'd been swinging me around the kitchen minutes before
was gone.

He hardly ever mentioned his ex-wife. Maybe two or three
times since we met. All I knew about her was that he thoroughly
despised her. And now he was comparing me to her. Unfairly, it
seemed to me. I hadn't listened to him and rejected what he had to
say. He'd refused to talk. But trying to get him to talk when he
didn't want to was like beating my head against a wall. The only
satisfaction I'd get was that it would stop hurting when I stopped
banging. I'd get nothing from him. "You want some more coffee?"

His eyebrows went up. "Is that a truce? Are we going to stop
beating the dead horse now?"

"Not exactly. I don't think the horse is dead," I said, "but sitting here butting horns won't get us anywhere." I got the pot and
poured us each more coffee. We drank it in silence. The brilliant
May sunshine still poured in through the windows and the curtains still billowed, but the charm had gone out of the day. This
was not the weekend I had so eagerly anticipated, driving home
on Friday. The aspirin were taking the edge off my headache, but
now that I was generally discouraged, it was easier to notice how
tired and spacey my tortured sleep had left me.

He got up, still without speaking, and started clearing the
table. I carried my coffee out to the deck and admired the view. I
might as well enjoy it, I was paying enough for it. Through the
open door, I could hear him loading the dishwasher and cleaning
up the kitchen. That was our arrangement. If one cooked, the
other cleaned up. At least he wasn't in such a rush he was going to
take off and leave me with the mess. I sat back in my chair and
closed my eyes, basking in the heat of the sun, gradually slipping
into a trance.

"I'm leaving," he said from the doorway. "May I have my shirt?"

I got up, still half-asleep, and went inside, unable to focus at first after the blinding sun outside. I fingered the first button, hesitating, unwilling to part with the shirt. Things might be unpleasant between us right now, but I still liked him, still loved him, still liked wearing a shirt that smelled like him. But for all I knew, it might be one of his only good shirts. He might need it for court. I was used to seeing him in casual clothes. "Please, Thea," he said impatiently. I stripped it off and threw it at him. He caught it and stuffed it into his bag.

"I'll call you," he said. He put his hand on the knob, hesitated, and turned around. "Don't get drawn into that mess between Eve and her father. They're both accomplished manipulators. Between them, they'll grind you into powder." He knows I hate being told what to do, and dislike even more being told what not to do. His advice practically guaranteed I'd do the opposite. He knew he'd made a mistake as soon as the words were out of his mouth. "I'm sorry. I shouldn't have said anything. But I'm serious, Thea. It's a nasty business and you should stay as far from it as possible. It's not like with Carrie. You don't have a personal stake in it." He looked worried.

"Except that Eve is my friend."

"So be a friend," he said. "Call her once in a while, see how she's doing. But don't get involved, unless you want to spend a lot more nights like last night."

"You were the one who insisted I call."

"That was before I met the family."

"I thought you'd like Eve."

"Whatever made you think that? She's unstable, Thea. And dangerous."

Usually I was inclined to defer to his judgments about people, especially in his area of expertise, but this time he was wrong. He didn't know Eve like I did. "You just saw her at a bad time. She was upset. Her mother had just been killed."

"I'm not going to argue with you," he said. "Just please consider what I said."

I stood there in my black running shorts and black bra, arms folded over my chest. Where did I find this guy, I wondered, this man who refused to talk to me about things that were very much his business and insisted on meddling in things that weren't. "Go on," I said. "Leave. We don't have anything to talk about, remember?"

His face closed like a slammed door. "I should know better than to waste my time trying to help someone as pigheaded as you," he said. He pulled the door open and shut it loudly behind him.

"I never said I was nice," I yelled at the closed door. Behind me, in the kitchen, the dishwasher slurped happily to itself. I knew if I went in there, everything would be sparkling and tidy. It was one of the things I liked best about him. He wasn't hung up on job descriptions, what women did, what men did. He was just a very straightforward man. I already missed him. I could probably run out now, still catch him, and tell him I was sorry and I was wrong. But I didn't want to. Because I wasn't sure I was sorry and I didn't think I was wrong. And I was in my underwear. So I turned my back on the door and Andre and went to bed.

CHAPTER 5

I WOKE UP about seven on Sunday night with the phone trilling next to my ear like a demented toad, reached out without even opening my eyes, and muttered the appropriate greeting. "Thea? You sound strange. Are you okay?" Suzanne said.

"Fine. I was asleep, that's all."

"Ah," she said knowingly. "I assume that means Andre has finally surfaced."

"Surfaced long enough to spend Saturday hanging around while I comforted a friend whose mother had been killed. Long enough to mope about hinting that he wanted more from our relationship, but not long enough to talk about it. He beat a hasty and huffy retreat when I suggested dialogue."

"You're kidding. No nude mud wrestling or anything?" Suzanne finds our obvious physical attraction amusing.

"Oh, we're a very practical pair. First we wrestle, then we argue. And I'm not really being fair. He didn't so much refuse to talk about it as admit that he wasn't ready to talk, partly because he thought he knew what I'd say, and partly because he didn't know what he wanted to ask for."

"Well, you can work it out next weekend. I can't see you guys staying mad at each other for long."

"I don't know if he's coming."

"That's a bummer, isn't it? Well, I bet he shows up." Suzanne is an optimist, a good balance to my pessimism. "I'm sorry to hear about your friend. What happened to her mother?"

"She was stabbed."

"Oh, Thea, not that awful murder that's been all over the papers?"

"Yes."

There was a silence. Then Suzanne said, "So the daughter, Eve, is your old roommate. I've met her, right? Small and dark and very intense?"

"That's Eve," I said.

There was another silence at Suzanne's end. "Look, Thea, it's none of my business, but I've never let that stop me, so I'll say this—don't get involved. You can console Eve and be a good friend without getting sucked in. You don't need any more murder or grief in your life."

"You're the second person who's said that."

"Andre being the other, right? Look, I know you hate being told what to do, but this time, he's right. You don't need this."

"Eve didn't choose to have her mother murdered."

"Don't get huffy with me, Thea, I'm just trying to be your friend," Suzanne said, "and now I'm going to change the subject." A very good idea, since I was getting huffy. "I feel really stupid admitting this, but I've got the prewedding jitters. Everything I've eaten all weekend I've thrown up. Every time I look at that beautiful white dress my skin gets clammy. And I can't miss it. It takes up half my bedroom. I was hoping we could go out and eat something wicked and fattening, have a few drinks and I could cry on your shoulder."

"Think you could handle clams?"

"I can't handle anything, so it doesn't make much difference. You weren't thinking of Monty's?"

"Where else? I've been dreaming of clams all weekend."

"Sometimes you are so weird. What time?"

I looked at the clock. "Quarter of eight?"

"You're on. Hope you don't mind pale green."

"Suzanne, you never wear green."

"I don't mean my clothes. I mean my skin. Paul's out with some of his friends tonight, celebrating the end of his single state. So I'm supposed to be out with a bevy of my girlfriends, doing the same. Only I don't have a bevy of girlfriends. Been too busy working. Paul's sister called and asked if I wanted to get together, but she's so serious. Can you imagine spending the evening in an earnest discussion of the best reference books on the blended family, or what *Consumer Reports* recommends in vacuum cleaners? Well, neither can I. See you there." She hung up.

I imagined her dashing around her neat, feminine bedroom, pulling on some perfectly coordinated casual outfit in sandwashed silk. Suzanne likes clothes. I, on the other hand, mostly wear them for the sake of decency, except for things I like a lot, which I wear to death. Most of them have come from Suzanne, my personal shopper. She spots them when she's shopping, buys them, and leaves them on my desk with little notes. If I like them, I keep them and write her a check, otherwise she returns them.

But this was no time for daydreaming, not if I wanted to get to Monty's on time. I grabbed an emerald green shirt and my favorite jeans, stuck my feet into some green flats, and went into the bathroom to check my hair. Not spectacular. I looked like me. That would have to do. I found my purse and was looking for my keys when the phone rang again. This time it was Eve.

She sounded exhausted. "Sorry I was such a beast yesterday. It must have been the shock." Her words came with difficulty. "I sound weird," she said. "I know. I've been on the phone all afternoon. Helene's funeral is on Tuesday. I was hoping you'd go with me."

Surely even those who didn't want me to get involved would agree I ought to go to the funeral. "Of course, Eve. What time? Shall I pick you up?"

"I'd like that," she said, "if you don't mind. The service is at two-thirty, so maybe around two?"

"Two is fine. I'll see you then. Call me sooner if you need me." I hung up the phone, scooped up the keys, which were hiding behind the malevolent ceramic cat on my sideboard, and went out.

It was still light, and the clear mild air was scented with salt. I drove with the window down and the sunroof open. It didn't matter if the wind messed up my hair, my hair is chronically a mess. Untamed hair. My mother used to try to impose order on it, forcing it into braids so tight I could barely blink my eyes. I suffered for a while until I figured out that I could unbraid it as soon as I got to school. She had untamed hair herself, so she believed me when I told her that the braids had come undone when I was jumping rope. I complain about my hair a lot but the truth is that I like it. Back when I was a kid, I read in some romantic trash book that a woman's crowning glory is her hair. That's how I feel about mine. I could cut it short and it would be neat and manageable, but I like the mass of it, its wildness, the feel of it on my bare shoulders.

As I got away from the sea, the air smelled of flowers, damp earth and fresh cut grass. Everyone seemed to be outside weeding, mowing, planting or just savoring the last of the day. On the radio, Jackson Browne sang over a swirl of guitars and piano, wanting me to "Stay," but I had places to go. I put the pedal down and my turbo engine responded with a burst of speed. As I skimmed along the highway, everyone seemed to be smiling. Balmy weather does that. It's hard to be grumpy in May. I hoped the weather would work a little magic for poor Suzanne.

The parking lot at Monty's was jammed. The lines at the take-out window were impressive, and the picnic tables that looked over the salt marsh were crowded. I wasn't the only one who had longed for clams. I beat out a slower car for the last parking spot, ignoring the other driver's flashing finger, and headed for the door. The guy rolled down his window and yelled, "Bitch!" but I ignored him. Women these days can't leave home without their epithet repellent. Anyway, he was just plain wrong. Suzanne was waiting inside, a confection in turquoise, with dangling turquoise and magenta earrings and a bright jewel-toned scarf around her neck. "Beat you," she said, grinning.

"I paused for a manicure."

"Are you ladies ready now?" We followed the host to a window table that looked out over the water. How it was possible in a place this crowded to walk right in and get a table was beyond me, but Suzanne had a knack for making things happen.

When we were seated, and he had handed out our menus and left, I asked. "Very nice. How did you manage this?"

She smiled wickedly. "Simple bribery. I told him this was my bachelor party, slipped him a twenty, and told him I wanted a window table."

"Well, you don't look the least bit green."

"It's the tonic effect of spring air, I guess. I feel green. Well, actually, now that I'm here, inhaling all these incredible smells, I feel like I could eat a horse."

"Fried horse? It doesn't sound appetizing."

She gave me a quelling look.

"Will you stop being flippant. How can I pour out my heart to you?"

I tried to look contrite. "Just defending myself against a hostile world. I'll stop."

Our waitress appeared, so fresh and young I felt old as Methuselah. She must have tipped the scales at 102, and her tiny lycra mini clung to a bottom the size of two softballs. "Can I get you ladies something to drink?" Looking at her, I needed one. "Beck's dark," I said. Suzanne asked for white wine. "You can't drink that with fried clams."

"Right," she said. "Sam Adams." The girl slipped away through the crowd to get our drinks. "You looked like you wanted to eat her, Thea. What's with you tonight?"

"Drank too much vinegar this weekend, I guess. Sorry. I'll try to stop." Outside, a rising tide was creeping in, covering the mud and stirring the fresh green grass. "Tell me about these jitters."

She set one elbow on the table and rested her chin in her hand, her straight blond hair falling forward on each side, her face half-hidden. She looked about sixteen. "I can't figure it out. I love Paul. I don't have any doubts about that. I like his kids, and they seem to like me. I think I've got a pretty realistic picture of what those complications are going to be like. And I want to get married. You know that."

"I sure do. And you and Paul are great together. So what is it?"

She just looked back at me with puzzled eyes. "I don't know. I want this. I'm happy. I've looked forward to this for years. So why do I keep having the feeling of the prison door clanging shut behind me?"

"Because for the last seventeen years or so, you've been making your own decisions, and running your own life. You're a rational, independent person, and even if you want to start sharing with someone else, that doesn't mean you don't have regrets, second thoughts, and awareness about what you're giving up."

"But what am I giving up?"

"Spontaneous dinners like this. A movie when you feel like it. Saturdays when you never get out of your nightgown. White wine and brie on toast instead of a proper dinner. Those evenings after an impossible day with some pompous, uncooperative administrator when you want to curse the armchairs and kick the cat, but your spouse wants to chat about coordinating calendars and planning your next vacation and the kids keep throwing up on the rug. A part of you is just being realistic. Your life will change. Mostly for the better, but it's naive not to recognize that you also have to make compromises, and they aren't always easy."

"You make me wonder why I'm doing this. I hate getting out of my nightgown on Saturdays."

Our waitress arrived with the beer, slid it onto the table, and pulled out her order pad. "You ladies ready to order, or would you like a few minutes." No reasonable person ever lets a waitress go in Monty's. We ordered now, or we risked dying of starvation.

I flipped open the menu and scanned it quickly. "The fried clam platter. Extra tartar sauce please."

"The regular platter, or the jumbo," she asked, not meeting my eyes.

"The jumbo." The jumbo platter would feed half a football team, but it was just fine the next day, reheated.

"I'll have the regular," Suzanne added.

"Fine." She snapped her pad shut. "You want another round of beer when I bring the clams?"

"Please," I said. She hurried away.

Suzanne sipped her beer, staring out the window. "I don't know if I feel better or not," she said. "If it's going to ruin my nice, comfortable life, why do I want to do this?"

"I didn't say it was going to ruin your life, just change it. It will also change all those lonely Saturday nights when you went to the mall or Frugal Fannie's because you couldn't stand being home alone. No more awful blind dates, first dates, disappointing dates. No more late night wrestling to get the reluctant date out the door. Someone to bring you aspirin when you wake up with a headache. Or bring you soup when you're sick. Someone to share jokes with. Bike with. Maybe to carry in the groceries. Or even buy them. Someone to take showers with who can wash your back. Someone who can put sunscreen on the parts you always miss. And think how warm the bed will be at night." She was smiling now.

"But remember how angry you used to get when I didn't want to stay late at the office and work, because I wanted to go home to David?" I said. She nodded. "That's going to happen to you. Suddenly you will find that work is only a part of your life, and the other things will tug at you and make you feel conflicted and guilty, as well as happy."

"I remember," she said. "Boy did I resent him, at first. But he was so direct about it. About competing with me for your time. There was nothing subtle about David. He was like you. Strong willed. Direct. Honest. Dependable. Do you still mind talking about him?"

"Sometimes it's okay. But in the context of a wedding, it's kind of a bummer. That's why it was so important that Andre come. And now I don't know if he will."

"He'd better," she said. "I don't want a depressed matron of honor."

"I can still be happy for you, even if he doesn't show up."

"That's the spirit," she said. Our waitress delivered enough clams to feed the extras in *Ben Hur*. I looked around at table after table groaning under the weight of clams. It was a wonder there were any left in the sea. It looked like some of the people here ate Monty's clams every night. It wasn't just the tables that were groaning. There were plenty of bulging guts, sagging over belts, slipping out from underneath shirts, pressing dangerously on buttons, and a wealth of ponderous thighs, spreading like un-baked dough over chair seats. But everyone looked happy. The din was incredible, and as it grew dark, the recessed lights shone down through air that was thick with smoke and grease. I loved places like this, dark enough for privacy, and so alive with the in-teractions of happy people. How could I feel sorry for myself? It was a wonderful place to be on a warm May night, with a good friend and grand, greasy food.

CHAPTER 6

THE FOG WAS so thick I couldn't see two feet beyond my deck, but I knew it was raining, because the water had finished pouring through my coffee pot and I could still hear the sound of dripping. It's not such a bad thing to have it rain on Monday, it makes everyone feel a lot less sorry for themselves about having to go back to work. I was eager to go to work. What I'd said to Suzanne last night, about an advantage of marriage being that you didn't have to sit home feeling lonely, was true for me, too. If I'd stayed home, I would have probably embarked on a cleaning frenzy accompanied by a long, self-pitying brood about whether Andre was going to show up for the wedding.

Instead, I had a power breakfast of raisin bran and skim milk, grapefruit juice and black coffee, followed by a vanilla yogurt, ignoring the temptation to follow it up with a dozen fried clams. I put on silky navy blue slacks, purchased by Suzanne, and a crisp white cotton shirt with beach-umbrella wide navy and red stripes, also purchased by Suzanne, a red belt and shoes, and fastened my hair back with the antique silver barrette Andre had given me. I was ready to knock 'em dead. Of course, the day I'd planned involved slaving over a crowded desk, but one must always be prepared. You never knew when a potential victim might stray across the perimeter of your patch.

Suzanne was already in, wearing a suit, which meant she was meeting a client. My secretary, Sarah, was at her desk, making faces at the pile of stuff I'd left on Friday. She grimaced as I passed her desk. "Jeez, Thea, it's Monday morning, and I already have a week's worth of work. Can't you ever take it easy?" She knew I couldn't, it was a rhetorical question. She's used to my habits. If she ever came in on Monday and didn't find a stack of work, she wouldn't know what to do. Today, though, she looked tired. She has two children and a husband who doesn't help out much. She handed me a stack of pink message slips. "These were on the machine," she said. I was late, arriving at nine. In the academic world, they get going bright and early, right along with the students.

I skimmed through the messages, arranging them in order of priority. I'd been a little dishonest on Saturday, telling Cliff that business was booming. Things were going well, but we were in a little lull. Neither of us had worried much about it. The business has always had cycles, and we'd just finished an impossibly busy year. Besides, Suzanne was planning to take a few weeks off, to revel in her newly married state, and I had enough to keep me going. We had several proposals out, some of which were bound to result in contracts, but still, I checked the messages carefully for anyone who needed stroking. There were a couple of people who did, and two more people who wanted to get together to talk about our services. The last message was a surprise. From Cliff Paris. Please call him at work.

I got some coffee, kicked off my shoes, grabbed a pad of paper, and lifted the receiver, ready to reach out and touch someone. By eleven, I was convinced that the medical community ought to pay more attention to the workplace ailment I called "crushed ear syndrome." I cradled the miserable piece of plastic and took a restroom break. Outside my insulated cubicle, the office was humming. Besides me and Suzanne, we had two full-time secretaries and one who worked three days a week, two full-time staff people, and six or seven people on call to do telephone surveys, large mailings and other big projects for us. Suzanne says it's just sensible business practice, creating a pyramid underneath us that earns us a lot more than we pay them, but it makes me nervous being responsible for supporting so many people.

Suzanne was in the ladies' room, putting in her eyes. She snapped the case shut, put on a dab of pink lip gloss, and gave me a dazzling smile. "How do I look?"

"Like a million dollars," I said. "Who is it today? Brockelman or Braddock?"

"It's Paul." She smiled foolishly, as though Paul were the most magical word in the language, then caught sight of herself in the mirror, and tried to put on a more solemn face. "Just look at me," she wailed, "grinning like a hyena."

"Better that than the alternative. But this is Monday. You know, haul that barge, tote that bale, all that sort of stuff."

She nodded, the unstoppable smile sneaking back onto her face. "We're picking up the rings, he's taking me to lunch, and then we're meeting with the minister."

"Dangerously traditional, if you ask me. And your jitters?"

"Vanished in the light of the day."

"Bravo. See you later. I'm gonna go beat some bushes."

"We're not headed for the poor house, you know."

"I know. It's just how I am. Not happy unless I'm in the middle of a frenzy."

She snapped her purse shut and headed for the door. "Didn't know people could get into the middle of frenzies. Are they anything like funks?"

"Quite different. One gets into frenzies in order to avoid funks."

"I'll store that little gem away for a rainy day," she said, and beat a hasty retreat before I could get her into further conversation. I like conversational ping-pong better than she does, but usually she'll play, unless she's too busy. She wouldn't have been any fun today anyway. Her quickness was tamped down by too much happiness.

Sarah stuck out a hand as I went by. Two more pink slips. My ear ached just looking at them. "And your mother wants to know if she should wear that cobalt blue jacquard to the wedding," she said. "I told her I thought the peach sounded better, but she still wants you to call. I have to go out to get Joanne a new bathing suit. Want me to bring you back a sandwich?"

Because I'm always busy, and my mother refuses to admit that I work for a living, Sarah spends a lot of time talking to her on the phone, answering the questions I'm not there to answer. I'm very happy with the arrangement. I don't know how Mom and Sarah feel about it. "Thanks, but I'm not hungry." I went into the office and shut my door. I called the two people who wanted to set up appointments, made one for Tuesday of next week, and one for this Wednesday. I called my mother and concurred with Sarah on the peach. My mother is a large, handsome, rather fierce woman. The peach would soften that image a bit.

Then, my first slate of tasks complete, I looked at the new messages. One from someone named Dom Florio. I didn't recognize the name. The other a second message from Cliff. I couldn't imagine what he wanted, unless it was to tell me when the funeral was, and for that he could have left a message, but I obediently dialed the number. He turned out to be guarded by a bevy of dragons determined to protect Dr. Paris from any intrusions. Patiently I worked my way through the dragonesque hierarchy. It was tiresome but not surprising. In any bureaucracy where a person has even a shred of importance, dragons go with the territory, and Cliff was very important. Right now he was probably also very much in demand by reporters, voyeurs, and other people who didn't have his best interests at heart. Finally, after explaining who I was and that I was returning Dr. Paris's call to the fourth person, a sullen sounding male, I got a slightly more promising, "I'll check for you," and seconds later, Cliff's familiar voice came on the line.

"Thea? I'm so glad you called back. I hope you didn't have too much trouble. We're really being hounded by the press. They're making it very difficult for patients and staff. You'd think they'd have more decency."

I'd done a brief stint as a reporter, back when I was just out of college. The first thing I'd learned, and one reason I'd given it up, was that since all the other reporters were so craven and opportunistic, you couldn't respect people's privacy, or their grief, or their feelings, or you wouldn't get stories. I hadn't covered much crime, but the bit I did, and what I saw other people do, turned my stomach. If reporters have a motto, it has to be "the end justifies the means." It's a philosophy I just don't buy. Graphic photos of tears and anguish may add a bit of drama to the evening news, but that doesn't justify bullying your way into someone's house when they're disabled by grief, asking them upsetting questions, and then recording their responses. So I could imagine what it was like at Bartlett Hill.

"I'm sorry, Cliff. It must be terrible. I know how the press can be. They haven't any decency."

"That's true, isn't it?" he said. He sounded surprised, as though he'd assumed they were just forgetting their manners and would soon come to their senses. "Well, I didn't call you to cry on your shoulder, though I must say you did a pretty good job of taking care of us on Saturday. I called because . . . I hope this won't seem too odd, coming at a time like this . . . but I was sitting this morning in one of our Monday breakfast meetings where we were agonizing, as usual, about the bottom line and I had an idea. Hospitals these days are getting as competitive as car dealers, and believe me, it does take some of the satisfaction out of being in what was once termed a 'helping profession.' Excuse me."

He cleared his throat and came back on the line. "Sorry. On top of everything else, I'm getting a cold. Despite the chicken soup. It was delicious, by the way. I'm afraid I'm rambling a bit here. As I was saying, I was sitting in the meeting, listening to our financial brothers telling us that we have to find ways to attract

more patients, to make our outpatient services more attractive—
can you imagine it, Thea, wanting more people to need psychiatric services? It hardly sounds compatible with the oaths we took.
And I thought about what you were saying on Saturday about the
work you do. I wondered why it should be limited to independent
schools, and whether we could do something like that here.
Maybe it would help to get a clearer understanding of our image
and figure out how to market ourselves." There was a clattering in
the background, like he was playing with the pens and pencils on
his desk, or one of those little magnetic sculpture things. I didn't
know whether psychiatrists went in for desk toys.

"Well, what do you think?" he said. "Can we get together and
talk about it? It's just an idea, but I'd like you to talk it over with
your partner and then the two of us could sit down and discuss it.
What about Wednesday?"

I was completely bowled over. By his suggestion. By how
much he remembered of my babbling on Saturday. By all the
questions his suggestion raised—could we do it, did we know
enough, were our skills so readily transferable?

And by how functional he was just two days after Helene's
death. It was sort of scary, even from a man whose whole professional life involved control. It was unreasonable to compare him
to myself, but that was what I was doing. After David was killed, I
tried to go to work, but everything I saw was David. Everything I
did reminded me of him. I finally gave up and went home and
stayed in bed. But Cliff was at work and apparently functioning.

"I can't do Wednesday morning, but how about Wednesday
afternoon? Any time after two."

"Three-thirty?"

"That would be fine." I wrote it on my calendar. "How do I
find you?" He gave me directions, which I wrote in the memo
section on the corner of the page.

I thought we were at the end of our conversation, but he
coughed and cleared his throat again, and then said, "Have you
talked to Eve?"

He sounded like he felt guilty asking the question, though there was nothing odd about it. Maybe he felt uncomfortable telling people about the funeral. It was a difficult thing to do. "Yes. Yesterday. She asked me to pick her up and drive her tomorrow."

"That's good," he said. "How did she seem?"

"Weary but calm. Not like Saturday."

"That's a relief. I'll see you on Wednesday, then." He hung up before I could respond.

Odd that he hadn't realized he'd also see me tomorrow, but maybe he didn't think it was appropriate to speak of seeing someone at a funeral. Too social. I could understand that. I looked at the other message, trying to remember who Florio was. I hate making cold calls. It always helps to know the identity of the person. "Florio," I muttered. "Dom Florio." Sure didn't sound like a headmaster, though it might be a trustee. I tried again. "Florio. Mr. Florio." It finally clicked when Mr. Florio didn't sound right. Florio was a cop. A nice cop, but still a cop. I stuck the message under the corner of my blotter. He could try and catch up with me and I'd talk with him if he did, but I wasn't going to call him. He'd want to talk about things I didn't want to talk about. Besides, I had a living to make.

I dictated a few letters and spent some time going over a draft questionnaire Valeria, our newest employee, had prepared for a telephone survey we were planning. Most of the basic material was there but it was awfully primitive considering how many of these we'd done. For phone work, the questions need to be simple and clear. Hers would have baffled even our very competent phone team. Her resume and references had been impressive, and she'd been great in the interview, but she was insecure and an awkward writer. The things she produced were useless. It made me wonder why her other employers had found her work so good. And she was lazy. In after nine, always out by five, never putting in the effort necessary to put a professional finish on her work. She didn't like spelling or proofreading, believing they were someone else's job. This was the third thing she'd done for me that was unsatisfactory. Suzanne was having the same problem. It was time for a constructive talk, my euphemism for shape up or ship out. I finished reading it, dug a sample out of the files, and asked her to come into the office.

She sat down across from me and immediately shook her head so her face was hidden behind her hair. "You hated it, didn't you?"

"Why should I hate it?" I asked, tossing the ball right back.

"It wasn't really finished. It needed simplifying. But you wanted it right away, so I didn't bother with the rewrite. I see questionnaire writing as rather difficult, really. A technique that's perfected over time. It might have been easier if I'd had a sample to work from."

"The office is full of samples."

"But no one gave me one." There was a faint whine in her voice.

"Did you ask?"

"Oh," she said, tossing her hair back, "I might have tried to say something to Suzanne, but she's got her head in the clouds, thinking about her wedding, so she's useless. And you're so busy I couldn't bother you, so I just struggled along."

"But you think you could have done better work with a sample?"

"Of course. No sense in reinventing the wheel, is there?"

"But you did reinvent the wheel."

"Only because I didn't have any choice. No one would help me."

"Did you ask Bobby?"

She glared at me. "Of course not. I couldn't very well ask him, could I?" She was wearing a cheap, shopgirl's idea of business dress. An ugly mustard rayon oversized jacket and miniskirt, and a lime green tee shirt. The colors went well with her hennaed hair, but the top was too tight and the skirt was too short, and the overall effect was rumpled sleaze. What she meant was that she couldn't ask our other professional employee, Bobby Neville, for help because he was her rival. The idea that we needed to co-operate to achieve a common goal, rather than compete, hadn't occurred to her. I suggested as much.

She stared at me with that "you just don't get it, do you?" look she used too often. A leftover adolescent sneer she should have shed at graduation. "But Bobby's gay," she said.

I almost asked her what that had to do with the price of onions in Spain, an old expression of my mother's, but instead I said, "Maybe I'm being dense, but I don't see what his sexual preference has to do with asking him to help you find materials that would let you create a better product. Can you enlighten me?" The musky scent of her perfume was overpowering in the closed room.

She raised her chin truculently. "In these tight economic times, a person has to look out for herself."

I didn't press the point. So far this apparently charming girl with the glowing resume had told me she was self-centered and homophobic. My next question was going to test her common sense. "Did you look through the files for a sample?"

"Sort of. I couldn't find one."

"Did you ask Sarah to help you?"

"Sarah? But she's just a secretary." Valeria's expression said that this time I'd insulted her dignity.

"Just a secretary?" I was beginning to lose my temper. Instead of apologizing for a poor job, she was blaming everyone around her, and seemed to think it was okay not to even make minimal efforts to produce a better product because no one helped her. Besides, Sarah and our other secretary, Magda, are the lifeblood of our organization. Without them, we wouldn't just be paper pushers, we wouldn't even have paper to push. Suzanne and I aren't very tolerant of people who look down on secretaries, who act as though they're just slightly above the earthworm in terms of intelligence and ability. "You're telling me that the woman you rely on to correct your grammar, spelling, and punctuation wouldn't be able to find a sample of the work she files every day in the files she maintains?"

To my astonishment, instead of answering, Valeria got up. "I think we should continue this conversation when you've calmed down, Thea."

That did it. Any vestige of desire to try and shape this girl into a useful employee evaporated. "I don't think we need to prolong it, either, Valeria. I'd meant to have a serious discussion of your project, to give you some guidance, and let you have another chance. But I would just be wasting all of our time. We're a small organization, and to be effective, we need to cooperate. You haven't been a team player, and I don't think you want to be. Your work hasn't been satisfactory, and you aren't willing to take the steps necessary to make it satisfactory. You need to find yourself a more competitive arena. We will pay you for two weeks, but I'd like you to leave now. It shouldn't take you more than half an hour to clear out your desk."

Her small mouth, painted a garish orangy red, pursed into a prissy O and she shook her head. "My my, Thea. That's quite a speech. I'm not sure you want to be so hasty, though. I know my rights under the law." I waited patiently, wondering what rights she was going to assert. "I know I'm protected from a retaliatory firing."

"An employer may fire an employee for unsatisfactory work. There's nothing retaliatory about that."

"That's not why you're firing me," she said, smirking. "You're firing me because I complained about sexual harassment."

"Bullshit," I said, amazed at her brazenness. If this girl had put half the imagination she put into protecting herself into her work, I wouldn't need to fire her.

The smirk sat there, growing wider. "You made advances to me, and I refused them," she said. "I wrote a memo to Suzanne, complaining about it. You'll find a copy in her files and naturally I kept a copy for myself. And now you're trying to fire me." She paused to let her words sink in, and then continued, "So maybe you'd like to think again about firing me?"

I wanted to tell her she was crazy, that I was as heterosexual as a person could be and that even if I was attracted to women, she'd be the last one I'd choose, but it wasn't my sexuality which was at issue here, it was her character. One thing was finally clear. I knew the source of her glowing recommendations, her fine resume. Blackmail. It was certainly true that she could make a lot of trouble for me, for us. Trouble we didn't need. But I wasn't going to be manipulated by an incompetent little sneak. She probably didn't expect me to fight back; it didn't look like the others had. But I wasn't somebody else and I hated duplicity and intimidation. This time Miss Valeria Davie, that arrogant, dishonest, incompetent, illiterate, homophobic despiser of secretaries, had found someone who wouldn't roll over and play dead. "There's nothing to think about," I said. "Your accusations are garbage. I want you out of here. Now."

She was surprised, but maintained the arrogant tilt of her head. "I'll leave," she said, "but this isn't the end, you know, it's only the beginning." She swept out, trying to look regal, but it's hard to look regal when you're wearing ugly clothes. When the door banged shut behind her, I put my head down on the desk and moaned. This was the last thing we needed right now. A Commission Against Discrimination investigation, even though it was bound to result in a finding in our favor, would be a major distraction, and I needed to concentrate on getting business. I had to believe she would carry out her threat.

I buzzed Sarah on the intercom. "I just fired Valeria," I said. "Watch her carefully. Don't let her take anything from the files, and call me when she's about to leave."

"I probably shouldn't say this, but oh goody," Sarah said.

Acting on the theory that the best defense is a good offense, I called my father. The dragons who protect him knew better than to keep me out, and I was connected without delay. After we got through the familial preliminaries, I told him why I was calling.

"Dad, I need some legal advice." Unlike the shoemaker whose children had no shoes, my dad loves to use his legal knowledge to help out the family. He listened very carefully to the whole story, and immediately started planning our defense. By the time I got off the phone, I had a laundry list more than a page long. And that was just the beginning.

I hoped Suzanne was coming back after her meeting with the minister. I needed to talk to her. Badly.

Sarah buzzed. "You'd better get out here. She's heading for the door."

"I'm coming. Tell Bobby to block the door and not let her past until I get there."

"I already did," she said. Sarah had that invaluable attribute of a good secretary, the ability to anticipate what needed to be done. Like me, she'd figured out that even though Bobby was as gentle as a lamb, his imposing size and Valeria's open fear of gays would keep her from trying to pass.

By the time I got there, Valeria was practically frothing at the mouth, screaming expletives at Bobby, who was lounging calmly in the doorway. "Just one more thing, Valeria, before you go," I said. "I need to check the papers you're taking to be sure you aren't violating your employment agreement." I waved a copy of the agreement she'd signed and reached for the briefcase.

"Don't you touch that, you disgusting lesbian," she snapped.

"No problem. If you don't want me to go through it, Mrs. Dillon can do it." Mrs. Dillon, of course, being Sarah. Valeria stood clutching the briefcase a little longer. Finally, she tossed it onto the floor at my feet.

"Go ahead. Search," she said. "You won't find anything."

I took everything out of the briefcase, carefully checking all the pockets, and piled it on Magda's desk. "Magda, can you make a list of everything that's here as I check it."

Magda got her steno pad and a pencil. "Ready," she said.

I started going through the papers, sure that Valeria would try to take something she shouldn't, unless she'd already taken it with her another day. I felt like the central character in a badly scripted spy novel, feeling more and more foolish as each paper proved to be perfectly harmless. I was almost at the bottom of the pile before I found it. But what she was trying to take away was dynamite from a business standpoint. In her pile of "personal" papers, Valeria had copies of our client lists for the past four years, copies of the list of clients we were currently courting, and our target list of potential clients. Lists which are kept in Suzanne's office, in a locked filing cabinet. After that were the file copies of our two most comprehensive reports, and taped to the back page of the second report were two computer disks. By the time I found the disks, I was ready to strangle her.

I held out the client lists, so she could see what they were. "Where did you get these?"

There was that idiotic smirk again. She shrugged. "I forget. They were in my desk. I must have just picked them up with all my other papers."

"What are these computer disks?"

"Just my working disks, the ones I did my drafts on."

Neither disk was labeled. I stuck the first one into Magda's computer and pulled up the index. It was my personal correspondence disk. From my supposedly locked desk. The second disk was the corresponding disk from Suzanne's desk. I held out my hand. "Let me see your purse."

She clutched it tightly to her side. "No way," she said, "that's personal."

"That's what you said about the papers. I'll give you a choice. You can let me look in the purse, or I can call the police, and we can wait here until they come and then I will look in your purse. They will back me up. I guarantee it. Employers do have rights with respect to employees like you."

"Oh, all right. You can look. But you're going to be sorry you treated me like this. Very, very sorry." She opened her purse, took out her wallet, checkbook, car keys, and makeup bag, and tucked them into the baggy pockets of her jacket. Then she took her purse, aimed it at me with the top open, and heaved. A heavy shower of stuff bounced off my shirt and pants and landed on the floor by my feet. I didn't look at it. I was watching Valeria. She marched up to Bobby, holding her breath, and croaked, "Out of my way, queer." He looked at me. I nodded, and he let Valeria go. We all stood in a stunned circle, listening to the *clackity clack* of her high heels until she disappeared down the stairs.

"Boy howdy," Sarah said, "are we ever lucky to be rid of that little witch. She tried to steal half the office." She looked down at the floor by my feet. Among the loot Valeria had stuffed in her purse were four packets of computer disks, five dozen pens, six printer ribbons, eight rolls of stamps, and the elegant, expensive pen Paul's mother had given Suzanne as an engagement present. "I wonder what else she took."

Magda shook her head sadly. "There have been other things," she said in her slightly accented English. "I was trying to decide whether to bring it up. But Suzanne has been so busy. I didn't want to trouble her just now."

"Didn't want to trouble me with what?" Suzanne said. She stared at the mess on the floor and Valeria's collapsed pocketbook. "What's this mess?"

"I fired Valeria."

"And she tried to steal half the office when she left," Sarah said.

"Worse yet, she tried to take your pen, that you had from Paul's mother," Magda added.

"And worse than that, she tried to steal our client lists, our reports, and our personal correspondence disks, and she has threatened to sue us for firing her, claiming that it was a retaliatory firing."

"Retaliating for what?" Suzanne said. "Incompetence? Since when is that forbidden?"

I figured I might as well let the whole staff in on the problem, so I didn't wait until we were in her office to tell her. "She claims that she will say I made advances to her, and when she complained to you, you refused to act and I fired her." Magda made a disgusted face and started picking up the stuff on the floor. Sarah bent to help her. Bobby, looking extremely confused, wandered back to his desk. "Let's get some coffee, take it into your office, and talk."

"I'll get the coffee," Sarah said. "You'd better sit down, Thea, you don't look so good."

I hadn't realized, until I sank into a chair in Suzanne's office, how much of a strain the last hour had been. It didn't help that it was after three, and I hadn't had any lunch. Suzanne stayed behind to give some instructions to Magda. I waited for her, my head in my hands, experiencing a crisis of conscience. Suzanne didn't need this kind of aggravation right now. Why hadn't I waited until next week? Had I really needed to fire her at all? How messy were things going to get if she really did file a complaint? All the questions that hadn't bothered me before, when I'd been so certain I was right, were hammering at me now, and I wasn't sure I knew the answers.

She came in quietly, shut the door behind her, and handed me some coffee. "Come on," she said, "it's not that bad. We would have had to do this sooner or later. She was hopeless."

"I know that." I showed her the list I'd made. "I called my father. Got some free legal advice. Looks like a busy afternoon ahead of us."

She made a face. "And I was having such a good day, too. Well, those are the breaks. Before we plunge in, is there any good news? Proposals accepted, serious leads, anything like that?"

I almost said no, but then I remembered Cliff. "Maybe. Something completely different. I'm not sure it's for us, though." I told her about my conversation with Cliff, and his suggestion that we consider trying a project for him. She listened thoughtfully, tapping her lip with her finger like she often did when she was thinking.

"I don't know, Thea. It might not be a bad idea. The principles are the same, if he could help us identify the client market. It might even be fun to try something new and see if we could make it work. After all, someday we might run out of schools."

I was surprised. "You mean you'd really consider it?"

"Why not? Nothing ventured, nothing gained, you know. There is one thing, though. This is the same man whose wife was just killed, right? He may just be trying to create a smoke screen of work to distract himself from his personal situation. We'd need to be sure he's serious about this."

"I'm seeing him on Wednesday. I can find out then." I picked up my list. "You want to go over this now?"

She made a face. "I'd rather talk about flower arrangements and rings, but I do understand about priorities. Where do we start?"

"You won't believe this," I said, "but the first thing we need is a bunch of those disposable plastic gloves, like you use for painting, to wear while we go through the files, to see if she's planted anything there. And whatever you do, don't touch those computer disks until you put on the gloves."

"You're kidding. We're worried about fingerprints? Our little old consulting firm?"

"What we're worried about is our reputation, partner. That and a quick and successful defense to an MCAD investigation. My father is sending us his paralegal, Karla Kaplan, to help out. She's done document searches like this before. And she's bringing the gloves."

Suzanne rubbed her forehead wearily. "Casting out visions of sugar plums," she said with a wry smile, "or rather, orange blossoms. I'm beginning to see why you look so discouraged. This is more work than I thought."

"Should I have handled it differently?"

"I don't think so. It's obvious she knew she was in trouble and was already planning how she'd handle things when we fired her. She'd already looted the files and the supply closet. I wonder how she got the disks?"

"Probably picked the locks. Or just sneaked in when you were out of the office for a minute."

"It's so ugly," she said, shaking her head. "She seemed so nice. Had such fine recommendations. . . ."

"And now we know how she got them."

Her eyes widened in surprise. "Oh, of course. I hadn't thought of that. I'm not usually so naive, am I?"

"No. Naive is not a word I would use to describe you." I handed her the list and stood up. "You might want to look this over. I've got to get a sandwich. You want anything?"

"No thanks," she said, "I had a big lunch."

"All right for you," I said, "but we've got a long night ahead, and I can't fight evil on an empty stomach."

CHAPTER 7

I STOOD IN front of my closet, my eyes gritty and my brain working like it was buried in sludge, trying to find something solemn enough for a funeral. We'd worked until the wee hours of the morning, Suzanne, Magda, Karla Kaplan and I, finding the memos Valeria had referred to, as well as some other suggestive personal memos in both Suzanne's and my files, all of which were also on our personal correspondence disks. The disks I'd taken from Valeria turned out to be copies of ours. Our own disks, augmented by Valeria's forged memos, were still in our desks. Where each item had been, Karla had inserted a pink form, indicating the identity of the document removed, the date it was removed, and that she had removed it. Each of the mystery documents had been placed in a clear plastic envelope, and Karla had taken them with her to give to a fingerprint expert. It had been absurd and high-tech and sinister, all at the same time. I'd come away feeling soiled, a feeling that a long, hot shower didn't erase.

I settled on a purple and black linen suit with a long jacket and pleated skirt, with a black linen blouse. At the last minute, I pinned on the silver Art Nouveau pin David had given me for our first anniversary. A talisman against an evil world. It wasn't raining but it was cool and overcast, the right kind of weather for a funeral.

The public radio station was offering its usual menu of interesting items, but I couldn't seem to focus on any of them, and when a plummy British voice began delivering the news, I turned it off. I'm not a dedicated "buy American" type, or I wouldn't be driving a Saab, but I do think that a radio station supported by public contributions ought to give us our news in American English, and not be getting it from the BBC. We Americans can be so absurd. Fiercely anti-intellectual, yet we glom on to the mediocre products of a dying nation as though every word was Shakespeare.

The traffic on 128 was as thick as sour cream. Half the traffic, now that it was after one, was no longer cars, but vans and small trucks, many of them being driven with a sort of "it's not my car, I don't care what happens to it" insolence. One of the favorite tricks of Boston drivers is to refuse to look at other drivers. If you don't see someone, after all, you don't have to yield to them. Normally I'm comfortable enough in my Saab to drive on autopilot, so I can think about things other than driving. This would have been nice, because I hadn't had much time after we finished flushing Valeria out of our files to prepare for what I expected to be a challenging day. But I'd allotted an hour for a drive that should have taken forty-five minutes, and I'd be lucky if I got there on time.

I found a parking space around the corner from Eve's apartment, jammed the car into it, and literally ran back to her door. It was almost ten past two, and she was waiting on the steps, raincoat draped over her arm, looking forlorn. She jumped up when I got close, the lost look replaced by a relieved smile. "I was afraid you'd forgotten," she said.

"As if I would, Eve. I almost ended up in jail, but I'm here." I put an arm around her and gave her a quick hug. "Let's go. I'll tell you about my adventures in the car." She climbed in obediently, tossed her raincoat in the back with mine, and buckled her seat-belt. "Where to?" I asked.

"The Unitarian Church. I'll direct you," she said. "Do you have any tissues? I forgot to bring mine."

"In the glove compartment."

She opened it, found the box, and stuffed a handful into her purse. "What do you mean, you almost got arrested?"

"I broke the law. I got caught in this horrible traffic jam, and after sitting there a while watching the precious minutes ticking away, I got impatient and tried to go around it in the breakdown lane. Good old law-abiding me. Only time in my life I've ever tried that. I'm usually the one waiting patiently in the jam, cursing the ones who are zipping down the breakdown lane. Anyway, I was racing along and suddenly there was a police car blocking the lane, and nowhere to hide. This giant policeman gets out and strolls over to my car. You know the type—the clean-cut, larger-than-life product of Wheaties with the aviator glasses and ridiculous Smokey hat. Walking with that stiff-hipped gait that comes from having a poker up his ass."

Eve gave a little snort she tried to stifle with her hand. "Stop it, Thea," she said, "I really shouldn't be laughing. I always thought they walked that way because of those silly jodhpurs and motorcycle boots they wear."

"You don't want to hear the rest?"

"I do."

"I rolled down my window and waited. He sauntered up and just stood there, staring down at my chest with that infuriating smirk that says 'I can stare as long as I want, lady, and there isn't a damn thing you can do about it.' Then he leaned down and said, 'In sort of a hurry, aren't you, ma'am.' I agreed that I was, and I told him I was going to a funeral. The bastard actually smiled, and he said, 'I don't think the deceased will notice if you're late.' Then he swelled up like a toad and got ready to give me a ticket, but I batted my lashes and talked him out of it."

I didn't tell Eve the rest. The way I'd talked him out of it was to tell him whose funeral I was going to, and that I was late to pick up Eve. I'd pulled no punches. I'd painted a dramatic, not-too-far-from-the-truth picture of poor, suffering Eve, alone, desolate and motherless, waiting in vain for her dearest friend, and then invited him to still give me a ticket. Instead, he'd given me an escort down the breakdown lane to the end of the jam, and then blocked traffic to let me back in. It's so often that way with cops. First they push you around to prove they can do it and then they indulge in some magnanimous gesture.

I really didn't have any reason to be mad at him. I had been breaking the law, and he was just doing his duty, but, with the exception of Andre, I have a real distrust of the police, dating from the night David died. David had been lying there in the hospital, dying, asking for me, and I was in the waiting room, desperate to be with him, but the police wanted to ask him about the accident, and they wouldn't let me see him until they were done. So they got the last moments of his life, and by the time I was allowed to see him, he was still warm, but the light had gone out of his eyes. I never had a chance to say good-bye. It left me with a big chip on my shoulder.

I put my hand over Eve's, which was cold as ice. "Doing okay?"

"I guess so." She sat stiffly, biting her lip, staring straight ahead. "I still can't believe it. I . . . ." She took a deep breath and slowly let it out. "I'm okay as long as I don't talk about it. Then I start to cry."

"You're allowed to cry, you know."

"But I hate being weak and defenseless, looking pathetic in front of others. I ought to have more self-control."

"It's a pretty screwed-up world we live in if the list of shoulds and oughts includes not being sad at your own mother's funeral, Eve."

The church parking lot was jammed and there was no visible street parking except a small space behind the hearse, marked by a little yellow tented sign that said FUNERAL PARKING ONLY. It was almost 2:30. I pulled into the space and explained our dilemma to the black-suited functionary who was working the street. "You can leave it there," he said, frowning at my lack of taste in arriving in a red car. He opened the door for Eve.

"Will you sit with me, Thea?" she asked as he closed the door.

"If you want. Wait a sec and I'll walk in with you." I locked it and tossed the keys into my purse, aware that he had checked my dress carefully to be sure I didn't favor red clothes as well as red cars. He needn't have worried. I may not have a wardrobe of vehicles, but I do know how to dress. My mother was very conscientious about teaching me the rules: no black or white to a wedding, no red or yellow to a wake, and her own personal one, somber, dark clothes to a funeral, but not black. Black was for the family. Eve was wearing a trim, black, Chanel-style suit edged in white. Walking beside her, in my loose jacket and flowing skirt, with my hair escaping around my face, I felt unkempt and ungainly. It reminded me of walking with Carrie, who had also been very short. I quickly pushed thoughts of Carrie out of my mind.

Eve stumbled as we went up the steps, and another of the black-suited functionaries was instantly at her elbow to support her. He stayed with us all the way down the aisle, until Eve was safely installed next to Cliff. I felt odd sitting there with the family when I didn't belong, but reminded myself again that I was there because Eve wanted me. I could hardly forget. She was clinging to my arm like a lifeline. Then the minister began the service and I put my mind on autopilot.

I guess it was a good service. At least the minister knew Helene, and could say meaningful things about her, and at least there were meaningful things to be said. Helene had lived a significant life. I think about that sometimes, about what might be said at my funeral. That my hair had never once looked combed? That I always got my reports in on time? That I was steady and dependable and could be relied on to fix things? That I had "quite a little temper for such a solemn child," as my Aunt Ella used to say?

That I loved a good meal, but was always forgetting to eat? Not an earthshaking bunch of epigraphs to mark the chapters of my life. I sat there in the pew, considering my own funeral and trying to still the wambling of my stomach, not paying much attention, until the minister stopped and a woman got up to speak.

She was a small, timorous woman in a plain dark dress, and she approached the lectern as cautiously as though it sheltered a mugger. Her voice, when she introduced herself, was inaudible, but it grew in strength as she spoke. "I was a battered woman," she said. "Helene Streeter saved my life." She scrubbed at her reddened nose with a handkerchief. "It would probably be more accurate to say that Helene gave me a life for the first time. Before a friend of mine literally dragged me into Helene's office, I thought it was all my fault. I believed that my husband beat me because I deserved it. I deserved it because his dinner got cold while he was watching T.V. I deserved it because I couldn't get all the stains out of his shirt. I deserved it because sometimes I complained that we never went anywhere, or that he didn't pay any attention to me. He told me that I was worthless and incompetent and demanding and I deserved to be punished. And I believed him. Until Helene taught me that I didn't have to. Until she taught me that I had rights, that I had value, that I deserved to be treated decently."

She seized the lectern with both hands, standing on tiptoe so she could lean out over it. "I am not alone. I am but one of the many, many women Helene helped. I came here today to speak for all of us, to say how much we valued her, how much we honored her, and how much we will all miss her. Our sympathy is with her family today, who knew her so much better, and therefore have so much more to miss. So we are sad, for her family, and for ourselves. Her death is a terrible loss. But . . ." Her voice rose, high and proud now, so very different from when she had begun to speak. ". . . there is a way in which Helene Streeter is not dead, because she lives in all of us to whom she has given a chance at a decent life. She lives in us every day, in the small triumphs she led us to, in each tentative but successful attempt we make to realize our selves, recognize our worth, and demand recognition of it from others. As each of us women she has helped goes through our lives, each small, shining triumph, like tiny beacons in the darkness, illuminates not just our individual lives, but also her memory. We shine because she taught us that we can." She stopped, smiling and tearful. "That's all I had to say. Thank you for listening." She stepped down and walked calmly back to her seat.

She was received there by two other women, their faces glowing. Her place was taken by a confident gray-haired woman who strode to the lectern with the manner of someone accustomed to public speaking. "Helene Streeter was my colleague, my mentor, and my friend," she said. Her voice was strong and clear, with just a faint touch of New York. "As a friend, I loved her for her warmth, her availability, her beauty and her cooking. As a colleague, I valued her for her wisdom and insight, her clear values, her compassion, and her ability to see both the forest and the trees. Helene was always there, as a peer, to serve as a sounding board, or give a second opinion, or to serve as a resource. She never stopped learning, thinking, discovering. She had an extraordinary mind, and she devoted it to helping others."

I glanced at Cliff, to see how he was handling this. Sometimes it can make you very sad to hear even the good things, or especially the good things, about someone you loved. His reaction shocked me. He was staring at the woman with a look of intense distaste.

"Most of you knew Helene in one, or both, of these roles, and so I don't need to dwell on them. We all know that Helene was a beautiful woman, a generous friend, and a gifted therapist. It is in her role as mentor that I think she should be remembered. For many of us, in what is often rather derisively called the 'helping profession,' Helene Streeter was a courageous pioneer. Through her writing and her speaking, she argued persuasively and forcefully for recognition of women's differences, women's values, and women's voices, in psychological theory. She used to say that she

often felt like an invisible woman, as at conference after conference, in seminar after seminar, she would question her male peers'
assumptions, pointing out that their research was done only on
males, or that the assumptions they were using were based only on
males, and of questionable value, since they excluded half the population, only to be met with bland smiles, or cheery nods that she
'had a point,' and to see the discussion continue as though she
hadn't spoken."

She paused, gripping the lectern as her predecessor had, and
looked out at us. "I'm sorry if I may offend some of you with what
I say. This is not meant as some feminist diatribe, but as a tribute
to Helene. In paying her tribute, I would remind you that Helene
lived life passionately, without reservation. She worked hard,
she ate heartily, she played enthusiastically. She met life head-on.
She wouldn't want me, in recalling her, to mince words. She considered the recognition of a woman's point of view in life-cycle
theory, and in the assessment of personality development, to be
the most significant effort in her life. She should not slip out of
our lives without some recognition of that effort. She was an early
voice, and a strong voice, for women in psychology."

She smiled, and when she spoke again, there was a trace of
humor in her voice. "Helene said that the way her male colleagues
treated her—and even some of her female colleagues, for that
matter—listening to her thoughtful, detailed, documented papers
and then dismissing them as insignificant, reminded her of
Humpty-Dumpty. You are all current on your Lewis Carroll,
aren't you? So you will recall the conversation between Humpty-
Dumpty and Alice, in which Alice attempts to make sense of what
the Egg Man is saying, but there is no sense there to be made?
The conversation goes like this:

" 'When I use a word,' Humpty-Dumpty said, in rather a
scornful tone, 'it means just what I choose it to mean, neither
more nor less.'

" 'The question is,' said Alice, 'whether you can make words
mean so many different things.'

" 'The question is,' said Humpty-Dumpty, 'which is to be master—that's all.' "

Beside me, I heard Cliff mutter, "For God's sake, Lenora, Humpty-Dumpty at a funeral?"

"Helene believed that if you looked behind the words, there were truths that would require them to be given their proper meanings. That was the dreamer in Helene, the woman who believed in what was right. Who hoped that others would see what were to her such obvious truths. The realist in her recognized that everyone twists words and uses them for their own purposes and that part of Helene wanted to be master. She was a complicated person, and *de mortuis nil nisi bonum* notwithstanding, I loved her while I didn't always like her. Her death—let me not speak euphemistically—her murder, her slaughter, was a terrible loss institutionally, and personally. It is up to us—those of us who are left—to continue her work and ensure that her ideas and her ideals did not die with her. Her killer may think he has finally silenced her. We must not let him!" She struck at her chest with her fist. "There will always be a hollow spot here for Helene and an even bigger void is left in the psychiatric community." She left the lectern abruptly and strode back to her seat.

Her eulogy, or speech, or whatever it should be called, seemed to have lost momentum and wandered oddly before returning to that call to arms at the end. When I glanced around, I could see mine was not the only puzzled face. The minister moved quickly to get on with things, perhaps fearing that another strange speech might follow. Before long, her coffin was gone and we were leading the surge of people down the aisle and out into the street.

"Lenora was as batty as usual," Eve announced. "She's probably been waiting to use that quote from Humpty-Dumpty all her life."

"I wish she'd waited a while longer," Cliff said. "I could hardly refuse, when she called and said she wanted to speak. She was Helene's closest friend. I don't know what it is about her, though, but she always does something odd which undermines the efficacy of what she's trying to say. Are you coming back to the house with us, Thea?"

"Yes, shortly. I just have a few calls to make first."

"You're welcome to use the phone."

"She's got one in her car, Cliff," Eve said. "These are the nineties, remember?"

He shook his head. "Can't think of much I'd less rather have in my car. Except, perhaps, a drooling Saint Bernard." He turned away to greet some of the people who were coming up to him. Eve stayed with him while I retreated to my car, eased it out of the parking space, and headed off in search of someplace quiet to park. I ended up at what David used to call the IHOP, the International House of Pancakes, a wonderful place to spend Sunday mornings, lingering over their bland, generous American breakfasts and endless cups of coffee. There's nothing nouvelle about the IHOP, but if you're hungry in the morning and want a serious breakfast, it's a good place. Sitting there in the car, thinking about food, reminded me that once again I'd missed breakfast and lunch. There would be time for food later. I disciplined myself to stay in the car and use the phone, instead of rushing inside and throwing my hungry self on the mercy of some bored waitress.

After that I reluctantly drove to the house, glad to see, when I got there, that the street was jammed with cars. That would make it easier to carry out my plan, which was to stay a few minutes, tell Eve she could call me if she needed me, and get back to the office, a plan which assumed someone else could drive her home and that she wouldn't decide she needed to cling to me. I wanted to review the file before tomorrow's morning meeting, and put together some stuff for my meeting with Cliff, if he was still serious about it.

I was barely through the door when the tall woman who had spoken at the funeral, Lenora, grabbed me by the arm and asked if I could help her in the kitchen. Actually, she didn't so much ask as simply impress me, much as sailors were forced into the British navy. Soon I was circulating with a tray of delicious looking snacks, which vanished like mist in the sunshine before my hungry eyes. I reached for the last one just as someone else did, and found myself looking at a man who seemed vaguely familiar.

"I gather you're one of those people who don't return phone calls," he said.

"Please don't take it personally, Detective. Right now you're in a queue with about forty other people. I almost got to you yesterday, but then we had a staff emergency and I didn't get home until very late last night. I haven't even gotten to the office yet today. And you'd better let me eat that, or I may collapse at your feet. I've had nothing but one sandwich since yesterday morning." He took his hand away, leaving me free to eat the last delicious morsel on my tray, but he didn't look mollified. He looked annoyed. I was sorry to have annoyed him. On Saturday, when we'd met, I'd liked Florio immediately. The tiny bite of food hit my empty stomach so hard I could almost hear it, and suddenly I felt strange and lightheaded. It must have showed in my face, because Florio grabbed the tray, stuck it on the nearest level surface, and steered me through the kitchen, out onto the terrace, and into a chair.

"Don't move. I'll be right back." He returned before I could collect my scattered wits, carrying a glass of milk and a sandwich. He hovered over me like a nanny over a recalcitrant charge until I'd finished eating. "Better?" he asked, when I'd set the plate and glass down on the bricks.

"Much better. Thanks."

"Andre said you were like this. Like a dervish, is how he described you. Rushing around in a great swirl of activity, completely forgetting about eating or sleeping, and getting great mountains of work done. He thinks you need a keeper."

"Not that he's available for the job," I said. "The man needs a keeper himself, so he's a fine one to talk. Every bit as wrapped up in his work as I am in mine. But you're not here to talk about Andre."

"No. I'm here to talk about Eve."

"I thought we went over all that on Saturday."

He shook his head. "I'm sorry if you find it tiresome, but sometimes I have to go back over the same ground several times, and you're an excellent source. Actually, we talked about Eve and her mother but we didn't talk about Eve and her father. I was going to offer to buy you lunch and ask you a few more questions if you'd called me back."

"I told you I was sorry about that. I'd be glad to help you, Detective. But this hardly seems the time or the place."

He tipped his head slightly sideways and stared at me. In the harsh gray daylight I could see how tired he was, the lines around his eyes etched deeper and a weary droop to his mouth. His shoulders sagged under his neatly pressed suit. "You're right," he said, "but if I let you go, how do I know you won't whirl away and not touch down again for days?"

I rubbed my forehead, which felt tight and sore. I could feel a headache coming. It could have been the low pressure system but it was probably from not eating. "I'm not trying to be difficult, Detective. Sometimes in my business, we have to scramble to make a living and right now I'm scrambling as fast as I can. What are you doing for breakfast tomorrow?"

"Breakfast?" he said warily. I could see him unhappily contemplating a predawn drive to the North Shore. "How about lunch instead? And can you call me Dom?"

"I haven't got time for lunch. I mean breakfast. You know, the first meal of the day. Supposed to be very important, nutritionally speaking. What if I meet you at the Ihop at eight?"

"Ihop? The pancake house?"

"I'll even buy you breakfast. You'll love it."

"You mean right here in Anson?"

"Wherever it is. You know where I mean. The one right down the street."

"You've got a deal, Thea. You've made this worn-out old man very happy." He was neither worn-out nor old, but it sounded like he felt both. Before I could stop myself, I was giving him advice.

"It's not the years, Dom, it's the mileage, you know. Why don't you take a break, go home and whirl Mrs. Florio around the room. Use up some of that energy you were going to use to dump on me."

"Rosie is in a wheelchair," he said.

"Wheelchair or not, I'll bet Rosie is a hot ticket."

He considered that and nodded. "She is."

"I'm sorry about the wheelchair."

"It was a drunk driver. Smashed right into her while she was crossing the street. After that, I single-handedly doubled the number of OUI arrests in Anson. That's how I got to be a detective," he said.

"By making so many arrests?"

"Yeah." He grinned. "I'd arrested just about everyone in town who was important. They were dying to get me off patrol so they promoted me. Rosie thought it was hilarious. She kept making rude remarks about the Peter Principle. But I've come to like it. Shall we rejoin the company?" He held out his hand. I took it and he pulled me to my feet. "Maybe you're right," he said at the door, "maybe I'll go home and bother Rosie. She'd like that. On the other hand, considering the case of characters assembled, I should probably stay here and detect."

"But these are her friends. These are the people who loved her."

"Ah, but 'Heaven has no rage like love to hatred turned. . . .' "

"So these are the usual suspects?"

"Correct."

"Then there is truth to the old saying about the criminal always returning to the scene of the crime?"

"There's more truth in the old police adage that victims are most often murdered by people they know. And these are the people she knew." I remembered that Andre had said the same thing.

"But the paper said that a witness had reported a suspicious young man who looked like a street person lurking in the bushes around the time she was killed. Surely that's more likely, in a crime so senseless and violent?"

"Unless someone hated her."

"But who? Except for some rather strident psychological politics, I think she lived a rather staid life. Surely psychologists don't kill each other over things like that, they merely argue them to death." An image of two psychologists, lying on the floor in extremis, having argued themselves literally to death, flashed into my mind, followed by an image of the first woman who had spoken at the funeral. "But she treated battered women, didn't she? What about an enraged husband?"

"We're pursuing it," he said. "I thought you were in a tearing hurry to leave?"

"It's your fatal charm," I said. "You could get a stone to talk."

"Probably wouldn't have anything interesting to say, though, would it? See you at breakfast." He opened the door and went inside. I went back to the chair where I'd been sitting, picked up my plate and glass and took them to the kitchen. Then I went to say good-bye to Cliff and Eve.

Eve was sitting on the couch next to a very large man. They were holding hands. "Oh, there you are," she said. "I thought you'd gone. This is my friend Waldemar Becker. Thea Kozak." We shook hands. Becker had a brooding, Neanderthal sort of attractiveness. Protruding forehead with thick blond eyebrows, jutting cheekbones and a prominent jaw. His mouth was half-hidden by a bushy bronze mustache and his teeth, when he smiled, were sturdy and white and looked like they'd been designed to crush corn. "Waldemar will drive me home." She regarded him with a gaze that was possessive to the point of being icky.

"So you don't need me anymore?"

"No. But thanks for picking me up." She stuck her small hand back into his and nuzzled his shoulder with her chin.

I'd planned to urge her to call me if she needed someone to talk to, but her curt dismissal stung. Good-bye, Thea. Thanks for everything, you've been replaced. I felt a twinge of what I'd felt in eighth grade when I was supposed to go to the movies with my best friend Sherry and she stood me up without even calling because a boy had asked her to go with him instead. The twinge only lasted a few seconds, though, before it was swept away by a wave of reason reminding me I wasn't the center of everyone's universe. Besides, I'd been planning to abandon her, hadn't I? I left Eve playing an intimate finger-game with Becker and went to look for Cliff.

After passing through three rooms of guests in somber plumage, I found him in the library, sitting on another couch next to another attractive blond male, and they were also holding hands. It was beginning to be a scene worthy of Fellini. His companion was slight except for extremely broad shoulders which gave him the unbalanced physique that broadcasts "swimmer." I'd seen him on Saturday in Cliff's living room. "Thea," Cliff said, getting up as I approached, "I'd like you to meet my friend Rowan Ansel. Thea Kozak."

"Pleased to meet you," I said. Standing, Dr. Ansel was short and his oversized shoulders made his hips seem unnaturally narrow. His pale hair was straight and fine and the features on his pale face were delicate, almost feminine. His whole demeanor projected uncertainty and discomfort, like a teenager trying to seem at home at an adult party.

He dropped my hand and stepped back. Cliff took it and held on, his other hand on my shoulder. "Thanks for taking care of Eve," he said. "She really needed you. It was so important for her to have someone to turn to. Maybe she'll be okay now that her Viking is back. But if you could keep an eye on her . . ."

"Of course I will. Are we still on for tomorrow?"

"Certainly," he said, seeming puzzled that I'd needed to ask. "Three-thirty, right?"

"Right."

"I have a map for you someplace around here," he said, crossing to his briefcase and rummaging through it. "Here it is. I've marked my building in red. Oh . . . and Thea?" I waited. "Eve might make some odd suggestions . . . about me. Don't encourage her, please. It's just her own way of dealing . . . No. Never mind. Forget it." He turned his attention back to Ansel, dismissing me. I wasn't supposed to have noticed the urgent gesture Ansel had made which stopped whatever he'd been about to say.

I took the map and stuck it in my bag. "Thanks. I'll see you tomorrow then." I was in the front hall when someone tugged on my arm.

"Thea. Wait." Eve dragged me into the little powder room and locked the door behind us. "I was afraid you'd gone. There's something I have to tell you. I mean something I want you to do for me," she whispered.

"Sure, Eve. Of course. But why all the secrecy?"

She put a finger to her lips. "Quietly, please. You'll understand soon enough," she said. "Cliff says he's going to have you do some work for him? Up at Bartlett Hill?"

"We're going to discuss it."

"Good. So you'll be working there?"

"Maybe. If we take on the project. Why?"

"I want you to spy on Cliff and Rowan for me."

"You what?" I burst out.

"Quiet. Please. Look, I'm sorry for the mysterious act. I might as well just come out with it. But it's hard. You see . . ." She leaned against the sink, breathing hard, her eyes downcast, then said with a rush, "I think Cliff . . . my father . . . killed Helene."

"Eve, that's absurd." It was the same thing she'd said on Saturday, but then I'd assumed it was just the product of hysteria. Now I didn't know what to think. She seemed deadly serious.

"Look at him," she said, "does he seem like a grieving man? Sitting in there holding hands with that wretched Rowan at his wife's funeral! And hasn't he already called you up and invited you to do business? I told you how he left her at the hospital to go . . ." She choked on her words, steadied herself, and went on.

". . . to go walking with Rowan. He did the same thing at dinner on Saturday. You were there. You saw him. Just a bland 'excuse me, I've got to go walking with my friend now.' How could he? How can he? How can he not mourn? What kind of a man is he?" She stopped, breathing like a runner at the end of a race.

"I'll tell you what kind of man he is—a happy one. Freed of the burden of her disapproval, her challenges, her causes. All you have to do is look at him to see it. He's not bowed down by the sadness of her loss, he's a man who has had a great weight lifted from his shoulders."

"Eve," I interrupted, "it's natural for people to turn to their friends. . . ."

She raised her eyes from her study of the nondescript carpet. "Not like this. Not holding hands and looking happy!" Her voice rose, shrill and unsteady. "I need your help, Thea. I want him found out. I want my mother's murder avenged." Though she seemed wildly out of control, I didn't doubt that she believed what she was saying.

"People sometimes show their grief in odd ways," I said.

"Yeah. Right. By smiling and curling up with their lovers."

"That's what you're doing," I said.

"Exactly my point. In his case, it's completely inappropriate. He is . . . was . . . married. To Helene. To my mother. He shouldn't have a lover to curl up with. She wanted him to give up Rowan, so he killed her!"

There was no way to make her see how absurd her accusations were, so I tried a different tack. "If you really believe Cliff was involved, it's not me that you want, it's the police. Why not tell this to Detective Florio and let him handle it?"

"Sure," she said bitterly, "and make myself the laughingstock of the entire psychiatric community. They'd dismiss me as hysterical or as having unresolved Oedipal conflicts or something. Cliff would manage it beautifully and I'd come off as an overwrought fool. Besides, he has those two cops wrapped neatly around his

finger. They think he walks on water just like everyone else does."
I hadn't observed any such thing. To me, they'd seemed skeptical
of everyone.

She gripped my arms, her nails digging deep into my skin.
"You're the only one who can help me. You can understand . . .
and you know what to do. You found Carrie's killer when no one
else could. This is so perfect, don't you see? You'll be right there.
You can ask questions, look through his things, watch what he
does. See how far this thing with Rowan has gone. Don't you see,
Thea? There's no one else I can ask. I don't have a whole lot of
friends. You know how I am. You've got to do this for me. I can't
live with this awful doubt. I'm not asking for much and it's so
important to me. I have to know if it was really him."

When Andre had insisted that I call her, he'd had no idea what
he was getting me into. I'd forgotten how irrational and demanding Eve could be when she was emotional about something. She
was still clinging to my arm, nails dug deep, her eyes glued to my
face. I felt claustrophobic, shut up in that tiny bathroom with her
hysteria. I had to get out. "Look, Eve," I said, "I know this has
been very stressful for you. You're upset and you're worried." I
broke her grip and put my hands on her shoulders. "I don't mean
to diminish or devalue your feelings but right now you are in no
state to make decisions about something like this. You need to
calm down and consider this rationally. In a few days maybe we
can talk about this again."

"Don't patronize me, okay?" she said, shaking me off. "I'm
not some pathetic, anxious admissions director who needs to be
soothed. I have a reason to be upset! My mother has just been
slaughtered. I'm telling you that I'm afraid my father did it. All
I'm doing is asking for some help. Don't try to placate me with a
pat on the head. I am not a pet! Either say you'll help me or say
you won't, but can the smarmy bullshit, okay?" She jerked the
door open. "Go ahead. Leave. You can call me in a few days and

give me your answer after *you've* had time to calm down and consider this rationally. I'm in the book." She stalked out without looking back. A few people who were standing in the hall stared at me curiously as I left.

CHAPTER 8

IT HAD BEEN a thoroughly unpleasant day. It had left me feeling grouchy and overburdened and it wasn't over yet. I wanted to go crawl under a rock but I had to go back to the office to catch up on the "affair Valeria," and do some work for tomorrow. Luckily, I knew exactly how to revive my unwilling body. There was a new health club in the businessman's hotel near our office which offered a series of afterwork aerobics classes to help counter the spread of the desk-bound butt. They also had a weight room, a lap pool and a whirlpool. I had just enough time, barring another traffic jam, to suit up and make the 5:30 class. All that bouncing and leaping and panting was great for working the poisons out of my system, even if the instructor was an irritatingly enthusiastic young thing with great hair and perfect nails who had probably never tipped the scales at more than 103.

I rolled into the parking garage at 5:15, grabbed my gym bag out of the trunk, and raced down to the locker room, pausing to give my membership number to the sleek blonde behind the reception desk. Deftly, I spun the dial on the lock, jerked the door open, stripped off my business clothes, and hung them in the locker. Then I transformed myself into a creature of the lycra per-

suasion. I fastened my hair back with a blue band, and raced upstairs. I had a particular place I liked to stand, and if I didn't get
there early, someone else would take it.

I knew most of the people there by sight and we exchanged the
casual greetings of people who share a common interest but don't
even know each other's names. The conversation died out when
an ad-agency handsome man in a gleaming white version of a
1920s bathing suit glided in carrying a handful of tapes, put them
down, and turned to dazzle us with his matching white teeth.

"Good afternoon, ladies, my name is Aaron, and I'm going to
be your instructor today."

I heard a low moan from the young mother behind me. "Just
what I needed," she said softly, "I can't cope with my two left feet
if I have to stare at that adorable little ass." I tried to keep the grin
off my face. I knew how hard aerobics could be if you were distracted. I have to watch myself pretty carefully. Someone my size
can do a lot of damage in a small room full of bodies.

The dazzling Aaron slipped in a tape and glided to the front of
the room. "All right, ladies," he said, "let's start warming up." It
was immediately clear that he wasn't going to baby us. Fifteen
minutes into the class, I already had a large circle of sweat around
my navel and my hip flexors were threatening rebellion. When he
bared his perfect orthodontia and told us we had only five minutes
left before we began the cool down, I could have hugged him,
even though he was glistening with sweat.

It wasn't the usual sweetly rhythmic cool down, either.
Aaron's version of a cool down was a "serious upper body workout," as he called it, since women's upper bodies tend to be underdeveloped. I glanced down to where my feet were barely visible
below my underdeveloped chest. I knew that wasn't what he
meant. He meant that in the lats, pecs and delts area, I'm bony
rather than bulgy. No knotted ropes of muscles ripple the surface
of my skin. By the time he finally allowed us to drop our weights
and get mats for floor work, I had sweated Valeria, Andre, and
Eve's strange request right out of my system along with about two

gallons of water. Afterwards, in the locker room, Aaron was the hot topic.

I emerged from the shower limp as a wet noodle, but feeling spiritually revived, pulled black stirrup pants and an oversized sweatshirt over my trembling limbs and dragged my weary body out to the car. I've read that vigorous exercise is supposed to suppress the appetite but it sure doesn't work like that with me. Foremost in my mind was the image of a gigantic hamburger. Like a weary pilgrim, I followed that vision to Burger King and bagged a large coffee, a Whopper with cheese and a large fries. Clutching my booty and my briefcase, I climbed the stairs to the office, unlocked my door, and fell into my chair, greedily stuffing a handful of fries into my mouth as I picked up the stack of pink message slips Sarah had left for me.

Beneath them was a lengthy memo from Suzanne, responding to my phone call, suggesting some approaches for my meeting with Cliff Paris, and updating me on steps she'd taken in anticipation of Valeria's MCAD complaint. The last line of her memo was, "Call me as soon as you read this." I set the memo down and picked up the phone. She answered on the first ring.

"Hello?"

"Hi," I said, making my voice low and gruff, "this is Paul and I'm calling the whole thing off."

"I almost wish you were," she said, "and I almost wish you would. Call it off, I mean. I am reduced to dealing with the most excruciating mountain of minutiae. Which is why I asked you to call. Did you get your shoes?"

"Shoes?" I said.

"That's what I was afraid of. Paul's sister reacted exactly the same way, like I was saying something both inappropriate and offensive. Since when has shoes been a dirty word?"

"Since about one minute ago," I said. "Look, I'm a busy woman. The many and varied problems of independent schools are weighing heavily upon me and you want to talk about shoes? I don't have time to sit around and worry about elusive and nebulous concepts like shoes. What exactly is it about shoes that you wanted to discuss? I have fewer pairs than Imelda Marcos, even after she left the Philippines. I wear a nine narrow and I like expensive ones. What else is there?"

"There is whether or not you have a pair dyed to match your dress?"

"No. I do not. Am I supposed to?"

"Why else would I ask?"

"Good question. Okay, I'll stop giving you a hard time. When and where am I supposed to get these shoes?"

"They were supposed to come with the dress. You do have your dress, don't you?" There was an edge in her voice that suggested imminent breakdown. It was time to stop kidding.

"Calm down. You know I have the dress. You were with me when I picked it up. You picked yours up at the same time, remember? And I did go home and try it on, so I know that it fits. But there weren't any shoes. I'll go by tomorrow and ask them where the shoes are."

"That's the problem, Thea," she wailed. "They say they don't have the shoes. They insist that they gave you and Connie the shoes when you picked up the dresses." I'd be glad when the wedding was over. Suzanne doesn't wail, and she doesn't usually let herself be browbeaten by anyone. Cast in the role of the frazzled bride-to-be, Suzanne was acting the part beautifully, but it didn't suit her. It wouldn't be helpful, right now, to tell her to pull herself together. She already knew that's what she should do.

"How many pairs of shoes are missing?"

"Three. Connie's, yours, and a pair for Paul's daughter, who is going to be a junior bridesmaid."

"What colors and sizes?"

"Green in nine narrow and seven medium, and rose in a size five."

"They'll be on your desk by noon tomorrow." She didn't argue, just thanked me and hung up. I pulled out my calendar, wrote in my breakfast meeting with Detective Florio at eight, and between that and my eleven o'clock meeting I wrote SHOES. Then I got the files I needed and started preparing for tomorrow's meetings. Sarah, anticipating me, had left a new yellow pad and a stack of sharpened pencils.

My mother worries about me being alone in the office late at night, but I like it. The phone doesn't ring, no one stops in to ask questions. I can do as much work in three or four hours at night as I can in a whole day, sometimes more. I like my office. Early on, I realized that I was going to be spending a lot of time there and figured it was worth spending some money to make it comfortable. I have a little portable CD player and desktop speakers, with good old friends like Jackson Browne and Linda Ronstadt to sing to me, or Tom Petty to get the blood humming, or Vivaldi and Albinoni, if I'm feeling moody, and the Gordon Bok disc from Andre, which reminds me of some of our good times. I have a wonderful oil painting of a rocky beach in Maine on the wall, and a wacky and wonderful Art Deco lamp. My desk chair is extremely comfortable. Suzanne refuses to let me get a couch. She says if I had one, I'd never go home. She worries about me sometimes, which is silly, since she's a workaholic too.

By 10:30 I was ready to hit the road. I reached into my drawer to get my correspondence disk, to write a quick memo to Suzanne, couldn't find it, and searched frantically for a minute before I remembered that Karla Kaplan had taken it with her. I got another one from the supply closet, and while it was being formatted, I sat staring at the screen, thinking about Valeria. Suzanne and I hadn't discussed it, but it seemed like a good idea to talk to some of her former employers. Not by phone, it would be too easy for them to be unavailable if they were reluctant to talk about her. The best thing would be to simply drop in and surprise them. I got her resume and reference letters out of her personnel file and coaxed duplicates out of the copying machine. The machine, like a one-man dog, worked properly only for Sarah. It hated the rest of us and showed it in a multitude of infuriating and nefarious ways.

I stuffed the copies in my briefcase, typed a quick memo to Suzanne, and left, dropping a small stack of work on Sarah's desk on the way out. I didn't want her to feel underutilized.

The ride home was pleasant. I was tired enough to avoid obsessing about work and the workout had left me feeling good. There was time enough to worry about tomorrow's problems tomorrow. Sometimes I wonder if I lack a thirst for living. I don't feel a need to see a lot of movies, or go bowling, or drink with my friends, or even to veg out in front of the television. Mostly I go to work, I go to meetings, I come home, do some more work, and go to bed. I like my work, that's why I do it. I tried some other things, right after college. Social work, because I wanted to work with people, but it was too depressing, and working as a reporter because I like to write, but that was even more depressing. Now that I'm living at the ocean, I've added walking on the beach.

And there are weekends with Andre. Or there were. I wished I felt more optimistic about that. I knew he'd been badly hurt by his failed marriage even if he never talked about it. I wasn't the only one with emotional baggage that tended to pop open at the thought of weddings. I just wished we could talk. Nothing infuriates me more than stubborn silence. But tonight I was feeling good. I was not going to let him get to me.

I drove through the soft spring darkness with the music turned up loud. Road music. Springsteen, Tom Petty, The Stones, Creedence Clearwater, Canned Heat.

My answering machine squatted mute and unfriendly on the counter, its unblinking red eye glowing in the darkness. I marched past it. Who cared if Andre hadn't called. I had more important things to think about, like sorting the mail and hanging up my clothes before they got irretrievably wrinkled. My mother the compulsive neatnik had trained me well. When I die, they will find my clothes on hangers and my papers sorted into piles. And I won't be around to be embarrassed by the amazing variety of molds in my refrigerator or the sticky bourbon glasses on the coffee table or the pile of shoes under my chair.

I threw my balled-up workout clothes into the hamper and put my suit on a hanger. It was only as I closed the closet door that I realized I hadn't seen my pin on the jacket. I pulled the door open and checked. Nothing on the lapel. I searched through the bag, and it wasn't there, either. There were so many places it might be. It wasn't that it was valuable. It was just a simple silver pin. But it had come from David. A finely etched woman's face. A woman with fine features and a cloud of curly hair. He said he'd bought it because it reminded him of me. When I wore it, it brought me luck and this was no time to lose my luck. I kicked my shoes—my expensive Italian shoes—into the closet, mangling my toe in the process, and hobbled into the bathroom to find a Band-Aid and brush my teeth.

The woman in the mirror looked the same as always. A pale, heart-shaped face with straight dark brows, wide cheekbones, too much mouth and a determined chin. She didn't look worried or unlucky, just solemn. "A lot you know," I told the mirror. "Show a little emotion." The face tried to smile, but I could see her heart wasn't in it. "Oh, forget it," I muttered, and stomped off to bed. I was tired but sleep was a tease, lingering just beyond my grasp, too close to let me get up and read, too far away to seize. I curled up, hugging my pillow tightly, and tried to clear my mind. I'd just managed to crawl to the edge of sleep and slide over when the phone rang. I fumbled for it in the darkness and pulled the receiver to my ear. "Hello?"

"Thea? I'm sorry. Were you asleep?"

Andre. "Yes. Just."

"I'm sorry," he said again. "I just didn't want to leave you hanging. About the weekend." I should have hung up right then. I knew from his tone what he was going to say. I could even see his face, hard and angry, the way it got when he had to say something he didn't want to. "I'm not coming to the wedding. I can't. I'm sorry I left in such a hurry on Sunday. I guess I should have stayed and talked about things."

I wanted to tell him to stop, that I wanted him to save that deep, resonant voice for words of love, or for trivial, time-passing things, but part of our contract is that we're honest with each other. I wasn't sure how much honesty I could handle right now. "Andre . . ." I began.

"Please, Thea, let me get this out. It isn't easy, you know. I don't want to hurt you. I don't even want to disappoint you. If I could come and just walk through it, I would. I tried to imagine doing that, after you said it was no big deal, just something that a polite grown-up ought to be able to do. And maybe you're right. Maybe it is, in which case I guess I'm not a polite grown-up." He paused and this time I didn't interrupt. You can't value a person for their honesty and then refuse to let them be honest. "I guess that if I were a true romantic I'd show up and be there for you no matter how much it bothered me, since I know that you'll be sad going by yourself. But we both know that what you'll be sad about is not being there with David, not being married to David. If I'm there, it will be easier for you not to think about that."

"But if you're there, I wouldn't even be thinking about David."

"Maybe not," he said, "but I think you would. Listen, I'm not trying to be melodramatic, but it took me hours to get up the courage to make this call. I have a whole prepared speech to deliver."

"I'm listening."

"It's not that I think we should be married or anything. I'm no more ready for that step than you are," he said. "All I know is that I want . . . no, that I need . . . something more than this casual, good-times-when-our-schedules-permit thing we have now." He sighed. "I wish I were there, so I could see you. I thought this would be easier by phone. I wasn't brave enough to tell you in person that I wouldn't come to Suzanne's wedding. I was afraid I'd back down. But now I wish I were there. Damn. This is hard. I'm usually the one trying to get someone else to talk. I really said it all on Saturday. I need you around, to come home to. To anticipate. To offset the bad stuff. I need more of you in my life. I know it sounds childish, but if I can't have more, I don't want any. I'm not the type who is satisfied with just a bite of the cake. I want the whole piece." It was the perfect analogy, given how he felt about cake.

"But what is it that you want? Are you saying we should live together? Or spend all our weekends together, or what?"

"I know. I know." He sighed again. "I shouldn't get into it if I don't have the answers. If I don't have a plan, right? But I don't have a plan. I just can't go on like this. It's not good enough."

"It's been awfully good for me." I really didn't know how to respond. This wasn't a conversation to have over the phone. Or to have when I wasn't awake. He didn't know what he wanted, and I'd been content enough with what we had not to bother to analyze where it might be going. As he talked, I was waking up fast. The relaxed state I'd finally achieved was being replaced by anxiety creeping through me like an internal fog bank. "I don't know what to say, Andre. I guess I don't know what you're saying. Is this an ultimatum? More or nothing? Are you trying to tell me we shouldn't see each other anymore?" There was silence on his end, but in the background I could hear some sort of commotion. "Where are you? At work?"

"Where else?"

"So even if I was there, sitting in some apartment waiting for you to come home, I'd still be alone."

"You'd be closer. Besides, you haven't been sitting at home. I called three times, earlier, and you weren't there."

"I'm not a pet, Andre, to be kept at home, waiting for her master's return. I was at work just like you."

"Goddamnit, Thea, I know that. You aren't going to make this easy for me, are you?"

I thought of that day last fall when he'd told me, brutally and explicitly, how Carrie had died. I'd hated him then, raging out of his office physically sick and emotionally devastated, only to have him show up on my doorstep with a bag of groceries. Ignoring my hostility, he'd cooked me dinner, overcoming my dislike and resistance with his surprising candor and kindness. Since then he'd seen me at my worst, and I'd seen him through some pretty bad times, too. We had a lot of history, and even when I didn't like him, I loved him. This relationship wasn't something to be discarded like worn-out socks. "Honestly, I'm not trying to be difficult, Andre, you know that. I just don't know what to say. Or what to do. Or even what we could do. We both have our jobs. You have to be in Maine, and I have to be here."

"You could get another one."

"So could you, probably more easily than I could, but that's not what either one of us wants to do, is it?"

The commotion behind him got louder. "Hang on a minute," he said, and I could hear the buzz of low voices. When he came back on, it was to blurt out in an anguished rush, "I've got to go. I'll call you."

"I've heard that one before."

"Thea . . ."

"I'm sorry. I know you have to go. I'll be here. Call me. Anytime. Day or night."

"As soon as I can." He was gone in a click. Inert, I sat clutching the phone as the silence became a buzz, and then the buzz became an officious recording informing me that if I wanted to make a call I should hang up and dial the number. God how I hated those contented, corn-fed voice boxes. They reminded me of the worst kind of elementary school teachers, the kind that treated students like idiots. Maybe the phone company knows the truth and the majority of people really are idiots, but I hate to be patronized by a recording. I dropped the phone forcefully back into its cradle and went to find the bourbon bottle.

CHAPTER 9

My friend Jack Daniels and I were sitting out on my deck, listening to the sound of the waves. Jack was wearing a smart black label, tight fitting, simple and smooth. I was wearing a black velour robe, also tight fitting, simple and smooth. Overhead, the sky had cleared and the stars were winking at me knowingly. Jack was trying to persuade me to let him take his hat off so we could get to know each other better. I knew what Jack wanted. What all the guys want. To get inside me and make me feel good. But Jack doesn't know me as well as I know him. In the morning Jack would have his hat back on and would be sitting around contentedly awaiting his next encounter, maybe a little drained, but still full of heat and vigor. I'd have a headache, bad breath, a full schedule, and the unpleasant awareness that Jack was another thing I had to deal with.

Sometimes Jack can be a good friend, but in a crisis he usually does the wrong thing, or provides the wrong insights, and leaves me worse off than if I'd never gotten together with him. Still, his approach was so smooth, his warmth so inviting, I had to struggle to resist. Finally my sensible side won out over the weak, sensuous side of my nature. I grabbed Jack by the neck, dragged him inside, and shut him up in the closet. I got a bottle of seltzer and poured it over the disappointed ice cubes. They like Jack as much as I do.

Eventually the steady sound of the waves, combined with satisfaction from my victory over Jack, lulled me into a more placid state. I lay back in the lounge chair, sipped my seltzer, and looked up at the stars, trying to clear my mind. I'd managed to put Andre and work out of my mind, but I wasn't having the same success with Eve. She'd always had that effect on me. I thought back on our long friendship. When she wanted something from me, a conversation, help in sorting out a problem, or to borrow a favorite piece of jewelry, all she'd had to do was lurk there on the edge of my consciousness until I gave up and dealt with her. Eve had always suffered from the only child's fallacy of assuming she was the center of the universe. A great friend and a good roommate, but a person who wouldn't be ignored. Sly as a weasel while appearing perfectly innocent. She wasn't even here tonight and I still felt her bright eyes watching me and felt the pressure of her expectations. Trying to get her out of my head was like sweeping down a big cobweb and then trying to get rid of it. The little sticky bits cling and won't be swept away.

It was bad enough that Dom Florio kept showing up and making me think about Eve and Cliff and Helene. Now the whole mess had followed me home. This was supposed to be my castle. I was in charge here. "Go away, Eve," I said aloud. "Go away. I am not going to get involved in any more murders." My voice sounded strange out here in the quiet darkness. And my thoughts of Eve and of Helene, so abruptly and brutally dead, wouldn't go away.

I considered what she'd suggested—that Cliff had killed Helene—and why I didn't want to believe it. It wasn't very complicated. Viscerally, I didn't believe that Cliff killed Helene, but it was also true that I didn't want Cliff to be the killer. Because I knew him. Because I liked him. Because I wanted to believe that he was a good man, that he'd loved Helene, that good people didn't kill each other even if they were involved in midlife crises and alternative lifestyles. And because, like the woman who'd spoken at the funeral, I had admired and looked up to Helene and I couldn't bear the thought that someone so special could have been killed by someone I knew.

The part of me that likes to play devil's advocate said that was all very well but what about the facts? What about Cliff's lover? What about his apparent lack of grief? What if he had wanted a divorce and Helene refused to give it to him? It wasn't enough to support even a weak suspicion, let alone an assumption, my rational side responded. But the devil's advocate wouldn't stop. If Cliff wasn't guilty, it wouldn't hurt to do what Eve had asked. All I had to do was keep my eyes open and ask a few questions, that was all Eve wanted me to do. It wouldn't do any harm. I was going to be there anyway, wasn't I? Assuming we got a contract. It would be a good way to show Eve how wrong she was. "But I don't want to. I don't want to get involved," I told the darkness, feeling like a damn fool.

The devil's advocate just smirked and told me I already was involved or I wouldn't be thinking about it so much. It was this impulsive, do-gooder side of my nature, the side that thinks I have to do what I can to help people, to "fix" things, that Suzanne and Andre had been warning me about. They know me too well. I leaned back in the chair and closed my eyes.

Sometimes I wish I could be a little girl again so I could go and dump all my problems in the lap of some big, all-knowing grownup, to say, "Daddy, Andre and Valeria are being mean to me and Suzanne's happy and having a big party and I feel left out and my friend Eve is trying to get me to do things I don't want to do that I know I really shouldn't do. Fix it." Sometimes it's no fun being an adult. It isn't comforting to realize that no one is all-knowing, and it's wearing as well as empowering to know that you're responsible for supplying your own answers. So here I was, Thea "the buck stops here" Kozak, adult, sitting by myself on a cool, damp night, feeling like my mind was overrun with industrious black ants, and I was the exterminator.

I breathed deeply, relishing the salty tang of the air. Oddly enough, once I'd acknowledged them, the ants were very willing to go back to their nest for the night. Overhead, the stars twinkled against the velvet sky like tiny jewels. I would have fallen asleep, but it was too cool to be comfortable.

I tottered inside, my legs stiff and sore from the intense workout Aaron had given us, and crawled into bed. If I was this stiff now, I didn't want to think about what I'd be like in the morning. I buried my head in the pillow and made one last wish. I wished for a sleep without dreams, and my wish was granted.

When the alarm went off I groaned out loud. What had possessed me to arrange breakfast with Dom so early? It must have been his fatal charm. Cursing the dazzling Aaron, I limped into the bathroom and turned on the shower. My body felt like I'd been beaten with a hose and tomorrow I was supposed to go back and do it again. Maybe it wouldn't be Aaron. To compensate for my pain, I decided to show off a little and wear the new suit Suzanne had picked out for me. It was a superfine wool crepe in sage green, with a short, tight skirt and a swingy trapeze jacket over a slightly greener silk blouse. Eve always used to say when I wore green that it showed off my cat eyes.

Just thinking Eve's name was like having a bucket of cold water dumped on my head. What was I going to do about Eve and her crazy obsession? With anyone else I might be able to wait a few days and then get her to listen to reason, but Eve had always been adamant once she made up her mind. Luckily, this morning the solution seemed clear. I didn't have to do anything with them. I could dump them in Dom's lap and get on with the pressing problems of my own life.

I pulled back the hair that always straggles into my face and secured it with some small gold barrettes. I found some gold and jade earrings and green shoes. I checked the whole business in the mirror. Not bad. I'd struck a neat balance between someone's wet dream and Sister Mary Catherine. I grabbed my briefcase, hurried out to the car, and joined the morning rat race.

I was only a few minutes late, but Dom was already there, drinking coffee and staring happily at a steaming mound of pancakes. He smiled when he saw me, gave me a brisk head-to-toe inspection and shook his head. "Good thing Steve's not here," he said. "The poor guy'd be drooling."

"They don't give you guys a course at the academy in drool management?"

"Sure they do," he said, "but you know how it is. Some guys just do better at it than others. I shouldn't make fun of Steve, though. He's a good, solid guy. And smart. It's just that sometimes he lets the little one-eyed guy do his thinking for him."

"The little one-eyed guy?" I said, puzzled. Then I realized what he was talking about. I could feel a hot blush rise up my face. "Well, we're off to a good start, aren't we?" I slid into the booth and picked up the menu, waiting for the blush to fade.

"I already ordered for you," he said, "assuming that you may not eat again all day." The waitress appeared and set a staggering amount of food before me. Dom poured my coffee and waited for my reaction to his selection.

Two poached eggs on toast. Bacon, sausage and home fries. A side of pancakes. A large glass of orange juice. Enough for the Russian army or one hungry woman. "Well, what are we waiting for?" I said, picking up my fork. "The day is getting old."

"Interesting funeral yesterday, wasn't it?" he said.

I stopped trying to dissect my sausage and met his half-hidden blue-eyed stare. "I guess we need to get a few things straight, Dom. I never find funerals interesting. I hate them. And I don't like to play cop games. If you want to ask a question, ask it, but don't try oblique approaches, don't try to trick me, don't try to screw around with my psychology because of things you know, or think you know, about me, okay?"

"Whew," he said, shaking his fingers like he'd been burned. "You change moods almost as fast as your friend Eve."

"I don't think so," I said, slicing into the first egg and watched the yellow yolk roll out and ooze across the toast. It's a treat to get a poached egg that isn't hard-boiled. Dom was dealing with his pancakes in a much more methodical way. He was just eating them. "And don't judge Eve by the last few days. She has every reason to be upset. She's not normally so difficult."

"Was Helene Streeter a faithful wife?" he asked.

"How the hell should I know . . ." I began, then backed off. "I'm sorry, Dom. I guess I am a little edgy this morning. As far as I know, yes. At least, Eve never said anything to me to suggest otherwise. But it isn't something she would necessarily tell me. I told you, we haven't seen much of each other lately." Feeling slightly guilty, I shared what Eve had confided in me. "She did say her parents weren't sleeping together."

"By which she meant they were occupying separate bedrooms or weren't having sex?"

"I don't know about their sleeping arrangements. I assumed she meant they weren't having sex." As I said this, the waitress leaned across me to check the coffee pot. Waitresses and waiters have special built-in intimacy receptors that compel them to interrupt the most private parts of conversations. You can spend a whole evening undisturbed having a personal conversation with your lover, but the moment you finally get up the courage to blurt out "you need to take more time to get me aroused," the waiter will refill your water glass and drown out the word "aroused." He will hear it, but your lover will not. It never fails.

"Interesting," Dom said. "Cliff Paris told me theirs was a happy marriage in all respects, and Eve said nothing to contradict that."

"You know why, don't you?"

He smiled, an amused smile that reminded me of Andre, the first time I met him. It was the experienced cop's "who does this civilian think she is?" smile. "Tell me," he said.

"Eve doesn't trust you. She thinks Cliff has you wrapped around his finger, so you won't believe anything she says. And Cliff has spent a lifetime protecting his privacy from people who are trying to get at him. He'd probably have a hard time talking to you even if he truly wanted to. I think shrinks reach a point where they only feel safe talking to people in their own profession."

"Thank you, Dr. Kozak."

"Shut up, Dom. I like you. Don't spoil it by being an asshole, please."

He seemed genuinely shocked by my bad language. Because I'm pretty, and abundantly female in design, men tend to expect me to be delicate, feminine and a sweet thing. Treating me like a fragile blossom when they can't wait to get their hands on my petals. It is wickedly iconoclastic of me to shatter those illusions, but I love to.

He concentrated briefly on his pancakes before he spoke again. "Okay," he said, "truce. I guess you aren't the only one who's edgy this morning. I just want to find the person who did this. We both know there's no such thing as a good murder, but this one is just so nasty. Not just a stab wound or two, like you might expect from a random attack, but deep, deliberate slashes, designed to kill."

"Just don't show me any pictures, okay?" I interrupted.

"No," he said, "I don't think you'd like to see the pictures. But why did you think I might?"

"Andre did, when he wanted my cooperation and he thought he wasn't getting it."

"It never occurred to me. But you know cops. We just do what works." He pushed his glasses back into place. "Within the bounds of the Constitution, state law, and our own personalities, that is. What Eve said about her parents is interesting because the autopsy showed that Helene Streeter had had sex with someone on the day she died." As soon as he'd said it I could tell he regretted it. It was one of those facts cops like to keep to themselves.

"So maybe they'd reconciled." I was very uncomfortable talking about Helene Streeter's sex life. "I thought you wanted to ask me about Eve and her father?"

"I do. But other things occur to me, so I ask."

I tried to drop my problem in his lap. "Eve thinks her father killed her mother. Has she told you that?"

"Obliquely. She keeps hinting at it and baiting him. Like she did at dinner."

"And you know about Rowan Ansel?"

"Paris hasn't exactly been subtle, has he? Holding hands with the guy, for God's sake, right after the funeral. I understand these guys in the touchy-feely business are maybe a bit more demonstrative than other folks might be, but they've gotta have limits, too. I guess it would make more sense if Paris was the one who got killed. Then I'd assume it was his wife in a minute and understand why she did it, too. People have a hard time when their mates are unfaithful. It leads to a lot of violence. But it's harder than hell to take when your spouse leaves you for a member of the same sex. It's just too weird. People really freak out."

"I'm not detecting a bit of homophobia here, am I?"

Dom massaged his forehead wearily. "Oh, hell no, Thea. I don't care if people wanna sleep with anteaters, as long as they're peaceful and don't do it in the streets. I just think people would be a lot better off if they'd just sleep with each other, get close, get some of that tension out of their systems, instead of bargaining with sex like it was poker chips."

I thought I was beginning to understand another source of the sexual overlay on today's conversation. "Do you take your own advice? You didn't go home and whirl Rosie around, did you?"

He stared down at his plate, refusing to look at me. "She was tired. That physical therapy really wears her out. And makes her glum. She thinks she'll never get anywhere. Never get any better. So I left her alone."

"Thought you just said people ought to make more love? Get close, get the tensions out?"

"Yeah?"

"So after you leave here, you should go right home, scratch that itch, get sex off your brain so you approach your work with a clear mind and let Rosie know that accidents, disability and physical therapy notwithstanding, she is still a sexy desirable woman. And if you say 'yes, Dr. Kozak' again I will pour syrup on your head." His eyes came up from his plate and he was grinning. I wondered how I'd ever typed him as plain and dull. "What?" I said.

"That Andre Lemieux is a lucky man." He put on a leer and twirled an imaginary mustache. "As some actor is alleged to have said about Sonia Braga, 'you are much woman.' Tell me about Eve's relationship with her father."

"She's mad at him. She thinks he betrayed her mother by having a relationship with Rowan." I told him everything I could remember about Eve and her father, the current stuff she'd told me, and things from back when we'd lived together. It seemed odd that he thought I was a useful source, but Eve had always been sort of a loner, a one-friend-at-a-time kind of person, so maybe there weren't many people around he could ask about her. Waldemar Becker didn't look like the talkative type, and anyway, he was a newcomer. Now that we'd gotten our cards out on the table, we got along fine.

"Cliff wants to talk to me about doing some work for him and Eve thinks it's the perfect opportunity for me to do a little spying for her." I guess I'd expected him to tell me I wasn't even to consider such a thing, because his answer disappointed me.

"Oh, really?" he said. "She wants you to be her spy? Do you think he did it?"

"Of course not."

"Why 'of course not'?"

"Because Cliff loved his wife. And he's not the killing type."

"So, are you going to do it?" he said.

Disappointment made me grouchy again. "I thought finding killers was your job."

"We can always use a little help."

"You're supposed to tell me to stay out of it," I said.

"Oh, right," he agreed. "Missy, you keep your pretty little

nose out of this, you hear? This is police business. Too dangerous for a nice girl like you. You just leave the crime solving up to Uncle Dom and Uncle Steve and when we're done you can bake us a cake, okay?" I wanted to be mad at him but I was laughing too hard.

"Seriously, though," he said, "by a little help I don't mean you should go around interviewing witnesses or give Cliff Paris the third degree. Just keep your eyes and ears open and if you hear something, call me. Anytime. Day or night. The lines are always open." And then, sounding a lot like Andre, he said, "You be careful around these people. *All* of these people, you hear?"

"There's nothing wrong with my ears, Florio. Does that mean you've narrowed your pool of suspects?" I wanted him to say no, but he just gave me that mocking cop's look again—the old "trust me, I'm trying to help you but don't expect me to tell you anything" look. The one that always makes me bristle. On the bright side, even if he hadn't quite taken my problem off my hands, he'd given me some direction, as in 'stay out of it unless you overhear something useful.' That felt better.

When the check came, I grabbed it before he could over his protests that he couldn't let a witness pay. "I'm not a witness," I said, "I'm just an informant. A sweet young thing, remember? Besides, I invited you." He still seemed uneasy. "Come on, Dom, relax," I said, "you don't think I did it, do you?"

He shook his head. "So far, you're about the only person I don't suspect."

Grateful for small favors, I went forth to tackle the next task on my list. The Elegant Aisle, which is a nauseating name for a bridal shop, opened at 9:30, and I was camped on the doorstep ten minutes before that, waiting for shoe showdown time. I was feeling invigorated by my breakfast with Dom. It was strange how exhilarating a bit of banter and conflict could be first thing in the morning. Andre often gave me the same feeling, and I knew one of the reasons I liked Dom was that he reminded me of Andre. I wasn't literally on the doorstep, of course, I was in my car, and I used the time to review the notes I'd made for my eleven o'clock meeting. I wasn't worried about that one. It was a straightforward job, something Suzanne and I could do with our hands tied behind our backs. It was the afternoon meeting with Cliff that I was more concerned about.

Finally, at 9:40 the place began to show some signs of life. I guess I shouldn't have been surprised. Weddings never start on time, why should wedding suppliers? Besides, these were the dim folks who had lost three pairs of shoes and now were trying to weasel out of their responsibilities by passing the buck. I was about to pass it right back. I shouldered my briefcase and went inside.

The woman who came to greet me was probably in her fifties, well corseted and elaborately coifed. She was wearing a fussy pink silk number unsuitable for any occasion occurring before four in the afternoon. I got right to the point. "Good morning, Mrs. Leslie," I said, "I'm Thea Kozak. I don't know if you remember me. I'm in Suzanne Begner's wedding party. She asked me to stop in and pick up the shoes."

Mrs. Leslie's face, which had begun to smile, fell into a frown when I reached the word "shoes." "I'm afraid there's been some misunderstanding, Mrs. Kozak," she said, "we don't have the shoes. They've already been picked up."

"That's odd," I said, "Suzanne just called me last night and asked me to pick them up this morning. Were you open at ten last night?"

"We closed at six," she said. "The shoes were picked up along with the dresses. We always do it that way. To avoid confusion. You know how flustered brides can be."

"I do," I agreed, "brides can get very flustered, especially when something that is supposed to be delivered is never delivered. To whom did you deliver the shoes?"

"I'll have to check the records," she said. "Excuse me just a moment."

I waited impatiently, shifting restlessly from foot to foot. The room was so decorated it was oppressive. It looked a lot like I'd always imagined a French bordello might look, and it wasn't big enough for the three mannequins in full bridal regalia who stood around me. The carpeting was so deep I could hardly see my feet.

After an extremely long moment she came back clutching two order forms which she laid down on the desk facing me. "Now, as you can see from this," she pointed to my order form, "we put a check mark in these boxes when the items are delivered. Here is your form, with a check next to your dress, and one next to your shoes, and here," she pulled my form back and slapped another in its place, "is Constance Webster's, also with two check marks." She pointed out the marks with the pen she was holding.

I looked at the marks, and then at the pen. "I'm still confused," I said. "I picked up my dress myself, and there were no shoes. Suzanne says Mrs. Webster got no shoes either. Isn't it possible that someone simply forgot to hand them out but inadvertently checked the box, and the shoes are somewhere in the back, still waiting to be collected?"

"Certainly not," she snapped without even considering my suggestion, "we're very careful about things like that." I doubted that she'd even looked for the shoes.

"How does your pickup usually work?" I asked. "Does one person coordinate the order and deliver both the dress and the shoes, or do you have a dress person and a shoe person, each of whom must check off the appropriate space on the order form?"

"One person," she said, looking puzzled. "We're a small business."

"Well, then perhaps you can explain to me why the checks on the forms are written in two different colored inks, one blue, and one red like the pen you're holding, and why they are so obviously made by two different people? And perhaps you could also explain," I said, pulling out my own copy of the form, which I'd gotten when I picked up the dress, "why only the box for the dress is checked on my form, which is supposed to be an exact copy of yours."

Mrs. Leslie bent down and peered at the form I was holding, then straightened up and looked at me like I'd just tracked something nasty across her carpets. "I'll have to check on this," she said, and stalked out, her tightly corseted rump rocking stiffly up and down like an anchored tugboat in a rising tide. She stumped back five minutes later with two shoe boxes which she dumped in front of me. "Here you go," she said grudgingly. "I don't know how this could have happened."

I opened the first box. A gleaming pair of green satin shoes. So far, so good. Opened the second box. Another green pair. The boxes confirmed that one was nine and the other seven. Great. I was two-thirds of the way to victory. "This is terrific," I said, "now I just the need the rose shoes for the junior bridesmaid and I'll be on my way."

"She hasn't picked up her dress yet," Mrs. Leslie said stubbornly.

"That's okay. I'll take the dress, too."

"I'm afraid I can only release that to the bride or the young lady herself."

I was losing my patience with her administrative bullshit. Systems put in place to make things go more smoothly I can understand, but I have no tolerance for rigid adherence to systems which only inconvenience the customer. "I promised Suzanne I'd deliver the shoes today and I intend to do that. You can give me the shoes, or the shoes and the dress, whichever you prefer. But I will not leave without the shoes, and if you delay me any further," I made an elaborate display of looking at my watch, "I will take out a very large ad in the local papers detailing exactly how you've behaved here today and urging people not to patronize this shop, and I will do it for at least four weeks."

"You wouldn't dare!"

I shrugged. "You want to try me and see? I can afford it. And I hate people who screw things up and then try to shirk their responsibility." I moved closer, so I was towering over her, invading her personal space. "Why don't you go get the shoes."

She scampered off and came hurrying back with the dress and shoes. She practically threw them at me. "There," she said, "take them and go. I have never dealt with someone so rude."

I put the dress over my arm and picked up the three boxes of shoes. "I can't say I've never seen anyone more dishonest," I said, "but you do puzzle me. What were you going to do? Return the shoes and pocket the money? It's pathetic, Mrs. Leslie. Unless it's just incredible incompetence." She started to say something, but I didn't wait to hear it. I took the loot and left. From the car I could see her standing behind the counter, sagging like an inflatable doll with a slow leak.

Flushed with triumph, I went to the office. Magda's normally sad face lit up when she saw me coming with the dress and the shoe boxes. "This is very good, Thea," she said. "Now maybe Suzanne can get some work done today." She shook her head and made a spiraling motion in the air with her hand. "All of this stuff is making her crazy. Myself, I will be most relieved when this weekend is over." Suzanne wasn't in, so I left the stuff in her office and hurried to get the stack of pink slips Sarah had been waving at me since I came through the door.

"Thanks," I said, grabbing them.

She smiled wryly. "I'm not sure you should be thanking me. I've been wondering, is telephone ear a covered disability under workers' comp?"

"Not until you have open sores," I said. She made a face and went back to her typing. I carried the messages into my office, dropped into my chair, and went through the stack, sorting them into three piles—ASAP, respond when I have time, and into the circular file. The ability to prioritize is an important skill. I ended up with three messages from someone called Lenora Stern I didn't know what to do with. I stuck my head out and asked Sarah.

"Any idea who Lenora Stern is?"

She shook her head. "The only thing she said was that Eve had asked her to call you." That wasn't very illuminating, but at least I knew I could put her in the "when I have time" file. I threw most of the messages away, stuck Lenora and the rest of her group under the corner of my blotter, and began to work my way through the ASAPs.

A while later Suzanne blitzed in, thanked me effusively for the shoes, and dumped an administrative headache on my desk. "Bobby says he has a hot prospect for Valeria's job. Can you see her sometime tomorrow?" She thrust a resume at me and hurried out.

Praying for light traffic and green lights, I grabbed my stuff and went to my meeting. I was sitting at a red light, drumming impatiently on the steering wheel, when I remembered who Lenora Stern was. The imperious colleague who had spoken at the funeral. The one who'd impressed me into slavery. I experienced a momentary irritation with Eve. I didn't know what she was up to, but I did know I had no intention of returning Lenora's call.

CHAPTER 10

My MEETING WITH Cliff Paris wasn't going well. "Bear with
me," he said wearily, "I know I initiated this and I should be more
helpful but I have a lot of trouble thinking about our clinical services as a product and about referring therapists and HMOs as
target groups or feeders. All these words. Networking. Height-
ened awareness. Name recognition. The Yellow Pages. Jesus! Is
this really what we have to do?" He closed his eyes, leaned back in
his chair, and scrubbed at his forehead like he was trying to wipe
his confusion away. "I'm glad you understand this stuff," he said,
"because I'm totally at sea here."

"It is a lot of stuff to grasp all at once, Cliff. Would it be better
if I put something in writing for you to look at? Something you
can show the rest of your board? Or would it be easier if I just met
with you and the board and tried to explain it to all of you?" He
stared at me helplessly, not responding. I wasn't used to seeing
Cliff helpless. He was the parent of a friend. As long as I'd known
him, he'd always been a grown-up. Wise and invincible. I stared
back at him, this man I'd known for nearly a decade, seeing him
for the first time vulnerable and confused. He was so clearly suffering. How could Eve possibly believe he'd killed Helene?

Today he looked as haggard and distressed as everyone had been suggesting he should. The skin beneath his eyes was smudged with purple and he had an unhealthy pallor. He was nothing like the charismatic man I knew. He was doddering and confused and looked suddenly old. He had to make a physical effort to follow what I was saying and even then he wasn't getting much. As I watched, waiting for him to answer my question, his eyes gradually closed and his head dropped forward onto his chest. I sat very still, not wanting to startle him with any sudden movements. When I was sure he was fully asleep, I took his jacket, tucked it around him, and quietly let myself out.

In the outer office, his assistant Roddy Stokes gave me a surly nod, grabbed a stack of papers and headed for the door. "Don't bother him right now," I said. "He's asleep." He paused before the door, literally trembling with indecision. He wanted to defy me because he disliked me. He seemed to dislike everyone. I knew that from Eve and I knew that from dealing with him. It didn't take long. This time, though, he was frustrated. He couldn't defy me without disturbing Cliff. Finally, with a shrug and a sigh, he walked dejectedly back to his desk, sat down and stared at me angrily.

"It was very inconsiderate of you to insist on seeing him the day after the funeral," he said petulantly. His whiny, nasal voice made me want to cover my ears. I couldn't understand how Cliff had ever hired Roddy. According to Eve, no one else could stand him. Eve's dislike bordered on hatred and I could see why. He had a supercilious nastiness that infused every transaction. Today he'd kept me waiting ten minutes before telling Cliff I'd arrived just for the sake of making me wait. Dealing with Roddy made it easier to understand how you could come to hate someone so much you didn't feel badly about doing horrible things to them. His appearance didn't help. He was plump in a way that made his pinkish skin seem bloated. He was only in his twenties, but his pale hair was receding, and it rose in tufts from his high, domed forehead and straggled untidily down over his collar, reminding me of a troll doll. His mouth was large, loose and wet, his glasses loomed over his tiny nose, and he didn't smell fresh. His one virtue was that he adored Cliff and zealously guarded him from intruders.

"He insisted on the meeting," I said. "Can you tell him that I'll call him tomorrow?" I was reaching for the doorknob when the door burst open, slammed into me, and literally knocked me across the room. Rowan Ansel stood there, clutching a blooming zebra plant, his fair skin gradually turning bright red.

"Oh goodness, Mrs. Kozak," he said, "I'm so sorry. Are you all right?" Behind the desk, Roddy watched him with a look so venomous the poison practically oozed across the floor. Ansel put the plant down and crossed to where I was leaning against a desk, rubbing my face, feeling slightly stunned. He took me firmly by the arm and steered me to a chair, setting the briefcase I was still clutching on the floor beside me. "Where did it hit you?"

"Here," I said, pointing to my cheek. I could already feel it swelling. There was a knife edge of numbness running down my face, with pain radiating out on either side. Another line of pain ran down from my right shoulder to my breast. "And here." My first thought was not about broken bones or nerve damage, it was Suzanne's wedding. Wouldn't it be great to stand up in front of a church full of people looking like I'd been punched in the face? And ruining her wedding pictures? "I'm okay, really. It was just a bump." I tried to get up. Being fussed over makes me uncomfortable.

But Dr. Ansel, having creamed me with a door, wasn't going to let me go until he'd made sure the damage wasn't serious. "Roddy, can you go down to the staff kitchen and get some ice, please." It wasn't a request. It was a command, and Roddy showed his displeasure by making a great deal of noise getting out of his chair and stomping to the door. Ansel watched his departure with a look of intense distaste. It was clear there was no love lost between the two of them. A lot of tension left the room when the door closed.

Ansel bent over me and probed my face very gently with his fingers. Then he slipped his hand inside my shirt and began doing the same thing to my shoulder. I stiffened involuntarily when he did. "Relax," he said, smiling for the first time. "I'm a physician." I tried to relax, but his concern was making me nervous. I just wanted to gather up my things and get out of there. Gently he felt my shoulder and my collarbone, his face thoughtful, his eyes watching me, observing my reactions, moving slowly and carefully back and forth. "Mmm," he said, finally, withdrawing his hand and straightening up. "Feels okay. I can't be sure nothing's broken—you'd need an x-ray for that—but there's nothing obvious."

Roddy came stomping back with a Styrofoam cup of ice, which he stuck in my face and rattled loudly. Ansel pushed his hand back. "Don't be so thick, Roddy," he said, "see if you can find a plastic bag or some wet paper towels or something. She needs to put the ice on her face, she's not going to take it for a walk." Roddy left again in search of a plastic bag.

"I'll just give this plant to Cliff and we can go back to my office," Ansel said. "It's not very restful around here, is it?"

"Don't bother him," I said. "He's asleep."

"Asleep?" he said, as shocked as if I'd said Cliff was dancing a jig.

"He fell asleep in the middle of our meeting."

"You're kidding," he said, then recognized that I might find that offensive. "Is he okay? I mean, it's just not like Cliff to just fall asleep in the middle of the day." It was obvious he wanted to see for himself, to reassure himself that Cliff was okay.

"Yes, he's okay. He was just terribly tired. And the stuff we were discussing was hard for him. I think it wore him out."

"He falls asleep on you and then you get bashed by me. We're not treating you very well around here today, are we? Look, we'll go down to my office and you can lie down and put some ice on your face. If you do it right away, you should be able to prevent some of the swelling."

That seemed like good advice since the last thing I wanted was a swollen face, so I let what I would call "practical vanity" win out over my urge to flee and let him lead me down the corridor to his office. He carried my briefcase and clutched my arm like he expected me to collapse at any minute. Halfway down the hall we met Roddy, clutching a plastic bag. Ansel took the bag and the ice and ushered me into his office. He quickly removed two stacks of books from the couch and gestured for me to sit down. Then he dumped the ice into the plastic bag, wrapped a handkerchief from his pocket around the bag, and gave it to me. He moved the two throw pillows to one end and thumped them. "Lie down, put your head here, and then rest the ice on your cheek for at least twenty minutes."

Reluctantly, I slipped my feet out of my shoes, curled up on my side with my head on the pillow, and pressed the improvised icepack against my stinging cheek, wincing at the initial pain. I closed my eyes and slowly counted to ten, waiting for the ice to start having a numbing effect. "I can see you're uncomfortable. You want to get out of here as quickly as possible, don't you?" he said. "Is that because you can't stand being taken care of or because Eve has told you that I'm an ogre and should be avoided?" I started to say something, but he stopped me. "Never mind. You don't have to answer that. I was just thinking out loud. I'm sorry. It would be unfair for me to keep you here because I want to be sure you're not suffering some shock from a sudden blow like that and then ask you troubling questions."

He knelt down beside the sofa, studied my face and then felt my hands. "You're cold," he said, getting his jacket from the back of the door and draping it over me. Then he went to sit behind his desk, obviously ill at ease.

His first guess was right. I felt ridiculous curled up on a stranger's couch being fussed over because of a little bump from a door. Well, it hadn't been such a little bump. The ice had numbed my face, but my shoulder and chest still throbbed. Not something that needed medical attention. I just needed some aspirin and a hot bath. A bath, I thought sadly, that was a long time away. I still had too much to do today. But Dr. Ansel ought to be able to scare up a few aspirin. The sooner, the better. I felt vaguely stunned and enervated, tempted to just close my eyes and nap. I sat up and set the ice down beside me. "I've got to get going," I said. "Could you get me a couple of aspirin?"

"Of course. But I wish you wouldn't go. Twenty minutes with the ice really would be better than ten." He smiled, a sweet, self-deprecating smile. "I know you think I'm being a fussy and old maidish, but I'm not. I admit it, I do feel horribly guilty for crashing into you like that, but it's quite sensible to watch you for a while. Sometimes people think they're fine and they go marching off all pumped up with adrenaline and then later, when the chemical rush subsides, find themselves dizzy and unstable and shaken." He tapped his fingers together nervously. "I'm just being cautious."

Okay, he'd convinced me. I could spare ten more minutes if it meant he'd feel better. I put the ice back on my face and curled up on the sofa. This time I didn't close my eyes. I was taking no chances with old man sleep. Instead, I studied the lair of this man Eve believed had led her father astray.

Everywhere else I'd been at Bartlett Hill had been decorated in early chocolate-and-vanilla pudding—yellowing white walls and utilitarian brown woodwork—but Ansel's office wasn't dark and dim at all. Three walls of the office were white and the fourth was a bright apple green. There was a dhurrie rug on the floor with lots of bright green and rose and sunny yellow. The sofa I was lying on had a bright flowered slipcover. On the walls were two large pastels of summer gardens, and behind his desk, on another wall, were four smaller pastels of a river at sunset. "Nice pictures," I said. My face hurt when I talked. It reminded me of the first, last and only time I'd ever been punched in the face. At least this time my nose wasn't broken. I have such a facility for looking on the bright side.

"Thanks," he said, "I did them."

"I especially like that one." I pointed at a picture of a lone canoeist about to enter a ribbon of gold laid on the water by a sinking sun. "It reminds me of the river behind my parents' house."

He got up and took it down off the wall. "I'd like to give it to you, if you'll take it. Just a little thing to say I'm sorry."

"I couldn't," I said. "It's too much. Besides, it was an accident. I know that. You don't owe me anything. And it looks so nice there with the others."

He stood there, awkwardly holding out the picture. "Is it that, or has Eve convinced you that I'm a bad person, and you shouldn't take things from bad people like me?" There was a trace of bitterness in his voice.

"Are you a bad person?" I asked, wondering why he cared what I thought of him and why he believed Eve's influence was so important.

"I'm a gay person," he said, setting the picture down. "In the minds of a lot of people, that makes me bad. Maybe I am bad. I had an affair with a married man. Not that that's so unusual." A smile as faint as a whisper crossed his face. "But usually that's something women do, isn't it? Having an affair with the boss. I'd be less than honest if I didn't admit I felt bad about it. I felt wicked. Sometimes completely wretched. But Cliff was irresistible and I didn't resist. I didn't reject him and send him back to his astringent marriage. I saw him and I wanted him and I yielded to temptation. I didn't give much thought to how Helene might feel. Cliff said she didn't care and I accepted that at face value because that's what I wanted to believe."

He sat down behind the desk, pushed the picture away so that he had room for his elbows, and sat there, chin in hands, watching me. He looked like a kid talking to his mother at the kitchen table, but what he was saying was anything but childlike. "You've known Cliff for a long time, haven't you? So you know how good he can make a person feel. How special. How central. And I'll bet you know how compelling and irresistible that kind of attention is. Who wouldn't want that?"

It was obviously a rhetorical question because he didn't wait for an answer. "So I took what I wanted. So what. That's what everyone does. At least he was honest with her. We weren't going behind her back. Then she decided she didn't like it and asked him to stop seeing me."

I abandoned the ice pack and sat up. The only reason I was staying was to be sure I was calm and together before I went on my way, and because Ansel had seemed to need reassurance. There was no way I could relax and recover while listening to true confessions, even if this was precisely the sort of snooping Eve wanted me to do. I could tell I didn't want to hear what Ansel had to say. "I appreciate your frankness, Dr. Ansel, but I really don't want to know about your relationship with Cliff. It's none of my business."

"Hold on a minute," he said. "I'm sure Eve has filled your head with venom, with inflammatory stories, about how I induced Cliff to betray her mother. She's probably even shared her nasty little theory that Cliff, or Cliff and I, killed Helene because she was opposed to our relationship. It's bullshit, you know, pure and simple."

I opened my mouth to protest, to remind him again that I didn't want to hear it, but he waved me off angrily.

"I've got a right to be heard," he said. "Unresolved Oedipal stuff, Cliff says. Eve's always been insanely jealous. Even jealous of her own mother. Naturally she'd be upset by our relationship— Cliff's and mine. I've tried to talk to her about it. She won't even listen. She says I disgust her. Stupid girl. It must be such a burden for Cliff, having a child like that. I've tried to be nice to her but she won't warm up no matter what I do. And Cliff is so blind . . ."

What arrogance, I thought, calling her a child. He must have been close to Eve's age himself. If he approached her with this attitude, no wonder she disliked him. It was hard enough to deal with a parental affair without all this pseudohonest and condescending openness. "Dr. Ansel, please, I . . ."

He wasn't listening. He was lecturing. "Cliff needed me as much as I needed him," he said. "Helene was a strident, manipulative bitch. She didn't want to be a wife or a companion to Cliff, to share his life, not anymore. She didn't care if he was happy, she only cared if she was happy, but she would never have let him go. She wanted the semblance of a marriage, the protective shell of monogamy, even if she didn't want the reality. It gave her a security that freed her to concentrate on her real interests." He stared out the window.

I followed his gaze to the reddish green, fan-shaped leaves that were sprouting on the tree outside. It was spring, and they would be growing larger every day, the red fading away, leaving only a rich, true green. It was the time of year to be outside, reveling in the beauty of the world, letting the warm wind caress my skin, breathing in the rich earthy smells. A very physical time of year. And my very physical man, Andre, seemed to be about to take a hike, while all the other people I was spending my time with seemed to want to talk only about murder and death and sex and school problems. Right now, I'd even have welcomed a little of Suzanne's wedding talk. At least weddings were happy occasions. I'd certainly gone wrong somewhere, to be in this situation. Either that, or the gods really had it in for me.

Dr. Ansel, who earlier had seemed to have some facility for reading my mind, had withdrawn into a world of his own, continuing his confession, or whatever it was, oblivious to anything I might be feeling. "Their sexual relationship became nonexistent long before I even met Cliff. Any claims she may have made that they had to stop having sex because of the dangers of sleeping with a bisexual man were just a pretext. A sham. Helene wasn't turned on by monogamous sex. It wasn't dangerous enough for her. She was like a female tomcat." He stopped abruptly as though recognizing that he'd gone too far.

In spite of my reluctance to be drawn in, I found myself asking, "What do you mean?"

But Dr. Ansel, after a barrage of frankness, had decided to be secretive. He tilted his head coyly to one side. "I just know," he said. "But I don't want to talk about her. I was telling you about Cliff . . . about how we have a right to be happy."

I'd heard enough. More than enough. Mother Kozak did not hear confessions on Wednesdays. "Dr. Ansel," I said, "I have to leave. I have another appointment."

He stared at me blankly for a moment as his focus returned to the present. "I'm sorry, Mrs. Kozak," he said, "I didn't mean to impose on you like that. It was unfair and unprofessional. It must be the strain . . . this situation . . . it's been so confusing. I don't know what came over me. And here I was, supposed to be making sure you relaxed. I hope . . ." He rubbed his forehead in a gesture almost identical to the one Cliff had made earlier. "I hope you won't think too badly of me."

I'd sort of liked his gentle, caring quality. Too bad he'd had to show me his self-centered, too-intimate confessional side; too bad I'd seen the unpleasant glimpses of a greedy, selfish side. Now he was being gentle and apologetic again but it was a little too Jekyll-and-Hyde for me. If his purpose had been to get me on his side, he'd failed. My sympathies were all with Eve and Helene. I couldn't imagine what it would be like to have a husband or father involved in an affair with anyone, let alone a man like Rowan Ansel. Even for an open-minded and generous woman like Helene, it must have been terribly difficult. I stood up, slipped my feet into my shoes, and picked up my briefcase. "Thanks for looking after me," I said, carefully refraining from answering his question. I didn't say anything else, and neither did he, he just stared at me, a peculiar, brooding stare that I could feel even after the door closed behind me.

The campus of Bartlett Hill, and campus was the only appropriate word, despite its being a mental hospital, was rolling and lovely and bursting with spring, but I wasn't at all tempted to savor it. I was eager to leave it, and the peculiarities of Dr. Rowan Ansel, behind as quickly as possible. I sped through the soft spring evening oblivious to my surroundings, wondering whether I'd be able to work for Cliff if it also meant working with Ansel. As soon as I got off the campus, the traffic claimed all my attention, and I filed my reservations under "later." Spring weather has a way of making people inattentive to their driving, and the famed "Boston drivers" seemed particularly inattentive today. I pressed my hand lightly against my bruised cheek, thought of everything I still had to do—and wished the day was over.

CHAPTER *11*

I'D PLANNED TO sleep a little later in the morning, since I didn't have any appointments until eleven, but that hope was shattered when the phone rang at seven. A ringing phone has an intrusive, imperative quality that makes it hard to ignore, and I finally gave up, took the pillow off my head, and answered it with a very grouchy "Hello?"

"This is Lenora Stern," a voice said, "and I was just so pleased to hear from Eve that you're going to try and help her nail that bastard."

"Excuse me? I think you must have a wrong . . ."

"This is Theadora Kozak, isn't it?" the imperious voice demanded.

"It is," I said, trying to rearrange the phone so it didn't hurt my face. This was Lenora Stern, the wacky speaker from Helene's funeral. "But I'm afraid I don't understand what you're talking about."

"About him," she said impatiently, "Clifford Paris. The bastard who killed his wife. Who killed my friend Helene. I've been trying to reach you, but I guess you're one of those people who don't return phone calls."

Not more than twenty or thirty a day, I thought. "I don't know what Eve told you," I said, "but it was wrong. I am not involved in this. If you have information which you think is relevant, tell it to the police. I can give you the investigating detective's number if you'd like."

There was a silence. I hoped she'd hang up, but this wasn't my lucky day. "The police. Hah! As if they'd look beyond the ends of their noses. I'm very disappointed in you. That poor girl has just lost her mother and she's sitting there believing that you're her friend—and just about her only friend, I might add—and that you're going to help her. If you aren't going to help, you should at least do the decent thing and tell her that, so she doesn't go around with false hopes. It's cruel to string her along."

I felt like a schoolgirl summoned to the principal's office and I didn't like it any more now than I had when I was in school. "Ms. Stern, before you waste any more time lecturing me, you should know that I never told Eve I would help her. . . ."

She cut me off in a way that made it eminently clear that she'd only called me to deal with matters on her own agenda and wasn't going to listen to a word I said. "She thinks you did. Now I have just one more thing to say and then I'll stop bothering you. You can do whatever you want to with this information, I don't care. I'm just doing this for Helene. That little worm Ansel isn't the first, you know. There's been at least one other. Maybe more. Before Ansel it was that toadlike creature that works for him. Robby or Rowdy or whatever it is. Helene couldn't bring herself to say his name. And he gave her a sexually transmitted disease, too. Cliff, I mean. When she finally put her foot down and said she'd had enough, he killed her to keep her from spoiling his fun."

She hung up before I could say anything, which was okay. I was speechless anyway. I have a pretty good imagination but no way could it stretch to encompass Cliff and Roddy Stokes. I was beginning to wish I'd listened to Andre and Suzanne and stayed away from the whole business. But that's what I had done, really. All I'd done was visit Eve once and go to the funeral. Nothing more than any friend would have done. So why did I feel like I'd lifted the lid on a beautiful enameled box and found it was filled with cockroaches?

I pulled the pillow back over my head and tried to sleep again. I'd gotten as far as that warm, drifting state just before you doze off when the phone rang again. This time I let the machine answer it. I didn't care who was interested in a piece of my time. I stayed under the pillow, kept my eyes closed, and ignored the thing, letting my mind drift. When I'd lingered as long as I could, which meant it was closer to eight than to seven, I got up, ran a hot-bath, poured in a generous measure of bath oil, and climbed in. There was a nasty bruise on my shoulder, but my face looked pretty good. Nothing that a little makeup couldn't cure.

Since I don't have a maid, I also had to make the coffee. Before I got dressed, I took my coffee out onto the deck to sample the day. A soft warm breeze tugged at my robe and tried to get my hair to play. It was going to be a nice day. To my right, in the distance, I could see that people were already on the beach, jogging, walking their dogs, or just out getting some air. I was tempted to play hooky and go to the beach. It was a risk I'd weighed when I bought the condo. But I was too much of a Puritan. Why have fun when you can go to work? Besides, if I didn't do my work, and secure some of these contracts, I'd be spending all day every day at the beach, and going to the beach isn't any fun unless you feel slightly decadent and wicked because you're there.

I went inside and studied the stuff in my closet. What felt like spring? A lavender print shirtwaist in a Liberty cotton so soft it felt like silk, with an oversized lavender linen blazer in case I had to go somewhere that already had the air-conditioning on. On my way to the door I passed the answering machine, still blinking sadly. Curiosity made me press the button. The message made me wish I hadn't.

"Hello, Thea Kozak," an unfamiliar voice said, "my name is Martha Coffey. I'm a neighbor of Cliff Paris. This is probably going to sound strange to you, but Eve Paris told me that you were some sort of a detective helping her investigate her mother's death, and she asked me if I could help you prove that her father is a murderer. I didn't want to upset her—Eve's a very high-strung girl and I can see she's having a hard time right now—but I don't believe Cliff would ever have done such a thing. Still, I thought if you were investigating, there were some things you ought to know. Please call me."

She'd left her number on the tape, and some times when I might reach her. I wrote them down and stuck them in my pocket. If I got any more of these damn phone calls I was going to kill Eve. And there would be no mystery about it, either. I'd go immediately to the police and turn myself in, claiming temporary insanity. I should have expected something like this from Eve. The remarks she'd made at dinner about Helene's perseverance and determination went double for Eve. Eve was exactly the opposite of a quitter. She had a hard time knowing when to quit. It meant she was a friend through thick and thin; it also made it hard for her to give up on anything, even lost causes. That was why I was so surprised when she was able to break up with Padraig and go to Arizona.

I got in the car and slammed the door unnecessarily hard, probably slamming it on Eve in absentia. I was really furious with her for going around giving my name and number to people. Driving calmed me, as it often does, while Linda Ronstadt and Aaron Neville provided some nice soothing backup. By the time I reached my first stop of the day, Eve had been cleaned right out of my mind.

I'd noticed from Valeria's resume that one of her former employers was right on my route to work, and I was going to pay him an unexpected visit. According to her resume and my notes, Advotech was a public relations firm that produced promotional materials for high-tech companies. Valeria had been a copywriter for them, and according to the glowing reference Robert Hillyer had given her, she'd been nothing short of a marvel and a genius.

When I came through the door, the Advotech receptionist was

staring with the face of doom at a broken fingernail. She could barely tear herself away from it to bother to greet me. I gave her my best professional smile and handed her my card. "I'd like to see Mr. Hillyer, please. It's about some writing that he did which I found very interesting." I tried to make it sound like I was a business possibility without actually lying. She took my card and disappeared, still casting occasional sad glances at the broken nail.

A minute later she reappeared, followed by a pleasant looking middle-aged man in a pink shirt with an absolutely insane tie. He held out his hand. "Ms. Kozak? Why don't you come into my office and tell me what piece of writing it was that intrigued you." I shook his hand and followed him into his office. He waved me into a chair, sat down himself, and looked at me curiously. "You aren't trying to sell me something, are you?"

I shook my head. "I'm a consultant, Mr. Hillyer, not a saleswoman."

"But the two aren't mutually exclusive, are they?" he said.

I was beginning to like Mr. Hillyer and I decided not to string him along. I reached in my briefcase and took out his reference letter. I passed it across the desk. "This is the piece of writing I was curious about."

He took it and read it, a puzzled frown on his face, then handed it back to me. "I'm afraid I don't understand."

"I'm sorry to barge in here unannounced like this," I said, "but I wanted to talk to you directly, and I was afraid if I called, you wouldn't see me. You see, partially on the strength of your recommendation, my firm hired Valeria Davie to assist us with our educational consulting." I paused, watching his face. "She turned out to be an unqualified disaster. She was lazy and disorganized, foolishly competitive, and she certainly couldn't write." He winced as I described her shortcomings. "We had to fire her, and she was, to put it mildly, extremely difficult when we told her to leave. I'm trying to figure out how an employee who performed so well for you could work out so badly for us. For starters, Mr. Hillyer, I was hoping you could tell me why she left."

He didn't answer right away. Instead, he stared at his fingers. "I don't recall," he said finally. "Maybe she found the work too boring. Some people just don't like technology. I do, but it's not for everyone." He seemed uncomfortable with his answer. "I don't remember, really. Writers come and go." On the bookcase behind him was a large framed picture of Mr. Hillyer with a pretty woman and two little boys who looked just like him. He swung his chair so he could see the picture, as if he was hoping it might give him the answer.

I decided not to beat around the bush any longer. "Mr. Hillyer, I'm going to be blunt, and I hope you'll be honest. Wasn't it actually the case that you tried to fire Valeria and she threatened to charge you with sexual harassment unless you gave her a glowing reference?"

His face was a mix of astonishment and anger. "That's absurd. Who told you that?"

"You did," I said, "just now." I knew I'd scored a bingo. Hillyer's demeanor had gone from genial to unsettled to frigid in a matter of seconds.

"I didn't tell you anything," he said, "and I'd appreciate it if you would get out of my office. I have work to do."

"Of course, Mr. Hillyer. I didn't come here to upset you. But Valeria is doing the same thing to us, and I wouldn't be surprised if she did it to the employer before you. She'll go on doing it as long as people let her get away with it. She's threatened to go to the Commission Against Discrimination, and we'd be in a position to get things resolved at a very early stage if we could show them that this sort of thing is a pattern with her, something she does whenever her competence is challenged."

"I'm afraid you're mistaken, Ms. Kozak. I don't know what you're talking about."

"I can just see her sitting here," I said, "staring through her hair, right past you at that picture of your family, and saying in her girlish voice, 'I'm not sure that's what you want to do, Mr. Hillyer. I know my rights under the law. I know that this is a retaliatory firing, and you can't do that to me.' And I can imagine your reply, too. 'Retaliatory firing, Ms. Davie? An employer is entitled to fire an incompetent employee.' And dear Valeria looking you square in the eye and saying that you were firing her because you'd made sexual advances and she'd rejected them, and wouldn't your wife be pleased when she learned about that."

He stared at me in astonishment. "That's practically word for word," he said. "How did you know that?"

"I told you. Because I saw her do it."

"She was so inept and pathetic," he said. "I felt sorry for her at first. Tried to help her out, be nice to her, you know, in a kindly sort of way, so when she accused me of harassment I thought she might have just misunderstood. I tried to explain that to her. She just smirked and told me to tell that to the judge, and after she'd let me squirm a little, she suggested her alternative. The reference letter and a month's salary. She even had the letter all prepared. The only competent thing she wrote while she was here. I just wanted to get rid of her as quickly as possible, it was so sordid, you know, so I signed it and paid her and she left. It never occurred to me that she might have done it to someone else."

"Well, now we know, don't we. I wonder whether there's the same story behind this," I said, pulling out another letter and handing it to him.

He took it and read it through. "This is the one that hooked me. I think we should ask." He picked up the phone and dialed the number on the letterhead. "Mr. Kramer, please. Bob Hillyer calling." There was the usual pause while the call passed through the dragons. He drummed his fingers impatiently on the desk. "Joey? Yeah, Bob Hillyer. How's the old backhand? Still having trouble with the follow through? Is that right? Great. Yeah, that new pro really knows her stuff, doesn't she? Born to wear tennis skirts, too. Yeah. My wife says it's all that lateral movement. Look, sorry to bother you, but I had a question I hoped you could help me with. Yeah, right. No, it's not about my backhand. I'm still working on getting it over the net, you know?"

I've never been much good at the old chitchat. Hillyer's bon-homie was probably the right approach with Kramer, but it made me want to drum *my* fingers impatiently on the desk. Finally he got to the point. "It's about a former employee of yours that we hired. Girl named Valeria Davie. Yeah. Yeah. That's the one. Smallish, wore a lot of mustard-colored clothes. Yeah. You gave her a great reference. Greatest thing since sliced bread. I was wondering why she left."

He listened, nodding and mumbling. "Is that right? Well, look, I might as well be blunt here. She was an incompetent with an attitude, so I fired her, and she came back at me with a threat and a proposition. Give her a chunk of change and sign the refer-ence she'd written for herself, or get slapped with a sexual harass-ment complaint. I bought her off, of course. A lot less hassle, but now I've got her next employer sitting here telling me the same thing's happened again. So tell me honestly, Joey. She do the same thing to you?"

Now I was sitting on the edge of my chair, watching his face, trying to read the answer, while he listened and nodded and hummed. Finally he said, "Exactly. And I think it's time we stopped the little bitch before she does it to someone else." His voice dropped into a series of mmms and yeahs. "Okay, yeah Joey, if you'd be willing to do that it would be great. Yeah. Umm. Look, why wait, you can just fax it over, shouldn't take you long. Right. Advotech. Sure. Terrific. I'll be watching for it. See you round the club." He gave his fax number and hung up. "And you make num-ber three. Unless there are more we don't know about. Astound-ing, isn't it?"

"If she'd put half that amount of creativity and effort into her work, none of us would have had to fire her."

"Right," he said. "Joey's going to write up a little something and fax it over pronto, and I'll do the same. You want to wait for them?" I nodded. "Shouldn't be long, but I need to do my com-posing alone. I feel like a bit of a fool, being taken in like that, even if I'm not the only one. You mind waiting outside? We've got lots of exciting magazines, like *Laser Technology*, and *Silicon Signals* and *Business Week.*"

I settled down in the waiting room, passing on his offer of high-tech magazines. Across the room, the receptionist had assembled her own range of high-tech equipment and was reinstalling the dislodged nail. I pulled out Yanita Emery's resume, which Suzanne had given me yesterday, and looked it over. Yanita was in her late twenties, had studied education and management at BU, and was presently working as an assistant dean of students at a small women's college. Before that she had done some teaching and worked at a real estate management firm. On the surface, she looked great, but Valeria had made me wary. I was also concerned that what we had to offer might, quite frankly, be beneath her. I scribbled a few questions that occurred to me in the margins and stuffed her resume back in my briefcase.

I was in the middle of a memo about my meeting with Cliff Paris, when I became aware that I was being watched. Hillyer was standing across the room, papers in hand, staring at me. "You're a real workaholic, aren't you," he said.

"People have suggested that," I told him, holding out my hand for the papers. He surrendered them with an amused smile. The top sheet was a simplified affidavit, setting out the details of his experience when he tried to fire Valeria for incompetence. It was well organized, coherent and very honest. Hillyer hadn't spared himself in describing the event. "This is great," I said. "Thank you so much for doing this. Do you mind if our lawyer contacts you if he has further questions?"

"Not at all. And I'm sure Joe Kramer won't mind either. His statement is so much like mine we sound like Siamese twins." I shifted the papers and read Kramer's account. Hillyer was right. Their experiences were nearly identical, the only difference was writing style. Kramer had bludgeoned the language into shape and Hillyer had twisted it deftly to fit.

"I see what you mean," I said. I tucked the papers into my briefcase and held out my hand. What I felt like doing was jumping up and down and shouting hooray. I couldn't wait to shove copies of their statements in Valeria's mean little face. "I was playing a hunch when I came here. Your frankness and cooperation are going to make my life a whole lot easier."

He took my hand, and his grip was warm and enthusiastic. "No problem. Actually it was fun. Made me feel like one of the good guys for a change, writing the truth instead of just promo stuff."

"Don't put yourself down, Mr. Hillyer. I get the impression that you are very good at what you do."

"Thanks." He turned and headed for his office, but paused halfway across the room and came back. "I don't want to sound too dramatic, but be careful, okay? I have the feeling Valeria isn't going to take this very well."

"I know what you mean. Don't worry. I'll only confront her in well-lit rooms full of witnesses."

"Good idea," he said, disappearing from view. I took my briefcase and left.

CHAPTER *12*

SARAH JUST SHOOK her head when I gave her the affidavits and asked her to make six copies of each of them and six copies of the reference letters right away. "Copier's busted," she said, "and Louie says don't count on using it again before two." She pointed at the legs and feet of a person whose torso and head appeared to have been swallowed by the machine.

"It's demanding human sacrifices now?"

"I guess so," she said, shrugging her shoulders. She tapped the papers with an unmanicured nail. A real, live human fingernail. It was one of the reasons I liked Sarah. "This an emergency, a real emergency, or a really, truly serious emergency?"

"See for yourself. This is dynamite designed to blow Miss Valeria Davie right out of the water."

"You're kidding. What'd you do, break into her psychiatrist's office?"

"Only Republicans do that."

"Well, Lucy next door will let me make some copies. We've helped them out when their copier was broken. That guy Florio wants you to call him and so does everyone else in the western world. If the guy who invented the telephone had realized what he

was letting us all in for, he would have shot himself in the head."
She handed me a fat stack of pink slips and went next door to
make the copies.

I kicked off my shoes, sat down and finished dictating the
memo I'd begun in Hillyer's office. Recalling yesterday's meeting
had the unfortunate side effect of also making me recall my uncomfortable encounter with Rowan Ansel. In my own office, and
when I wasn't being treated like a shock victim, his behavior
seemed more annoying than disturbing. Perhaps, like Cliff, he
was shocked by Helene's death. A shock like that, as I well knew,
can make people behave strangely. Put in perspective, he no longer seemed like such an obstacle to working with Cliff. I followed
the memo with two assignments for Bobby, follow-ups to yesterday's meetings. If things heated up like they appeared to be doing,
we would need a replacement for Valeria quickly. Maybe Yanita
would solve that problem.

I carried the tape out and put it in the middle of Sarah's desk
with a note indicating that I needed it ASAP and went back to sort
my pink slips. A call from Cliff Paris, apologizing for his inexcusa-
ble conduct and asking me how quickly I could put together a
proposal to present to his board. Then there were a bunch of
other business calls. Florio's message was intriguing. Sarah had
written, "Rosie says 'thank you' and will you come to breakfast on
Sunday?" At the bottom of the stack were two messages from Eve,
asking me to call her at work, and a message to call Norah
McCarty, Cliff Paris's housekeeper.

I checked my watch. Almost eleven. I had just time to call Eve
and give her a piece of my mind. After being shuffled around a few
times, a helpful person informed me that she was out and could
probably be reached after three. I left a message for her to call me
and hung up, disgruntled. Now I'd committed myself to a round
of telephone tag, and it's a game that I hate.

I called Dom Florio, who was out, and left a message accept-
ing his breakfast invitation. I figured Saturday I'd be busy with the
wedding but by Sunday I'd need some distractions to keep me

from dwelling on Andre's absence. I did fine during our separations when I knew it was just a matter of time until I saw him again. Now that things were up in the air and I didn't even know if I would see him again, the other half of my bed seemed vast and lonely. Staying busy was the only way I knew to stave off a bad case of the "poor me's." Staying very busy.

I tried Eve again, but she was still out, and so was Norah McCarty, so I stopped worrying about Helene Streeter and solving the mystery of her death and immersed myself in my own work.

At one Sarah brought me a stack of typed memos, some mail and a sandwich. "Sorry I was grouchy," she said. "When I'm mad at Brad I take it out on everyone, and I'm real mad at him today."

"No problem. I'd forgive anything for this sandwich."

"That's what I was hoping," she said. "Brad better come home tonight with a heck of a lot more than a sandwich. He won't though." Sarah is tough and bright and pretty, with a generous ration of good humor and common sense, and vastly unappreciated. Brad, her husband, is so distressed that she's a size twelve instead of size eight that he can't see around that to enjoy what she is. If he were mine, I'd be tempted to hit him over the head with a cast-iron frying pan, but he's not, so I try to keep my opinions to myself.

I flowed around the sandwich like a hungry amoeba, made it a part of me in a matter of seconds, and went back to work. Sometime in the middle of the afternoon I met the blushing bride-to-be in the ladies' room. "Great news," she said, "Lisa is coming back. Says she finds unadulterated motherhood unbearable and wants to know if she can work thirty hours a week."

"No kidding. When did you talk to her?"

"Just now." Suzanne smiled. "Someone up there likes us, I guess. I'm glad some thing is going right for a change."

"Speaking of things going right, what did you think of the affidavits?"

But Suzanne wasn't listening. She was staring at my face. "What happened to you?"

"Ran into a door."

"Right," she said, "that's what they all say. What really happened?"

"A door ran into me. Let's get some coffee, go into your office, and I'll tell you all about it. Does your lack of enthusiastic response mean you haven't read the affidavits yet?"

"That's right. I'm so busy I don't know whether I'm coming or going. I haven't even looked in my 'in' basket yet. There's an ominous heap of messages and more than half of the darned things have to do with the wedding. Paul's mother has called me three times, his sister twice, I've even had a call from his ex-wife. Magda's doing her best to protect me, but there are some that she can't handle. Don't ever get married, Thea."

"It's a little late for that, Suzanne."

She hit herself in the forehead with the heel of her hand, mocking herself for being stupid. "What I meant was, don't ever have a wedding. I don't know what possessed me to think I wanted this. All I wanted was Paul."

"The good news is two more days and it'll be over, and you'll be Mrs. Paul Merritt. Are you going to be Suzanne Merritt? Or stay Suzanne Begner?"

Suzanne dipped her little finger into a pot of lip gloss and smoothed it over her lips. "Merritt, I think. I've changed my mind about six times. The only thing I'm sure of is that I don't want a hyphenated name. Merritt-Begner sounds like the name of some obscure congressional bill, you know, the Merritt-Begner Act, requiring underground road crossings for salamanders." She straightened up and put the gloss back in her purse. I noticed that she'd been losing weight. The skirt of her carefully fitted suit hung on her hips.

"How much have you lost?" I said.

"Six pounds. Any other time I'd be delighted, but if I lose any more, the dress isn't going to fit. Just another ridiculous part of this whole ridiculous business. Let's go get that coffee. Maybe I'll have Magda go out and get us some doughnuts or something."

"Make mine jelly," I said. "I don't like a doughnut without a challenge, and I love the feeling of the jelly oozing up the back of my hand."

"Not me, boy! It's like eating a slug. I'll have Magda call you when the supplies arrive."

Our partners' meeting reconvened in Suzanne's office about twenty minutes later looking vaguely like a scene from "Twin Peaks." On each side of the desk was a napkin, a pristine square of white in the sea of pink messages, and on each napkin sat a small heap of doughnuts. "Looks like about six pounds' worth right here," I said, grabbing the one on the top of my stack and biting into it. A sticky wad of white goo burst out and headed for my lap, but I was too quick for it, catching it in midair, and stuffing it into my mouth.

Suzanne made a face. "That's disgusting."

"Your idea, not mine."

"True." She grinned triumphantly and picked up the affidavits. "This is brilliant, Thea. How did you ever manage it?"

I threw back my shoulders, stuck out my chest and batted my eyes. "Feminine wiles," I said.

"I could believe that, but I don't. What really happened?"

"I marched in, said 'can you help me?' and asked the guy why Valeria left if she was such a dynamite employee. Guy stared at his wife's picture and said he couldn't remember. So I said 'let me suggest a scenario,' described what Valeria did here, and the guy almost fell off his chair. Started to deny it, backed down, and admitted she'd accused him and then offered him the out of signing the reference letter. He knew her previous employer, so he called the guy, Kramer, and it turned out she did the same thing to him, so we all agreed it was time to put a stop to her little scheme. And without further ado, they offered to write the affidavits, on the spot, and gave them to me."

"What does your father say?"

"I haven't told him yet. Honey, I'm just busy trying to make a living."

Suzanne delicately licked the sugar from her first doughnut off her fingers and picked up a second. "Well, I think we can relax about this one. Moving right along to the next item on our agenda, what happened to your face?" I described my meeting with Cliff and how Ansel had bashed me with the door on my way out and then gotten sidetracked into true confessions. "It's just a little too weird, Thea," she said, "don't you think? Are you sure you want to work with those people?"

"No, I'm not sure. But Cliff did call today and apologize, and wants me to put together a presentation to his board, and aside from the folks yesterday morning, who need some help with grant proposals and a couple of other little things, we don't have much on the drawing board right now."

She made a face. "We still don't have to take it, Thea. Things will work out fine. They always do."

"I thought you were excited by the possibilities of exploring a new field."

"I was. I am. But maybe this isn't the right entree. Maybe you're too connected to Cliff Paris. As I recall, I was the one who suggested you give that whole family a wide berth. And then I go and encourage you to undertake a project with him. I'm not thinking very clearly these days. I regard it as a form of temporary insanity, from which I will have recovered by Monday." She finished another doughnut and licked her lips. "God I love to pig out on doughnuts. I might as well enjoy this. It may be the last time in my life I'll ever eat doughnuts without guilt."

"I hope not. You're just getting married, aren't you? You're not getting a life membership in some weight watching organization. Don't tell me Paul thinks you're too fat?"

There it was again—that idiotic smile at the sound of his name. "No. Paul likes me just the way I am. In fact, he thinks I'm a little too thin."

"The man is a paragon. An angel."

"Oh, come on," she said, "I'm sure Andre thinks you're just right, too."

"Andre who?"

"Ahh," she said, raising her delicately arched brows, "so he didn't come to his senses after all. He's not coming?"

"He called and said he couldn't. Said he'd call me as soon as he was ready to talk about it, and he was going to tell me more, I think, but something came up and he disappeared into a morass of sirens and ringing phones. Hard as we work, his life makes all this seem easy."

"I'm sorry he's not coming," she said. "Man's a fool, what can I say? Are you doing okay?"

"Trying not to think about it. I don't know what to do, how to fix things so we both have what we want. And I don't want to start wondering if I was a fool to let myself get involved again. So I'll just apply the Kozak solution."

"Which is immerse yourself in work, right?"

"Right."

"Excuse me." Magda stuck her head around the door. She looked like something extremely distasteful had just dropped onto her desk.

I looked at Suzanne, who met my gaze and nodded. "It's Valeria," we said together. Magda nodded.

"Give us a minute, and then send her in," Suzanne said.

We gathered the pink slips into a neat pile, threw the napkins away, and brushed the doughnut crumbs off the desk. I found copies of the affidavits and reference letters. We toasted each other with the dregs of our coffee, tossed the cups into the trash, turned on the tape recorder and sat back to wait for Valeria.

She sailed in with the smirk we'd hoped for set firmly on her lipsticked mouth, sat down without being invited, and thrust a wrinkled paper at Suzanne. "I've brought you a copy of the complaint I filed with the Commission Against Discrimination. You might like to read it."

Suzanne picked it up, scanned it briefly and passed it to me without any comment. I read it and set it down on the desk. "What puzzles me, Valeria, is why you put so much effort into dishonest manipulations like these but won't put enough effort into your work to do a decent job."

"My work was fine," she said. "That's not why you fired me."

"That's why we fired you," Suzanne said, "and that's why your last two employers fired you."

"Don't be ridiculous," she sneered, "I left voluntarily. They were very pleased with my work. You know that. You've seen my references."

"Which you wrote yourself and blackmailed them into signing," I said.

"That's complete bullshit." She was beginning to sound uncertain. "You know it is."

"We've talked to your previous employers," Suzanne said. "Both Hillyer and Kramer have confirmed that your work was unsatisfactory and when they tried to fire you, you threatened to accuse them of sexual harassment unless they gave you generous severance pay and signed the reference letters you'd prepared. Why didn't you offer us the same deal?" Suzanne has a talent for sneaking zinger questions in very innocently. And it worked.

"It was too soon," Valeria said without thinking, "I couldn't leave another job so quickly, no one would believe . . ." She stopped and glared at Suzanne. "Oh no. You're not going to trick me like that. She made advances to me." She pointed at me. "I've never been so shocked in my life. It's all right here in black and white," she said, tapping her complaint.

"And right here in black and white," I said, "we have written statements from Mr. Hillyer and Mr. Kramer describing how you blackmailed them into signing those great reference letters. The three of us conferred this morning and decided we had to cooperate to put an end to your 'bad habit,' before you tried it on any more employers." Valeria snatched the papers from me, scanned them quickly, and dropped them onto the desk like they were too hot to handle.

"It would have been you, of course," she said, her voice trembling with rage. "You just waltzed in there with your gorgeous legs and those great big breasts, and they did exactly what you wanted, didn't they? They probably never even looked at your face." Her reaction was so unexpected neither of us could do anything to stop her. She jumped out of her chair, picked up Suzanne's big wooden "In" box and threw it at Suzanne. Suzanne ducked, and it hit the painting on the wall behind her, smashing the glass and showering the floor with papers and shards of glass. "And that," Valeria raged, "is just the beginning. You conniving bitches haven't seen the last of me. I won't be treated this way." She ran out of the office, shoving Magda, who had rushed in when she heard the crash, roughly aside. The three of us stared at the mess on the floor.

"Incredible," Suzanne said. "She doesn't believe that she's done anything wrong."

Magda tapped her forehead. "I do not think that she is entirely right up here." She reached out and picked a sparkling bit of glass out of Suzanne's hair. "I wish I could think it is over, but I worry about what that girl may do. She won't see that you must defend yourselves, she will only see this as an unfair attack on her." She crouched down, picked up the "In" box, shook out the glass that was in it, and started picking up the papers, shaking each one before she put it back in the box. "I think we still have a vacuum cleaner in one of the closets, Thea. Do you think you could find it?"

I was on the floor beside her, picking up the big pieces of glass and putting them in the wastebasket. The crumbs from our merry feast were being buried under glass, a tangible reminder of how quickly things can change. Suzanne sat in her chair watching us, looking confused. I abandoned the glass for a minute, picked up her purse, and handed it to her. "Go to the ladies' room and comb the glass out of your hair."

Her hand went uncertainly to her head. "I have glass in my hair?"

"Of course you do. You practically took a shower in it," I said, realizing that Valeria's sudden attack had had an unsettling effect on Suzanne. Maybe I was less surprised because I'd already seen Valeria explode or maybe I was calmer because the box hadn't been aimed at me, and I hadn't had my possessions smashed and been showered with glass. Besides, she had a lot on her mind right now and it made her vulnerable. At her most feisty, Suzanne would have picked up the box and thrown it right back.

"I'll go with her," Magda said, setting the box of papers back on the desk. "You get the vacuum." She gave me a look that suggested I was somehow to blame for letting this happen. It didn't bother me. Magda fussed over Suzanne like the daughter she'd never had. Sometimes her protectiveness got annoying, but she was talented and loyal, and as long as she wasn't trying to mother me, I thought it was better to have too much caring rather than too little. I might have felt differently if Sarah had tried to mother me, but that would never happen. I'd had enough of the controlling mother growing up, and Sarah did enough mothering at home to be glad of an adult relationship at work.

I went to get the vacuum, and walking back to Suzanne's office, I found Bobby standing by my desk looking troubled. He looked at the vacuum. "What happened in there, anyway?"

I realized he hadn't seen the affidavits and didn't know what was going on. "I'll show you." He followed me into Suzanne's office and I handed him the affidavits, which Valeria had neglected to take with her. He read them quickly, a satisfied smile on his face, a smile so malicious it seemed totally out of character. I was ashamed that I hadn't recognized sooner how awful working with Valeria must have been. "She didn't like them, so she threw Suzanne's 'In' box and broke the picture."

"I'd like to hope we've seen the last of her," he said, "but I doubt it." He reached for the vacuum, which I'd set on a chair.

"Would you like me to finish cleaning up? I'm pretty good with one of these things."

"I never argue with a man who wants to vacuum."

Sarah stuck her head in the door. "Excuse me," she said, "it's Eve Paris on the phone. You want to take the call?"

"I certainly do." I left Bobby with the vacuum and went to give Eve a piece of my mind.

CHAPTER *13*

I PICKED UP the phone and wasted no words getting to the point. "Eve, I am not your personal private detective, and I want you to stop giving my name to people. I don't think your father killed Helene and I don't want to get involved. Can't you understand that?"

"I thought you said you'd help me."

That was Eve in a nutshell. I'd said I wouldn't, but she'd decided I had to help her, and in her own mind transformed that desire into my consent. I couldn't begin to count the number of double dates, unwanted restaurant meals, and movies I'd endured because Eve had decided I should. Ann Landers says people can't make you do things if you don't let them. She's right, of course. And I had to admit that some of those times I'd had fun, but there was no way what she wanted this time could be fun. I tried to shut the picture of her disappointed face out of my mind. "No, Eve. You weren't listening. I said I wouldn't."

"You haven't talked to them yet," she said, "or you'd understand. You have to help me. I need you. I'm afraid he'll come after me next."

"Eve, don't be ridiculous. . . ."

"You don't understand, Thea," she said. "I'm serious this time. I'm scared. Come to dinner tonight and I'll explain everything. I promise after you hear what I have to say it will all make sense to you. About seven, okay? I'll make that stuffed cabbage casserole you like."

Not even her "heartburn special," which I adored, was sufficient inducement, but I felt I owed it to her to spend a little time listening, and besides, she wasn't going to give up until I said I'd come to dinner. "Make it seven-thirty and you've got a deal." That would give me time for aerobics, which I needed for my emotional well-being as well as to hold the flab line. I hung up with the uncomfortable feeling that I'd neither given her a piece of my mind nor gotten myself off the hook. Oh well. Tonight I would.

Friendship is a funny thing. To outsiders, my relationship with Eve might seem strangely one-sided. Maybe it was, right now, but I don't keep score, and Eve and I had been young together when we were hatchlings fresh from the nest, supporting each other as we moved from home and college out into the world. She could be demanding, frustrating and impossible—but she was also a great listener and a kind, supportive friend. There had been laughter and tears, confessions and closeness. She'd nursed me through a broken heart, I'd tried my best to help her with Padraig. We had a history and that counted for a lot with me.

Sarah brought me the memos I'd dictated, along with the ones for Bobby. I called him in and spent an hour going over what I needed him to do. Then I put on my thinking cap and started working on a proposal for Cliff. I was immersed in a sea of yellow sheets containing my notes when Suzanne came in to tell me she was leaving. "I won't be in tomorrow," she said. "Don't forget the rehearsal, and we're having dinner afterwards at Cipio's. Try not to run into any more doors between now and Saturday, okay?"

"I'll do my best," I said, wondering how a person might behave who truly wanted to avoid doors. Stay in one room, maybe? Suzanne's departure was quickly duplicated by Magda and Bobby, but Sarah showed no signs of leaving. "You can go if you want," I told her.

She grinned. "Nope. Told Brad I had to work late, so he's picking up the kids and taking them to his mother's for dinner. And I'm going shopping. Guess I should have realized by now that no one is going to give me what I want except me. So tonight is 'be good to Sarah' night. I'm going to get exactly what I want to eat, and then I'm going to buy myself a birthday present. Can you believe that asshole forgot my thirty-fifth birthday?"

"Going alone?"

"No way!" She laughed. "My friend Jeannie told her husband she had to work late, too. We're going to work very hard at shopping. I'm going to use that gift certificate you gave me for something completely frivolous." She checked her watch. "Oops, gotta go. Don't work too late. I don't want to come in tomorrow to a mountain of typing." She waved a hand at me. "Don't want to break my nails, you know." She scooped up her coat and purse and left.

It was so blissfully quiet after she departed I decided to skip aerobics and work on my proposal instead, even though I could feel my thighs spreading, my bottom drooping and my biceps and triceps growing weak. Against my better judgment, I'd let Cliff talk me into a three o'clock meeting tomorrow. For a while I worked quite hard, identifying for myself the similarities between the service Cliff had to offer and what a private school had to offer, trying to identify the sources he needed to reach to attract new clients, and determining what methods he might use to reach those sources. It was a start, but I'd need a lot of help from him, and a much better understanding of how Bartlett Hill worked, how the staff, patients, and their families perceived it, and how it was perceived by the referring community.

I could see Cliff sitting there in his chair, rubbing his fore-head, struggling to follow what I was saying, and gradually drifting off to sleep. Seeing Cliff so vulnerable had scared me. It's not that I don't want to grow up, or be responsible, or any of that stuff. I like being a grown-up. I hate it when anyone calls me girlie or acts like I'm mindless or tries to tell me what to do. But I also secretly believe in another group I call the "real grown-ups"—the people like Cliff and Helene, and Uncle Henry and Aunt Rita, who have been grown-ups as long as I've known them. I want them to stay ageless and infallible forever. I know better, of course. I know my parents have feet of clay. Their behavior after Carrie died was a real eye-opener for me, and now I loved them but with a more realistic view. But Cliff . . . Well, I suppose that like all of his female patients, and like any insecure young girl exposed to such a charismatic man, I was more than a little in love with Cliff Paris at one time. All that was left now was some gratitude to him, for making me feel beautiful and special and worthy when I otherwise felt like such an ugly duckling, and from that gratitude, an urge to protect him.

That was my conflict and why I'd agreed to have dinner with Eve. I felt a need to set things right by convincing Eve that her father couldn't have killed her mother. Very early on, my family assigned me the role of the "fixer." "Thea will fix it" was practically a family motto. It meant that I was called in to mediate family disputes, sort things out, pick up the pieces, do the dirty jobs that no one else would do. Michael was moody, surly and inflexible; Carrie insecure, silent and rebellious. I was the good kid, and after a lifetime of being expected to sort things out, I found it hard to shake off the yoke of responsibility, even in a situation I wanted to avoid as much as this. What I wanted was to be left alone to do my work and live my life, but Eve and Cliff, two people I cared about, were locked in a struggle that could destroy their relationship forever.

My reverie was interrupted by the phone. "Knew I'd find you

there," Florio said. "Thought I'd better give you guys directions."

"I hope this won't break your heart, but there's no us, just me," I said.

"I'm sorry I won't see him, but my heart's fine. What about yours?"

"Bruised," I said.

"I'm sorry." He sounded like he meant it. "Guy must be crazy. What does he want?"

"A little woman at home, and a player to be named later, I guess."

"Glad to see you've still got your sense of humor," he said. "I don't suppose anyone has called you up and confessed to Helene Streeter's murder yet?"

"No, Dom. All the people who are calling me say someone else did it."

"Seriously," he said, "people are calling you up, other than your friend Eve, I mean?"

"I'm afraid so. Eve seems to be organizing a whole cadre of people who are supposed to tell me why they think Cliff Paris did it. Except some of them don't seem to think he did."

"So that's what she meant," he said with a sigh.

"What's what who meant?"

"Say again?"

"What's what who meant?"

"Gotcha. For a minute that sounded like a foreign language. The neighbor across the street said she'd rather talk to Eve's detective. I suppose that's you?"

"Involuntarily. I'm being impressed, shanghaied, hijacked, entrapped. You get my drift?"

"Not exactly."

"Eve keeps calling people up and telling them I'm helping her out and giving them my number so they can talk to me."

"Why?"

"I don't know why. Because she wants me to help her prove Cliff did it, and I won't. This is her way of getting me involved. First it was look around at Bartlett Hill, now it's this." My watch said ten past seven. Time to go. "Better give me those directions, Dom, I've got a date."

"You work fast," he said.

"With Eve."

"Got a pencil?"

"Does a bear . . . oh, never mind, of course I've got a pencil." He gave me the directions and I wrote them down. "Thanks, Dom. I'll see you Sunday. Can I bring something?"

"An appetite. Rosie does great breakfasts." There was a silence on his end, then he said, "Maybe you should talk to them."

"You mean be a spy for the cops?"

"Why not?"

"We already talked about this. Because I don't want to get involved. Because I'm busy. Because I don't want to hear the sordid inside story of the Paris-Streeter marriage. And because I already got involved in one murder investigation, one I had a whole lot bigger stake in than I have in this, and I almost got myself killed. I may like the excitement of living a little close to the edge, but I draw the line at murders. Besides, Uncle Dom told me not to. He said just listen."

"How else are you going to convince Eve that her father didn't do it?" It sounded like Uncle Dom had changed his mind.

"What makes you think that's what I want to do?"

"Isn't it?" he shot back. That's the trouble with good cops, they tend to be mind readers, and Florio was a good cop.

"Don't mess with my head, Florio," I said.

"Thought I had a read on that." He sounded pleased with himself.

"I hate it when people try to manipulate me."

"Golly gee, Miss Thea, was I trying to do that or were you referring to Miss Eve?" he said, in a high, singsongy voice.

"I have to go now. I'll see you Sunday."

"Just think about it, okay?" he said, and hung up.

"What do you think I've been doing?" I said to the empty line. I grabbed my jacket and stuffed the jumble of yellow papers into my briefcase. In my car, I slipped in a tape, opened the sunroof, and headed out into the tail end of the rush hour traffic, glad that Springsteen and I were "Born to Run." At least, I was. I plunged through two yellow lights and one red, swore at other drivers at least six times, gave an older woman the finger—I could imagine what my mother would say about that—and beat out another car for the last space on Eve's street. By the time I rang her bell, I had committed enough bad acts to flush my irritation with Florio out of my system.

Eve gave me a warm hug, which I returned, noticing that her still-damp hair smelled like coconuts. I'd forgotten all about him, but Eve's new hunk, the hulking, brooding Waldemar, was sitting in her living room with headphones on, singing along loudly and badly to the inaudible music. After she let me in, she went over and waved a hand in front of his face until she had his attention, then pointed at me. He gave me a broad grin that showed about seventy-five teeth, shook my hand, and went back to his music. "He writes music reviews for *Altermath;* it's a new alternative paper," she said. "He's got a deadline, or else he'd take those things off. Sometimes it's like living with an alien."

"Sometimes living with any man is like living with an alien."

"I know. I'll bet they feel the same way. Must be that all of us have a fascination with the unknown," Eve said. "The guys I've been involved with have all been so different from me, and so different from each other. Where'd you meet Andre, anyway? He seems almost human, for a cop."

"He was the investigating detective when Carrie was killed."

"Not the greatest way to meet someone, huh? She was such a sweet kid. You still miss her?" I nodded. Carrie's murder still wasn't something I could talk about. Eve could tell. She changed the subject. "Come in the kitchen and have some wine while I finish making dinner." She had an open bottle sitting on the counter with two glasses. She filled one and handed it to me, then poured one for herself. The kitchen was filled with the delicious smell of baking sauerkraut, the principal ingredient in the heart-burn special. She started putting things out on the counter. "You make the salad dressing, okay? Just like the other night. That was great. I'm sorry I was such a bitch."

I hung my jacket over a chair and made the dressing while Eve unwrapped a loaf of pumpernickel bread, stuck it in the oven, and started tearing up lettuce. It was pleasant to be hanging around a kitchen, cooking with a friend. It was something I didn't do enough of, I'd let myself become such a hermit.

Eve looked like her old self tonight, no longer pale. Her eyes were bright and her cheeks rosy, and she was bustling around with her usual energy. "I'm sorry about the way I behaved after the funeral," she said. "I know I didn't handle things at all well. And I know," she peered at me from under her bangs, reminding me once again of a small, black-capped bird, "that you're annoyed by the people who've been calling you. But you can really help me here, and you're the only person I know who can."

She took a cucumber out of the refrigerator. "Look, I know you're worried about divided loyalties. You've always admired Cliff, and he was nice to you when you thought no one should be. But that wouldn't be a reason to let him get away with murder, would it?"

"What about the stranger people saw lurking in the bushes, Eve? Why are you so sure that it was Cliff? He's a doctor. If he was going to kill her, he could have found some neat, undetectable way to kill. It doesn't make any sense for him to do it out on a public street at a time of day when there were likely to be people around. In his own neighborhood. Besides, if he didn't want to be married anymore, he could have just gotten a divorce."

"It wasn't just a killing, Thea, it was a slaughter. It was done in anger, and it was done so that the killer could be certain that she would die. By someone who intended to kill and knew how to kill. And who knows the human body better than a doctor?"

"How do you know that?"

"That's what the police said."

"You still haven't answered. Why Cliff?"

"Because he hated her. Had for a long time. And because he couldn't get a divorce. Not easily, anyway. She would have fought him tooth and nail, resisting any threat to her comfortable life-style and her position. Can you imagine the insult to her ego if her husband divorced her for another man? A beautiful woman like Helene? She'd asked him to stop seeing Rowan, you know. And she had a terror of being poor. She was very poor as a child. Did I ever tell you that? A divorce would have been a nasty, protracted affair, and Cliff doesn't like conflict. Easier to kill her. Or have her killed. I'm not saying he did it himself. There are people out there who will kill for drug money, or just for fun. Just consider it, won't you, Thea? You remember how things used to be. But they'd changed."

I shook my head. "But there are so many other possibilities. A stranger. An angry patient. The husband of one of those abused women. A jealous colleague. If all it takes is someone who was angry with Helene, anyone could be a suspect, even you."

"But he knew her habits," she insisted. "Whoever killed her knew her routine."

She was peeling the cucumber, and the peeler slipped and gouged a piece out of her finger. She shook it angrily, spattering blood on the counter. "I'll never be a cook," she said, wrapping a paper towel around it. "I'm just not good around sharp things. Always cutting myself. I never make a meal without a sacrifice."

"I'm sorry," I said, "that was my fault. I should know better than to argue with someone while she's peeling. I'll get you a Band-Aid." There weren't any in the bathroom, but I knew that Eve sometimes kept some loose in her desk, so I looked there.

Rummaging through the drawer I found a stack of catalogues, most of them for lingerie, a few for the outdoorsy clothes she liked, and some for fishing, camping and hunting which I assumed reflected her new interest in outdoor sports. I pulled them out to look underneath. No Band-Aids, only a poem she'd been working on.

Back in our early twenties, in those days of late adolescent angst, Eve had worked out a lot of her problems through poetry, and some of it had been quite good. This one wasn't, though. It was just bleak and depressing. She'd written:

> Into the warm heart of trust
> Creeps the cold black head of despair.
> Ruthless, taking what it will, at will
> Heartless, leaving cold heart hollowed,
> Hopeless.
>
> Into the nest of nurtured joy
> Creeps the pale white hand of greed.
> Merciless, solely satisfying self,
> Pitiless, leaving crushed heart hollowed,
> Hapless.

I was staring at it, the Band-Aid forgotten, wondering what tragedy she hadn't shared with me that had led to such a sad poem, when Eve came looking for me. She rushed across the room, snatched the poem out of my hand, and stuffed it back in the drawer.

"That's none of your business," she said. "What are you doing in my room?"

"Looking for a Band-Aid."

"Going through my drawers."

"Just looking for a Band-Aid," I said. "There were none in the bathroom, and you used to keep them in your desk."

She just stared at me coldly and walked away. "Dinner's ready," she said over her shoulder.

Our earlier camaraderie had vanished. We ate dinner in an uncompanionable silence, whatever rapprochement we'd achieved lost in disagreement. There were three of us, as Waldemar had deigned to leave his headphones long enough to eat. The food was good, but I had no appetite for it. Finally Eve broke the silence. "I don't understand you anymore, Thea," she said. "You say you're my friend, yet you won't help me when I need it. It seems like you're more loyal to my father than you are to me. And then I find you snooping through my things."

Her crazy accusation was the last straw. I'd run out of patience with Eve, with her persistence, her mood swings and her total self-absorption. "I wasn't snooping through your things, Eve. Why would I? I already explained that. I don't care whether you believe me or not." I didn't like having this conversation in front of Waldemar but he seemed oblivious. Maybe he was tuned into the music zone even when he didn't have headphones on.

She poured more wine into our glasses and sat staring glumly at me. "I'm sorry. I overreacted, that's all. You know how it is when someone you loved is dead, Thea, I know you do. My feelings are just all over the place." She sounded genuinely contrite. I picked up my wine and started to relax and she hit me with another zinger. "But I'm not wrong about my father. . . ."

"What did you mean when you said you were afraid he'd come after you next?"

She smiled triumphantly and jumped up. "I'll show you." She led me to the back door, which opened into a little hallway behind the kitchen, pulled the door open, and showed me a series of marks along the jamb which had dented the paint, in some places leaving splintery edges of raw wood. "Someone tried to break in yesterday," she said, "and I found this on the stairs." She held out a brown plastic pill container with no label, twisted off the top, and shook out some pills. "I've been having trouble sleeping, and

Cliff gave me some pills to take which look a lot like these, only these are three times as strong. I came home from work yesterday afternoon with a headache. I was sleeping when I heard noises and came back here to investigate. When I opened the door, I saw a man running down the stairs. I ran down to the street and saw a man getting into a car just like my father's. Now you see why I think he's after me?"

"You're sure you saw your father?"

"It might have been Rowan. It was dark on the stairs, and he was pretty far down the street."

"What kind of car does your father drive?"

"A gray Saab 9000."

So did a hundred other people in Cambridge. She couldn't identify the man on the stairs or the guy getting into the car. "Maybe it was just a burglar, Eve."

"Then how do you explain these?" she said, waving the pills.

"Maybe the burglar was a druggie."

"You just don't want to believe me."

"What time did this all take place?" I asked.

"Midafternoon. You know. Around four or four-thirty."

"Then it wasn't your father."

"How do you know?"

"Because I was with him in his office yesterday at four."

"Then maybe it was Rowan."

"Nope. He was at Bartlett Hill, too."

"Maybe it was later, then," she said, "I don't really remember. Not that any of this matters, since you won't help me anyway. Maybe after something happens to me, then you'll believe me. I'm sure Helene never expected anything to happen to her, either." She shook her head angrily and returned to the table.

In our absence, Waldemar had finished his dinner and gone back to his headphones. I wondered what Eve saw in him. He hadn't uttered a word or even looked at me, so there was no way I could form an impression of him.

Eve sat across from me, scowling as she pushed little bits of food around on her plate. Neither of us had eaten much. "Are we having fun yet?" she said. I didn't answer. "Look, this isn't what I had in mind at all. Now I'm mad at you and you're mad at me, when I was hoping to have a pleasant dinner. I didn't mean for things to turn out like this. Honest. I mean, you're practically my only friend. Can we backtrack or something? Start over? Please? All I want you to do is talk to a few people; it's not so much to ask. Just talk to Lenora and Mrs. Coffey and Norah. Listen to what they have to say, think about what I've told you about my parents, about Cliff and Rowan, and see if you're still so sure my father is an innocent lamb."

She ate a teeny bit of lettuce. "You're wondering about me and Waldemar, aren't you? Thinking he's not my type? He's big, but he's very peaceful. Sorta like your Andre, maybe. I had my fill of intense guys with Padraig."

She was trying hard now to be nice and patch things up, but it wasn't working. I wasn't interested in a girlish chat about her new boyfriend and the way things stood, I couldn't chat about Andre. I was trying to be patient, trying to keep in mind her recent trauma, but it didn't help. When we were younger I hadn't minded but now I found her mood changes and her demands tiresome. Nothing she had said moved me any closer to thinking that Cliff was a murderer, or to understanding why she thought he was. Nor did I have any idea how to convince her that he wasn't.

My common sense told me to walk away from the whole mess but she seemed so pitiful and sad that I couldn't do it, so in the name of friendship I compromised. "I'll do this much for you," I said, "I'll talk to some people, the ones who've been calling. I'll keep an open mind, I'll listen to what they say, and I'll report back to you. But that's as far as I go. I won't snoop around at Bartlett Hill. I have to establish an honest working relationship with those people, and I can't do that if I have a secret agenda."

She smiled and clapped her hands together gleefully. "I knew I could count on you, Thea . . ." she began.

I held up a hand to stop her. "One more thing. You have to agree to listen to what I have to say and keep an open mind, too. Agreed?"

"Of course," she said, though, knowing her as I did, I was sure she hadn't paid any attention to my conditions. "I'm very grateful."

I left immediately after dinner and went home feeling like I'd made a complete mess of things. Why hadn't I just said no? It didn't help that my answering machine was blinking like a crazed traffic light and most of the calls proved to be from people Eve had sicced on me. Lenora Stern, with something she'd forgotten to tell me. The neighbor, Martha Coffey, calling to see if I'd gotten her message. Norah McCarty, who grudgingly surrendered her name and nothing more. Coffey was the only one I called back.

"I saw you with Eve at the funeral, didn't I?" she said. "You're the tall girl with the long hair?"

"I am." No sense in telling her I wasn't a girl, I didn't want to alienate her before I even heard what she had to say.

"It's a terrible tragedy, what's happened to that family. When Eve came to see me and asked me to talk to you, I didn't know what to say. She seemed to assume that I agreed with her theory that Clifford was the killer, and I don't, Ms. Kozak, I truly don't. I decided not to argue with her—Eve's such a sensitive girl—and just talk to you instead. Since you're a detective, surely you'll be able to sort things out. And that's just what I told the policeman when he was asking me questions. That I'd tell everything I know to you, and you can decide what to do with it. I'd just feel more comfortable talking to a woman, you can understand that. Come to lunch tomorrow. Twelve would be good. It's the house across the street. Directly across the street."

After she hung up, I realized the only words I'd said in the entire conversation, once I'd identified myself, were "I am."

What I am, I thought, is tired. Weary. Exhausted. Sick of weird people and their weird problems. I was awfully tempted to rouse my friend Jack and tell him my troubles, but I didn't, and I was asleep as soon as my head hit the pillow. Not even the grumbling of my stomach, gnawing on its meager bit of sauerkraut, disturbed me.

CHAPTER *14*

I'D EXPECTED TROUBLE sleeping. I had a lot on my mind after the crazy ups and downs of the day, starting with my very successful meeting with Robert Hillyer and ending with my very unsuccessful meeting with Eve. I wasn't surprised by the mercurial swings in her moods. She'd always been prone to them, and I knew she was deeply disturbed by her mother's death. What surprised me was how unsympathetic I was becoming. I'd always been very patient with Eve, maybe because the relationship had been a two-way street and I was getting something back from her. Now all I seemed to be getting from her was demands and hostility. Her reaction when I looked in her desk for Band-Aids was just plain nuts. Maybe Waldemar was a snoop and I'd accidentally trespassed into a sensitive area. When we'd lived together she'd never been so suspicious and territorial.

Irritated, I turned over and buried my head in the pillow. Eve had disrupted enough of my nights. I didn't need her sorry figure lingering in my brain and making me feel guilty. I willed her out of my head and out of my house, and this time, my mind obeyed, leaving me alone in the big bed. Too alone. The other half of the bed seemed very empty and none of the messages on the machine had been from Andre. I'd been secretly hoping he'd call and say he'd changed his mind. It could happen. The guy was a cop, and pretty stubborn sometimes—he'd once been described to me as that guy with the poker up his ass and the bristly hair—but he was also reasonable, and honest, and he could be astonishingly romantic.

Like last Valentine's Day. A cold, drizzly, miserable Thursday. I'd left work early because I had a rotten cold, one of those colds where my head felt like it was packed with sawdust, I'd blown my nose until it was scrubbed raw, coughed until my ribs felt broken and my chest ached, and every time I bent over I felt like the top of my head was going to come off. I'd crept home through the snarl of traffic, taken a shower and changed into my softest old sweats, and then discovered that the only cold remedy I had left in the house was one teaspoon of cough syrup. No decongestant, nothing for the aches and pains of flu or the incredible pain in my head. And not a single tea bag or even a can of soup. Too sick to drag myself out again, I was curled up on the couch, wallowing in self-pity and dully watching the talking heads on the screen deliver what passed for news, when the doorbell rang.

When I opened the door, Andre was standing there, holding two brown paper grocery bags, looking exactly as he had the first time he cooked me dinner. He carried them to the kitchen and picked me up in a bear hug, waltzing me around the room. "I figured you must be pretty sick to leave the office so early. I was in Kittery on business, so once I was that close, I had to come and see you. I called your office and Suzanne said you'd gone home sick, so knowing your refrigerator like I do, I stopped for some supplies." I watched in awe and wonder as he pulled out what he'd bought.

First he took out dinner. Boneless chicken breasts, broccoli, snow peas, cashews and a spicy sauce for a stir-fry. "I assumed you'd at least have rice and an onion," he said. A bottle of dry white wine. A chocolate cheesecake. And cocktail shrimp with sauce for starters. "You take the shrimp like this," he said, opening the package, "dip it in the sauce, and feed it to the woman you love. Says so right here." He pointed at the label.

I bent down to read it. "It says '$8.25 Seafood.' "

He pointed to the bar code. "And feed it to the woman you love. It's in code," he said, dipping one into the sauce and feeding it to me. He put his ear against my stomach and listened. "Heard a splash, and I know what that means. Poor little guy is down there all alone. When's the last time you ate?"

I shrugged. "Maybe breakfast, maybe yesterday. I haven't felt like eating."

"Too busy to eat is more like it. But tonight," he tapped himself on the chest, "vee hef zee premier chef du Maine ici, end 'ee vill mek you somesing sooo delicieuse, you weel faint."

"And then you will have your way with me, is that it?"

"Have you seen yourself in a mirror lately?"

I nodded glumly. "Zee premier chef du Maine must be pretty hard up."

He took my hand and brought it to his body. "Maybe not hard up, lady, but definitely . . . well, I leave that to your imagination."

"I'm not sure my imagination's working right now, mister. My head's too full of sawdust." It was a lie. Getting close to Andre always excites me. If I was in cardiac arrest, he could probably restart my heart just by coming close. "So what's in the second bag?"

"Magic potions." In went his big, blunt-fingered hand, and out came a gigantic box of tissues. He gave me his sexy, sardonic, eyebrows-raised look over the top of the box. "Freud just made it all too complicated. I know what women want." He hummed a little of "Try a Little Tenderness," and handed me the box with a flourish. "The softest money can buy," he said, pulling out a bag of scones, cough syrup with a decongestant, throat lozenges, aspirin, and several cans of soup.

"You are so wonderful I can hardly stand it."

"I saved the best for last," he said, handing me a box of Sleepytime tea.

"Just another ploy to get me into bed."

"No, this is the ploy for getting you into bed." He grabbed me and kissed me, and a deliciously warm, languid feeling started in my toes and made it to my head before the kiss ended. "And this." He released me, reached into the bag once more, and pulled out a huge bouquet of roses.

"Andre! They must have cost the earth!"

"You're worth it," he said, dangling another shrimp in front of my eyes. I snapped it up like a trout. We ate the shrimp at seven and the rest of the meal at ten. Despite my cold and the weather, it was a great Valentine's Day.

Why couldn't I have it all? The man I loved and enough freedom in my life to work my absurd hours, be by myself when I needed to be, and still have someone warm in my bed, someone to play with on the weekends. Someone to feed me when I was hungry, to feed when he was hungry, someone who . . . Right in the middle of my meditation on relationships, I fell asleep, plunging down through the darkness to dreamland like an angel falling off a cloud.

I slept the deep sleep of the just, or tired, until about 3:00 A.M., when I was suddenly wide awake. I lay in the darkness, trying to breathe quietly. There was a noise out there that was neither the wind nor one of the many noises I'd learned the sea can make. Yes, there it was again, a sound like the creaking of footsteps on wood. I rolled out of bed, quickly pulled on my robe and went into the living room. As my eyes gradually adjusted to the dark, I could see a faint shape on my deck, a twisting figure, holding something in its hand. Without thinking, I snapped on the outside light and charged toward the window, fumbling the sheer curtain out of the way and struggling to open the lock. Something thudded loudly onto the deck and the intruder turned and ran away into the darkness.

I opened the door and gave chase, leaping down off the deck and dashing around the corner of the house. There was only a sliver of moon, and the night was very dark and still. Ahead of me

I could hear the sound of shoes slapping the pavement of the driveway, a stumble, a muttered curse, and the running resumed. A robe is not the best thing to jog in and in my bare feet I kept stepping on rocks and prickles and couldn't make any time. Finally I gave up and bent over, breathing heavily. So much for aerobics. Where was that stamina I was supposed to be building? The running footsteps disappeared up the drive.

I limped back to the house, pausing on the deck to look for whatever my intruder had dropped. In the bright light, it wasn't hard to spot, and when I spotted it, a chill ran through me like I'd been dipped in ice water. Lying on my deck, shining against the dull gray boards, was an evil looking hunting knife. I ran inside, slammed the door shut and locked it. Then I grabbed the phone and dialed 911.

I wasn't dressed for a police visit, not even a nocturnal one, but I was afraid to let the knife out of my sight. I compromised by dashing into the bedroom for some sweats. My hands were trembling so badly I could hardly get them on. After what seemed like an eternity, and which was only four minutes according to the glowing red display on my digital clock, there was a vigorous knock on the door. The kid who was standing there was so neat and crisp and spit-shined he looked liked he'd just come out of the box. He swept me with a quick head-to-toe, introduced himself as Officer Harris, and stuck one shiny black shoe inside the door. "What seems to be the problem, ma'am?"

I opened the door wider, and he walked past me into the room, sweeping it with his eyes just like he'd swept me, making it easier not to take his scrutiny personally. He was probably just doing what they'd taught him at the academy. "There was an intruder, a person, out on my deck trying to break in. The noises woke me up. I came out here and turned on the lights and there he was." There was an annoying quiver in my voice. "He ran away. I tried to catch him, but I couldn't. When he ran, I saw him drop something, and when I came back, I found the knife."

He'd been listening with routine politeness until I mentioned the knife, then his head came up and he stared at me. "Could you show me the knife, please?" I led him to the window and pointed at it, lying bright and nasty, and, in my eyes, looming as large as an elephant on my deck. "I'll just take a look around outside. I'll be right back," he said.

I stifled my impulse to grab his arm and say "don't go," even though that's what I felt like doing. I didn't want him to think I was some helpless female intimidated by knife-wielding intruders in the night. Instead, I huddled on the couch, bits of conversation about Helene running through my head. "She was butchered, Thea," I could hear Eve say, "I've never seen so much blood. Two of her fingers were nearly cut off."

And Dom. "Not just a stab wound or two, like you might expect from a random attack, but deep, deliberate slashes, designed to kill."

Or as Eve had said last night, "it was done so that the killer could be certain that she would die. By someone who intended to kill and knew how to kill." The paper had said they'd found a hunting knife nearby that might have been the murder weapon.

Outside the window, Harris peered intently at my sliding door, then stooped and examined the knife. He pulled a flashlight off his belt, snapped it on, and went down the steps to the lawn. I couldn't see him anymore, but I followed the progress of the light as he slowly searched the yard. He was gone about five minutes, while I sat and shook, furious with myself for being such a wimp, and resisted the urge to grab Jack out of the cupboard to comfort me. It does not look good to the cops to dash for the liquor bottle. I could imagine what Harris would think. A few footsteps in the night and the broad heads straight for the bottle. They like you to wait until they suggest a good therapeutic slug of whiskey. He didn't know about my connection to Helene.

He was back at the front door again, shaking his head as he replaced the flashlight. "Whoever it was, they're not out there now. Did you see or hear any sort of vehicle?"

"No. Just the footsteps."

"Whoever it was used a screwdriver to dismantle the lock on the fence and got into the yard that way, but left the screwdriver by the fence, so he was using the knife to try to break the lock on your slider. You wouldn't happen to have a couple of plastic bags I could use to put the knife and screwdriver in, would you?" I could tell that he hated to ask. Cops like to keep the upper hand. They don't like to ask favors. But I didn't care, the sooner that knife disappeared from sight, the better. I got him two bags from the kitchen. He went outside again, bagged them both, and came back in, setting the bags down on the coffee table.

Close-up, the knife looked even more evil and menacing. My stomach was being squeezed by a big fist and my muscles were tensed like they were anticipating pain. I've always had a horror of knives, nightmares of knives coming at me, bright and shiny, with no way to fight them off. I thought of Helene, with all her defensive cuts, holding up her arms while the knife kept slashing. I thought of my father and Uncle Henry, going deer hunting, rifles in the crooks of their arms and hunting knives in worn leather sheaths strapped to their belts. Remembered the deer strung up in the garage, its slit throat like a gruesome smile and hollowed belly gaping, and my father's knife, having done the deed, wiped clean and back on his belt. Harris was saying something to me, and I hadn't heard him.

"Ms. Kozak? Did you hear me? Are you okay?"

"Could you put that thing away please? Somewhere out of sight?" I couldn't quite keep the tremble out of my voice.

"The knife? It bothers you?" he asked.

He couldn't know how it was for me. It hadn't been found outside his door in the dead of night—an apt expression—and he probably hadn't spent the last week constantly regaled with stories about someone who'd been knifed to death. "Yes, it bothers me. When I look at it, I can't stop thinking about Helene."

"Helene?"

"Streeter. The woman who was killed last week in Anson."

He'd had his notebook out, ready to ask me questions, but

suddenly he seemed a lot more interested. "You knew her?"

"I knew her. Her daughter Eve is an old friend."

He picked up the knife. "And you think this knife might have some connection?"

"That's not what I meant, Officer. It's just that looking at that knife makes me think of Helene. She was killed with a knife, you know." Against my will, my lips were trembling and my voice sounded shaky even to me. I stretched out a nervous hand, picked up the knife and handed it to him. "Please. Put it somewhere out of sight." He looked around for a moment, puzzled, then set it on the floor behind his chair. "I'm going to make some tea," I said, "would you like some?" I had to move around, do something to shake the panic that was gripping me. My hand, when I touched it to my face, was frigid.

"I'd prefer coffee, if you have it," he said. "Instant is fine."

I got up and headed for the kitchen, closing the drapes on my way. The clock said 3:30. I was getting a nice early start on the day. I turned on all the lights. It didn't make me feel any better.

Andre always complains that I never have any food in the house. About most things he's right, but I always have coffee. Good, rich, freshly ground coffee. Bad for the stomach, the bladder and maybe for breasts, but an essential element of any civilized diet. Made with spring water. No sense in bothering to buy good coffee if you're going to make it with chlorinated, fluoridated water. I put an unbleached filter in the pot, spooned in some Kona coffee flavored with macadamia nuts and poured in the water. Presto. A push of the button and the machine began to gurgle happily. Harris had come into the kitchen and was sitting on a stool, watching me.

"Boy that smells good," he said.

"Cream or sugar?" I asked, rummaging through the freezer for something to serve with the coffee.

"Black is fine."

I felt better with something to do. Before long, Officer Harris and I were sitting at the table with our coffee and a pecan coffee cake, chatting like old friends. I'd stopped regarding him as a toy just out of the box, and he'd stopped regarding me as an over-reacting knife-phobic high-strung female weirdo. He'd taken seriously my fears about the knife and what had happened to Helene, and promised to call Dom in the morning. We were both disappointed that I couldn't give him more information about the intruder, but whoever it was wore dark clothes and I hadn't seen the face or hair. I couldn't even tell him if it had been male or female. All I could tell him was I thought the person was shorter than I was and had a slight build, but that was true of at least half the people I met—the shorter part, anyway. Not a lot to go on, but maybe they'd find something on the knife or the screwdriver. When he left at four, I was wide awake and I'd almost stopped shaking.

I locked the door behind him and switched on the alarm, which I normally used only when I was out of town. I got out the stuff I'd been working on for Cliff, but a wind had come up, and after an hour of jumping every time a twig brushed the house or a board creaked, I gave up, got dressed, and went to the office.

CHAPTER 15

BY NINE I'D finished the proposal and left it on Sarah's desk. Bobby and I were discussing some things I needed him to do when Sarah knocked briskly on the door and came in. She was wearing a wonderful salmon-colored dress that suited her coloring and emphasized her curves. She was holding the sheaf of papers I'd left on her desk and frowning. "Detective Florio on the phone," she said, "you want to call him back? And didn't I tell you not to do this to me today?" She shook the papers.

"I need that stuff as soon as possible," I said. "Eleven-thirty latest. Good thing you're the best typist on the East Coast. You get that dress last night?"

"You bet," she said. "We had a great time. I spent a bundle and I don't feel one bit guilty. And Brad did give me a birthday present. The asshole."

"What did he give you? Cookware?"

"Worse. A stair-climbing machine. Stood there with a foolish grin on his face and told me it was for my thighs. I can't wait, really. I'm gonna use it daily until I have thighs like Wonder Woman and then I'm gonna squeeze his little head between them and crack it like a nut. You want to take the call?"

I'd almost forgotten about the call, listening to her. Funny as she was, Sarah was getting to be one angry woman. I hoped Brad woke up soon, before she really did lose her patience. "I'll take it." I picked up the phone. "Hi, Dom."

"What the hell is going on, Theadora?" His voice thundered out of the phone.

"Excuse me?"

"I said what the hell is going on?"

"I'm sorry," I said sweetly, "I don't understand the question."

"I mean what's this stuff about someone outside your place in the middle of the night with a goddamned hunting knife?" he thundered.

I sighed. I hate people who call up and yell at me first thing in the morning. "I put it there myself and called the police because I was dying for attention."

"Cut the crap, Kozak," he said.

"That has a nice alliteration, Dom."

"I don't know what the hell alliteration is, but if you don't stop kidding and tell me what happened I'm going to come over there and shake you."

"Don't threaten me with police brutality, Dom. If you've talked with Officer Harris then you know as much about it as I do. Noises woke me up in the night and I saw someone outside on my deck. I switched on the light and went to investigate and whoever it was dropped what they were holding and ran. I followed but they got away, and when I got back I found this big hunting knife on the deck."

"They? There was more than one?"

"No. One. They is the preferred sex-neutral at the moment, pronoun even if it is grammatically incorrect," I said.

"Are you okay?" His voice was calmer now.

"As long as the sun is out and I'm surrounded by people."

"We need to talk."

"We are talking."

"Boy you *are* a real bitch today, you know that?"

"Lack of sleep and mortal fear will do that to a person, you know. That and being yelled at by one of the few people I trust. Besides, I never said I was nice. That was just an assumption you made."

"Sorry," he growled. "I was worried about you." Bobby was observing the whole interaction, goggle-eyed.

"I'm going to be in Anson later. You want to meet for coffee at the IHOP? Around two, maybe?" He agreed reluctantly. It sounded like it was hard for him to resist his urge to come right over and see for himself that I was okay. He should have been able to tell from talking to me. If I wasn't too intimidated for a little sharp repartee, I was doing okay. I wondered how much of his concern was for me because he liked me, and how much was the product of fraternal bonding, guarding the territory of a fellow homicide detective.

"Okay, Kozak. I'll meet you," he said. "Meanwhile, watch your back."

Yeah, sure, I thought, I'll spend the next five hours looking over my shoulder and bumping into walls. Bobby shook his head. "Boy, you sure do lead an exciting life. Everyone around here does. Well, you and Suzanne anyway. And it doesn't sound like Sarah's life is exactly uneventful either."

"She's just got a man who's a bit disappointing to live with."

"Funny," he said, "I never have that problem. The man I live with is as nice as the day is long."

"Well, maybe you got the last good one, Bobby. Or maybe you made a wiser choice, though I wouldn't suggest that to Sarah, if I were you."

"Don't worry. I try to steer clear of anything that looks like confrontation, and Sarah's been loaded for bear—don't you just love that expression?—all week. Back to work?"

"Please." I finished with Bobby, called Lisa and lined her up for Monday morning just in case Bartlett Hill wanted to get started that fast, and sneaked out to the 10:00 A.M. aerobics class. Last night's anxiety and lack of sleep had left my body feeling like a loosely assembled collection of knots. I needed to work them out before lunch with Martha Coffey. I might have denied it in my conversation with Dom, but he was right, I was bitchy. My nerves were ragged and I kept having these little spurts of anxiety, like shorts in an electrical circuit, that left me momentarily breathless.

Sarah gave me a bleak smile when I passed her desk. "You coming back for this, or can I spend the rest of the morning chatting on the phone with my girlfriends?"

"I'll be back for it by eleven-thirty. Proof it when you're done, and make me eight copies."

"If the beast is working today."

"If not, use Lucy's. Please?"

"I hate to keep imposing on her."

"Maybe I should have given you a new copier for your birthday."

She plucked at the fabric of her dress. "Rather have this, thanks. Makes me feel great. Don't worry, you'll have your copies."

I rarely went to morning classes, so I didn't know any of the instructors. I was surprised to see it was Aaron again. I guess I was just being sexist, but I'd assumed it was an after-work job for him, something he did after his "real" job. It was a different crowd from the evening group. The women in front of me and behind me had small children in tow, and waiting outside for the class before us to be over, the talk was all of day care and childrearing. Even the outfits were different. Everyone was coordinated, down to their shoes and socks, and there was a lot of makeup and jewelry. The evening group is quieter. Tired. A lot of lank hair and tense faces waiting for the jolt to jump-start their evenings.

There was a lot more chatter, too. The ladies were clearly taken with Aaron, and wanted him to notice them. I waited restlessly, doing stretches and pliés, impatient for class to begin. Finally Aaron switched on a tape, positioned himself in the front of the room, and said, "Let's warm up." After that it was okay. He gave another workout that left me drenched with sweat and trembling but I felt a thousand times better when I walked out.

Back at the office, Magda was on the phone, a harassed look on her face, speaking slowly and firmly to someone. "I am sorry," she said, "but as I have already explained to you three times, this is Ms. Begner's office, not her home. I am only her secretary, not her mother. I will give her the message if she calls in, but I do not know where she can be reached." She banged down the phone and wrote something on a pink slip. The pile of them on her desk was already gigantic. "Only one more day. I'm not sure I can stand it. All of these people are so stupid! Why can't they keep things straight? This person here," she tapped the note angrily with a forefinger, "wants to know if the rehearsal dinner is tomorrow night or Sunday night? Of course I said it was tonight, and they told me it was impossible. Tonight they are completely booked. And no way to reach Suzanne."

I patted her on the shoulder and took the note. "I'll take care of it. Anything else of crisis proportions?"

"I will check." I waited while she sorted through the pile. "No. That's the only one."

Sarah was sitting behind a small mountain of papers, looking as harassed as Magda. We weren't a very happy family today. The only unlined face in the office was Bobby's. He was sitting at his desk, bent over his work, a happy smile on his face. I could have hugged him just for being there. I paused and asked Sarah what was going on. "Damn collator won't work. I swear someday soon I'm going to execute this machine."

"Make it easy on yourself. Call the company rep, get him in here, and order a new machine. None of us needs this frustration."

"You mean it?" Her face lit up. She was awfully pretty when she wasn't angry.

"You ought to smile more often," I said. "It suits you. Of course I mean it."

"I'm so happy I could dance!"

"Maybe after you finish putting those together?" She made a face and went back to her sorting. I kicked off my shoes, put my feet up on the desk, and grabbed the phone.

A cheerful little voice answered, "Cipio's."

I asked for the manager and was transferred to a man with a slight accent. I explained why I was calling and asked what was going on. "I will check. Please hold."

In the time I was on hold I could have knitted a sweater, and I had places to be. I drummed impatiently on the desk with my fingers. I was still waiting when Sarah brought the proposals in. She looked odd, like someone who has just heard bad news and can't quite absorb it. "What's wrong?" I asked.

"Miss Kozak?" said a voice in my ear.

"Can you hold on a moment, please." I put him on hold. Sarah was hesitating by the door.

"I'm not sure I should tell you."

"It can't be that bad. Not unless you're quitting, that is."

She shook her head vigorously. "It's nothing like that. There was a phone call for you. Someone who wouldn't give a name. A very faint voice, gruff, asking for you. When I said you were on another line the person said to give you a message." She stopped and stood there looking miserable.

"So?"

"So the message was 'last night was only the beginning.' "

Once again I felt the cold chill of fear go through me. I wrapped my arms protectively around my body. "Don't worry about it, Sarah. Probably just a prank."

"I hope so," she said, leaving me alone with my fear.

I punched the button and got Cipio's manager back on the line. "What's the story?" I said.

"We have no record of Miss Begner's reservation."

"What is your name, please?"

"Roscoe," he said. "Mark Roscoe."

"Can you hold on a minute please, Mr. Roscoe?"

"We're rather busy right now, Ms. Kozak. Perhaps you could call back later. . . ."

"Look, Mr. Roscoe, we're talking about a wedding rehearsal dinner. An event that was planned months ago. A dinner that has to take place tonight. . . ." I buzzed Sarah. When she came in I asked her to have Magda bring me Suzanne's wedding file. Magda was at my side in an instant, and just as quickly sorted through the file and handed me Suzanne's letter to Cipio's making the reservation and their letter confirming it. Suzanne was much too organized to do anything that important without leaving a paper trail. "Okay, Mr. Roscoe, you don't have to go on hold. I have here in front of me a letter dated January 23 to Cipio's from Suzanne Begner, making the reservation for tonight, and another letter from Cipio's dated January 27 confirming that reservation. . . ."

"There must be some mistake," he interrupted.

"The mistake would be for you to continue to pretend this reservation does not exist. The signature at the bottom of the letter is Mark Roscoe. Now as I see it, you have two choices. You can honor the reservation, or you can have me very mad at you."

His response was huffy. "I guess I shall have to have you mad at me. . . ."

This time I interrupted him. "Let me tell you what I will do if you make me mad, Mr. Roscoe. First there will be a lawsuit. A consumer complaint under Chapter 93A, the Consumer Protection Act. A breach-of-contract claim, and a claim for intentional infliction of emotional distress. We are talking about a bride here, Mr. Roscoe, and your negligence ruining one of the most important occasions in her life. I will hire people to pass out leaflets outside your restaurant during business hours containing copies of both letters and a description of your despicable behavior. I am not naive, Mr. Roscoe, I know that you like to attract wedding parties to your private dining rooms. I've seen your advertising. We both know how skittish brides can be. They worry about things going wrong."

"Are you some kind of a nutcase? You wouldn't dare do those things."

Being scared makes me angry, and Mr. Roscoe was getting the brunt of that anger. "I am the matron of honor, Mr. Roscoe, and it is my job to make sure that things go smoothly. If that makes me some kind of a nutcase, then perhaps I am, although it doesn't seem at all nutty to me to have a strong reaction when someone claims they will not honor a confirmed reservation the day of the event. As for what I will not dare to do, I haven't finished my list. . . ."

"I don't have to listen to this. . . ."

"You'd better. I am going to hang up now, Mr. Roscoe, and if I don't get a call back from you within the next ten minutes, assuring me that the dinner is going ahead as scheduled, my next call will be to the board of health, complaining about bugs in my food, followed by a formal complaint to the town that you are abusing your liquor license and it should be reviewed. I seem to recall an automobile accident last month caused by an intoxicated person leaving your parking lot. And wasn't there a fight there recently? That's all for now, but I could go on and on. I'm hanging up now, and remember, Mr. Roscoe. Ten minutes."

I hung up, out of breath, and collapsed in my chair to the sounds of vigorous applause. Magda, Sarah and Bobby were all standing in the doorway watching me.

"Bravo," Magda actually smiled. "You should have been a lawyer."

"Now we wait," Bobby said, checking his watch.

"Don't you people have any work to do?"

"Don't be a party pooper," Sarah said. "That was the best show I've seen all week."

I stuffed the proposals into my briefcase and scribbled Martha Coffey's number on a piece of paper. "I'm going to run to the ladies' room. Can you call this woman and tell her I'll be a few minutes late? And if Roscoe calls, put him on hold."

When I came back, Sarah was on the phone. She pointed to

the blinking light. I went into my office and picked up the phone. It was Roscoe. "All right. You win. We'll honor the reservation."

"Great news, Mr. Roscoe," I said. "I hope the service won't be as grudging as your capitulation. You're doing the right thing, you know." He hung up without answering. I got my papers and ran, pausing at Magda's desk. "You can call the bride and tell her the little mix-up is all straightened out."

"She's lucky to have a friend like you," Magda called after me. My shoes seemed amazingly noisy in the hall as I rushed out to my meeting with Martha Coffey.

CHAPTER 16

MARTHA COFFEY'S HOUSE had the static look of a place decorated by the book because someone doesn't trust her own taste. Martha Coffey's physical appearance matched. Fiftyish, her hair was frosted blond to cover the gray, but it was neither a shade nor style that particular suited her. She wore makeup that had a sort of built-in glitter designed to give her skin a fresh, dewy look, but that didn't suit her either, nor did her shiny purple, teal and black warm-up suit, or the purple-framed glasses she wore. She would have looked better with gradually graying dark hair, little makeup on her nice ivory skin, and simple, tailored clothes. I think she knew it, and was uncomfortable in the costume she thought she was supposed to wear.

Although she'd initiated the meeting, she was shy and uncertain, seeming as uncomfortable with her ideas as she was with her house and appearance. I wondered why she'd bothered to inflict what was obviously an unpleasant experience on herself, and as soon as we were seated in her tidy living room, I asked.

"I see you're very perceptive," she said. "Eve said you would be. She said I should feel free to tell you everything." She hesitated, picking nervously at her hair. "I don't think she realized what I might tell you."

"It sounds like you have quite an extensive relationship with Eve. Is that right?"

She plucked at the hair again. "I guess you could say that. I've always been very fond of Eve. She was a little younger than my daughter, Amanda, and being an only child, she'd get lonely. She was always appearing on the doorstep and asking if Mandy could play." She laughed nervously. "Mandy didn't really like Eve. She found her annoying and she said Eve was a terrible liar, but I felt sorry for the child, so I encouraged Mandy to play with her sometimes, and sometimes I'd just let Eve hang around in the kitchen with me. She was good company. She'd just sit on the stool and chatter away about school, or ask what I was cooking, or tell me things." She glanced across the table at me, her troubled brown eyes magnified by the glasses. "I'm afraid sometimes she told me things I really didn't want to know."

"How long did that relationship continue? Did she still come around when she was a teenager?"

Martha Coffey studied the ceiling, trying to remember. "Not so often, but sometimes. Especially when she had boy trouble. It's kind of ironic when I look back on it. My children never wanted to confide in me. They thought I was a complete fuddy-duddy. Just not with it. Or so they told me all the time. And there was that girl, with both her parents professionals in the field of listening to people's troubles, and they couldn't hear a word she said and whenever they gave advice, it was totally wrong." She plucked at her hair once again, then blurted, "I was the one who went with her when she had the abortion. Not Helene. That's pretty sad, don't you think? I don't claim to be any kind of great mother, but imagine a girl having to go to her neighbor under those circumstances."

"It sounds like she was lucky to have you."

Her rather severe face brightened. "It's nice of you to say that. Oh, and here I am forgetting my manners, I was so nervous about talking to you. You're probably wondering if I'm ever going to get around to serving lunch. I'll just be a minute. Everything is ready." She got up and rushed into the kitchen.

I followed, pausing in the doorway. This room, at least, reflected Martha Coffey's true self, the generous woman who had opened her house to a lonely little girl. The rest of the house was rigid and restrained, but not the kitchen. The floor was gleaming natural wood, the walls up to the chair rail a light, slightly grayish green, and above that white wallpaper with green trailing ivy. The cupboards were white, with glass doors, the appliances also white, and the countertops some marblelike stuff in green to match the walls. The backsplash was shiny white tile, with occasional tiles handpainted with ivy to match the wallpaper. There were lots of vibrantly healthy flowering plants in a greenhouse window over the sink, and a green bowl full of lemons on the counter. "I really like your kitchen," I said.

She smiled again, the smile of someone who would like to smile more often, but wasn't sure how it would be received. "I always wanted to redo it, but my husband thought the old one was perfectly functional. He's a real 'if it ain't broke, don't fix it' type. But it was terribly dark and uninviting. When my mother died and left me some money I just threw caution to the wind and redid it. And every day, I'm glad I did."

In the middle of the room was an old bleached pine table set for two. As I watched, she lifted the lid on a big pot and stirred, filling the air with the delicious scent of curry and apples. "This is really a winter soup, I think," she said, "but I was in the mood to make it today." She ladled it into two bowls, took a napkin-lined basket out of the oven, and put it all on the table. "I'm afraid this is all there is," she said. "I hope you won't be disappointed."

"If it tastes as good as it smells, I'll be disappointed if you don't give me the recipe."

We ate in silence for a few minutes, and it took all my willpower not to gobble my food. The soup, which she called Mulligatawny, was a delicious combination of chicken, corn, apples, raisins and curry, and she'd set out little pots of coconut and chopped peanuts to sprinkle on top. Finally she broke the silence.

"I'm not, by nature, a gossip, but what I have to tell you is exactly that. Gossip. And I don't know what good it will do, either. I know that many people feel you should say only good things about the dead, but what I have to say about Helene isn't very flattering. I hope you don't mind."

I wasn't sure how to respond. I didn't want to know bad things about Helene. I'd always admired her enormously for what she did, for her outspokenness and her sense of mission, and for having the courage of her convictions, even if I didn't always agree with her. She might not have been a great mother, but as the women who'd spoken at her funeral had recognized, she'd been a great role model, and also a dedicated champion of women afraid to speak for themselves. She'd also been beautiful, organized and gracious.

It was probably closest to the truth to say I'd been in awe of her and wildly jealous of her, both at the same time. I'd sat at her table, awkward and uncertain, admired her perfect clothes, her perfect house, and her wonderful food, and despaired of ever being able to be a competent grown-up. Helene had seen that, reassured me, complimented me, and eagerly solicited my opinions. But I wasn't here to reminisce about Helene. I'd promised Eve I'd listen, and I hoped Mrs. Coffey was going to tell me something that would help me persuade Eve to abandon her vendetta against Cliff. "Not at all, Mrs. Coffey. Sometimes it's hard to know what's important."

"That's what the policeman said, too."

"Which policeman was it, Mrs. Coffey? Was it Detective Florio?"

She shook her head. "No, I don't think he had an Italian name. Nice looking fellow. Youngish. A bit pushy. He had this odd haircut." She moved her hand around her head, mimicking short on top and long in the back. "Rather a thick neck. From working out with weights, I guess. My son does that. I suppose it may be good for their bodies, I really don't know, but it makes it impossible to get clothes that fit." She stopped abruptly and put her hands over her mouth. "James, that's my husband, says I run on at the mouth like a brook in the spring."

"Not at all, Mrs. Coffey," I said. It looked like living with James wasn't exactly a barrel of laughs. No wonder she was nervous. She'd been told that everything she did was wrong. "Sounds like Detective Meagher to me."

"Exactly," she said, "that's him. Well, if you've met him, maybe you can understand why I wasn't comfortable talking to him."

I understood perfectly. What I didn't understand was why Dom hadn't interviewed her. She would have been comfortable talking to him. I supposed they'd just divided up the neighbors to be interviewed and each done their share. "I do understand, Mrs. Coffey. There is something about his manner, isn't there? But I believe he's a very good detective."

She just shrugged and then said something astonishing. "Helene Streeter was a slut." She watched me with satisfaction. "I've shocked you, haven't I? Well, I'm sorry if I have, but it's true."

"What do you mean?" I tried, not entirely successfully, to keep the surprise out of my voice.

"I mean she had a succession of men in and out of that house. Ever since Eve started school. I don't know what she did before that. Went to their houses, maybe. It was like something from a bad TV movie. Helene would come out with Eve and wait for the bus. Eve would leave on the bus. Helene would open the garage, get in her car and drive away. Cliff would come out right behind her, get in his car and drive away. Sometimes they'd wait with Eve together, share a kiss in the driveway, and then leave. A few minutes later, Helene would arrive back and open both garage doors. A man in a car would drive into the garage and the doors would shut behind them. Then, about forty-five minutes later, the man would leave, and then Helene would leave."

"How do you know they weren't patients she was seeing at home?"

She gave me a sharp look, as if she suspected I might be stupid.

"Helene treated women," she said. "And therapy appointments usually last more than forty-five minutes."

This was shocking news. "There were different men?" She nodded. "Did you recognize any of them?"

"One or two. Not by name. Just from having seen them around town. One was a fireman. Another worked in the pharmacy. And they were all ages. Gray, blond, brunette, red. She had very catholic tastes."

"How often did you notice this?"

"It varied. Sometimes once a week, sometimes once a month. Then there would be long periods when it wouldn't happen at all."

"What about in the months before she died?"

"Sometimes she'd have men at the house, but usually she went elsewhere, I think. Her behavior had changed." She got up and cleared our dishes onto the counter. "I hope you're not one of those young girls who are always on a diet, like Eve. I've made us a lovely dessert." She set out clean plates and forks and took a picture-perfect fruit tart out of the refrigerator. She seemed completely oblivious to the discontinuity between what we were discussing and the normal rhythm of a ladies' lunch.

It was a struggle not to let her see how shocked I was, but I tried to behave like an unflappable female detective. "I have a terrible sweet tooth," I said, "and this looks delicious. What did you mean when you said her behavior had changed?"

"I'd see her come home from work, and then an hour later she'd come out and get in her car and leave. Sometimes she wouldn't come back until the next morning."

"How do you know she stayed out all night?"

"She was wearing the same clothes."

I thought about Helene's clothes, wondering if Martha Coffey might be mistaken. Helene had always worn wonderful clothes. Expensive, simple and elegant. I'd sometimes thought I'd learn to dress just like her as soon as I could afford it. But they tended to look much the same. Dark, subdued shades. Delicate blouses. Fitted jackets. One outfit might easily be confused with another, especially at a distance. "How can you be sure?"

"I can be sure," she said, "because they were unmistakable. You're thinking about Helene's professional clothes. But these were what I called—to myself only, of course, James would be shocked to hear me talk like this—her whoring clothes."

"I just can't picture it, I'm sorry. Can you describe what you mean."

"Of course," she said. "I understand your confusion. I was pretty shocked myself. She'd go inside in one of those demure suits the color of an overcooked vegetable, and come out an hour later in red suede shoes with four-inch heels and a skintight red leather dress that stopped about five inches above the knee. Black stockings. Her hair teased out to here." She held her hands about six inches from her ears. "And the next morning she'd come back around six, hair uncombed and with runs in her stockings, still in the same red dress." There was the trace of a smile on her face, but I didn't think it was malice. It was because she'd found the courage to say "whoring" aloud. She probably read detective novels and assumed you could say anything to a detective, at least, to a woman detective.

"Do you have any idea where she went?"

"None. I'm not sure I'd want to know. Eve might, though. She was watching. She doesn't know that I saw her, but this is a pretty quiet neighborhood. Anything unusual tends to stand out. A couple times I saw Eve sitting in her car, just around the corner, watching the house. She might have followed her mother. Or she might have been watching her father—she's been very angry at him lately—or she might have just been being nostalgic. I wouldn't ask. Eve always wanted so much for them to be a normal family. She used to tell me that, you know. How much she wished for regular parents like me and James. Parents she could call Mom and Dad instead of Cliff and Helene." She sliced the tart and put a generous wedge on my plate. "Would you like coffee?"

I was stunned by what she was saying but I forced myself to

respond. "No, thanks. I drank too much of it already. Getting back to the men, did you notice makes of car or license numbers or anything like that?"

"I'm just a neighbor, not a spy. I didn't keep a journal on her comings and goings, I just noticed things."

I'd offended her without meaning to. "I'm sorry. I didn't mean to offend you. It's just that on the phone you said you didn't think Cliff was the killer, so I wondered if you suspected one of Helene's lovers."

She shook her head. "No, I'm afraid not. I see what you mean, though. It might easily have been one of them, mightn't it? But I didn't keep track. No. It's not that I have any idea who did do it, only that I don't think Cliff did it. That's why I agreed to talk to you. I assume she's going to listen to you—after hiring you and all. Tell her that Cliff's no killer. I've known him a long time and he isn't the type. He's really quite a gentle man. Some days . . . now I know this is hard to believe . . . but some days, when she'd come back early in the morning . . . she'd be dead on her feet. Staggering. And that poor man would go out and help her into the house. Once or twice he even carried her. That was quite a sight. The man was practically a saint. Well, I suppose he loved her so he was willing to put up with a lot."

She took a bite of tart, chewed it thoughtfully, and nodded in satisfaction. "Helene gave me this recipe. She was a wonderful cook until she got that foolish notion into her head that if she cooked it was a sign she was inferior. She had some strange ideas. Not, you understand, that I don't agree with a lot of the feminist positions. But Helene took things way too far. She was never satisfied. James said that Cliff was just a pussy-whipped fool, but I always admired his tolerance." She sighed, cut another bite with her fork, and pushed it around her plate without eating it. "I wonder what it's like to be beautiful."

"Helene thought it made it harder to be taken seriously," I said. "She was probably right about that. Did Eve tell you why she wanted you to talk with me?"

She nodded. "To help you prove that Cliff killed her mother."

"Any idea why she thought you could help?"

"Eve has some stubborn notions about loyalty. I expect you already know that. She believes that if it is important to her, her friends should consider it important, too. Eve is . . ." She searched for a word. "Obsessed. That's the word I wanted. She's obsessed with the idea that Cliff was having a relationship with another man." She stopped and looked nervously about, as though we might be overheard. "Personally, I didn't believe it. I think the poor man was just lonely and sad, after the way she—Helene, I mean—treated him, and needed a friend. Why shouldn't the man have a close friend? Look how much time Helene spent with her women friends, but that didn't make her a lesbian, did it? Of course not."

She shook her head emphatically. The rigid hair didn't move at all. "Even if it was true, even if Cliff does have a . . . uh . . . male lover . . . so what?" she said. "Of course James would be delighted if Cliff turned out to be a faggot. He's never liked Cliff. But as I say, I don't care. It doesn't seem like a good enough reason for murder, especially such a gruesome murder. I mean, if he already had what he wanted, and she had what she wanted, and they both still had the façade of a respectable marriage, what more did they need? I don't suppose Cliff wanted to marry the man?"

I just shrugged. I couldn't imagine it any more than she could. But I was still confused about why she'd been anxious to talk to me. Was it loyalty to Eve? Had she felt compelled to tell someone about Helene's odd behavior, but couldn't bring herself to talk to Meagher? Or was it because she wanted to defend Cliff? I was betting on the latter. I returned to something she'd said earlier that seemed odd. "You said you noticed Eve watching the house? More than once?"

"Yes. A couple of times."

"Recently?" She nodded. "Did she just sit there? Did you ever notice Eve following her mother?"

She thought about that. "I don't know. Because I didn't watch, exactly. I didn't want them to see me snooping. So I'd just look out from time to time and see what was happening. Anyone looks out their window once in a while," she finished defensively.

"Of course they do. So you looked out once and saw Eve, and when you looked again she was gone?"

"Exactly," she said, nodding vigorously, "so I wouldn't know whether she followed Helene or not."

"I'll have to ask Eve, won't I?"

"Oh, dear." She had resumed tugging at her hair. "I'd rather that you didn't. She'll think I've been disloyal and then she'll get mad at me. She expects me to be giving you the dirt on her father."

"Well, we detectives have some pretty subtle ways of asking our questions. She doesn't need to know the information came from you." I felt like a complete phony as I said it, but it was exactly the right thing to say. Part of the reason she was talking to me, it was clear, was that she relished the excitement of being part of a real live mystery. Too reserved to talk to the police the way she'd talked to me, but under that stiff exterior, James hadn't completely succeeded in reducing his wife to a cipher. "Do you think Eve knew about Helene's other men?"

She shook her head. "I'd like to think she didn't, but I don't know. Certainly not when she was younger. She was more naive then. As for now? Who knows? In that family they told each other everything. Maybe Helene told her."

"Can you think of any other reason she'd be watching the house?"

"Unless it was her father, rather than her mother, that she was spying on." She shrugged. "Who can say? She always had such a high opinion of her mother. All I know is she's never said anything about it to me and a blunt kid like Eve would have said something if she suspected."

"But you think Cliff knew about the other men?"

She nodded reluctantly. "How could he help it, the way she was behaving, having to help her into the house like that. I told you. The man is a saint."

Knowing how she felt about Cliff, I could predict her answer to the next question but I asked it anyway. "You said Eve expected you to implicate Cliff in his wife's death. Do you have any reason to think he might be involved?"

"Other than the way his wife behaved?" She shook her head. "I do not. Much as she provoked him, he was a gentle man and it was a brutal murder."

I got up and took my dishes to the sink, thinking that it was time to go if I wanted to keep my appointment with Dom. I didn't really want to see him, but he was enough like Andre so that I knew what would happen if I didn't. He'd track me down, show up somewhere, and demand my attention. Better to keep the control in my hands. "Thank you for the lunch, Mrs. Coffey. It was delicious. May I call you if I have more questions?"

"Of course, dear," she said, "though I don't think I have anything else to tell you that could possibly be useful." She followed me into the living room, watching as I picked up my jacket and briefcase. "That shade of green suits you perfectly. A cute style. Swingy, is what I used to call it. Of course, Mandy would die if she heard me say that." She tapped her jaw with a finger. "Was there anything else? I did tell you that Helene and Cliff used to have huge fights sometimes, didn't I? Great loud brawls in the yard, shoving each other and calling names? Not often, mind you. Perhaps three or four times over the years. Very embarrassing. Everyone watched and then we'd gossip about it for weeks. Oh, and you know that flashy redhead Eve used to date? Who beat her up? The one she dumped when she moved to Arizona?"

"Padraig?" I said.

"That's the one. He was one of Helene's visitors." She glanced at her watch. "Oh dear, I'm late. Hate to rush you like this. I almost forgot it's tennis day." She held out her hand. "Nice to meet you, Mrs. Kozak. And good luck."

I was out the door and it had shut behind me before I realized what was happening. Martha Coffey was an odd duck and a whole lot more complicated than I'd given her credit for. I could picture her inside, watching me covertly from behind her staid blue drapes, smirking over the explosive effect of her parting bombshells. Her husband James might think he had the upper hand but I wasn't so sure.

CHAPTER 17

THE CONSTANT BARRAGE of murder and death and intrigue was beginning to take its toll and my sleepless night wasn't helping. Between work and the wedding, I had enough to do. I didn't need this wild-goose chase for Eve as well. If I asked myself what I knew now that I hadn't known before, the answer was plenty, but if I asked myself what earthly good it did, or whether it made things clearer, the answer was none and no. Unless Dom was in a better mood than I was, we were about to waste the next half hour yelling at each other. I didn't know whether he was going to fuss over me, as he'd done on the phone, or press me to continue to help Eve so I could gather information for him. I wasn't feeling very receptive to either approach. I can be very unpleasant when I'm overtired.

As I walked from my car to the door, little warm currents of air teasing at my hair and skirt, I was struck by the depressing realization that I was letting the lusty month of May, one of my favorites, slip by while I raced around like a rat in a maze. I paused in a patch of warm sunlight, closed my eyes and savored the warmth, so weary I could have curled up on the pavement and gone to sleep.

Someone grabbed me around the waist and pulled me roughly

sideways. "Jesus H. Christ, Theadora, what are you trying to do, commit suicide? This is a parking lot."

"Good to see you, too, Dom," I said as I regained my footing. "Nice to know there are still people like you around to rescue maidens in distress."

"Happy to oblige, ma'am. We live only to serve and protect, as you know."

"Yeah. So where were you last night around 3:00 A.M.?"

He ignored the question. "You hungry? Or you just want coffee?" he asked, steering me through the door and into a booth.

"Just coffee. I've come from a delicious lunch with Mrs. Coffey."

"Oh no." He frowned and ran a hand through his graying hair.

I felt a flicker of anger, but I was like a lighter low on butane today. Not much spark. No charm, either. I'd used the last of it on Martha Coffey. "What do you mean, 'oh no'? Aren't you the guy who thought I should help you folks out, talk to people, ask a few questions? You want to know how many things I've learned that I never in my life wanted to know? Plenty, mister, that's how many. Why in hell don't you catch this guy so I can get back to a normal life."

But Dom was concentrating on the first thing I'd said. "Well, I don't want you involved anymore. That was before last night. Suppose these things are connected? Suppose someone doesn't want you asking questions?"

"But you told me to . . ." I stopped abruptly as the impact of his words hit me. "Connected? I never thought . . . I mean, I was upset by the knife because Helene was killed with one, but I never thought about a connection. Why should anyone care if I'm asking questions? It doesn't make sense, and anyway, I wasn't asking questions until today."

He shrugged. "Eve has told half the world you're her detective. Say it's not related, you have some other enemies who should be checked out?"

I thought about that. Last night, the idea that it was personal hadn't occurred to me. I just figured it was some stranger. A robber. But that was before the phone call. Whoever had called me at work had aimed their threat specifically at me. There was at least one person I could think of who might be crazy enough to do something like that. Valeria. Once I thought of it, I was astonished that it hadn't occurred to me before. Too much on my mind, or too many irons in the fire, as my mother might have said. "There is someone," I said, "an employee we just fired." I told him all about Valeria and her threats, my encounter with her former employer, the affidavits, and her bizarre behavior during her visit to the office.

He nodded. "Sounds like a possible. I'll pass that information back to Harris. You got an address and phone?"

"At the office. But I'm not going back there for a while. I've got another meeting. You can call my secretary, Sarah, and she'll give them to you. Tell her I said it was okay."

"Seems to me you've got more meetings than the president. Aren't you the one who told me you've gotta stop and smell the roses?"

The idea of Dom stopping to sniff roses made me giggle. Maybe I was just getting a little punchy. "Got no roses to sniff right now, Dom. It's a whole lot easier if I just keep busy." The waitress brought my coffee. I bent over it and inhaled the steam, wishing the introduction of fumes directly into my head would work some sort of a miracle. My brief pause in the sun, before Sir Galahad knocked me off my feet, had left me stunned and sleepy. Not a good state to be in when I was facing a meeting with Cliff and his board.

"That sounded a lot like self-pity," Dom said. "Are we feeling sorry for ourselves?"

"I don't know about you, Dom, but I am."

"About Andre?"

"None of your business," I snapped and retreated behind a wall of silence.

"What about Andre?" he said. "What's he done?"

"He's being a jerk. Now let's drop the subject."

He folded his arms across his chest and leaned back, a disapproving look on his face. I ignored him, concentrating on my coffee. If it weren't for him and people like him who wanted to push me around and make me do things for them, my life would be a whole lot simpler and I might be less grumpy. I went back to brooding about my awful interview with Martha Coffey.

Dom snapped his fingers in front of my face. "Earth to Thea. Come in, please. Got any exciting things planned for the weekend?"

"Tonight a wedding rehearsal dinner, tomorrow a wedding, and on Sunday I'm having breakfast with you and then I'm going to bask in the sun for the rest of the day."

"Bad for your skin," he muttered. Now we were both in foul moods.

He was getting on my nerves. First he was fretting because I might not have enough to do, then he acted angry because I did have plans. What did he want from me, anyway? What was I doing here? "What's bad for my skin? Weddings? Or breakfast?"

"Shut up and tell me about your talk with Martha Coffey."

"Can't do both," I said. He gave me a look I knew well from Andre. It was the "stop being a smart-mouth broad and give me a little cooperation here" look. I didn't feel like cooperating. I felt like sulking. But the stuff she'd told me might be important. I took a sip of my watery, warm, drink-all-day-and-never-feel-a-thing American coffee and told him about my lunch with Martha Coffey. He sat impassively and listened, saying nothing, until I had finished.

"This case is like a maze. Every time we talk to someone, things get stranger instead of clearer. What do you make of the boyfriend?"

"Whose?" I said, repressing the urge to add Tonto's famous line, "What do you mean we, white man?"

"His."

"Unpredictable. Superficially kind and mild mannered. But preoccupied with Cliff and scathing in his criticism of Helene. If you're asking me did he kill her, I have no idea. He doesn't strike me as the murderous type, but I'm not sure there is a murderous type. He's accustomed to functioning on the edge of convention and making his own rules, because he has to, and if he wanted to possess Cliff, who knows what he'd do?"

"What about Paris?"

"I've been there. I like it. Great food."

"Thea . . ."

"I'm sorry. I've got a conflict. I like him. I've always liked him. I just can't imagine him doing something like that. He's got too much of those old-fashioned things like honor and dignity."

"Even if she was being unfaithful? Flagrantly, embarrassingly unfaithful? Even if he was desperate to be with Ansel?" I shook my head. "What if his lover was pressing him? What if he wanted a divorce and knew she'd refuse?"

"That's no reason to kill someone, Dom."

"Murder is rarely an act of reason. Passion, maybe. Confusion or desperation, but not reason."

"I'm working for him," I interrupted. "I wouldn't do that if I had the slightest doubt. . . ."

He sighed. "Ah, youthful certainty."

"You can save remarks like that for the sweet young things, Dom. I'm not exactly a stranger to violent death. I just wish you'd solve this thing. Why haven't you? What do you think? Who did it?" I knew I wasn't going to get an answer but I was feeling smothered by the pressure on me. And it was his problem.

He just leaned back from the table and smiled.

I'd been hanging around cops long enough to know that smile. It was the 'you don't really think I'm going to answer that' smile. "Unfair," I said, knowing I sounded like a child. "Why should I share things with you if you won't share things with me?"

"I don't suppose you'd settle for 'that's just the way it is'? No, of course you wouldn't."

"Damned straight I wouldn't."

"I think you have a pretty good idea what we're facing," he said, and changed the subject. "Tell me about last night."

"I was in bed. Asleep. I heard noises outside. . . ."

"What sort of noises?"

"Footsteps. Then scratching noises."

"What time?"

"Two-thirty, three. I'm not sure. I got up to see what it was. When I went into the living room, I could tell the sounds were coming from my deck. I have a fenced-in yard in back that goes down to the ocean. Big glass sliders out to the deck, and steps down to the lawn. I thought I saw a figure out there, so I switched on the lights. Whoever it was dropped the knife and ran."

"And you chased after him? Was it a man?"

"Yes, I chased the person. I don't know if it was a man or a woman. I guess I assumed it was a man, but now I'm not so sure."

"How was he dressed?"

"All in black. Shoes, pants, top. Maybe some sort of hat or a hooded sweatshirt? It all happened so fast. I never saw his face."

He nodded. "You didn't hesitate? Just ran out and chased after him? You didn't worry about whether he might have had a weapon?"

"It didn't occur to me."

"But later," he said, his voice dropping, growing gentle, "you were scared." I didn't say anything. I was reliving the moment when I came back up on the deck and saw the knife. Dom put his warm hand over mine and held it there. "You were sensible to be scared. People who come in the night with knives are scary." It was very reassuring to have his hand there. He went on in the same gentle voice. "I wish I knew what was going on, so I could tell you how to be safe, but I don't. The best I can offer is be careful. And don't take chances. Use your alarm. Leave your out-side lights on. Arrive and leave when your neighbors are arriving and leaving. No late night arrivals or departures. Chances are good it was just a burglar. Harris said there's been one, up there. All the same, don't take chances."

I wondered why Harris hadn't told me about the burglar. "If this were an Agatha Christie novel, we could assume they all did it," I said, trying to shake off my fear and lighten things up.

"Did what?"

"Killed Helene."

"Who is they?"

"Well, let's see. The stranger who was seen lurking in the bushes. There was one, wasn't there?" He nodded. "The husband of one of Helene's patients who was furious that his wife had found the courage to resist his absolute control. A jealous colleague angered by Helene's success. A clinical student she supervised who's been nursing a grudge. A bitter former client. Cliff and Rowan. Eve. One of Helene's lovers. The wife of one of Helene's lovers. Have I left anyone out? The housekeeper who has been nursing a secret passion for Cliff, or a grudge against Helene, for years. And Mrs. Coffey, for the same reasons."

The waitress came and refilled our cups, giving our clasped hands a disapproving look. "It's okay, Sally," he said. "Rosie doesn't mind." Sally gave a sniff and stalked away. He shook his head. "Now it'll be all over town that I was here holding hands with a gorgeous young woman." He tipped his wrist and checked his watch. "Sometime in the next half hour, Rosie will get a phone call."

"I'm sorry," I said, reluctantly pulling my hand back. Despite our verbal battles, I liked Dom, and I felt very safe with him.

"Hey, don't be," he said, "she knows I'm faithful, and that's what counts. Besides, a world's not worth much where you can't comfort a person who's scared because someone might get the wrong idea."

"Thanks. It was comforting. You'll check up on Valeria?"

"I will. And you be careful, you hear? Don't take chances. And just in case these things are connected, don't talk to anyone else, no matter what your friend Eve wants."

The man had spent enough time with me to know better than to tell me what to do. Besides, now that he'd prodded me into considering Valeria as a possibility, I didn't feel so threatened. It was so like something she would do but a few questions from the police would scare her off. We paid the check and he walked me out to my car.

At the car he paused, dropped his hands firmly onto my shoulders, and leaned into my face. "I meant it, Thea. Don't go flying around playing girl detective, okay? This is serious business." He saw as soon as he'd said it that he'd said the wrong thing. He could probably feel my resistance surging right up through his fingers. "I blew it, didn't I?" he said, maintaining a firm grip.

I nodded. "But if it's Valeria, it's got nothing to do with Helene's murder, so why shouldn't I talk to people? I'm just doing it to placate Eve. Besides, you told me to."

"And now I'm telling you not to. What if it's *not* Valeria?"

But I was content with the Valeria solution, and already moving on to the next item on my agenda. He stood a minute, hands in place, as though he was trying to bring me to his way of thinking through sheer force of will, but it wasn't working. Finally he dropped his hands and turned to go. There was a stoop in his shoulders that I knew was my fault. He had enough to worry about without adding me to his list. "Okay, Dom, you win," I said, "I'll back off. Let me know what you learn about Valeria, will you?"

"Of course," he said, walking away.

I realized I'd forgotten to tell him about the phone call. "Wait," I called. "There's something else. I had a phone call at the office today. My secretary, Sarah, took the call. The caller said last night wasn't the end, it was the beginning." The relief that had been on his face at my capitulation vanished, replaced by a look composed of astonishment and worry. He probably thought I was the biggest damn fool on the East Coast, forgetting to mention a threat like that.

"Is there someone you can stay with?" he asked.

There was only Suzanne and she didn't need a guest right now. "I'll be okay," I said. "You can call Harris and tell him to keep an eye on me."

"That's not good enough. I don't think you understand how serious . . ."

"There's nowhere I can go. I'll just have to be careful."

He shrugged, a disgusted, resigned gesture, and walked away.

CHAPTER *18*

RODDY BROUGHT US two glasses of flavored mineral water, carefully handing the first one to Cliff, then hesitating with mine and finally setting it down on the desk as far from me as possible. Cliff noticed, and a flash of irritation crossed his face, but he said nothing. When the door had shut behind him, I was unable to control myself. "Why do you put up with him? He's a dreadful person. He's nasty to everyone but you. He creates a terrible public impression."

He looked at me sadly. "I think you're judging him too harshly. Public relations are such a small part of what he does. He's an excellent secretary. Superb typist. Very familiar with psychiatric jargon. He never makes a mistake. Maintains impeccable files and can always put his hands on whatever I need. Makes my appointments flow smoothly, and is zealous at guarding me from intrusions. Absolutely discreet. Reliable. . . ."

"You make him sound like the poster boy for National Secretaries Week. To me he's been rude, insolent, uncooperative. Kept me waiting for no reason . . ." He was looking at me like I was the one who was out of order.

"I'm afraid it's because you're a friend of Eve's. Roddy and

Eve don't exactly see eye-to-eye, as I'm sure you've noticed."

"I'd say he doesn't see eye-to-eye with Dr. Ansel, either."

"No, you're right about that, too. Roddy is a bit jealous where I'm concerned."

A bit? It was strange to find Cliff with blinders on, but on this subject that was definitely the case. It looked like he had no comprehension of how offensive his secretary's behavior was. It was both illuminating and discouraging. How could I work with Cliff to make Bartlett Hill more successful in selling itself if he couldn't see even the very obvious problems that were right in front of him. I said as much to him.

He sighed. "I see you're not going to let me get away with being evasive or obtuse. The fact is that you're right about Roddy. He's extremely difficult and I tolerate a lot from him that people think I shouldn't, but if you knew where he came from and how much progress he's made, I think you'd be more understanding. He comes from a terrible family, had an unbelievable childhood—every imaginable kind of abuse. It's a miracle that he's a functioning adult. It's all a matter of perspective, I guess. You're measuring him against some societal norm and deciding that he fails; I'm measuring him against the expectations for someone with his dysfunctional background, and find him a tremendous success."

I started to say something, but he held up a hand to stop me. "Don't misunderstand me, Thea. I know he's a liability sometimes. I know that he's difficult, particularly with women. I am not naive nor am I blind to it. Believe me, we're working on it, but if I were to fire him, it would be like kicking him in the teeth. Like telling him that any belief he had that he was a worthwhile person was wrong. You understand what I'm saying?"

I did. Cliff was giving me a new perspective on Roddy. Still, the consultant in me hoped I wasn't going to have to deal with a whole institution full of people with Cliff's brand of altruism, if indeed it was altruism and not just the ego gratification that comes from a successful project. It would be a personal challenge beyond the limits of my ambition to try and market an institution with functional clinicians and a primarily dysfunctional support staff. I had a brief vision of it. "Why, yes, Mrs. Kozak, my secretary spends an hour a day cowering in the closet, but otherwise she's a fabulous employee. Why, yes, Mrs. Kozak, our telephone operator is sometimes verbally abusive, but we're working on her medication. Why, yes, Mrs. Kozak, the janitor talks to himself, but his conversations are most erudite." I'm just a hard case, I guess. It might be great social policy, but it wouldn't be easy to market.

I gave Cliff a noncommittal smile, reached for my glass, and took a sip. Mandarin orange. An odd flavor to put in water, but good. Cliff was ready to leave the subject of Roddy behind, too. "Rowan says he's been trying to reach you but you won't return his calls."

I tried not to show my irritation, to keep things light. "Dr. Ansel and about forty other people. I'm right out straight this week, Cliff. As soon as I have time . . ." I trailed off, leaving a half-promise in the air.

He seemed satisfied. "I thought the meeting went well. The board is eager to go ahead with this. A real tribute to you, Thea, since they're normally so inert it takes them forever to decide whether to order tuna or egg salad. Are you really prepared to start on Monday?"

"There are some rather mundane details," I said, producing a consulting contract and handing it to him, "but assuming we can agree on them, I'm prepared to start on Monday. You know that the first part of our assessment involves a lot of interviewing. That's what gives us an overview of current conditions. Won't your people need more time to arrange their schedules to accommodate that?"

He shook his head. "If you can give me an idea of which people you'd like to see and how much time you'll need, I can have an interview schedule set up for you by nine on Monday."

I was impressed. Cliff might sometimes appear rather unworldly, but it was clear that his being head of the children's outpatient service wasn't just the Peter Principle at work. He knew what he was doing. I left half an hour later with a signed contract, a full Monday, and a bleary mind, heading for Suzanne's rehearsal.

The church had a hushed, expectant quality that seemed exactly right. The florist's minions were putting the finishing touches on the altar flowers and fastening the last of the white satin bows onto the ends of the pews. Off to the left, the organist, informal in jeans and a sweatshirt, was softly running through the music, the almost inaudible high notes underscored by the muted thrum of the low notes. I stood for a moment taking it all in. The air was already lightly scented by the flowers. The high stained-glass windows gleamed in the last of the day's light. There was a bustle up on the balcony, and then the bride-to-be leaned over the railing and disturbed the peace.

"Okay, campers, we don't have to wait. My father's stuck at the office as usual. Maybe he'll be on time tomorrow," she said. "Siobhan is going to sing and then we're going to walk through it." The organist began to play, and then a high, clear, beautiful voice filled the room. A Beatles' song, "In My Life." There was a clatter of high heels on the wooden stairs and Suzanne rushed over to me and gave me a hug. "You're wonderful," she said. "I heard what happened about the restaurant. Think they'll give us decent service, after all that?"

"If they don't, I'll have another talk with Mr. Roscoe."

"I'll bet he never knew what hit him." She patted my arm and turned away. "Got to organize the mothers." Paul was by the door, talking to a couple I assumed were his parents. Suzanne slid under his arm, which tightened around her, and said something to the other couple which made them burst out laughing. Then she slid away, and delivered the message to her mother. The minister, sweaty and garbed in the black and white of a soccer referee, slipped in a side door, waved apologetically to Suzanne, and beckoned for Paul to join him. Together they walked to the same door and disappeared. The soloist had finished, and the organist segued into some random prewedding Bach.

Paul's brother-in-law took Mrs. Merritt by the arm and led her down the aisle, her husband trailing behind. Then Suzanne's brother escorted Mrs. Begner to her seat. The organist switched to the march from *Aida*. Paul and the minister emerged from the side door. The two ushers and Paul's son Jeremy went down the aisle to join them. Then Paul's daughter Amy, pretty and solemn in a white sailor dress, began the tedious step, halt, step, halt walk down the aisle. Connie fell in behind her and I fell in behind Connie. Stately, solemn, and feeling self-conscious, I made my way down the aisle to the front, stepped to the left beside Connie, and turned to look back.

The organist switched to the traditional wedding march and Suzanne, looking small and neat and uncertain, started down the aisle. Pretty in a pink suit. Clutching a flowered scarf in place of a bouquet. I glanced over at Paul. The look on his face as he watched her come down the aisle was a delight to see. Beyond question, this man loved her the way she had always hoped to be loved. Partway down the aisle, she faltered. Casting aside any wedding conventions, Paul went down the aisle to meet her, tucked her arm through his, and they walked forward together. It was perfectly, exactly right, and I felt my cynicism drop away like a shed skin.

After that, even the incongruities seemed right, like Suzanne in her suit, Paul in his blazer, and the red-faced minister in his tight black shorts. Or Amy and Jeremy, Paul's children, squabbling on the way out of the church because Jeremy didn't want Amy to take his arm. Or the denim-clad organist ending the recessional with *dum dum da dum dum . . . dum dum*, and then turning to us and spreading her hands like a vaudeville comedienne.

I left the rehearsal dinner, where the service had been more than adequately attentive and the food delicious, about half a sheet to the wind, but I wasn't worried. My car knew the way, and with the windows down and a cool wind on my face, I'd do just fine. I'm much too practical to drink past my capacity to get myself home. When you live alone, you learn things like that. I buckled myself in, popped in a tape, and roared off into the night. The good feeling lasted until I turned into my parking space, and then the memory of the night before came back to me like I'd been slugged in the face with a big wet fish. The memory of last night, and of the follow-up phone call today.

Suddenly, I was soberer than I wanted to be. I slung my briefcase over my shoulder, grabbed my keys, and sprinted for the door. The night was silent except for my running footsteps and a dog barking in the distance. No one lurched toward me out of the bushes, no one was waiting in the shadows. I fumbled the key into the lock, dashed in, and slammed the door shut behind me.

I went straight to the wall to key in the alarm code and realized that something didn't look right. The alarm was already deactivated. I might have been shaken and sleepy when I left for work in the wee hours of the morning, but I knew I'd set the alarm. I was on my way to the phone when something the size of the Empire State Building landed on my head. The floor came rushing up to meet me. My last conscious thought, as I put my hands out to break my fall, was Suzanne's admonition not to run into anything else before the wedding. I wasn't doing very well, was I?

CHAPTER *19*

ALL MY LIFE I've been afraid of fire. I guess my mother did too good a job with her lessons about not playing with matches and her habits of calling our attention to any fire on the news where a child was killed and regularly reviewing with us the family fire escape plans. Sometimes I wake up in the night, convinced I smell smoke, and roam all over the house, turning on the lights and sniffing, until I'm sure it's safe to go back to sleep. Smoke detectors have made me feel a lot safer, but that fear of fire is still firmly implanted. Sort of ironic, since the only time we ever had a fire in the house when I was a kid was the time my mother set the kitchen wall on fire trying to make popcorn in a frying pan.

She called us into the kitchen, showed us the fire climbing the wall, and then stood by the door, mechanically repeating, "Everyone get out of the house. We'll meet at the driveway. Everyone get out of the house. We'll meet at the driveway." While she stood there doing her duty, Dad put the lid on the pan, smothered the flame, and put the pan in the sink. I got a pan of water and flung it at the wall, and Michael turned off the burner and doused the flames on the stovetop with baking soda. Then we opened a bottle of orange soda, got some potato chips, and went back to watching television. Our calm reaction was the product of enlightened self-interest—there was a raging blizzard outside and none of us was eager to leave the house.

This time, when I thought I smelled smoke, I didn't have to turn on the lights and look around to see if I could find any. The lights were already on, the smoke detector was screaming, and I could barely see across the room through the haze. I got carefully to my feet and used the wall to support me on my trek across the room to the phone. Experience has taught me that when something like a large building has landed on your head, it is wise to move slowly. Usually, it is wisest not to move at all, but another form of wisdom, unrelated to damaged heads, says when your house is on fire, you should get the hell out.

I dialed 911—an action that was getting to be a habit—and when the gruff voice answered I gave my name and address and asked for a policeman and the fire department. In response to his inquiry about the nature of the problem, I succinctly explained that someone had hit me over the head and set my house on fire. He had the grace not to pursue it, but only asked if I wanted an ambulance as well. I said I didn't think so and hung up.

Then, perhaps because the blow had jarred loose my common sense, I wet a dishtowel in the sink, wrapped it around my face, and began crawling through the living room, looking for the source of the fire. It was hard to tell through the smoke, but it looked like someone had piled a lot of stuff on the sofa and set the whole mess afire. I'm usually pretty sensible, so what I did next can only be explained as the product of the last twenty-four hours' adventures having a deleterious effect on my judgment. I decided to move the fire outside by opening the slider and shoving the sofa out. I pulled back the curtain, opened the slider, and bent down to give the sofa a shove. The fire, which had been smoldering sullenly, took a gulp of the fresh air pouring in and roared up in my face, sending me staggering backwards.

A lot of the mess looked like clothes, and then, like a warning bell going off, an idea made its way through the maze of my brain and pounded on the door of my consciousness. An absurd, middle-class, abominably female notion—that if it wasn't already burning in the pile, I had to find my bridesmaid dress and save it. I was halfway to the bedroom when I remembered it wasn't in there. I'd hung it in the hall closet where there was more room, and then absentmindedly hung my raincoat over it. I crawled back to the entry, opened the closet and dragged out the dress. I draped it over my arm, got my briefcase and keys, and opened the door. Officer Harris was standing there, his fist poised to knock. "I'll be with you in a minute," I said, "I just need to put this in my car. The fire's in there." I pointed back over my shoulder.

"Why don't we go sit in my car instead," he suggested, putting an arm around my shoulders and steering me toward the cruiser. He must have understood the situation better than I, because halfway to his car my brain started misfiring and the walk messages got distorted. I ended up leaning limply on him, then against the side of the car while he opened the door, and collapsing into the seat like a mechanical toy when the batteries run down. I should have used Energizers.

He took the things I was clutching and put them in the back seat. "What's this?" he asked as he took the dress.

"Bridesmaid dress. I have to be in a wedding tomorrow." He just gave me a curious look and laid it carefully on the back seat.

"Can you tell me what happened?"

"Not yet." I closed my eyes and tried to rest my head against the seat but the back of my head hurt. I said "ow!" and shifted restlessly, trying to find a comfortable position.

"Bend your head down for a minute," he said. I tried to cooperate, but it hurt. His fingers gently probed my head and neck.

"Be careful," I told him, just as he touched a tender spot. I jumped and he pulled his hand back in surprise, staring regretfully down at the blood on his fingers. "Relax, Officer. I don't have any communicable diseases." My mouth tasted like smoke and my lungs and throat burned from inhaling it. I felt weak and listless and cold. Harris was staring at me expectantly, ready, I was sure, to start asking a million questions, while all I wanted to do was take a shower and go to sleep. Not the easiest thing to do when your apartment is filled with firemen. "I'm cold," I said, "do you have a blanket?"

He did. Cops are real handy like that. You wouldn't believe the stuff they keep in their trunks. He got it and wrapped it around me, then started the engine and turned on the heat. It must have seemed silly to him, doing that on a warm May night. But maybe not. Cops spend a lot of their time with people who are in distorted physical states. It may be the normal which seems odd to them. "Please, Ms. Kozak," he said, "can you tell me what happened?"

"Here we are spending our second night together, and I hardly know you," I said inanely.

"Yeah," he agreed, "it's a hell of a way to get to know someone, isn't it? What happened?"

Through the windows I could see the flashing lights on the fire truck and the firemen moving in and out of the house. It had a magical, unreal quality, more like entertainment than reality. "Looks like something from a movie, doesn't it?" He didn't respond. "Sorry, Officer. I'm not trying to avoid the question. My brain is barely functioning." I tried to recall the sequence of events. "Dom—Detective Florio, that is—said don't linger outside, so when I got home I rushed to the door, let myself in, and slammed it behind me. When I went to turn off the alarm, it was already off. That didn't seem right. I knew I'd left it on. I was turning to look around, trying to figure out what was going on, when something hit me like the proverbial ton of bricks."

"You didn't see anything? Hear anything? Notice anything?" He sounded disappointed and disbelieving.

"Not that I remember. It all happened so fast, you see. I was inside less than a minute and then wham!"

"Do you know what hit you?"

"A large building?" I said unhelpfully.

"What time did you get home?"

"Between ten and ten-thirty. I didn't look at my watch. I was at a wedding rehearsal dinner. I left there a little before ten. What time is it now?" I had no idea whether I'd been unconscious for a minute or an hour.

"Almost eleven," he said. "Did you ask for an ambulance?"

I started to shake my head, but it hurt. "No. Well, not exactly. The person who answered asked if I wanted one, and I said I didn't think so. Do I need an ambulance?"

"I don't know," he said. "But you've got a head injury, plus the smoke you've inhaled. It would be sensible to check it out. Plus, judging from our long acquaintance, you're usually a quick, clear-headed person. Tonight you're hardly that."

His statement, meant to be helpful, annoyed me as did his next question, which was how much I'd had to drink. "So you think a night without sleep, two frightening encounters with a malevolent stranger or strangers, a blow on the head, and spending too much time in a smoke-filled room isn't enough to diminish my capacity to think clearly? Or are you suggesting I got drunk, hit myself over the head and then set my clothes on fire? What did you expect? Wonder Woman? Believe me, I'd like to be more helpful. I don't like this any more than you do. Less. I like it less. After all, I'm the one who got bopped on the head. All you have to do is show up and ask some questions."

As I talked, I got more wound up, and suddenly, irrationally, I was yelling at him. Taking out all the fear I'd felt on him because he was the only person around. "Gee golly, Mr. Officer, I hope I'm not keeping you up, or distracting you from some real important police work. I know it was damned inconsiderate of me to go and get myself knocked out and to let some bad guy set my house on fire and then not even be able to tell you who did it. I promise I won't let it happen again. I'll grow eyes in the back of my head." I wadded up the blanket, shoved it at him, and fumbled with the handle, trying to get out of the car.

He put a heavy hand on my shoulder and pressed me down into the seat. "You just sit tight," he said, "you're in no shape to be wandering around on your own, and you can't go back to your condo tonight. I'm taking you to the emergency room. You might need stitches."

I felt foolish and frustrated and dangerously close to tears but I was not going to cry in front of this guy. "I don't want to," I said. "I hate hospitals."

Ignoring me, he muttered something into his radio. "I'll be right back," he said, opening the door. "Don't you do anything foolish." I watched him cross the parking lot and speak with the fireman who was directing operations. Slim, boyish and still band-box new, but he was already 110 percent a cop, with the kind of "Father Knows Best" superiority that made him certain he knew what was right for me. Andre wasn't like that. He would have asked me what I wanted to do. Damn Andre. If he'd been here, none of this would have happened. I would have been safe.

I couldn't help it. Thinking about Andre, and thinking about being safe, the tears started flowing, and all my willpower couldn't hold them back. Good thing Officer Bandbox was out of the car. I reached down by my feet and fumbled through my briefcase for a tissue. I wiped my eyes and nose and the tissue came away black. I tilted the rearview mirror and looked at my face. I looked like a coal miner, with spooked, red-rimmed eyes staring out of my blackened face. I must have gotten the black on my hands from the sofa, and then smeared it on my face when I tried to protect it from the flaring heat. Why hadn't he told me, or offered me his handkerchief instead of grimacing at my blood and ordering me to stay put? Last night I'd thought he was an okay guy, but my opinion of Officer Harris, boy cop, was heading right down the toilet.

Another police car, lights flashing, raced down the drive, picked its way carefully around the fire truck, and halted abruptly just a few feet away. I heard a commotion of voices. My neighbors were standing together in a huddle just a few feet from where I was sitting, staring at the scene. The officer jumped out and walked over to meet Harris.

Someone called out, "Officer, can you tell us what's going on?"

"Fire," he said helpfully, pointing at the truck.

Harris and the newcomer immediately got into an animated conversation. I decided it was a good time to make my exit. I retrieved my dress from the back seat, thanking my lucky stars—what few of them I had left—that it was in a plastic bag, and got out on the driver's side, keeping the car between me and the police. Ignoring my neighbors, who were staring openly, I crossed to my car on wobbly legs, got in, and started the engine.

Suddenly Harris appeared, banging on the window. "Where do you think you're going?" he demanded.

"To the emergency room. Isn't that what you told me to do?"

"You're in no shape to drive. I'll take you."

"I'm driving. You can follow me if you want."

"I'm going to," he said, "and you'd better be careful."

Not an admonition about protecting my health, but a warning that I'd better not do anything he could give me a ticket for. I'd hurt his manly pride and he wasn't taking it well.

It's always hard to drive with a cop breathing down your tailpipe. It's a whole lot harder when it takes most of your energy and concentration just to keep your mind on the car and the car on the road. And I was further distracted trying to figure out where I was going to go after I left the emergency room. I weighed the options. I couldn't possibly go to Suzanne's. The last thing she needed tonight was a battered, smoky house guest. Even if I was able to make the long drive to my mother's, her censorious caring would do me more harm than good, and I'd rather sleep on the sidewalk than impose on Michael and Sonia. I needed a bed and a shower, and the solution presented itself as I drove past the Navigator Motel with its gleaming red vacancy sign. I flicked on my blinker and turned in almost too fast for my police escort to follow.

The man behind the desk looked very dubious when I asked about a room. I couldn't blame him. I'd be suspicious, too, if a disheveled, dirty woman wandered in at eleven at night and asked for a room. "I know I look awful," I said. "I live in those new condos out on the point, and I've just had a fire in my unit. I don't even have a toothbrush. I won't know how bad the damage is until morning—the firemen are still there now—and I need to be nearby so I can get back there first thing in the morning, check out my things, meet the insurance adjuster, all that stuff." I took out my prestige credit card and set it on the counter. "The best room you've got."

I heard Harris's footsteps coming up behind me and watched the clerk's eyes go over my shoulder to watch his approach. "Great idea, Ms. Kozak," Harris said, "you just get yourself checked in and cleaned up a little, and then I'll drive you over to the emergency room, just as a precaution."

He'd caught me neatly in my own trap, hadn't he? He'd given me credibility with the clerk and also ensured that I had to let him drive me to the hospital. The clerk handed me a registration form. "If you'd just fill this out . . . um . . . Ms. Kozak. Our . . . um . . . nicest room is the . . . um . . . bridal suite. It has a sitting room with a minibar, as well as the bedroom and bath/dressing room suite."

"Perfect. I'll take it. Do you supply bathrobes by any chance?"

"Certainly, madam," he said. "I'll get you one." I signed the registration card and traded it for the room key. I followed his directions to the suite and Harris came along behind, my faithful bodyguard.

Inside, I handed him the keys. "Help yourself to something from the minibar, if you want. I'm going to clean up." When I saw how awful I looked, I decided I was lucky Harris had come along, or I never would have gotten a room. I discarded the jacket, sponged as much soot and dirt as I could from the skirt, and washed my face and hands. It looked like my smart new suit was beyond repair. When I came out I didn't look a whole lot better, but at least I was recognizably human. I was tempted to just crawl into bed, but my bodyguard was waiting, set-faced and inflexible.

Reluctantly, I turned myself over to Harris and let him drive me to the hospital.

If there is one important truth about emergency rooms, it is that the only way to insure reasonably prompt treatment is to arrive unconscious or in the throes of a heart attack. I fell into neither category and there wasn't anything I could do about it. Maybe the soot would move them. Or my police escort. I'd rather forego treatment than hang around a dingy waiting room with frightened adults and wailing babies, surrounded by dog-eared old magazines with all the best bits torn out. In this respect, at least, it turned out to be my lucky night. They were having a quiet evening and happy to get a customer.

I went through the registration process with Harris at my side, glaring and breathing heavily. He was still mad at me, and the heat of his anger was softening the starch on his police-scout uniform. During the half hour it took to get through the preliminaries he said only one thing to me: "It was very irresponsible of you to drive." I said nothing to him. The tight little lines around his eyes and mouth said it all. I had transgressed one of the policeman's rules—that once you are a victim, you're supposed to act like one.

They put me in a little curtained cubicle and a nurse bustled by to say that the doctor would be along in a moment. I sat on the edge of the examining table, staring at the runs in my stockings. Harris leaned against the wall and glared. "Oh, come off it, Harris," I said, finally. "If something's bothering you, spit it out. I'm too tired to bear the weight of your silence any longer. If you don't have anything to say, or to ask, why don't you just go away and leave me alone?"

"I need to know the nature and extent of your injuries," he said.

"You could call the hospital in an hour and I'm sure they'd be happy to tell you." He just shook his head and went on leaning against the wall. I tried again. I really wanted him to go away.

"You could get us some coffee. I promise I'll still be here when you get back." He didn't respond, so I gave up.

The nurse came back and began to fuss over me. "Now, dear, let's just get you up on this table and see what we've got to deal with, shall we?" I swung my legs up on the table, but I didn't lie down because it hurt my head. As she listened to what had happened, she gently washed my face and hands again, discovering, in the process, that I'd gotten a nasty burn on my left hand. Then she asked me to lie down on my stomach so she could look at the back of my head. "You can take your shoes off if you'd like."

"Can't," I said. "Hurts my head to bend over."

"That's okay, dear, I'll do it." As she bent over me, I caught a faint whiff of her perfume.

"Wait a minute," I said. She stopped, staring at me in surprise. "Oh, I didn't mean you. I just remembered something."

Instantly Harris was away from the wall and standing by my head. "You remembered something," he said triumphantly. "What is it? What did you remember?"

I tried to get it back. "I can't remember. When she bent down it reminded me of something. I can see it in my mind, but it's so fuzzy . . . like trying to read a sign through a mud-splashed windshield." I struggled with it for a while. I wanted to remember it as much as he wanted me to, but it stayed just beyond reach. He had her repeat the motion a few times but it didn't help. If looks could kill, I would have been wounded, if not dead, but I couldn't help it. He just stood there and glared at me until I couldn't take it anymore.

"Cut it out, Harris," I said, "or take your glaring and your sulks somewhere else."

"You're not even trying to cooperate," he said. "You could remember if you really wanted to."

At that same moment, the nurse probed an extremely tender spot. I sat up abruptly, almost knocking her over, and jumped off the table. "You don't know what you're talking about, Harris," I yelled, "why wouldn't I want to tell you? You think I like being hit over the head?" There was a lot more I might have said, but the world chose that moment to begin doing a strange dance, the floor and the walls and the lights all moving at once. So much movement had a disturbing effect on my stomach. The nurse, instantly understanding what was happening, tucked her shoulder under my arm and steered me back to the table. Gratefully, I lay down, closed my eyes, and worked on controlling my nausea.

"Officer, I think you'd better wait outside," she said.

"But she might remember something."

"And if she does, I'll call you. Right away. I promise." Carefully, I opened my eyes, and was treated to the sight of the small nurse firmly steering Harris away from me and closing the curtains behind him. When she came back, she bent down and whispered in my ear, "You can come out now."

"Thanks," I said. "He was beginning to get on my nerves."

"So I observed," she said dryly. "You want to flip back over on your stomach now?"

"I think a flip is beyond me right now. How about I just struggle over?"

"Whatever you can manage, dear." I managed an awkward, elephantine shift, and even that seemed like too much work, then lay there wearily while she poked and prodded. "You certainly do have a lot of hair," she said. "Maybe I can find an elastic and tie it out of the way. Be right back." She found an elastic and tied back my hair and then the doctor came in and the two of them began doing nasty things to my head.

"Do you know what hit you?" the doctor asked.

"It felt like a large building."

"Well, it wasn't a building. Something glass, I'd say, from the amount we've taken out of the wound."

Except for the needle pricks as they anesthetized the edges of the wound, it didn't hurt, but the pulling and poking as they picked out glass and stitched it shut was very unpleasant. "How many stitches?"

"This is seven," the doctor said. "One more should do it." I closed my eyes, let my mind drift, and was swept back to my child-hood. To another examining table and another doctor who was giving me stitches, closing the gash on my foot I'd gotten when my father had accidentally left a paint scraper lying in the grass and I'd stepped on it with my bare foot. Even then I'd found the drama and the fuss hard to take. My mother had wrapped my foot in a towel and driven me to the doctor. I remembered bleeding all over the car and all over his office. He hadn't been nearly as gentle as this doctor, and had done the stitching without anesthesia while I clenched my fists, bit my lip, and tried not to cry, even though it hurt a lot.

"There," he said, "all done. Let's have a look at that hand." Then some more gentle probing, their soft voices murmuring, and someone was bandaging my hand. The image I'd been trying to recall came back. I was lying on the floor and not far away I could see a black shoe and then a glimpse of face. I was trying to focus on it, recognize it, when the doctor asked me a question and the image vanished. "Can you sit up, please, Mrs. Kozak, and open your eyes?"

Reluctantly, I abandoned my dozing state and came to atten-tion, trying to cooperate while he put me through the standard repertoire of "does this woman have a concussion" questions. In the end, we agreed that although my head hurt like hell, as did my lungs, throat, hand, and various other parts that must have gotten whacked when I landed, I probably was not badly concussed but only in need of a good night's sleep. Finally, weak, weary and ach-ing, I was given some sheets entitled "Aftercare Instructions— Head Injury" and released to Officer Harris's tender care.

He wasn't at all pleased when I insisted we stop at the all-night grocery store, and followed me around with an insufferable look of disgust on his face while I acquired a toothbrush and tooth-paste, some deodorant, some cheap black sweats, socks, sturdy cotton underwear, sneakers, and an extra-large tee shirt to sleep in. Acquiring in a rush all the junk I normally complained about the store carrying. It had never occurred to me before that someone might need to come to the store at midnight and buy an entire wardrobe.

By the time we got back to the motel, I was dead on my feet, far too tired to argue when he insisted he was going to stay there and sleep on the sofa. I hauled my weary carcass into the bathroom, put on my new sleepshirt, washed out my bra and hung it up to dry, and brushed my teeth. I swallowed two painkillers and crawled into bed, said goodnight to another fun day, and threw myself with complete abandon into the arms of Morpheus.

The next thing I knew, someone was pounding on the door, and then there was a babble of voices. I wasn't even curious; whoever it was, friend or foe. Harris could handle it. I slipped back down into sleep. Sometime between four and five I woke in the first gray light of morning with my head and my hand aflame. I staggered into the bathroom, shook out some more painkillers with trembling hands, swallowed them and went back to bed. Relief seemed a long time coming. The next time I woke up, it was because I had the uneasy sensation that I was being watched. When I opened my eyes, I found Harris and Dom Florio bending over me.

"Rise and shine, princess," Dom said, "the insurance investigator and the police are anxiously awaiting your presence."

I bit back my first response, which was a series of most unladylike words. "As they say in the play, Florio, 'I'll rise, but I won't shine.' You guys got any coffee?"

"Better than that. We've got breakfast," Dom said. I noticed that Harris wasn't saying anything. Probably still mad at me. I threw back the covers and swung my legs over the side of the bed, moving slowly in case my body decided it wasn't ready for this. I looked up to find them both staring at me and realized my tee shirt was up around my waist. Thank heavens for decent cotton underwear.

"Whazza mattah you guys, eh? You nevah see legs before?"

"Not such nice ones," Dom said and went on staring. Harris lowered his eyes.

"You're a jerk, Florio," I said, "I don't know why I like you." But I did know. Part of the reason I liked him was that Dom was the kind of guy who could look at my legs and like them without an overpowering desire to get between them, and I appreciated that.

"Just bad taste, I guess."

I stood up, tugged the tee shirt down, went into the bathroom, taking my bag of grocery store finery with me. The woman in the mirror looked gray, grimy and depressed, and her hair smelled like smoke. I did the best I could with one hand and emerged clean, dressed, and somewhat the worse for my exciting night, to find that they'd been telling the truth about breakfast. Over eggs on English muffins, OJ and coffee, we went back over the night. I told them that I'd seen a face, but couldn't bring it into focus, and a black shoe. Harris was all for giving me the third degree until I cooperated and remembered, but Dom told him to relax, it would come back to me eventually.

"Have you checked up on Valeria?"

Dom shook his head. "We did but we struck out. Her roommate says she was home all evening and they had a pizza and watched TV."

"She could be lying."

"Yeah, but Valeria could describe the plots of the shows they watched."

"She could be lying. The roommate could have briefed her. They could have time-shifted the whole evening."

"Could have. But her mother also says that she called and spoke to her daughter."

"But my prowler came at 2:00 A.M. Was she talking to her mother then?"

"I was talking about last night."

"What about the night before?"

"Roommate says she is a very light sleeper. She would have heard if Valeria went out. She heard nothing."

I didn't know what to think. As long as I had suspected Valeria, everything made sense. If she wasn't the one, nothing made sense. It hurt my head to think about it, so I pushed the whole thing out of my mind. Dom left after breakfast, apparently satisfied now that he'd seen for himself that I was alive and well. I'd promised to call him if I remembered anything more. I packed my things in my grocery bag, checked out, and then Harris and I drove, in separate cars, back to my condo. There were so many people waiting to talk to me, I felt like a visiting head of state.

I received them on the back deck. Below us, on the lawn, the remains of my sofa, topped with my ruined wardrobe, sat in a soggy, ruined heap, looking like a dejected elephant.

CHAPTER 20

THE REST OF Saturday went by in a blur. After the insurance adjuster left and the arson investigator left and Officer Harris left, the condo manager and I spent a while working out plans for getting my place back in shape. He suggested a cleaning service that specialized in cleaning up after house fires, and offered to haul my ruined sofa away. It wasn't purely altruism, I knew—he was anxious to restore things to normal and reassure the other tenants—but that was okay with me. I was anxious to restore things to normal, too. To my surprise, the cleaners offered to come right away, and while I waited for them, I opened all the doors and windows to air the place out and stripped the curtains so I could drop them at the laundry. The cleaning service would have to shampoo the rugs and upholstery. The whole place had an irritating chemical smell.

A surprising bit of normalcy in the midst of the mess, my answering machine sat on the counter, grimed with a layer of soot, its little red light blinking energetically. I stared at it, wishing I ran on electricity. There wasn't anything about me that felt even slightly energetic. I got a pad and pencil out of the drawer and pushed the button, listening in despair as the disembodied voices tried to haul me back down into the morass of Helene Streeter's murder.

The first message was from Norah McCarty. I had to listen carefully to understand her. "Hello, Thea Kozak? This is Norah McCarty, Mr. Paris's housekeeper. I've been trying to reach you but you're never home, so I'm leaving you this message. Miss Eve said you were lookin' into things, so I thought you should know that Mrs. Streeter and that Ansel fellow that was a friend of Mr. Paris, they didn't get along at all. In fact, the week before she died, they had a huge fight when he came by to tell her that he thought she ought to give Mr. Paris a divorce. Normally, I'd leave things alone, people's private business being none of mine, but the way they were hollering and shouting and shoving at each other, I was afraid he might hurt her, so I came and stood in the doorway, just in case. He gave me a real mean look and told me to get lost but I didn't. I didn't work for him." There was a pause and then she said, quickly, "I don't know if it means anything, you understand, I just thought someone ought to know. When they were hollering, he said he wished he had the guts to just kill her and get it over with." A click and then silence. I wondered if she'd told Dom.

A message from Rowan Ansel, this time with a distinct whine in his voice, complaining that I wasn't returning his calls and that he had to speak with me. Then a short message. "How can I talk to you when you're never home? Call me," from Andre. And another message from Lenora Stern. "Hi, this is Lenora Stern again. It's very rude of you not to return my calls. I'll just tell you what I wanted to talk about, and the rest is up to you. Helene was afraid something was going to happen to her. That's why she signed up for an Armed and Dangerous course. Call me and I'll tell you about it."

The last one was a message with no name, but I knew who it was from. "Here's one for you, Thea. Guy goes to the doctor for a checkup. The doc examines him and does some tests and tells him, 'I'm sorry, there's nothing I can do, you're going to be dead by morning.' Guy gets in his car, goes to a bar, has a few drinks and broods a while, then goes home to his wife. The wife says, 'So, how'd it go at the doctor?' 'Not too good,' says the husband, 'he says I'll be dead by morning. So I've been sitting around thinking, how would I like to spend my last hours on earth, and I've decided I want to spend the night making passionate love to you.' 'That's fine for you,' the wife says, 'you don't have to get up in the morning.' " One of David's old friends. Maybe four times a year he calls up and leaves a joke on the machine. It's his way of keeping in touch. Of looking after me. He had no way of knowing how welcome his joke was.

The doorbell summoned me to find a small wiry guy with a clipboard, a blond ponytail, and a tee shirt that said BURNOUT. "You Thea Kozak?" he said, holding out his hand. "Hi, I'm Geoff from the cleaners." I shook his hand and led him into the living room. He prowled swiftly through the place, taking notes. Then he stopped by the window, in a pool of sunlight like a cat warming itself, and did some figuring, humming to himself as he worked. "This is what it's going to cost," he said, pointing to an astronomical sum. "Don't worry. Your insurance will take care of it. You go away for a few hours, leave the place to us, and when you come back, it will be just like new. Trust me. I've done this dozens of times. We've gotta repaint this room, though. You realize that, don't you? No way we can make it look right otherwise."

"You want to start right now?"

He shook his head. "Nah. In an hour. I've got to pick up the paint and stuff and get the rest of the crew. That all right by you?"

I felt like I was being run over by a steamroller, but if he could do it quickly, that was great. "Fine with me."

"Well," he said, "see you in an hour, then. You want the same color?" I nodded. He pointed at the mound of curtains on the counter. "You want me to drop those at Sudz? They do a good job on soot."

"Sure. I mean, that would be nice." He gathered up the curtains and headed for the door.

At the threshold he paused. "You ought to take it easy today, you know. Go down to the beach and soak up some sun. A fire can really shake you up." Thank you, Dr. Freud, I thought and he opened the door and was gone. Now all I needed was someone selling sofas and area rugs door-to-door, and a new wardrobe. I forced myself to go into the bedroom and see how bad the situation was. The closet doors were open, but only one part looked empty. All my business clothes. I heaved a sigh of relief. There were only a few things I cared about losing, and none of them had been in that part of the closet. I found the green satin shoes, got out some clean underwear and stockings, and ran myself a bath. I was going to spend the next hour on R & R, and try to get myself in shape for the wedding.

By the time my energetic savior returned an hour later with his cleaning crew, I had done my best to restore myself to vintage Kozak, and it hadn't been easy. For one thing, parts of my hair were sticky with dried blood, but I wasn't supposed to get the stitches wet, and the whole business was complicated by the bandages on my hand, which I also had to keep dry. My bath had been an acrobatic feat worthy of Barnum and Bailey, but I'd emerged with my morale considerably improved, some color in my face, and the confidence that someday soon I'd feel human again.

My morale took another big leap just minutes after the titan of tidiness had deployed his troops, a bizarre crew of three, each with a different tee shirt. There was a tiny blonde with skin so pale she looked liked the sun had never touched it, lugging a vacuum as big as she was. On her tee shirt was a picture of an identical vacuum with the motto SOOT SUCKER on the front and on the back SUCK YOUR WAY TO SUCCESS. Behind her came a mean-faced skinhead with four earrings in his ear, black jeans and motorcycle boots. His shirt had a picture of a guy standing behind a car pouring out clouds of black exhaust, covered head-to-toe with soot. Underneath, it said AFTERBURNER. He was followed by the gentle giant, a huge guy with a vacant face and pale blue faraway eyes, his head surrounded by a cloud of curly blond hair. His shirt said MOP-HEADS CAN OUTHINK DIRT.

"Don't let appearances fool you," Geoff the Burnout man said, "these guys know what they're doing. I uh . . ." he hesitated, "I hope this won't offend you or anything, but my dad's in the furniture business, and I uh . . . I took the liberty of stopping by the store and picking up a few things for you. No obligation, of course. He'll give you a good price, though."

"What sort of things?" I said suspiciously.

"A sofa. And a rug."

I almost laughed out loud. Hadn't I just been wishing for just this sort of service? So how could I complain now that he'd done it. "Let's see what you've got," I said, and followed him out to the truck. The "truck" was a heavily chromed, customized van with painted dragons, erupting volcanoes and other sci-fi stuff on it. With a flourish, he opened the back and stood aside so I could step in. The back was nearly filled with a sofa covered in buttery soft black leather. A radical replacement for the old faded chintz number I'd inherited from my mother. I squeezed myself alongside it and sat down on it. It folded itself around me like a glove, making me want to own it. "Okay," I said, refusing to get up. "How can I say no? I'll take it." It would go okay with one of my chairs, but the other chair was going to look frowzy and matronly beside this sleek monster.

Geoff, the consummate businessman, read my mind. "I can get you a chair to go with it."

In for a penny, in for a pound, I thought. "Why not?" I said. "Can you deliver that today, too?"

"Sure thing," he said. "You want to see the rug?"

I'd been expecting something contemporary, so the rug surprised me. It was an oriental, slightly worn, in shades of deep red, cream, black and gray. Once again, I fell for it instantly. "Are you sure you don't set these fires so you can sell people things?"

"That's a good idea," he said. "Never thought of that. Might have to try that, if things get slow. So, what do you think? You like it?"

"You know I do, don't you."

"Yeah," he said, "I know. The rugs are my hobby. I've had this one a while. Been saving it for just the right person. Goes nice with the sofa, too."

Once again I was reminded that you should never judge a book by the cover. This guy looked and dressed like a townie, ran a cleaning service, talked with the confidence of a broker, collected oriental rugs, and read people's minds. A pretty amazing combination. "Do you often bring along furniture to sell people after a fire?"

He nodded. "I sorta backed into it," he said. "Stopped by to give someone an estimate one day when I had a sofa in the back I was delivering for my dad. The woman saw it and asked if I'd sell it to her—turned out she was having her husband's boss for dinner the next night and her sofa had just burned up—so I said I couldn't sell her that one, but I could get her another one just like it and she was thrilled. You'd be surprised how often people are eager to skip the shopping and just replace the stuff as soon as possible."

"No I wouldn't. Look, I've got to run. How do you want to work the money?" We agreed on that and went back inside. Geoff joined his crew and I went into the bedroom to dress for the wedding. Twenty minutes later when I waltzed out, a vision in green satin, he stopped scrubbing long enough to whistle. "You look grand," he said, "but I still think you'd do better to spend the day at the beach."

"Would if I could, but someone's got to prop the bride up."

"I hear you," he said, "take it easy," and he went back to scrubbing.

I not only made it to the church on time, I remembered to bring "Auntie Thea's Emergency Kit," and it was a good thing that I did, because it was badly needed. The kit is something I always carry in my car to handle wardrobe emergencies. I'm not the type to care, really, but when you spend as much time as I do talking to people in situations where first impressions count, you learn to pay attention to your appearance. I have the predictable things like safety pins and a sewing kit. I also have Band-Aids and moleskin, in case new shoes give me blisters. Spare stockings in black, nude and ivory. Double-faced tape, for handling gaping blouses, too much cleavage, and falling hems. Aspirin, scissors, clothes brush, bobby pins. I was a veritable five-and-dime, and when I entered the little room where Suzanne was assembling her bridal party and saw the tense faces and watery eyes, I immediately began dispensing relief.

Two aspirin for the bride's mother. Double-edged tape for Connie, whose dress gaped a bit. Moleskin and a Band-Aid for Amy, whose high heels had given her a blister. Three bobby pins to secure Suzanne's headpiece and scissors to snip off a trailing thread. By the time we were ready to step off down the aisle, I felt a bit like Mother Teresa.

It was a splendid wedding. The bride was heartbreakingly beautiful, the groom joyous and handsome. Suzanne's father actually tore himself away from his work long enough to escort his daughter to the front of the church, and the minister didn't wear soccer shorts. I cried as I watched my friend walk down the aisle— tears of joy for all the good things she'd longed for and was finally going to have.

I managed to stay upright and coherent and kept a smile on my face through a two-hour dinner with my parents. I held my tongue and was sweet—and Lord knows, I'm not sweet, even though people sometimes make the mistake of thinking I am— even when my mother told me four times that I looked tired and was working too hard, though I faltered when she asked for the third time where Andre was. Then I admit to an edge in my voice when I said, "Working." The best man trod diligently on my feet when we danced and Connie's husband kept his beady eyes glued to my cleavage. Through a masterful exercise of will, I kept my heart from breaking by not letting Andre or David into my mind, but in the midst of that crowd of happy people, there were moments when I felt very much alone.

An eternity later, footsore and weary, but very happy that my friend's day had gone so well, I parked in front of the condo and jumped out of the car, eager for a glass of bourbon and bed. I was wishing, in a forlorn, fairy tale way, that Andre would be there waiting for me, when the reality of the situation hit me like a two-by-four. I was standing alone at night in my parking lot, about to enter my condo where, for the past two nights, someone had tried to harm me.

I'd never realized how dim and genteel the lights were. As I peered across the lot to my door, I could see that there was someone standing by the door, and it didn't look like Andre. Awash with confusion, I stopped dead in the middle of the lot, debating whether to scream or run for the car. I wasn't dressed for running. The green dress had a narrow skirt and the heels were high. Screaming would disturb my already severely taxed neighbors but I couldn't handle another attack. Even us tough guys have our limits. My body was churning out enough adrenaline to fuel a herd of charging rhinos as I prepared to fight or flee.

Over the choking roar of my rising panic I called, "Who's there?"

My old faithful companion of the past two nights, Officer Harris, with the displeased look that was becoming chronic firmly in place, stepped into the light. "Sorry if I scared you," he said, and just to be sure I didn't get the idea that he wanted to be there, he added, "the chief sent me."

He looked so unhappy I felt sorry for him, as sorry as my tense, aching, exhausted body allowed me to be. Ever The Fixer, I tried to create an ego-saving situation for him. "I wouldn't mind at all, Officer, if you'd stay with me until I unlock the door and have a look around."

He nodded and took a step toward the door. I unlocked it, pushed it open, and stepped back to let him go ahead of me. "Would you mind going first?"

"Not at all," he said and stepped inside.

I followed Harris in, and went around behind him as he checked all the rooms, windows and closets. My heart was still pounding and I felt the drained, woozy aftermath of a bad fright. Harris didn't seem to notice. He was focused on the apartment. The place smelled rather strongly of cleaning products, but it looked great. He stared at the new sofa in astonishment. "How'd you do that so fast?"

"Guy from the cleaning service sold it to me."

"Geoff Poldari?"

"All I know is his name is Geoff."

"He probably stole it."

"He said his father was in the furniture business."

"Yeah?" Harris said. "Well maybe his father stole it. A light-fingered bunch, those Poldaris. Do a great job cleaning, though. He bring his brothers and his sister?"

"He didn't introduce me to the crew."

"Bunch of weird looking morons. Big guy who looks like an imbecile? Scrawny girl who just crawled out from under a rock, and the motorcycle man?" I nodded. "Yeah, those're his sibs. He's got more, but those're the only ones that can function. His ma had a kid a year for about twenty years, then the old man decided he couldn't take it, so he built himself a shack across the yard, lives over there by himself, only comes home for meals and the occasional screw." He shook his head. "Sheesh, what a bunch. Gotta give Geoff credit, though. He does take care of all of 'em. Has to, I guess, he's the only one in the bunch got any brains." He tapped the nightstick, which he'd been carrying, against his thigh.

"Well, everything looks quiet. Hope I won't be seeing you later. You oughta be taking it easy tonight."

"I'm glad you were here. I feel safer now."

"The chief sent me," he said again. "He doesn't want any more incidents. The word gets around and women . . . uh . . . people get scared. It makes the department look bad."

"Sure you can't stay and have some coffee?"

"No thank you," he said, tapping his palm with the stick, "I've got to get back on the road."

I walked him to the door, reluctant to let him go and be left there alone. I was also aware of what a pitiful figure I would seem if I asked him to stay—the scared and lonely woman clinging to a man who was obviously desperate to escape. Well, there was no way I was going to appear vulnerable in front of this unsympathetic stranger. I grabbed the doorknob and pulled it open. The cool night air rushed in and enveloped me. Suddenly I was aware of the darkness, the enormous emptiness out there, and I was flipped back to the night before, to that dim figure coming at me and then the explosion of pain and nothingness.

It was a purely visceral reaction—I'm normally as brave as a barrel full of bears—but I found myself cowering against the wall with my hands over my head, making scared whimpering sounds.

Harris shut the door, put an arm around me, and steered me back into the living room. "It's okay, Ms. Kozak. It's okay. There's no one out there."

I bit my lip and willed my body to stop shaking. It didn't work. In a contest between will and primitive body chemistry, chemistry wins. I went on shaking and Harris seemed positively delighted by my vulnerability. I was finally acting like a victim. He offered me tea and blankets. I asked for bourbon.

"If you don't mind, I'd like to get out of this dress." Wedding clothes tend to be neither comfortable nor warm. Right now I was in the mood for soft, baggy things.

"Can you manage all right?"

I was going to say I'd been dressing myself since I was two but

I didn't. He was finally being nice to me; there was no need to make him grouchy again just because I liked to be assertive. I excused myself and went into the bedroom to change. There, too, everything was shiny and clean. I put the dress on a hanger, the shoes in the closet, and changed into black cotton leggings and a midnight blue velour tunic. It felt heavenly to be out of the tight, rustly satin. On the other hand, everything smelled like smoke and paint and pine cleaner. I was going to have to haul everything I owned—what was left of it—to the laundromat.

Harris was playing my new Marcus Roberts CD, and as I looked out from my bedroom door, it looked like a stage set for romance. Soft pools of light, a crystal glass of golden brown liquor, light jazz, a man on my sexy leather couch. The badge and nightstick and gun didn't fit in the picture, though. I sat down on the other end of the couch, curling my leg under me, and took a sip of my drink, wishing I didn't feel so much like putting my head down and crying.

"Are you married, Officer?"

"Yes."

"Children?"

"None yet. What about you? Are you married?" It was a purely conversational gesture. He knew there was no husband around. He'd been here in the middle of the night. Heck, in a way, he'd spent the night with me, and there'd been no husband then, either.

"I was. He died. A car accident."

"I'm sorry. Recently?"

"It's been almost three years."

"Significant other?" he asked.

"I'm not sure. There is . . . was . . . I don't know. I guess so. He's a cop. A detective. With the Maine Department of Public Safety."

He nodded approvingly. "Well, he can rest assured that we'll take good care of you."

Before I could comment on my elevated status or remind him

of how he'd been badgering me the night before, the doorbell rang. Suddenly I wasn't just a woman sitting in her comfortable living room enjoying a drink. Fear settled on my shoulders like a lead cape. I set my glass down with trembling hands, and headed for the door. "Would you just come and stand behind me, please?"

With Harris in back of me, I cautiously opened the door. Andre was standing there, half-hidden behind an armload of purple lilacs. "I'm sorry," he said, "I know I should have called, but I had to see you." His eyes shifted from me to Harris and back to me and the life went out of his face. I watched it close down, become hard and angry. "You work fast," he said.

"Andre, this is Officer Harris. He's a cop."

"I can see that Officer Harris is a cop," he said, "and of course you just happened to have the emergency he's responding to while you were barefoot and in skintight pants and your 'touch me' shirt at 10:30 P.M. on Saturday night, listening to the music I bought for you because I thought it was romantic. An emergency that's lasted so long his engine's almost cold. Or is his engine just getting hot?"

"Don't be an idiot, Lemieux," I said, "you know me better than that." But I could see things through his eyes, too. I was wearing this outfit because it was comfortable, but the last time I'd worn it around Andre, I'd also chosen it because it made me feel sexy. I was the one who'd told him it was my "touch me" shirt. I might get him to understand if I had an hour to explain why the last few days had made me too tired to think straight, but from the look on his face, I knew that at best I had two minutes.

"I thought I did," he said. "But I called you ten times last night. All night. And you weren't home." His voice was harsh, flat, devoid of emotion, but I knew him well enough to know that he could be mad as hell and still act cool as a cucumber.

Now we were both mad. "That's not fair. I wasn't here because I got hit over the head by someone who broke in and set the place on fire. I was at the hospital, and then I spent the night at a motel. If you don't believe me, call Dom Florio. He was there."

"You spent the night at a motel with Florio?" His tone was disbelieving. He peered past me at the living room. "And you expect me to believe there was a fire in here last night? What burned up, the hors d'oeuvres? The drapes? Don't bullshit me, Theadora. I wasn't born yesterday. There's no soot, no smell, no mess. . . ."

"It's not bullshit. I wouldn't lie to you. I got it cleaned up! Stop standing there and staring at me with those cold cop's eyes. Come in and let me explain. Ask Harris. He was here last night. You just don't understand. . . ." I felt, rather than saw, Harris retreat, trying to leave me alone with Andre.

"You're right," he said, "I don't understand. What I see with these cop's eyes is the woman I love with another man. I thought you understood that I loved you, I just needed a little time. You could at least have given me that." He opened his arms and let the flowers drop, then turned on his heel and strode away.

"Andre, wait," I said, running after him, "things aren't what they seem." I grabbed at his arm, trying to turn him around, trying to show him my bandaged hand, my stitches, anything that might get his attention and stop him long enough to listen.

"They rarely are," he said, shaking me off. He got in his car, slammed the door, and drove away.

Harris, looking miserable, was waiting to leave. "I take it that was your boyfriend?" I nodded. "Don't worry, he'll get over it. He was just surprised."

"I wish I could believe that, but I know him. He can be a real stubborn, righteous SOB."

He patted me on the shoulder. "I'm sorry," he said. "I really messed things up for you, and I'm sorry."

"It's not your fault. I asked you to stay."

He bent down and picked up the lilacs, lying abandoned and forlorn on the ground. "You want these?"

"Sort of like locking the barn door after the horse has been stolen, isn't it? But I do want them." I took the lilacs, closed the door behind him, and locked it. Clutching the flowers, I stood in the kitchen, rocking from foot to foot, my unwanted tears running unchecked down my face, dripping off my chin and onto my wretched "touch me" shirt. After a while, the shower passed. I put the flowers in water and set them on the coffee table. Then I checked all the windows and doors one more time to be sure that they were still locked, fixed myself another drink, and played Marcus Roberts again, sitting in the lilac-scented darkness, wallowing in self-pity and wishing I'd never let myself get involved. If you don't let them get close, they can't hurt you.

CHAPTER *21*

ROSIE FLORIO WASN'T at all like I'd expected. Despite Dom's descriptions of her courage and his obvious pride in her, I'd imagined a female Dom, someone plain and physically unimpressive, whose spark and impact came from personality. Not that Rosie didn't have personality; she had that in spades, but she also had a fierce, exotic face that was hard to stop looking at. Dark, heavy-lidded eyes, a strong nose, jutting cheekbones and a full-lipped mouth. I'd also assumed—which just goes to show, as I learn and forget repeatedly, one should not prejudge—that she'd have short, graying practical hair, easy for a handicapped person to care for, but instead she had a mane of thick, straight hair, dark with wide, sexy gray streaks. A striking, haunting, unusual woman who belonged in movies, to be glimpsed briefly and left to linger in your memory forever. Looking at her made me, in my tired, shop-worn state, feel dull and unattractive.

I'd come prepared to be on my best behavior, get through a polite breakfast, and leave. I didn't feel like I could sustain more than minimal social interaction. Without a schedule to meet, my body was taking the opportunity to experience all the aches and pains that had been inflicted on it and my spirit was in even worse shape. I still couldn't believe what had happened with Andre. Like a wounded animal, I wanted to crawl into my cave, away from the demands of the world, and lick my wounds. Instead I was sitting behind the luxuriant foliage of the fringed bleeding heart I'd brought, trying to smile and make small talk while Rosie and I waited for Dom to join us.

Rosie had seated me in the living room, next to a tray with a carafe of coffee, wheeled her chair up beside me, and poured us each some coffee. "You're exactly as I expected," she said. "Dom has a real talent for describing people."

I wondered how he'd described me. Stubborn? Difficult? An attractive witch? Maybe she'd tell me. I wasn't going to ask. "You're not," I said.

"Really?" The skin around her eyes crinkled with amusement. "What were you expecting?"

"Someone much more ordinary."

She smiled. "Should I be flattered or wonder what my husband says about me?"

"Your husband adores you. I'm sure you know that."

She tilted her head slightly sideways with a mischievous smile. "I hear you've been giving him advice."

Suddenly, my bantering advice seemed extremely presumptuous. "I hope you weren't offended."

She put a hand over mine. Hers was cool and strong. "On the contrary. It was good advice. That's why I was anxious to meet you. Dom can be so damned protective sometimes he forgets I'm still a woman."

"I don't see how he could forget that, looking at you."

"Look at me," she said, "not just my face . . . the whole picture. Remember, he's been looking at the same landscape for a quarter of a century, and now what he sees is this damned chair. Sometimes it blocks his view." She shook her head as though shaking off the whole conversation. "Let's not talk about me. I'm so bored with talking about myself." There was something there for a minute, in her voice, that gave me a window into her pain, into her struggle to get back to what she'd been, before she moved on to more mundane things. "I hope you're hungry. Dom loves a big Sunday breakfast. He promised me he was inviting someone with an appetite. I can't stand people who just push food around on their plates."

I didn't have a scrap of appetite, even though whatever she was making smelled wonderful. "I'm afraid I'm not myself today, Mrs. Florio. . . ."

"Rosie," she said, interrupting. "Mrs. Florio sounds like the old Italian widow down the block. Rosie. Well, from what Dom has told me, I'm not surprised. Strangers trying to break in. Someone attacking you and setting your place on fire. I asked him why he didn't just bring you here. You know what he said?"

"No, but I'd like to."

"He said you were just like me, stubborn as a mule, and the only way he could have gotten you here was to convince you that under no circumstances were you welcome in this house."

"Is that why he came and slept in my motel room? It was the only way he could keep an eye on me?"

"Short of hog-tying you and dragging you here, that's right," Dom growled from the doorway. "The other reason I stayed was to keep Harris from forgetting that you were the victim and trying to force you into cooperating. You gave that boy a pretty hard time." He was lounging against the wall, looking completely at home in gray sweats, his Clark Kent glasses gone and his hair awry, looking like an entirely different guy. Very appealing in his new avatar as the aging jock. His shirt was soaked with sweat. "If you ladies don't mind, I'll grab a quick shower?"

"We'd mind if you didn't," Rosie said, wrinkling her nose. "Go right ahead. We're doing fine."

"I did not give Harris a hard time, Florio," I said, unwilling to let him get away with that remark, "he showed all the humanity of a rotten log."

"He has equally complimentary things to say about you," he retorted, and went to shower.

"That guy wouldn't know a victim if it bit him," I told his departing back.

He stopped and turned around. "That's where you get it wrong, Kozak. The victim is supposed to be the one who's bitten, not the one who bites."

"Stuff it, Florio," I said sweetly.

Rosie laughed out loud. "Now I see what he meant," she said.

"Meant about what?"

"About you. Said you reminded him of me, as he put it, you were a deliciously spicy package."

I made a face. "Sounds like something you'd use to jazz up couscous."

She laughed again. "You're not really mad at him, are you? There's nothing smooth or flashy about Dom, but he's very good at what he does. I hear the two of you were holding hands at the pancake house."

"I'm sorry. It wasn't anything. He was just trying to comfort me."

"Don't apologize, Thea. I know that. A lot of people don't understand about Dom and me, especially since the accident. They assume since the poor guy's married to a cripple he's got to have a woman on the side. They think I need to know what's going on. I guess they don't have husbands who tell them things. The thing is that I know Dom would never be unfaithful to me, so I don't worry."

"I wish Andre had had the same faith in me." I said it without thinking and then it was too late to take it back.

Her eyes widened with curiosity. "Andre is the state trooper, right? Dom said you guys were having troubles. Would you like to talk about it?"

My throat tightened as I tried to hold back the flood of feelings. It was so easy to talk to Rosie. "No. I don't think so. I don't think I can."

"I think you should," she said, and I felt the dam I'd built to keep my feelings back slowly crumble, like a slow-motion film of an explosion, pieces of my resolve flying everywhere and misery pouring out through every crack. When Dom came back I was crouched on the floor next to the chair, my head in Rosie's lap while she stroked my hair with gentle fingers.

"If you're still hearing confession, I could come back later, but I want you to know that I'm starving out here."

"Don't be a jerk, Dom," she said. "If you're so hungry, maybe you could put the food on the table. We'll be right along."

I was in no hurry to leave my comforting spot, but the food he was putting out smelled wonderful. Somehow, in the course of my confession, my appetite had returned. I picked up my head and stood up. "Suddenly, Rosie, I feel like I could eat a horse."

"I hope you'll like it," she said. "Sorry about Mr. Impatient out there, but after he plays basketball he has an amazing appetite. You won't believe it."

"You should see Andre eat. Might be fun to watch the two of them together sometime. If there are anymore sometimes." Confiding in Rosie had made me feel better, but I hadn't completely shed my self-pitying mood.

"There will be," she said. "Give him some time to cool off, then call him, tell him you love him and that he's being a damned fool."

Dom was sitting at the head of the table with the plates stacked in front of him, surrounded by steaming containers of food. He put enough food on my plate to feed my whole family, then did the same for Rosie, and finally served himself so much food I half expected his plate to groan. He took a forkful, held it up, and said, "Cheers."

"Cheers," I returned, and attacked mine.

"So," he began, when he'd shoveled about half of it down, "did you listen to Uncle Dom and back off or are you still hot on the trial of Helene Streeter's killer?"

"I thought you weren't going to involve her in this anymore." Rosie said. "Didn't you tell her to stay out of it?"

"I can't help myself, Rosie."

"Yes you can."

I appreciated her protection, but I was torn. Part of me wanted to follow his advice and stay out of it while another part of me wanted to get the damn thing solved so we all could move on and forget about it. For the last day, I'd been too busy to think about Helene and Eve and Cliff, and that had been just fine with me. When I started to think about it, it all came rushing back. An incredible jumble, all the inconsistent things I'd been told, all the conflicting pictures of Helene. "Dom," I said, "have you ever gone into the funhouse at a fair or a carnival and looked in the mirrors?" He nodded. "People's images of Helene are like the reflections in those mirrors. Everyone has a different view of her, all very different and all distorted."

"That's perfect. You've captured it perfectly," he said. He rubbed his forehead wearily. "But who did it?"

"I don't want you two talking about this over my nice breakfast," Rosie said. "I mean it, Dominic Florio. You aren't going to drag the poor girl back into the middle of this mess."

But we were off and running, and not even Rosie could stop us. "I told you once before that if this were an Agatha Christie, they all would have done it. If I were writing the script—if it weren't so absurd—I'd say that she killed herself because she was as troubled by the unreconcilable pieces of herself as we are. But no one commits suicide that way."

"She couldn't have, of course. But who did?" He was leaning forward over his plate, his eyes fixed on me like he honestly expected me to have the answers. He'd hinted at it before, but now I could see how this case was obsessing him. He couldn't stand not being able to figure it out.

"Don't look at me like that," I said. "I've been following your advice. Staying out of it, just like you said." It was the truth. On the other hand, my withdrawal hadn't had any effect on the people who kept calling, so I might as well tell him about that. It was what he seemed to expect, anyway. He was waiting for my response with the air of a man who wasn't going to accept no for an answer. Some protector he'd turned out to be.

"Lenora Stern says Helene was afraid of someone. That she took some kind of a self-defense course because she was scared."

"Scared of what?"

"I don't know. It was on my machine. I didn't call her back. You can call her."

"Anything else?" His blue eyes were boring into me, searching for something I didn't have.

I felt my anxiety level rise to match his, as though the two of us had to figure it out before we could leave the table. "She had a big fight with Rowan Ansel," I said.

"Who told you?"

"Norah McCarty. The housekeeper. She also left a message on my machine."

He leaned forward eagerly. "What else did she say?"

"I didn't call her back."

"What else?" he repeated.

I couldn't look away. It was as though he had some indefinable power over me, holding me there and sucking out all the little bits like a mental vacuum cleaner. "She—Norah—said Ansel was trying to persuade Helene to give Cliff a divorce. I know Ansel didn't like her. When I talked with him, he wasn't the least bit sorry she was dead, only that it was so hard for Cliff."

He nodded. "What else?"

"Cliff told me that humoring Eve by going along with her crazy theories about his involvement was unhealthy for her and I must stop. And Rowan Ansel keeps trying to get me to meet him so we can have a private talk." I actually searched for more, even though I knew there was nothing, because I wanted to give him the answer just as much as he wanted it.

We sat there, eyes locked, until Rosie interrupted us by banging her coffee cup loudly on the table. "Stop it, you two," she ordered. "This was supposed to be a nice breakfast, not a goddamned interrogation. What is the matter with you, Dom? Why can't you leave the poor girl alone?"

"It's my fault, Rosie, I . . ."

"It's not your fault. My husband is just like a terrier, worrying at things until he's satisfied. But he shouldn't be using you." She turned her angry gaze on her husband. "Hasn't she been through enough?"

"I can't help . . ." Dom began.

"You can too, Dominic Florio, and you know it. The fact is that you don't want to help it." She folded her arms across her chest and glared at him.

Her remarks were directed at Dom, but I responded. "I'm sorry, Rosie. We can't leave it alone because we can't stand the fact that we don't know the answers. Not that it's exactly a two-way street. Dom knows everything I know, and I don't have any idea what he knows."

"That's life with a cop, though. You'd better get used to it," she said.

"I'm not sure that's anything I'll have to worry about anymore."

"What does that mean?" he interrupted. "So he didn't show for the wedding. That's not the end of the world. Hey, you're giving him the hook because of that?"

"That's none of your business," Rosie said.

"I'm afraid he's given me the hook," I answered, briefly telling him about Harris and the lilacs.

"Don't worry. I'll talk to him." Good old Uncle Dom. When he wasn't pushing me around, pumping me for information, or trying to tell me what to do, he was going to straighten out my love life. The guy was like a fishtailing trailer. First he swung a little in each direction, then a little more, than he began veering wildly.

"Don't bother, Dom. I can take care of my own affairs."

"Yeah," he said, "it sure sounds like you can."

"Shut up, both of you," Rosie ordered, "you're ruining everything, and I worked so hard to make it nice." That shut us both up in a hurry. We apologized and went back to eating. It was a fine

day and a fine breakfast, and if only an exorcist could have come in
and cast out the ghost of Helene, everything would have been
perfect, even if Andre wasn't there to share it. After breakfast,
Dom and I cleaned up and did the dishes while Rosie excused herself and went into the bathroom.

The stuff that wouldn't go in the dishwasher I washed and he
dried. "I'm sorry, Thea. Rosie says sometimes I can be a real jerk,
and she's right. Look at me. I tell you to quit—meant it, too—and
here I am, pumping you again. I can't seem to stop myself. . . ."

"I understand. It's like the invisible rock in your shoe. It just
keeps bothering you. You think you can ignore it and it will go
away, but it won't. And it never will until you solve it."

"No, I can't. She's gotten under my skin so that I have this
Helene Streeter obsession. I never even met the woman and yet I
can feel her staring at me with those gorgeous eyes, demanding
that I find her killer. But I can't get inside her head. I can't look
through those eyes and see what she saw. Usually I can do that,
but not this time. I don't mean to sound so melodramatic; I
haven't done that many murders. We don't get a lot of murder
here. Not in a white-bread community like Anson, so maybe I can
get into the heads of my crime victims . . . listen to me . . . sounds
pretty arrogant, doesn't it? My crime victims . . . but what I mean
is that I can usually put myself in the victim's place and see things
from their point of view. I can't do that here."

He wiped out the sink and leaned back against it, arms folded
over his chest. "It's too confusing. I don't understand her. Was
she a saint or a whore? A good person or a manipulative bitch?"

"You're trying to simplify a complicated woman," I said. "She
was all of those things and more. Intelligent and analytical and
charming. Strong willed, manipulative and ambitious. Gracious,
generous and controlling. Political. Paranoid. And beautiful,
Dom, really beautiful. When she was around it was hard to take
your eyes off her. It's too bad you never met her. She had this
presence . . . this mesmerizing presence . . . like Circe. . . ."

"Maybe that's why I can't stop thinking about her."

"Well, I'd like to forget the whole mess, but no one will let me. I'm like flypaper. All sorts of things seem to come my way and they stick even though I don't want to be involved."

"Yes you do."

"Why do you always think you know what I want? When I say I want to be left alone, I mean it."

"You do and you don't. . . ."

"Maybe you're right. You never knew Helene, but like people said at her funeral, she was very special. She had that same quality Cliff has, that facility for making you feel unique and welcome. And she was so passionate about her issues. So alive. It was exciting to be around her, intimidating but exciting. I used to want so much to be like her. . . ."

"Then it must hurt to hear about her secret life," he said.

"I'm not sure I believe . . ." Suddenly I didn't want to talk about it anymore. He was right. It did hurt. I'd been too busy to pay attention to my feelings, to what I believed and what I didn't, or how it felt to find more of my heroes with clay feet. It wasn't just the murder. The whole business was sordid and depressing and ugly. "She was important to me," I said.

"She was a decadent, self-centered bitch. . . ."

"Not always . . . not just that . . . she was so much more . . ." I shouted. I was angry at him. At Helene. At Cliff. At Eve. At Andre. "And it looks like I'll have to find her killer. None of the rest of you seem to be able to do a goddamned thing!"

"I told you to stay out of it. . . ."

"And I told you two to cut it out. This is just like having the kids at home." Rosie was standing in the doorway, glaring at us.

Then I realized what I was seeing. Rosie standing. She took a few careful, tentative steps, crossing from the doorway to the stove. Dom put down his towel and the dish he was drying and went to meet her, his face astonished and aglow. Carefully, tenderly, he took her in his arms. I dried my hands and went quietly into the other room, sat down on the couch, and pulled some work out of my ever present briefcase, waiting for a diplomatic moment to say good-bye. I was well into the third page of an interview outline to use at Bartlett Hill when they waltzed in looking radiant and embarrassed.

"I'm sorry, Thea. I'm afraid we've been very rude," Rosie said. "I wanted to do this when someone else was around, in case Dom collapsed from shock."

I joined them and put an arm around both of them. "I'm honored that you were willing to share it with me."

"Anything to get the two of you to stop fighting."

"We weren't fighting," I said.

"If fighting can get you to do this, we'll stay and fight all day," Dom beamed.

I said a quick good-bye and left them, feeling like I'd just witnessed a miracle.

CHAPTER 22

IF LENORA STERN was surprised to see me, she didn't show it. In fact, she acted like she'd been expecting me, leading me into her study with an air of satisfaction, and even her body language, as she settled into her chair, said, "It's about time." And that was, not surprisingly, the first thing out of her mouth.

"I'm sorry?" I said, all surprised innocence.

"You're not much of a detective, are you? Here I am, ready to give you information, and you won't even return my calls." She uncrossed and recrossed her legs, tossed her hair back from her face and tented her fingers on her knee. "Has anyone else told you about Armed and Dangerous?"

"Armed and Dangerous?"

She seemed pleased by my ignorance. "It's a self-defense course for women. Helene and I took it last month. She believed she was being followed and was afraid it might have been the husband of one of her clients. She wanted to be prepared to handle an attack."

"Why didn't she just get a gun?"

"Do you know how often women's own handguns are used against them?" she said. "Anyway, this was different. It wasn't about getting a weapon, it was about developing a whole new point of view. Very empowering. You can't imagine how good it felt, tossing those men around, screaming at them, hitting them." Her face grew flushed, remembering. "What they taught us was that no one has the right to hurt you. Women have a hard time with that idea, you know. We tend to just keep taking it, not making waves, trying to be conciliatory and not make a scene. The instructor said it is harder to teach women to have the will to fight than it is to teach the actual technique."

I could imagine Lenora enjoying herself; I had a harder time envisioning Helene hitting people and throwing them around. "Did Helene enjoy it?"

Lenora shrugged. "Not as much as I did. I admit I got a charge out of knocking those guys around, but she said it made her feel a lot safer. Said at least she'd know what to do if anyone came at her." She hesitated, studying her fingers. "That's why it doesn't make any sense."

"What doesn't make any sense?"

"That someone was able to come up to her and attack her like that, yet the neighbors heard nothing. It doesn't make sense unless you agree with Eve. Unless Cliff did it. No one else could have gotten close enough to her with a weapon before she made a scene. She'd been trained to make a scene. But Cliff could have walked right up to her and stabbed her before she knew what was coming."

"So could anyone, if they took her by surprise. . . ."

"You haven't been listening," she said, exasperated. "She was trained to expect surprise. That's one of the things the course was all about. About listening to your body. About sensing what's out there with your subconscious before your conscious mind even knows what's going on. About instinct. You probably don't realize this, but your body senses danger long before you actually know it's there. And when you sense danger, you take a deep breath, quickly assess the situation, and decide whether to fight, or scream and run, or whatever. Confronted by a sudden attacker with a knife, she would have run immediately, screaming for help, letting people know she was being attacked. And she didn't do that," Lenora finished, "so she must have known her attacker. The neighbors were home that night. And they didn't hear anything."

"Did you tell this to the police?"

"Of course I told them. Or him." She heaped immeasurable scorn on the word him. "I could tell that he thought I was totally off the wall. He hardly even bothered to listen. I could see it in his face, his disbelief in the possibility that a woman could handle herself capably in that situation. I'm sure he completely disregarded everything I told him. You look pretty skeptical, too, and you should know better."

I didn't like Lenora Stern, and evidently she didn't like me much, either. "I don't know how close you and Helene were. Were you aware that she had other men?"

She laughed. "Such a nice archaic construction. As long as she had them, rather than them having her. Yes, of course I knew she saw other men. She was a very physical woman. She needed sex. So what?"

"So what if the killer was one of her other men? Wouldn't one of them have been able to get close to her?"

She waved a hand dismissively. "They were never that important. Helene was very clear with them that the relationship was only about sex. She never let things get out of hand. Never let them get close. Never let them interfere in her everyday life. You have to understand. She was a very practical woman. Controlled and rational. Qualities that are admired in a man and disparaged in a woman. I suppose many men would describe her as a cold-hearted bitch. She knew what she wanted, she took it, and that was that."

"But what if one of them wanted more, was frustrated that he couldn't have it, and killed her so no one could have what he couldn't have?"

"Don't be silly. I told you. She knew how to manage them."

"Now who is being naive? You, of all people, ought to know about obsessions and people who lack impulse control."

"Of course I do. And the person who was obsessed and lacked impulse control was her husband, Cliff. Who wanted to be able to have his little affair, but wanted her to stop having hers. He was afraid she'd embarrass both of them. She could have, too. She had rather indiscriminate taste."

"In how she chose her lovers? Where did she find them?"

"Under every rock. Firemen, store clerks, taxi drivers. I wouldn't be surprised if she had a few cops, too, though they'd never admit it. She kind of liked men in uniform." She studied my face and nodded decisively. "You're shocked, aren't you? I don't see why you should be. When a man tomcats around and has a vigorous appetite for sex, he may come in for some superficial criticism, but secretly he's admired. When a woman does the same thing, she's a slut. So Helene was a slut. So what? She enjoyed herself. You know the line . . . I think they used it to sell athletic shoes . . . work hard, play hard. Well, that's what Helene did. She had strong appetites, and she indulged them." She shrugged. "Her work, you know, was emotionally demanding. Draining. After a day of listening to those pathetic stories, she needed an outlet. A physical outlet. She couldn't sleep with Cliff. Not after what he'd been doing. It wasn't safe. So Helene took lovers. So what?"

I thought the lady was protesting too much. Lenora Stern might have thought she was Helene's friend, and she might have admired Helene's style and bravado, but she'd also been extremely jealous. I could understand it. Like me, Lenora was tall. She was also big boned, carried a lot of weight, and her face, which must once have been quite attractive, was handsome but worn-out. Close-up, she looked old and hard. Distinguished, maybe, but not the face that could pick up a cop, or a fireman, or a store clerk in a two-minute encounter. Helene had been small boned, naturally elegant, and beautiful. Also respected in her field, with a successful private practice, a beautiful home and an apparently adoring husband. There'd been a lot there to resent, and Lenora Stern, however she might protest to the contrary, had resented it.

"Why are you so sure it was Cliff, when there are so many possibilities?"

"Because he wanted a divorce, and she wouldn't give him one."

"That's nonsense. No one can imprison someone else in a marriage. He could have gotten a divorce even if she didn't agree."

"Not without a bitter fight and significant financial losses. And his position at Bartlett Hill is sensitive. The place is paranoid that something might affect the bottom line. They would have frowned on messy publicity."

"That wouldn't have been necessary."

"You think she would have passed up an opportunity to broadcast the fact that he was cheating on her with another man?"

"But then she'd risk her own private life coming out. What about the husband of one of her patients? You said she was afraid a patient's husband was following her. The families and friends of battered women are killed all the time."

"No," she said. "No. It wasn't one of them. She recognized that risk so she was very careful. She never gave out her home number—she used a service. She was unlisted. She never saw patients at home. . . ."

"She could have been followed. Stalked."

Lenora shook her head vehemently. "I'm telling you. It was Cliff. Unless it was Rowan. . . ."

"She didn't like Rowan," I interrupted. "Why would she let him walk up to her on a dark street?"

But Lenora was on send and not receive. "Cliff was like all men," she said angrily. "He wanted the freedom to explore his own sexuality but resented the idea that Helene wanted to explore hers. He demanded that she stop and she refused, so he killed her."

"How do you know he asked her to stop?" I said, thinking this was distinctly at odds with Martha Coffey's description of a tender Cliff carrying his straying wife inside after a hard night.

She ignored my question. "I want him punished for what he did."

"What about Eve?" I said, so aggravated that I wanted to provoke her. "She could have gotten close to her mother."

"That's a sick idea," she snorted. "Eve was devoted to her mother." Suddenly she stood up. "Im afraid you'll have to leave now. I have someone coming in a few minutes and I need time to compose myself. This interview has been rather upsetting." She squinted her eyes and peered into my face. "I don't think you're really a friend of Eve's at all. I think you're just another one of those silly, impressionable girls who are always falling for Cliff. Poor Eve. She was always bringing friends home and having them go gaga over her father. Naturally he wouldn't do anything to prevent it. He thrived on their adulation. It's frightful to think he could do such a terrible thing and simply go on as though nothing had happened. I passed him yesterday in the hallway and he was humming to himself. Singing. Happier than I've seen him in years. Can you believe it, with Helene hardly cold?" She hurried me to the door, opened it, and practically shoved me through it.

The encounter left me feeling so good I decided to go stick my head in another lion's mouth. I was nothing if not a glutton for punishment. With Helene it might have been work hard, play hard. With me it was work hard, work hard. Play didn't enter into it. First I'd had an intense round with Dom. Then I'd let Lenora Stern abuse and patronize me. Now I had two more exciting choices. I could go confront Cliff and get his reaction to the whole mess, or I could go see Eve and tell her I'd talked to everyone on the planet and the whole thing was now as clear as mud. Since I was going to see Cliff in the morning anyway, I decided to try Eve. The alternative was to go home and brood about Andre.

I found her on the sidewalk in front of her building, doing something complicated to her bicycle. "Be done with this in a sec," she said. Waldemar, as silent as ever, was farther down the sidewalk, long legs straddling his bike, swaying slowly to whatever his headphones were piping into his head. He nodded and waved, but made no effort to disconnect. I repressed my annoyance and composed a letter to Miss Manners in my head, the gist of which was to ask why people felt that being plugged into mindless electronic devices exempted them from even the most rudimentary show of manners. More and more, I'd noticed, people plugged themselves into machines, thought they'd been removed from contact with others, and no longer bothered to say "excuse me" when they bumped into people, no longer bothered to hold doors for those coming behind them, and no longer returned greetings. Mr. Sony and his cohorts had turned us into a nation of zombies, and they hadn't even needed to use voodoo.

Eve gave the wrench a final turn, stuck it into a pouch at her waist, and straightened up, wiping her hands on her black shorts. "Convinced yet?" she asked.

I shook my head. "It gets more complicated, not simpler. But remember, you promised to listen. . . ."

"Can't right now," she said, "we're supposed to meet some people for a ten-mile ride and we're already late. We'll be back around six if you'd like to come by then."

"Can't. I've got work to do."

She looked up at the beautiful blue sky. "You should get a life, you know. It's too beautiful to be inside."

"I've been working for you," I reminded her.

She shrugged and bent down over the spokes. "Well, I guess that's something. I'll call you tonight."

"Would you mind if I used your bathroom?" I said, an idea suddenly brewing.

She sighed, then shrugged. "Why not. I'll come up with you and unlock the door. You can close it behind you when you leave. You don't mind if I don't stick around, do you? I really need this bike ride. Today is the first day I've felt even half human." Oh no, I thought, just because I was spending hours of my time on her, that was no reason she should waste any of hers staying to keep me company.

Quite the contrary. I'd expected that response. But I didn't tell her that. I couldn't tell her that I wanted to be alone in her apartment, and if a giant conscience had dropped out of a tree beside me and demanded in a deep and compelling voice to know why I was doing what I was doing, I wouldn't have had an answer, because I didn't know myself. They, the collective they who were driving me these days, had made me do it. That was all I could say. Don't blame me. I'm just a helpless victim, driven to do irrational things by forces beyond my control. Or by forces I wasn't controlling.

I pictured two angels, the good angel and the bad angel, sitting on a tree branch, looking down at me, discussing my behavior and giggling. Phooey on them. I was a detective, wasn't I? Or at least forced into being one. And detectives followed hunches. My hunch was that Eve knew something she wasn't telling me. That she was testing me to see if I could find it. Eve liked to test people.

Or maybe I was here because of my talk with Florio, trying to get inside Eve's head. The conversation had focused me again, clarified the fact that, like it or not, I was involved. Before, I'd put my right foot in and put my right foot out so many times I could have been doing the hokey pokey.

The apartment smelled like baking bread, a mystery I solved in true gumshoe fashion by going into the kitchen and discovering one of those handy-dandy do-it-all bread machines. Too high-tech for me. If I can't get half a pound of dough gummed under my fingernails and all over my hands while I knead the bread, I don't feel like I've baked. I pulled on the gloves Eve used to do dishes—a detective can't be too careful—and started searching through her bedroom.

It's maddening to search for something when you don't know what you're looking for. After an hour of prowling I hadn't located anything suspicious or helpful. Sure there were catalogues of hunting gear, but they also had kayaks, tents, sportswear and all sorts of things that I knew Eve was interested in. Then I experienced an aha! moment when I found a crumpled black jumpsuit in the bottom of her closet, but the dark spots on it smelled and looked like grease or oil. She probably wore it when she tuned her bike or worked on her car.

In the medicine cabinet were more drugs than you'd find in a pharmacy. Several different painkillers, mood elevators and tranquilizers, some prescribed by Cliff. Still trying to protect his baby from the cruel world. I wondered if he knew what the others had prescribed? Looking at the stuff made me uncomfortably aware that my head was aching and my burned hand felt hot and sore. I took a couple of my own painkillers and went to search the living room. I found a lot of dust, even more bad music, and several pairs of very stinky socks. But no diaries recording secret plans, no revealing letters, no photographs of Cliff stabbing Helene or Rowan Ansel in the bushes or Waldemar Becker with a knife clenched between his many teeth, nothing more incriminating than a grocery list.

The whole place was hot and stuffy. Despite her love of the outdoors, Eve hadn't bothered to open a window and let some fresh air in. My head was pounding and the pills didn't seem to be doing me any good at all. I tried to recall the instructions from my head injury aftercare sheet, wondering if I should be worried, but I was too tired to think. I went back into the bedroom and lay down on the bed. I'd meant to rest only until my head felt well enough to drive, but I dropped almost instantly into a catatonic sleep. Just like Goldilocks. And I didn't care what the three bears thought when they came back. My last conscious act was to strip off the gloves, roll them up, and stick them in my pocket. Once a detective, always a detective, even when you're running on empty.

What woke me was the eerie sense that someone was in the apartment. It must have been that primal instinct Lenora had talked about. I lay very still, keeping my eyes shut, and listened. Someone in the bathroom, moving around. I rolled off the bed and padded quietly to the door. I could see a man's back, bent over the bathroom sink, going through the medicine cabinet. A man too short to be Waldemar. I felt a prickle of fear lift the hair on the back of my neck. As he shut the door, the mirror gave me a quick glimpse of his face. It was Cliff.

There was no way I could leave without being seen. I tiptoed back to the bed and played possum. I heard him come into the room and lean down, breathing on my neck. As though I were asleep, I flung out one arm, groaned, and turned over. He jumped back, startled, and knocked the alarm clock off the nightstand. It crashed to the floor and began jangling crazily. I sat up, opened my eyes, and screamed. Cliff Paris dropped the clock again and jumped about a foot in the air.

"Jesus, Cliff. You scared me!" Hand to chest in my best Margaret Dumont imitation.

"Scared you? I just lost a year off my life. What are you doing here?"

The appropriate scripted response, I suppose, as to ask him what he was doing there, but I hate being a cliché. "I came to see Eve but I got here just as they were setting off on their bikes. I thought I'd laze around and wait until they came back, and then I fell asleep. It's been kind of a rough weekend."

I watched him slip from startled intruder to caring friend, relieved that I didn't ask the obvious question. Boy was I getting cynical. Pretty soon I was going to have to take a vacation away from the rest of the human race to get my perspective back. "I see you've hurt your hand," he said. "What happened?"

"It's a burn. When I got home on Friday night there was someone in my apartment who knocked me out and set the place on fire."

He sat down on the bed, shaking his head. "Sometimes it seems like the world is going to hell faster than we can comprehend. That must have been very frightening. And you have no idea who it was?"

"None. That is, I suspected it was an employee we'd just fired, especially since the intruder burned up my clothes, but the police say it wasn't her. So I have no idea . . . maybe a burglar who covers his tracks with arson?"

"Your boyfriend, that nice policeman, he wasn't around?"

"He appears to have ridden off into the sunset."

He put his hand over mine. Despite the heat of the room, I was chilled, and the warmth felt good. "I'm sorry to hear that. You deserve a lot more of the good stuff than you're getting. First your husband, then your sister. That's why you work so hard, isn't it?"

"I like my work," I said defensively.

"I know you do. It shows when you talk about it like you did the other night. I was very impressed. Too many people just walk through what they do without ever getting engaged. You're not like that. Whatever you get involved with, you take seriously. That's why I'm worried about this business with Eve."

"What business?"

He smiled. "Give me credit for some intelligence, Theadora, even if I am an old fogy, I wasn't born yesterday. We already talked about this. At my office on Friday. I must say, I'm a bit disappointed in you. I understood you to say you weren't going to get involved, didn't I?" I opened my mouth to speak but he shook his head. "Let me finish. I know who you've been talking to. Eve hasn't been exactly subtle, has she? And Norah is loyal, if a bit confused. And Mrs. Coffey?" He shrugged. "She's very confused. I don't know what she told you, but she hated Helene. It's hard to believe, but Martha once convinced Eve not to tell her mother that she was pregnant so that Martha could go with her for the abortion. Sort of sick, if you ask me. She sees everything through the filter of her own bad marriage."

Ordinarily, in my vaguely sick and dizzy state, depressed as I was about Andre, Cliff would have been the ideal person to be around. He'd always made me feel better. Not today. Today I felt like a twelve-year-old caught stealing from the local five-and-ten.

"That's the trouble with this so-called investigation you're conducting," he said. "Even if you had the time for it, which it seems you haven't, given how tired you look and the fact that you're falling asleep in strange places in the middle of the day, I wonder how you have the stomach for it. Getting the sordid details of Helene's and my life doled out in little bits and pieces by malicious informants can't be very pleasant, especially with Eve breathing down your neck."

"I'm just trying . . ."

"I know what you're trying to do. I think. You're trying to make her be reasonable. To see the whole picture. To stop being so obsessed. You've been trying to steer her straight as long as I've known you. I admire your loyalty, I truly do. She's very difficult. Most people would have given up on Eve by now. But I'm tired of this business. Tired of having her suspicions hanging over my head. What you're doing isn't going to help. You know Eve better than that. Nothing you tell her is going to change her mind. This is an emotional thing, not a reasoned one. Can you imagine how much it hurts me to have my only child suspect I murdered her mother?"

He had my injured hand between his, and as he spoke, he squeezed it tighter and tighter until my eyes stung with tears and I couldn't stand it any more. I jerked it back and cradled it protectively against my body, searching his face for signs of the malice I'd felt. All I saw was regret and sympathy. In his face. His eyes. His voice. "Oh, God! I've hurt you, haven't I? I'm so sorry. I was so carried away I forgot. May I see?"

He reached for it, and I fought the urge to refuse, to snatch it back as he pulled it toward him. To get up and run out of there and go home where I was safe. Ha. As if I was even safe there. Okay, so I'd let him look, make a few comforting noises, and then I'd get out of there. If there was still time before Eve came back. Why couldn't it be last Sunday? Then I'd at least have beer and clams and my good friend Suzanne to look forward to. It was very inconsiderate of her to go and get married just when I needed her most.

He started to peel the tape off and I closed my eyes. I wasn't good at blood, at pain, at injuries. It hurt more when he pulled the gauze loose, and when the air hit it, things escalated from just pain to agony. I clenched my teeth and tried to keep him from seeing. To distract myself, I said, "We didn't talk about Eve on Friday."

"Tuesday then. Or Wednesday," he said impatiently. "This hand is a mess. You haven't been taking care of it. I'll see what Eve's got."

I glanced at it. Ugly. A wide red swath across my palm with crusted, oozing blisters and raw skin underneath. Just looking at it made it hurt more. I reacted to the pain in my usual way—by getting angry and impatient. I didn't want to be fussed over. If he'd just left me alone, this wouldn't have been necessary. I knew Eve didn't have any Band-Aids, unless she'd bought more. Now I'd have to sit here while he tried to patch together some kind of makeshift dressing when I was chafing to be gone. I had to get to the office and do the rest of my preparation for tomorrow. Sarah was coming in specially to type the questionnaire. Then I had to get some food and get the sleep my tired body was begging for. He came back with gauze and adhesive tape. Despite the fact that I was seething like a pressure cooker, I managed to stay cool while he very competently and tenderly rebandaged my hand. As soon as he was done I jumped up. "Thanks, Cliff. I'll see you tomorrow."

"Shouldn't you take a few days off?" he said.

This from the guy who'd been breathing down the back of my neck for the past week, pushing me to get things underway. "I'll be fine. Really. This is nothing." Nothing but a hand that felt like I was wearing a red-hot boxing glove. "Tell Eve I'll call her later." It was a calculated remark. I didn't think he was there to see Eve. His response confirmed that.

"I don't think I'll stick around. Too hot in here." When he walked there was a rattling sound from his pocket. I stared. He noticed, then reached in and pulled out a vial of pills. "Eve puts too much faith in chemistry," he said. "From time to time I vet her medicine cabinet." He put the pills away.

Together we walked downstairs and out to our cars. It wasn't until I got out of the car at the office that I remembered the gloves. They were still in my pocket except for two little fingertips peeking out like tiny yellow ears. Well, it was too late to do anything about that now. I finished revising the questionnaire and left it on Sarah's desk, cursing Cliff every time I moved my injured hand. When I got home, I dug some heavy-duty oral analgesics out of the medicine cabinet and washed them down with a swig of fresh squeezed orange juice. If living well was the best revenge, I wasn't getting much. Revenge or anything else. No one had called, which was fine with me. I was feeling rabidly antisocial. I made myself a peanut butter sandwich and wolfed it down. Then, while there was still some daylight left, I put on my shorts and went for a walk on the beach. I had a lot on my mind and I didn't intend to think about any of it.

CHAPTER 23

I CAME BACK from my walk with a pocketful of shells and a better disposition. My good humor, inspired by the gorgeous weather and some healthy exercise, lasted through an hour of work out on the deck, where I basked like a happy turtle in the last warm rays of the sun. My hand didn't hurt much, thanks to the miracle of modern medicine, and the day was so lovely it was possible to ignore all the bad stuff that was going on. My good humor lasted until the phone rang. Even before I picked it up, I knew that it was going to ruin my mood. I should have trusted my intuition and let the machine get it. I almost said, "Hello, Eve," but it wasn't Eve, it was Andre. Asking a peculiar question.

"Thea, why do you have a bandage on your hand?"

No hello. No preliminaries. No apologies. Just that. Bastard, I thought. Here I am longing for you and you're cold as a stone. "Because I burned it in the fire." I could be just as terse as he could.

"Are you okay? Does it hurt?"

"No. Yes. I also have eight stitches in my head. Or maybe nine. I can't remember. They hurt, too. Was there anything else you wanted to know?"

"Who was that guy?"

That's right. Don't waste words, Detective, get right to the heart of things. "I told you. A cop. Officer Harris."

"He's a good looking guy, but awfully young. You should think about what you're getting into."

What was this? Yesterday the outraged lover and today he's trying to be my mother. After all this time, he ought to know better. "I always think about what I'm getting into before I take on a new project. I'm getting into the same things I always get into. Consulting contracts to help private schools. That's what I do, Andre. For a living. If you mean my midnight intruders with knives and arsonists and burglars, I didn't think about them because they were quite unexpected."

"Come on, Thea. I mean Harris. You expect me to believe he was there investigating? Over drinks at your place? At ten at night? With you dressed in your seduction clothes? What am I supposed to think?"

"You might have tried thinking the best, instead of the worst. You're supposed to trust me. You're supposed to believe me. You're supposed to be here for me when someone tries to kill me. When I'm scared and hurt and all alone. Not running away and then calling up and yelling at me."

"But I didn't know. . . ."

"Whose fault was that? I wasn't the one playing hide-and-seek. I called you. You were nowhere to be found. Maybe if you'd been here Friday night . . ."

"Okay, so I'm sorry. I thought you were calling to make me feel bad about the wedding, so I was avoiding you. And what happens? When I do show up, I find you with another guy. What am I supposed to think?"

He was breaking my heart. Why couldn't he just say he was sorry? That he'd missed me? That he was on his way? "Oh, I don't know, Lemieux. Maybe that I'm the woman who loves you, even if things aren't easy for us right now. That he was there for an innocent purpose even if he was male? Why can't you get it through your head that I'm not your ex-wife? That I'm not going to fall into bed with the next available man because we've had a fight. It doesn't show much respect for me, you know. What was wrong with listening to me? Hearing what I had to say? Why would I have lied to you about who he was?"

"You wouldn't be the first woman who ever lied to me."

There it was again. The specter of his ex-wife. She'd lied and manipulated and jerked him around till he was twisted like a pretzel, until he had the good sense to take a hike. It wasn't just being a cop that had taught him not to show his feelings; he'd learned a lot of it from her. If he didn't show her how he felt, there was less for her to work with. Surprisingly, he'd come out of it still open and decent, but when that distrust lined up with his temper, he could be a pretty pigheaded guy. That's what he was being right now and I didn't see how I could change his mind.

"I know that women have lied to you. But I didn't. I don't know . . . I might be the first woman who ever didn't lie to you, but I don't think there's anything I can do to convince you of that, not if you've already got your mind made up. You could call the police department and talk to Harris. You could ask him what was going on." I waited to see if he'd respond but his end was silent. "No comment? Well, right now, I'm tired and I hurt. I still have a lot of work to do before tomorrow and I have to figure out what to wear since all my work clothes got burned up. All I can say is that I love you and I'd be happy to talk, or walk, or sleep with you when you get over this heavy macho wronged-lover act, but as long as you're determined to be an asshole, please leave me alone."

I managed to be brave on the phone, but the call left me shaky, and the next one didn't help. One from Eve. Her earlier good spirits seemed to have vanished; like Andre, she was suspicious and unfriendly. I gave her an outline of what I'd learned, skirting carefully around the question of Helene's secret life by suggesting only that her mother might have had other men. I shouldn't have bothered. She was not at all receptive to what I had to tell her. Her position continued to be that I wasn't a true friend unless I could prove her father guilty, something which any true friend would find easy in the face of the overwhelming evidence available.

Despite our agreement, she wasn't at all willing to consider what I had learned, or to entertain the many possibilities it suggested.

"Lenora says you didn't really listen to her. She says you just kept suggesting other possibilities."

"Questioning her assumptions, Eve. Collecting information. That's what we agreed I'd do."

"We agreed you'd help me prove that Cliff..."

"No, Eve. We had an agreement that I'd talk to people and tell you what I learned. What I learned is that no one has any solid evidence that Cliff was involved. Things are no clearer now that I've spoken with people than they were before."

"You're just like all the rest, Thea," she said.

"What is that supposed to mean? That you have several other people out there asking questions who've come to the same conclusion, or that since I haven't been able to reach the conclusion you want me to, I am disloyal and unworthy and thus relegated to the scrap heap?"

"Exactly," she said.

"Exactly what? There were two choices in that question."

"You're on the scrap heap," she said. "This isn't some sort of joke, you know. My mother is dead. You can laugh about it. Cliff can go around being happy, but that doesn't mean I've forgotten. Maybe it would help if you could see some pictures. Maybe if you saw what he did to her, you wouldn't take this so lightly. . . ."

"Yeah, I noticed you looked as depressed as hell when you rode off on your bike today." Once I got started, I couldn't stop.

Eve had finally pushed the reject button, and for once, friendship, past loyalties and sympathy for her loss didn't override my impulse. "You're so fixated on your own situation you don't give a damn about anyone else. While you've been recruiting your sources to monopolize my answering machine, and while I've been scurrying around fitting in interviews with all those people around my busy schedule and my partner's wedding, I've had to chase away a midnight intruder with a knife and spent an evening in the emergency room after someone knocked me out, set my place on fire and burned up all my clothes. You aren't the only one with troubles."

"I had no way of knowing that," she said flatly.

"Except the only way people know anything about each other—by asking. Even if you were too distracted to trouble yourself with minor civilities, like noticing that I have a bandaged hand and asking if I'm okay, there's still the fact that I've done what you asked, and it hasn't been easy, believe me, hearing the things people have to say about Helene." I stopped myself, but it was too late. I'd gone too far.

"What do you mean? What are people saying about my mother?"

"She had an interesting personal life."

"They're lying, Thea. Lying. All of them. Which one was it? What did she say? I have a right to know."

"The people I've talked to believe they spoke in confidence. I can't tell you."

"You'd better tell me," she said, her voice shrill and rising. "They only talked to you because I asked them to. They were only supposed to talk about Cliff. Cliff and his relationship with Helene. That's all that was relevant. I can't believe they let themselves go and gossiped like that. Bitches. I want to know everything, Thea. I insist."

Now she had me yelling, too. "When I agreed to do this, you agreed to listen to what I had to say and consider it. Now I've told you there's nothing. There's nothing which singles Cliff out. So they fought? Most people do. So she took a self-defense course? Lenora says that's because of a patient's husband. It could have been that husband. So Helene wouldn't give him a divorce? He still could have gotten one. This isn't the Dark Ages. People can get divorces even if their spouses don't want them to. . . ."

"He didn't want a fight," she interrupted. "Have you told all this to the police?"

"Yes, I have . . . but listen . . ."

"Then why haven't they arrested him?"

"You aren't listening. Because they have no reason to, Eve. It could have been a case of mistaken identity. It could have been a stranger, or someone she'd been involved with. If she was scared enough to take a self-defense course, that suggests something on-going, someone she was afraid of. Lenora says someone was following her; Cliff didn't need to do that. If she was afraid of Cliff, she could have just moved out. It could just as easily have been someone who threatened her, or one of her lovers, or Martha Coffey, Lenora Stern, Rowan Ansel, or even you."

I was trying to make her take a balanced view, to see how inconclusive her information was. "I don't know what else I can do, Eve. But you've got to see that I tried. That like you, I only want to make things right again. I loved your mother. . . ."

She didn't take it that way. "I hate you," she said. "You're not my friend. How dare you accuse me . . . accuse our neighbors . . . her friends . . . suggest that my mother was a . . . I can't even bring myself to say it . . . it's obscene . . . filthy . . . indecent to even suggest. I never would have dreamed you could stoop so low, even to protect him. When are you going to stop seeing him through rose-colored glasses? No one stood to gain by her death the way he did. Would you see things my way if I was paying you? If I could offer you a fat consulting contract? My ever practical friend with her eye on the bottom line. I was a fool to suppose that our friendship meant enough to keep you objective."

I'd listened to enough. I didn't care if it was hysteria or grief. I was neither masochistic enough nor other-directed enough to take any more abuse. "I'm not the one who's having trouble being objective, Eve. I realize what I've told you is upsetting; I appreciate your frustration about not having your theory proved. I even admire you for being so determined to find your mother's killer. I was the same about Carrie, but what you're doing is trying to shoot the messenger because you don't like the message. You've got to face the facts, Eve. Your mother had a secret life—dozens of lovers, staying out all night. . . ."

Oops. I'd let her get me so upset I was blurting out everything. Well, too bad for her. There was too much pretending going on. It was time for the truth. "Didn't you know about that?"

"That's a lot of bullshit. I don't know what you're talking about. My mother wouldn't have . . ." she began. I hung up on her.

Her presence haunted me for a while. Images from our years together. Of her perched on the stool in Helene's kitchen, her head bobbing, her bright eyes fixed on me and Andre, shattered and helpless. The pain in her voice describing the way Helene had died. I was gripped by doubt. Was I being too hard? Judging her too harshly? Asking too much of her, so soon after the event? The "good kid, fixer" part of me wondered if I'd tried hard enough, but my common sense agreed with Cliff that she'd never listen to anything I said that didn't prove her point. It was time to let it go, give it up, and get on with my own life. Eventually I was able to put her out of my mind and get to work.

When Cliff called to see how I was doing and reiterated his request that I stop helping Eve, I told him that was exactly what I intended to do.

Comfortable in gym shorts and David's baggy old sweatshirt, I curled up on my new sofa and immersed myself in refinements of the Bartlett Hill project. The sofa gave off a rich, leathery smell and felt wonderful against my skin. I felt sinful and self-indulgent as I dug my toes down into its buttery soft surface.

Tomorrow Lisa and I were going to begin a series of interviews designed to give us an inside picture of what the hospital was like. How it worked. How the staff perceived it. Later, we would expand the picture by getting the views of patients and former patients, where possible, of their families and referring clinicians, and then the views of potential referral sources. When I wasn't being scared that it was too different from what we usually did for us to do a good job, I was excited about the possibilities of the project. I take challenges very personally, thriving on them even when they're scaring me to death.

At ten I got the munchies, made myself a big bowl of popcorn, and decided to let Jack take his hat off. I made him keep the hat right beside him, and banished him to the cupboard as soon as I'd seen enough of him. Before I met David, I considered bourbon and popcorn to be one of the basic food groups. He'd changed all that. The man was constantly hungry, rail thin, and extremely grateful for every meal. Feeding him was always a challenge. No matter how much I cooked, or how much he ate, he was always ready for more, and never gained an ounce. For a few brief years I was a model of domesticity, if you can be considered domestic when you and your husband do the dishes together as fast as you can and then play two hours of killer tennis. David embraced physical activity with the same enthusiasm he had for food. We were a pair of lean, mean, fighting machines. After he died, I filled up all my time with work, and often forgot about eating entirely. I rarely allowed myself the kind of leisure that goes with bourbon and popcorn.

I immersed myself in a black-and-white movie in which the voluptuous Jane Russell sauntered around from dawn till midnight in strapless, skintight dresses, wondering how my clients would react if I showed up at 9:00 A.M. in a sarong. Vincent Price was using his big-game hunting skills to save Robert Mitchum when the doorbell rang. The same instincts which had warned me not to answer the phone told me who, among the many possible suspects, would be standing on the doorstep. Nevertheless, I peeked cautiously through the peephole and determined that it was not a foe before I undid all the locks. I opened it to Andre, standing on the doorstep, holding an armload of lilacs.

"Instant replay?" he asked.

"More like a twenty-four-hour delay," I said, throwing myself at him. "What took you so long?" Once again the lilacs did not get much consideration.

When we came up for air, after a kiss that would have met "Crash" Davis's standards, he murmured, "Bourbon and popcorn."

"Great detecting, Trooper," I said, "you want some?"

"I was hoping for something a bit more substantial, but I know what your refrigerator is like. And there's something else I wanted first."

"I might surprise you." His eyebrows went up. "About the refrigerator, I mean."

"Later," he said, putting his arms around me and waltzing me toward the bedroom.

"Did I show you my new couch?" I asked.

"What?"

"My new couch." I led him over to it. "Just run your hand over that leather."

"I'd rather run it over you."

"I was just sitting here thinking how good it would feel against my skin."

He shook his head. "Uh oh. Sounds like the lady has been neglected."

"And whose fault is that?"

"And you want to try out your new couch?"

"Well, the idea had occurred to me."

"Not to be too blunt or anything, but as long as I can get close to you, I don't care if it's in a broom closet." I started across the room. "Now where are you going?" he said.

"To turn off the lights, unless you'd like this to be a public performance. The curtains are at the cleaners. They were a mess after the fire."

He took off his shirt and dropped it on the coffee table, then undid his belt. "Ready when you are."

"You usually are," I said, smiling for what felt like the first time in days, and snapped off the lights.

CHAPTER 24

WE HAD A midnight supper of steak and eggs and fried potatoes. Thanks to the miracle of microwaving I was able to precook the potato and defrost the steak while the grill warmed up and I sautéed the peppers and onions. Then Andre took the steaks outside and cooked them while I scrambled the eggs and mixed them with the veggies in one pan and fried potatoes with lots of fresh ground black pepper in another. I love fried potatoes so much it's a miracle I don't weigh four hundred pounds. Forget about fancy aftershaves. If a man came down the street smelling like fried potatoes, I'd follow him anywhere.

I was wearing my gym shorts and Yale sweatshirt. Andre was wearing a threadbare athletic shirt and cutoff sweats and we were truly an elegant couple. After a long winter being bundled up, all that exposed skin was almost too much, leading to a lot of not-quite-accidental touching and bumping. I was tempted to abandon the meal and drag him, like the cavewoman I am, back to my lair, but I exercised self-restraint, or maybe I just sublimated my desires onto the food. Neither of us approached the meal with finicky appetites. We washed it down with the champagne Andre had brought, accompanied by a mound of English muffins smeared with cherry jam. Nothing like a little exercise to stimulate the appetite. The couch had felt just as good as I'd imagined it would, but maybe I was prejudiced by the fact that everything in the past two hours had felt pretty good. "So what did you think of the new couch?" I asked.

"Nice," he said, "real nice, if you don't mind sex on a surface that creaks like a saddle. It gave things a certain down-home, outdoorsy flair. Come on." He put an arm around my shoulders. "These dishes can wait till morning. We need to get some sleep."

"As long as it's just sleep."

"Scout's honor," he said.

A foolish rhyme I'd heard once popped into my head.

> In sexual bouts,
> And nocturnal rides,
> The boy scouts,
> And the girl guides.

My mind was definitely grade B tonight. By the time I'd finished filling him in on what had happened while he was hiding out in the wilds of Maine, and he'd shared the latest trials and tribulations in pursuit of the bad guys, there wasn't much night left for sleeping, but we made the best of it, curling up like two spoons and falling, in a warm, companionable way, off the edge of the earth.

When the alarm rang at seven, it took a lot of willpower not to shut it off and go back to sleep. Not surprising, given my choices. Here I had Andre, warm and sleepy, his handsome face relaxed and dark with his aggressive beard, one strong bare shoulder uncovered, inviting me to touch him, wake him up and see his ready grin, the warmth in his shiny dark eyes. At Bartlett Hill there'd be Cliff, charming, enigmatic and irritated with me, his greedy, mercurial friend Rowan, and the decidedly unpleasant Roddy Stokes. What a choice. I lingered in bed another ten minutes, avoiding the inevitable moment when my Protestant guilt would take over

and march me to the shower, savoring the warmth, my contentment, my sense that here I was completely safe.

When I finally did try to get up, Andre threw a strong arm
around and pulled me back against him. "Prisoner," he muttered
sleepily. "Can't leave."

"I'm a working girl," I reminded him. "Gotta go."

"Mmmm. Yeah. You work just fine," he said, nuzzling my
neck.

"Don't start with me, Lemieux," I protested. "I absolutely,
positively must be at work at nine."

"I'll be quick."

"If that was what I wanted, man, I could find it on any street
corner."

"So I'll be slow."

His hands were doing irresistible things to me, and with a sigh,
I resigned myself to the inevitable. "But you'll have to make
breakfast."

"No sweat," he said. And sure enough, when I'd showered and
found the only serviceable summer dress that hadn't been in-
cinerated, the table was set, a slightly bedraggled pot of lilacs in
the center, and he was just pouring my coffee.

"You'd make someone a fine wife," I said.

"Sorry, not my thing. I'm into women."

"So I've noticed. What's this thing?" I pointed to what looked
like a large dried fish lying on a plate.

"Smoked alewife. Cute little thing, isn't it?"

"That's not quite how I would have described it. What does
one do with it?"

"One eats it. Like kippers, or smoked whitefish, or . . ."

"Or maybe we could save it for another day. I'm not sure my
public is ready for an interviewer with smoked fish breath."

"I'm hurt," he said. "That is a token of my undying love and
affection."

I scrutinized the thing. It was flat, with dried, wrinkled, yel-
lowish skin, sunken eyeballs and a bony, gaping jaw. "Yeah, I'd

say that's a fair characterization. Your undying love and affection, as demonstrated recently, was sort of flat, unresponsive and unappealing."

"No one, madam, has ever been so critical of my John Thomas before."

"Thought all you cops called it your Johnson. Anyway, lest we get confused here, I was not referring to your anatomy, I was referring to your behavior."

"If I promise never to do it again?"

"You'll do it again." I think we'd both learned something from the past week: the way to true love—or in our case, the way to a lasting relationship—was not going to be linear or smooth. There'd probably be more of these little glitches and maybe it wasn't such a bad thing after all. No one ever said life was going to be painless. "I think this is a relationship which is fated to have ups and downs. Right now I don't care."

"Maybe you're right," he said, snatching the last muffin from under my fingers. "Neither one of us is easy to live with. Whether you call it pigheaded or just strong-willed, we both want things our way and we're both sure we're right. We both tend to lock up our emotions to keep people out. We both need a lot of time alone. . . ."

"You make us sound like twins."

"No. You're a better cook. I'm neater. You're more willing to talk about things once you get going. I'm more controlling. I tend to tell you what to do. You're willing to give me more space, but I think we're connected by a bungee cord. Sometimes it's going to be stretched to the limits, but we'll always bounce back."

"Pretty poetic, mister. Can I assume from this we're ready to resume our commitment of an unspecified nature?" He nodded, and we left it at that. Gratifying as it was that he was finally willing to talk, we didn't have the time. Love in the fast lane, that was us. "Is there anything else around here to eat besides the fish?"

"You'd like it if you tried it." I made a face. "Guess you're out of luck, then. We ate it all last night. I can give you some more coffee, though. You know that's as much as you usually get. Unless you want popcorn."

"I'll pass. I assume when I get back you will have vanished like the morning mist?"

"I'm afraid so." The bantering tone had gone out of his voice. Neither of us was eager to face another separation. "The bad guys just keep shooting each other, stabbing each other, and killing their kids, with no consideration for me." Unfortunately, it was true. Even in supposedly peaceful, idyllic rural Maine, the level of violence was rising. People were shot, stabbed or drowned to keep them from revealing information about minor robberies. They might not be killing each other over jackets or high-tops yet, but the value of human life was definitely diminished. The State of Maine needed Andre Lemieux as much as I did, in a different but compelling way.

"I could come up for the weekend." A generous offer. Usually he came to me because he was the one with energy left on Friday nights.

"It's a deal. Bring a pot roast. And one of those great key lime pies? And homemade cinnamon rolls?"

One of the ways to this man's heart was definitely through his stomach. Ironic, though, that a modern woman like me should keep ending up with men who loved me for my body and my cooking. "What about my mind?"

"Okay," he said, "bring that, too. I'm sure we'll find a use for it."

I almost threw the fish at him, but he might have thrown it back, and not only would a game of fish toss waste time I didn't have, I had no more clothes to wear, and I wasn't sure the denizens of Bartlett Hill would react positively to an interviewer daubed with a large smear of smoked fish. I lingered until the last possible moment, knowing I'd have to drive like a maniac to get there for my first appointment. "You remember the alarm code?" He nodded. "And lock the door behind you." He walked me to the door, his face gloomy. "Please don't take this the wrong way."

He hesitated. "I know you didn't like it when I said this before, but I'm going to say it again. I'm glad you're giving up this inquiry for Eve. You shouldn't feel guilty about it, either. You did your best, I know, and I also know how much you hate to leave things unfinished, especially where friends are involved. Leave it to Florio. He's a good detective."

"They invited us for breakfast on Sunday. I think he was heartbroken you didn't show up. He liked you a lot."

"Probably likes you, too."

"We fight a lot."

His grin was wicked. "Why am I not surprised?"

"Cuz you know me so well, honeypie," I said, nuzzling his neck. "Don't worry, I'll be careful. No missions, causes or crusades. Eve was driving me crazy anyway. I'm gonna be a serious working girl until Friday and then I'm going to drive straight to you."

"You'd better. I'll be worrying. Seriously. I don't like the idea of being so far away when someone's hanging around who wants to hurt you. Promise you'll be careful?"

"Don't go all mushy on me, Andre. I like my men cold and hard."

"I think you mean warm and hard." He leered in a perfect imitation of his would-be friend Tiny Anderson, the three-hundred-pound car salesman, and closed the door. I trotted off to the car, keys out, jammed them into the ignition, and roared off like I was at Monte Carlo. For the first time in as long as I could remember, I'd had a decent evening and a decent morning. I didn't know if that was a good sign or not, but I was going to be too busy to worry about it.

They were mowing the grass at Bartlett Hill and the air smelled good. Lisa was waiting beside her car, watching the clouds blow by. "I should be taking my baby to the park on a day like this. Look at me. Pencil poised, my ruined figure squeezed into the only skirt I can zip, about to leave all this loveliness behind and begin stalking the dark corridors of mental health." She offered me a stack of papers. "I stopped by to get these. Charlotte came along and had a fit because she couldn't stay in the office and play."

This was no time for her to have an attack of maternal guilt. I needed her help. "Dark corridors indeed! Don't let the client hear you say that. They believe their work leads to enlightenment, insight, and clarity. Besides, if you stayed outside, you'd only get frustrated. Just as you were beginning to bask in the sun and relax, Charlotte would need to go home for a nap, or drop her pacifier in the mud, or the top would come off her bottle and cover both of you with apple juice."

She looked at me suspiciously. "How do you know so much? You've never been a mother."

"I haven't spent my life in a cave, either. What time do you need to leave?"

Her smile was impish. "I have to deliver some milk around noon, but after that I can come back until five. I was going to get a sitter, but Josh's mother insisted she wanted to watch Charlotte. I'd be a fool to turn down an offer like that."

It was good to have Lisa back. Clients loved her and she was a speed demon when it came to work. Despite her complaints about her ruined figure, today she looked very nice. Her suit was stylish without being showy, a short black skirt topped with a fitted magenta jacket detailed in black with shiny black buttons. One of the buttons was smudged. "Looks like you've got cereal on your button."

"If that's all that's wrong, I'll be lucky. I'm thinking of opening a business kind of like a diaper service that would deliver a week's worth of colorful dusters, kind of like the lab coats doctors wear, to working mothers, so they can get dressed for work, slip one of these on over their clothes, mother like crazy, and then slip it into a discard bin outside the door on their way out. Presto, leaving them with clean clothes. Once a week, the driver picks up the old dusters and leaves you a new batch. There is nothing more humiliating than walking around thinking you look like a million dollars and then discovering that all the while you've had a long white trail of baby spit down your back."

"A laudable idea, but only if you promise to wait until we've done these projects."

"Not to worry." She shook her head and her dark, precision-cut hair flew out and settled neatly back into place. I felt a twinge of envy. My hair has never, even for a moment, been neat. "The last thing I want is to be my own boss. I'd make me work too hard. You know what I mean?"

Which, of course, I did. Cliff was waiting in his office with a schedule. Today he seemed to have regained his enthusiasm for the project. He welcomed Lisa with a warmth and interest that quickly had her glowing. Over coffee, which Roddy served without scowling or spilling on us, we discussed how to proceed. "Would you prefer to be assigned a room, and have people come to you, or would you rather interview people in their own offices?" Cliff asked. "I assumed their offices, but we could change that."

"Where do you think we'd be likely to get better responses? People are always happier if you go to them. It makes them feel more in control. The question is whether, if they are in their own offices, they might also be reluctant to divulge information because they're so used to protecting privacy and keeping things confidential in those settings. What do you think, Cliff?"

"You've made a good point," he said, "but this is also a time-sensitive institution. Many of the people you'll be interviewing have busy schedules. It would help if you could go to them. Let's try it that way and see how it works. If, after today, you think we should change the method, we can. Now, here are your schedules, and Roddy has marked the locations in blue on these maps, so you should be able to find your way around. If you don't mind wearing them, these name tags will let you move more freely."

We each got our schedules, maps, and plastic badges that identified us as consultants. We also got a conference room to use as our headquarters, a small, airless, pale yellow cubicle which smelled of bad coffee and rotting apple cores. "Nice," Lisa said, inspecting it. "I wonder if he expected us to do our interviews in here?"

"Not exactly full of ambience, is it?"

She pulled out a chair, sat down, got up, tried another one, rejected that, and finally found a third that seemed to satisfy her. "Broken. Both of them. Do you suppose this is some kind of psychological test? I'll bet that's a two-way mirror." She pointed at the wall, where curtains were pulled back to reveal a gray, mirror-like slab of glass. "And I hate being watched." She got up and closed the curtains. "Well, boss. Any last instructions before we have at 'em?" We went over the things I'd identified last night, agreed to meet again at 4:30 to review the day, and then Lisa left to begin her interviews.

My first interview was with Rowan Ansel. Deliberate, I was sure. As long as he didn't hit me with any doors, and I kept the conversation focused on Bartlett Hill, it should be okay. No confessions. No conversations about Helene's death. No discussions about Eve. This was strictly business. I took a deep breath, located the questionnaire with his name on it, and marched down the hall to his office.

CHAPTER 25

LISA AND I conferred at the end of the day, declared our progress satisfactory, and parted company with a commitment to meet again the next morning. She looked a little guilty when she told me that she could only work half the day. "It's Josh's mother. She promised to watch Charlotte even after I explained I was committed for three whole days. I know I told her that and I know she nodded when I asked if she was sure she could do it. But at lunch when I went to nurse Charlotte, my mother-in-law informed me that she was only available until noon tomorrow because she always plays tennis on Tuesdays." She sighed. "I called my baby-sitter, but she'd already made plans. She can take her on Wednesday, though. Maybe I'm just being paranoid, but I think this is part of a plan to keep me from working."

It was frustrating, but I knew it wasn't her fault. Lisa needed to work to keep herself sane, and I needed her to work to keep me sane. It wasn't the first time Lisa's mother-in-law had conspired to screw up Lisa's life, and therefore mine. She liked to change appointments at the last minute, forcing Lisa to scramble around rearranging things to accommodate her. Any refusal to cooperate brought on sulks and accusations and a massive display of injured feelings. In the office, we'd devised a creative way of handling the woman. On days when Lisa planned to meet her mother-in-law, Sarah or Magda would field the call and declare Lisa either out of the office and then going on to a lunch meeting, or in conference where she could not be disturbed.

Sarah, especially, had enjoyed handling the calls. When asked to interrupt a conference to inform Lisa that the scheduled lunch would have to be moved to later, she always took great pleasure in informing Mrs. Elliot that Lisa's schedule could not accommodate a schedule change and suggesting she arrange for another day. That always left Mrs. Elliot sputtering and backing down and Sarah grinning maliciously. "It's too bad we can't just get Sarah to deal with your mother-in-law."

"Don't I wish! Well, it won't happen again. I'm afraid I'm about to be on her blacklist forever, because when I pick Charlotte up tomorrow, I'm going to tell her we can't do this anymore, that I need reliable child care so Charlotte will go to a sitter on Wednesday, and Mrs. E is going to get all huffy and treat it as my refusal to let her see her grandchild. Sometimes I wish we lived in another city."

It was a situation I could relate to. My mother, like Mrs. Elliot, liked to be in control and was affronted when I thwarted her. She also found my lifestyle unacceptable, both the romance and the work sides. She wanted me settled down and married and doing respectable things like polishing my furniture and joining the Junior League. As she kept reminding me, soon I'd be too old to join. She was also beginning to breathe down my neck about grandchildren. It looked like I was her only hope. My brother Michael's girlfriend Sonia, assuming they ever got around to considering children—an unlikely scenario since they were both so selfish—was so sour she'd curdle his sperm. And Michael was still a child himself. I laughed aloud at the notion of an army of little helmeted sperm, charging forth on a procreation mission, encountering Sonia's hostile environment. "Back up, guys," I could hear them shout, "it's a death trap ahead." Too many Woody Allen films, I guess.

"What's so funny?" Lisa asked.

"Thinking about your family got me thinking about my family. I guess every family has its dysfunctional elements."

"I think the functional family is a myth."

"So, speaking of dysfunctional, how'd your day go?"

"It was good. Can you believe no one asked me how I felt about anything?"

"As long as you found out how they felt about things."

"In spades. They were dying to talk about Bartlett Hill. If I had to summarize, I'd say: first, it's a great place. Best clinical treatment facility in the area. Second, they're too tight with money and regulations and don't understand how clinicians work. Third, Cliff Paris walks on water."

"Sounds like my day, too. Only one person suggested it might be a good idea to look into the water."

"Clever. Well, I'd better run, before the front of this suit gets soaked with milk. Nasty thing to think about, isn't it. See what you have to look forward to?"

"That was an aspect I hadn't considered. No matter. Motherhood isn't imminent. I'm still enjoying being a swinging bachelorette."

"Now there's an ugly word."

"Swinging?"

"Bachelorette. Sounds like the degree you'd get from a girls' junior college. Besides, you can't be one of those. You've been married. You want an ugly diminutive, try widowette. See you tomorrow."

I stopped to check with Roddy about picking up our appointment schedules in the morning. Once again it was a pleasure. He had a doughnut bag on his desk and powdered sugar down the front of his shirt. There was a smudge of jam on his cheek. He glared at me like I'd interrupted some very important work.

"Don't let me disturb your feast," I said. "I just wondered what time Cliff planned for us to start in the morning. Does he want to meet first or do we just pick up schedules?"

"Schedules," he said rudely. He picked up two sheets of paper, shook off the sugar, and handed them to me. "He doesn't need to see you." As if I wasn't there, he pulled another doughnut out of the bag and bit into it.

I couldn't resist antagonizing him a little. "You do understand why we're here, don't you?" He glared at me. "That's right. We're here to find ways of making Bartlett Hill a more attractive place to refer patients. How do you suppose your behavior and your attitude fit into that analysis?"

"I don't know what you're talking about," he said.

"That's what I was afraid of." I stuck the schedules in my briefcase and left. A lot of women can blame their hostile behavior on PMS, but I don't suffer from PMS. I just have a mean streak.

Outside, in the waning daylight, I felt the meanness recede, replaced by a kind of contentment. It's easy to be disagreeable in winter, when the weather matches my moods, but spring is so inviting and alive, it makes being grouchy seem silly. After the craziness and sadness of the past week, it was nice to be doing regular work on a reasonable schedule and not filling in all the crannies with hurried interviews, wedding preparations, phone calls and meetings. Sure I was on my way back to the office and I'd probably work there another couple hours, but it all seemed so normal without the wedding and Eve and Florio and Valeria also hanging over me.

My father had been delighted to get the affidavits and basically assured me that we were home free. I hadn't told my parents about the midnight intruder. They worry too much, and I wasn't about to try and fend off an invitation to go and live at home until the culprit was caught. I had no basis except intuition for my belief that the nocturnal visits were over—that and Harris's grudging admission about the local burglar—but I wasn't anxious anymore. I'd been in some pretty scary situations in my life, and when they were over I put them behind me and went on. I was too busy to dwell on the what ifs and what nexts.

How could I not feel good? With fear of the midnight visitor and the burden of Eve's request off my mind, I felt almost giddily light. So what if I'd earned her undying scorn? I wasn't Hercules. I didn't need to perform a series of difficult tasks to earn her forgiveness. I'd done what I promised and that was enough. I could sympathize with her situation and understand her grief without continuing to be drawn into her emotional morass.

No one could fix it for her. Eve would have to find her own happiness.

I knew very well how compelling the need for some resolution of a loved one's death could be. I'd gone through it with Carrie, determined to go ahead with my search over the objections of my entire family. In the end I'd found her killer, but it hadn't brought about a magical catharsis or a swell of satisfaction. Life isn't that simple. I'd achieved a resolution, but it had been a sad one. And Carrie was just as dead, still irretrievably lost. I'd had to learn to live with that. As with David, the hurt and the loss have never completely gone away. Yet I thought of myself as an optimist, remembering the good about them, and generally finding the good in life. Maybe that's why I could be so happy today.

I'd also resolved the Andre question. The mental daisy plucking, the "he loves me, he loves me not," that I'd tried unsuccessfully to ignore had been laid to rest. We were back where we'd been before, or maybe we were closer, though to what, whether it was commitment or just mutual understanding, I didn't know. Maybe romance is never clearer than that.

I stood there gazing out over the rolling green lawns, warm sun on my back, and indulged in an enormous stretch, throwing my arms wide, bringing them slowly up over my head and slowly back down again. It was time to get back to aerobics. I was getting stiff.

"Penny for your thoughts," a voice behind me said. A coin dropped with a metallic clang onto the hood of my car. Cliff was standing there with his briefcase, unlocking his car.

"Daydreaming, I'm afraid. Must be a touch of spring fever."

"It's awfully nice, isn't it. Though it takes me weeks to finally trust that it won't snow again. How did things go today?" I had the sense he was suppressing his interest, trying not to seem too eager. I'd forgotten how excited he'd been about the project—excited and hopeful—his board was looking over his shoulder on this one.

"It's too early in the process to reach any conclusions, but today went well. We're enjoying your staff, and they're being very cooperative. They all think you walk on water."

The wind ruffled his gold and silver hair. I studied him, taking in his slim, elegantly dressed body and his well-worn handsome face. Sunglasses hid his eyes, and nowhere else could I detect a trace of the sorrow I'd seen the other day. "Oh, I do," he said, "but the maintenance on the underwater structures is very expensive. That's why we need you. To help us bring in the money we need to keep the illusions alive."

"Illusions? I thought you were here to help people?"

"We are. Part of how we help them is creating the illusion that we are a special place where they can be confident they'll get help. Or the people who refer them can." He opened the door and put the briefcase in, then he took off his jacket and rolled up his sleeves. He pushed his glasses up onto his head and squinted at his watch, looking impatiently toward the building. He was wearing a light blue shirt with wide darker blue stripes which emphasized the blue of his eyes. "Are you feeling better today?" It sounded perfunctory, as if he didn't really care. Something was bothering him but I didn't know what.

"Much. I don't see how anyone could feel bad in this weather."

"It's hard." He looked over my shoulder at someone whose approaching footsteps were crunching on the gravel. "So there you are. I was afraid you'd forgotten." Whoever it was got the warm, welcoming smile I'd missed. Rowan Ansel, in white shorts and shirt, carrying a tennis racket, walked around to the passenger's side and got into the car, his greeting a mere nod. "See you tomorrow, Thea," Cliff said. "I hope you don't mind. I've scheduled you for appointments until seven. There were some people I wanted you to talk to who weren't available earlier. Did Eve find you?"

"Was she trying to?"

"She called this morning, looking for you. I didn't want to disturb you, so I told her to try you around lunch time. She was going to leave a message for you to call her. Guess you didn't get it?"

I shook my head. "I thought she'd stopped speaking to me." There was an odd note in his voice that I couldn't identify. A warning? An admonition? Too subtle for me. If there was something he wanted me to know, he'd have to be clearer than that. I'd told him my efforts for Eve were over. If he didn't believe me, he could say so. "A long schedule tomorrow is no problem. We're used to it. See you in the morning." I left them in a laughing, animated conversation, trying not to hear Eve's words about her father's unseemly happiness. Even sad people are entitled to the occasional light moment.

The stacks on my desk perfectly reflected the personalities of the three people who'd left them. Everything Magda had left for me was in a folder and the entire stack was capped with a detailed memo explaining what sort of action was needed in each of the underlying categories. On the other side of the desk Sarah had arranged my own stuff. First the inevitable heap of pink slips, held together with a giant acrylic clothespin that had my name on it. Beneath them were things she'd typed for me, some of them topped with little sticky notes featuring the Cheshire Cat's irritating smirk, raising questions in her untamed scrawl. Below them, clipped together, was the day's mail. The last sheet was a typed memo, but unlike Magda's, it was very simple. "When you get here," it said, "put everything back on the desk, go to aerobics, get yourself a sandwich, and come back refreshed. Bobby was sad and lonely today. You need to give him more to do. Sarah."

"Okay, Sarah," I said. "I'll do it." I left Bobby's pile, neat but with a daunting number of oversized question marks, for my return, and spent an hour sweating like a pig while the divine Aaron, barely clad in a brief, form-fitting unitard, leapt and danced like a maddened pixie. I showered, secured a sandwich and headed back to work. I was waylaid by the realization that I had nothing to wear to work and Suzanne wasn't around to help me. Grimly, I veered from my fixed course into the parking lot of a high-fashion discount store and forced my unwilling legs across the parking lot and into the too bright fluorescent interior. Like all such places, it smelled like old lady perfume. I resigned myself to a miserable hour.

Despite the fact that my build was supposedly every man's dream—a fact which had made my teenage years miserable, since most of the boys only came up to my chest, and that was all they wanted to look at anyway—clothes were rarely designed to accommodate my dimensions. By the time I found a size to fit my chest, the shoulder seams were halfway to my elbows and the sleeves came to my fingertips. And I have long arms. I headed for the suit rack, grabbed an armload of them and a few simple blouses, and carried them into the common dressing room.

My theory about common dressing rooms, where everyone stands around in a huge square walled with mirrors and tries on their clothes, used to be that we all have flaws so why be self-conscious. This place was an exception. Maybe the same people who care about fashionable clothes also care about their figures. I couldn't say. All I knew was that the women here seemed to have unacceptably nice shapes, no matter what their age. Grimly, I hung my possibilities on a hook, piled my own clothes up on the bench, and started trying things on. Ten suits later, I got dressed again, feeling like the hunchback of Notre Dame. How was it possible that nothing in my size fit me?

"Excuse me, dear," the pleasant-faced, henna-haired woman beside me said, "you're just not choosing the right things. Those were all dull and square anyway. With your height and looks, you can wear something with a little style."

"I hate shopping," I admitted. "Usually I have a friend who does it for me, but she's on her honeymoon. And I just had a fire in my apartment. . . ."

"I see." She tipped her head up and studied me for a minute. "Would you mind if I picked out a few things?"

Would I mind? Was she crazy? Assuming she had any taste at all, I'd be grateful. "Not at all," I said.

"Good. You wait right here. I won't be long." On her way out, she snagged two things, a suit and a dress, from the discard rack in the middle of the room. "Try these, for starters. You were made to wear these colors."

I looked at the suit she'd given me and knew I'd found a savior. It was the same suit Suzanne had bought me two weeks before. One that had gotten ruined in the fire. The cleaner had tried, but there was too much blood and soot. I didn't need to try it, I knew it fit. The dress fit, too. I put it on, zipped it and looked in the mirror. It was a fitted sleeveless sheath in iris blue linen with a short, Chanel-style jacket. The fitting room attendant looked over and smiled. "It's perfect for you. You're lucky, you know. Mrs. Merriam is a genius at what suits people."

My mentor, who I now knew was Mrs. Merriam, returned, staggering under the weight of the clothes she was carrying. "Now, dear," she said, "I'm sure we'll find something suitable here." She scrutinized the dress. "Yes, that works very well, doesn't it, and I know where you can get just the right shoes for that." For nearly an hour, I played human Barbie Doll while Mrs. Merriam and the clerk she pressed into service as her underling dressed me in a mind-boggling succession of outfits. She was as efficient as a drill sergeant.

Even though I appreciated what she was doing, there came a moment when the absurdity of it finally got to me. My office was waist high with work, and here I was, standing in a room full of nearly naked strangers, taking orders like a ten-year-old from someone I didn't know. I sat down on the bench to rest my tired legs and said, "Enough. I'm sorry. I appreciate it, but I've got to get back to work." I was an energetic person, but she was tireless. She would have gone on until closing time, or even, such was her personal power, persuaded the store to stay open longer.

She looked at her watch. "Goodness, you're right. I've got to get home and watch 'Murder She Wrote.' I just love Angela Lansbury. Now, let's see what we've got." She went quickly through the keepers, pulling one out and rejecting it, then through the possibles, where she shifted three items over to the keepers. "Yes, I think that ought to hold you for a while. My but that was fun. It was so nice of you to let me help. I love doing this. I expect you think I'm batty, don't you?" She rushed on, not giving me time to answer. "But I have a daughter, about your age and with a very similar build. She hates to shop and I pick out all her clothes. Different coloring, of course. She can't wear any of those interesting greens. But that's why I knew what to look for."

"I'm grateful. I truly am. As you saw, I wasn't doing too well on my own."

"Excuse me." She turned away, lightning quick, as the attendant tried to put some abandoned clothes on the discard rack. "Letty, those are mine." The attendant practically curtseyed as she apologized and backed away. "Well, I hope you enjoy your new clothes. I guess we found quite a few, didn't we? Can you afford all that?"

"If it means not having to go shopping again, it's worth it." I picked up all the clothes I could carry, Mrs. Merriam's assistant picked up the rest, and we marched off to the cashier. The cashier had the bored look people get when they work late in the evening, but the boredom changed to something more like astonishment when she saw us coming. I was such an ingrate, too. Here I was, living out every woman's fantasy, doing what people enter contests to be able to do. I'd just gone on a megashopping spree and I only saw it as a chore. I flinched when I heard the total, but the feeling had passed by the time I handed over my American Express card. The insurance would cover most of it. But I did feel a little like the sultana of Brunei when the shop assistant followed me out to my car carrying the six shopping bags I couldn't manage.

I drove back to the office, careful to park my car right under a streetlight, and went to work. I let the Eagles serenade me while I worked my way through Suzanne's mail, then my own, and finally felt ready to face Bobby's big, insecure question marks. It turned out that he didn't have any hard questions. The question marks had been employed to flag some good ideas he had that he wanted my response to.

I tipped back in my chair, kicked off my shoes, and dictated two tapes full of letters and memos. It was kind of like taking a shower when you want the phone to ring. For weeks we'd been sweating about where we were going to get more work. Today, with all of us busier than ants in August, and Suzanne off in Bermuda embarked on an orgy of moon, June, spoon, jobs were pouring in. An embarrassment of riches. Feast or famine. I could spend the next hour thinking of clichés. That was how it always went. I'd just forgotten.

I pushed my weary old self out of the chair and redistributed the piles: one onto Sarah's desk, one for Magda, and the third to Bobby, including a note telling him I'd call him in the morning to discuss Bartlett Hill. Hopefully I'd given them enough guidance so that they could handle things tomorrow. I left Sarah my number at Bartlett Hill in case she needed to reach me. If only I had a maid waiting at home to hang up all my new finery I'd be in heaven.

The phone rang just as I was shutting off the lights, ominous and compelling in the silent office. I resisted the temptation to answer it. That was what we had an answering machine for. Besides, most of the calls I'd been getting lately had been more trouble than they were worth. Instead I snapped off the lights and left the phone sending its plaintive appeal into the empty darkness.

Remembering that Andre and I had eaten most of my supplies,

I stopped at a convenience store and got milk, bread, OJ, English muffins and a box of cereal. Now I was prepared for flood, tornado, hurricane or other acts of nature. I also got coffee for the road, in one of the handy-dandy cups with the peel-back lids that let you sip without spilling. In my experience, what they're really designed to do is funnel a thin stream of coffee down the front of my shirt and into my cleavage. To be safe, I tucked a napkin into the neck of my dress, pulled out the little tray that holds my coffee when I'm not drinking it, and roared off into the night.

CHAPTER 26

ANDRE HAD GIVEN me two presents before he left, handing them to me in a furtive, almost embarrassed way after our midnight dinner. From his behavior I'd expected risqué lingerie and the presents had taken me by surprise. The first was a little alarm you could carry in your pocket which, if you pushed a button, gave off a tremendous noise. The second was a canister of something called STUN, which he said worked like Mace. I'd given it right back, reminding him that the last time I tried something like that, I ended up having it used on me.

"I haven't forgotten," he said. "This is better. No top to remove. It fits in the palm of your hand. Just point it at your attacker and squeeze. This doesn't deliver some little squirt, either. This stuff comes out with a rich, throaty roar, guaranteed to stop the bastard in his tracks." He handed it back to me. "Please keep it. I'll feel safer, knowing you have it. I thought about getting you a gun, but that didn't make sense. Not until I have a chance to show you how to use one."

This was a different Andre from the one I was used to and what was different was that instead of trying to protect me by telling me how I should behave, he was acknowledging that I was responsible for my behavior and trying to help me be safer if I made risky choices. I took the presents and put them in my purse. "I really appreciate this, Andre," was all I told him, but he knew what I meant, just like I'd known what he meant, and we both knew we'd taken a giant step forward. I just hoped the next step wasn't going to involve lessons in marksmanship. I wanted a less dangerous life, not one that was more dangerous.

When I got back in the car with my coffee, I took both devices out of my purse and slipped them into my pockets. Intuition or not, I wasn't taking any chances. Being brave doesn't mean one has to be foolish.

Everything looked normal. All the usual cars in the usual parking spaces. Tonight, everyone had their outside lights on, and things seemed unusually bright. I wondered if they were behind their curtains, watching, saying to themselves, "That girl better get home soon, we want to turn out our lights and go to bed." Instead of parking in my slot, I parked the car right in front of the door, sprinted to it, unlocked it, and shut off the alarm. Then I began the tiresome chore of lugging in my new wardrobe. I was coming back for the second load when someone behind me said, "Can I help you with those?"

Without hesitating a second I dropped the bags onto the walk, stuck my hand into my pocket and hit the alarm button. As my dress began to wail loudly, I pulled out the STUN and Officer Harris went for his gun. Luckily we both figured out what was happening before I zapped him or he shot me. We both fell back against the car, panting, while I turned off the alarm and he put his gun away.

"Excuse me, Ms. Kozak," he said, "but what the hell was that?"

I couldn't answer. I was still trying to get my breath, trying to slow my heartbeat down to a reasonable level. Right now it was slamming against my chest wall like a wild bird trying to escape from a cage. I'd been in some tight situations in my life, but I'd never come face-to-face with a loaded gun before. There was so much adrenaline surging through my system I probably could have run all the way to Boston and back. He stared at me in confusion and I just went on leaning against the car, waiting for my stomach to unknot. My hands, when I touched my face, were icy and trembling.

"What's the matter? Are you okay?"

"The gun. You scared me."

"I'm sorry. It was that noise. It startled me."

"You always pull your gun when you hear a loud noise?"

"Of course not."

"Well, you could have fooled me. I think you just took ten years off my life."

"I'm sorry," he said again, at a loss for anything more helpful to say. "Why don't you go in and sit down. I'll bring the rest of this stuff in and park the car. What was that thing, anyhow?"

"Give me a minute to pull myself together and then I'll show you." He carried the rest of my wardrobe and the groceries inside, parked the car while I watched warily, then came inside and shut the door. "It was this," I said, taking the alarm out of my pocket and handing it to him. "Present from my boyfriend Andre." Harris and I had had our ups and downs, but if he hadn't frightened me out of my wits just now with his gun, I would have been glad to see him tonight. And he had carried in my stuff.

"Sure makes a racket," he said. He handed it back. "Good idea. Keep it with you. I don't imagine your neighbors liked it much, though."

"After the last week, I'll be lucky if I'm not ridden out of town on a rail."

"I don't believe they do that sort of thing around here," he said. "It's more like a big chill. Any chance I could get you to make some more of that great coffee?"

"Twist my arm," I answered, getting the coffee out of the freezer. When he wasn't being an asshole he could be rather sweet. Or maybe it was just that things were different seen with my new optimism. The light on my answering machine was blinking like a spastic with conjunctivitis, but I ignored it. Experience had taught me that it rarely delivered good news. I wasn't in the mood for bad. I poured in the water and pushed the button. The machine gave a happy gurgle, a hot steamy whoosh, and the smell of good coffee began to fill the room. "To what do I owe the pleasure of this visit?"

"I just wanted to see that you got home all right," he said defensively. Meaning the chief had sent him again.

I didn't needle him, as I might have done in a more prickly mood. Intense fright has a way of taking the starch out of me. I had all the stamina right now of an overcooked noodle. "Thanks," I said, "I appreciate it. I'd been wishing for someone to help me carry all this stuff in."

"Looks like you went shopping."

"That is an understatement, Officer. I went on a binge, a total, obscene binge. I bet no one has ever bought this much in the history of the world. But I had to. All my clothes were toasted."

He nodded. "I'll bet you hate to shop, too. My wife would have been in heaven."

It was impossible to imagine Harris with a wife. He seemed so awkward around women. Unless it was just me. I wondered what Mrs. Harris thought about her husband spending the night in my motel room. I fixed his coffee and offered him an English muffin. Over muffins and coffee, tea for me to settle my jangled nerves, he admitted he'd been told to keep an eye on me, direct orders from the chief. Maybe my intuition told me it was over, but the police didn't think so. "Why does the chief care?"

He shrugged. "Like I told you before . . . I don't mean to sound callous or anything, but it wouldn't look good for any of us if something happened to you. The people in this area have paid a lot of money to live in a nice place . . . they don't like the idea of midnight intruders and women being attacked."

"Can't say I'm too fond of the idea either." We didn't linger in conversation. I was tired and still had to hang up my new clothes before they got wrinkled, and now that I was in for the night, he was hot to get out there and serve and protect. I saw him to the door, locked it behind him, and lugged my stuff into the bedroom. I hung up the first five things and then ran out of energy. Ignoring my mother's voice, permanently installed in my head, which was ordering me to stay awake and finish the job before everything turned into a mass of wrinkles, I slipped off my shoes, fell across the bed, and sank into sleep.

I was sitting in my car, parked behind a screen of shrubs, watching Helene Streeter come out with a dog on a leash, turn away from me, and walk off down the sidewalk. As she walked away, I was conscious of a stir of activity around me. Ahead of me, in another parked car, the window went silently down and Eve stuck her head out, eyes fixed on her mother. In the dark house beside me, there was a brief flash of light as the curtains stirred. I knew that Martha Coffey was in there watching. Away in the distance, a man was waiting, hidden in the bushes. I knew he was there more by instinct than anything else, a sense of pale skin in the shadows. A shiny dark car came slowly down the street and pulled over fifty feet ahead of Helene. She approached it, leaned down, and said something to the occupant. Her head flew up once, white teeth exposed in a smile. A trace of laughter floated toward me on the still air.

She bent down again, and this time she pulled back violently, her arms clutched protectively around herself. The dog, no longer controlled, wandered off down the street, sniffing curiously at the bushes. The car moved silently away, turned a corner, and was gone. A movement caught my attention and I looked away from Helene. Silent dark shapes were moving down the street toward her. The figure from the bushes. Eve was out of her car and walking. Cliff came out of the house, down the walk, and strode briskly toward his wife. Martha Coffey came out, closed the door carefully behind her, paused and checked to be sure it was locked, and then went to meet the others in the street. They approached Helene, who had fallen to her knees, and clustered around her.

I heard a scream and then another cry, more muffled. Something was wrong! They weren't helping her. No one had left the circle to go for help. I groped for my car phone, picked up the receiver, tried to punch in 911, but the receiver was a banana, and all it did was yield under the pressure of my fingers until the skin split and thick banana ooze burst out all over my hand. I tossed it out the window, heard the clink of hard plastic hitting the street, and looked out at the shattered receiver. Then I started my car and drove toward them, my fingers sticky on the steering wheel.

I pulled up beside them, wiped my hand on my skirt, and lowered the window. Cliff was the first to turn away, handsome in a mango polo shirt and carefully creased slacks. Rays from the streetlight glinted off the knife in his hand. "It's always good to see you, Thea, but I'm afraid this isn't a good time. Maybe tomorrow?" he said, gazing at me with his intense, caressing blue eyes.

Eve was next, brusque and unfriendly. "Go away, Thea. We don't need your help. We've got everything under control." Blood was running up the blade of her knife and across the back of her hand. She shook it off impatiently. Behind her, on the ground, Helene moaned, a low, animal sound.

"Oh, be quiet," Martha Coffey said, nudging her with a foot. "I suppose you think we're just terrible, don't you?"

"Why did you do it?" I barely managed to choke out the words.

She shrugged. "For the good of the neighborhood. She was very disruptive."

The fourth person straightened up and stared at me with blank, incurious eyes. Waldemar. Still wearing headphones. Still tuned out. He was shuffling his feet to the music, making little bloody tracks in the street. None of them seemed concerned about what they were doing.

"Who was in the car?"

"Can't you guess?" Eve said. "Who's missing?"

I honestly didn't know. "The patient's angry husband? The one who was stalking her?"

Eve shook her head. "Guess again."

"A jealous lover?"

"Think globally, act locally," Eve said.

"I don't understand. What does that mean?"

"Nothing." She laughed. "Absolutely nothing. I was just testing your ability as a detective."

"Eve, don't be provocative," Cliff said. "Thea did her best."

"Oh, yeah, sure. She can't even figure out who was in the car."

"Rowan," I said, realizing who was missing. "It was Rowan."

"That pansy wouldn't know a blade from a hilt. Come on, Thea. Guess again."

"Eve, dear, you're being very rude to your friend," Martha Coffey chided. "Just tell her, please, and then we'd all better get out of here. Oh, look what that boy has done!" She reached out and grabbed Waldemar by the elbow, pointing toward his feet. He looked down, shrugged, and took a few steps back.

"Don't worry about it," Eve said, "I'll just kill him on the way home and leave him beside the road."

"Eve, you mustn't make this a habit. . . ."

"Why not, Cliff?" she interrupted. "Okay, Thea, no more games. It was Lenora in the car. I'm surprised you didn't figure that out. Now, Cliff, you go home, wait five minutes and then call the police. Goodnight, everyone. Thanks for coming." She stuck two fingers in her mouth, whistled loudly, and a flying carpet floated up. Waldemar helped her aboard, climbed on himself, and they disappeared into the sky.

Cliff walked down the street, tossed his knife over a hedge, and then walked back past the body and on to his house. Martha Coffey stared at her knife blade unhappily. "Guess I'd better go and wash this. We're having roast beef tomorrow." On the ground, Helene lay staring up at us, a surprised expression on her face.

My car phone was ringing but I couldn't answer it because the receiver was gone. I fumbled around in my purse, found the canister of STUN, plugged it in and said, "Hello?"

Eve's voice, low and harsh and furious. "You bitch. You searched my apartment, didn't you."

"You have a phone on your carpet?" I said, sleepily. The STUN made a pretty good receiver. I could hear everything she said. "The receiver turned into a banana," I muttered. "Martha went home to wash her knife and Cliff's gone to call the police. Don't you worry about falling off the edges?"

"What the hell are you talking about, Thea? Are you drunk? Why did you take my pills?"

"You're the one with the thirst for gore, not me. Anyway I didn't take them, that was your father. I'm going to drive home now. Someday take me for a ride on your carpet. Not in the winter, though." I unplugged the STUN and put it back in my purse. It wouldn't stay. It fell off and landed on the floor with a crash. It was the crash that woke me up. Not fully, but enough to pick the receiver up off the floor and put it back in the cradle. Then I went back to sleep, but everyone else had gone home and they didn't return to trouble my dreams.

CHAPTER 27

MORNING, AS WAS its habit, came too soon, but it came in the form of a glorious spring day with bright sun and birds sounding giddy with joy. I found myself humming in the shower and smiling over coffee on the back deck. I finished hanging up my new clothes, chose a crisp white linen shirt, flowing navy and white skirt and a navy jacket, and got dressed, feeling a little like Cinderella. The answering machine was still blinking—machines never get tired—and I went on ignoring it. I even remembered to put my alarm and STUN in my briefcase. I braided my hair and wrapped it around my head in a coronet, secured it with pins, and put on some big gold earrings. Then I grabbed a Vivaldi tape and went to work.

It was one of those days when it felt good to be alive, a feeling that didn't even dim when I greeted Roddy Stokes and got a sneer in return. Lisa was waiting for me in our gloomy borrowed office, but today she'd jazzed it up with a couple of bright posters and a jar of flowers. She'd also picked up croissants and coffee. "Morning, boss," she called as I came through the door. "How do you like the decor?"

"Don't tell me you're getting attached to this place? Looks like you're ready to move in."

"Oh." Her face fell. "You don't like it?"

"I do. I'm just amazed that you had the energy to do this."

"Must be the weather. Makes me lively. Or maybe it's because my baby-sitter's plans fell through so she was able to take Charlotte today, and when Josh's mother called him last night to complain that I was deliberately keeping her away from her grandchild, he firmly but politely explained to her that when I'm working I have to know I have reliable child care. You could have knocked me over with a feather. So I guess I was inspired to reach out and do a little something extra myself."

"Like going down to the basement and looking through the boxes you still haven't unpacked and finding two old posters?"

"Exactly. And cutting off a handful of flowers from the bed beside my front door. I got the jar from the women in the office." She handed me a croissant. "I can work the whole day after all."

"How'd your mother-in-law take it?"

"Besides calling Josh? She told me that I'm selfish and a bad mother and that I'm depriving her of an opportunity to bond with her grandchild. Nothing unexpected. That's a nice outfit. New?" I told her about my shopping spree with Mrs. Merriam. "Sounds perfect. I hope you got her phone number for the next time you need clothes."

"I've got Suzanne."

"Oh, right. I hope she's having a wonderful time. Just imagine those beautiful sand beaches, luscious meals, snorkeling through turquoise water."

"And unbridled lust." She looked a little shocked. I handed her a schedule. "Here's your list. They have us both scheduled until seven, but we can ask Roddy to cancel some of yours."

She gave a little shudder. "Ugh. He's repulsive, isn't he?"

"I think so. Cliff says I'm unsympathetic and should be more understanding."

"Well, that makes two of us. Mr. Paris is so charming. Maybe he keeps Roddy for contrast."

We stopped by and endured Roddy's scorn long enough to

explain that Lisa's schedule needed changing. That was long enough. His toadlike inertia gave new meaning to the word "sullen." As the door closed behind us, Lisa said, "Phew. I feel like I need to go wash after that." She shook her hands like she was trying to shake off something nasty. "Things can only go uphill from here."

We arranged to meet briefly before five and went off to interview. At noon I came up for air with the discomforting feeling that I'd spent my morning with the Stepford Wives. The picture of Bartlett Hill that I was getting sounded too much like a party line, like they'd all just come from a meeting where they'd decided what they would say. I wondered if Lisa's impressions were the same. I hadn't brought a sandwich but I wasn't really hungry. What I yearned for was some air, so I took a long walk around the grounds, cautious when I passed other people. In my last interview, I'd heard an anecdote about a seemingly mild patient punching a complete stranger in the nose. It made my own nose ache just to think about it.

I was lying under a tree, letting the wind shower me with apple blossoms, when Rowan Ansel came by. "I've been looking for you," he said.

I sat up and brushed the petals off my shirt. "Why?"

He seemed surprised at that. Probably another one of the misinformed people who think I'm sweet. "I wondered how things were going."

"Not bad," I said. He apparently didn't realize that I was imitating his behavior in yesterday's interview.

He shifted restlessly from one foot to the other, looking annoyed. "Too soon to reach any conclusions?"

"Right." Talking with him had been like pulling teeth. Unlike the day he'd hit me with the door, when he'd been confiding and talkative, yesterday he'd been formal, cold and unresponsive, making no secret of his displeasure that I refused to talk about Eve.

He tried again. "Cliff is unhappy with what you've been doing."

"I'm surprised to hear that. This project was his idea."

Now he was really annoyed. "Not the project. What you're doing for Eve."

"He told me."

"Oh. I didn't realize that. And you've agreed to stop?"

"I'd already stopped."

"You need to try and make her understand . . ."

"Do I look like a miracle worker to you?"

"Excuse me?"

I stood up, picked up my jacket and shook it, and draped it over my arm. "It would take a miracle worker to get Eve to understand anything she doesn't want to understand. You ought to know that. I've got to get back. Full schedule this afternoon."

"But you're her friend," he said. I stepped around him onto the path. "Wait a minute, I'm not finished. . . ."

"But I am."

He grabbed my arm and jerked me roughly to a halt. "I said hold on."

"What do you think you're doing, Dr. Ansel?" I said, staring pointedly at his clutching hand. He released me, but not before he'd made sure I understood the depth of his anger. I could see the marks on my bare arm where his fingers had been. For an instant, standing close to him, I was aware of the fresh, manly scent of his cologne. Something in my mind stirred and I almost had the memory I'd been trying to recapture since I was attacked, but as I reached for it, he spoke and it flitted away.

"You can be a real bitch, can't you? I'm surprised that Cliff hired you to do such a sensitive job."

"I wonder why it is that whenever a woman refuses to abandon her schedule or her point of view to accommodate a man, he immediately calls her a bitch? Not very creative, is it? You sought me out here so you could criticize my behavior and tell me what to do instead. If I choose not to take your direction or to discuss my decisions or my actions, personal or professional, that's my business. Business I should be able to pursue without being manhandled by you. And it is our policy not to discuss an ongoing project, except with the client. Am I making myself clear?"

"Quite," he said, trying to manage a placating smile. It fell off his face before it even passed from rictus to something pleasant. "I didn't mean to offend you, Thea. You don't have to be so hardnosed. . . ."

Foolish man, standing there dotted with flower petals, trying to make me think he was my friend when anger was glaring out of his eyes and he was clenching and unclenching his fists. When the marks of his anger circled my wrist like a bracelet. Did he think I hadn't noticed? It looked like Dr. Ansel's caring facade was about as thick as cheap veneer. "Sometimes it takes a hard woman to do a hard job, Dr. Ansel. If you'll excuse me?" I turned and walked away. I could feel his eyes on me but I didn't look back. I'd caught a glimpse of something there that was too unpleasant, like I was a cockroach and he was a giant shoe.

The afternoon flew by, and by four I was sorry I hadn't eaten lunch. Old habits die hard. Someday I'll reform and start carrying emergency rations. It would be better than letting myself get so hungry a candy bar seemed acceptable. I was interviewing a young woman, quite new to Bartlett Hill, and getting a refreshingly different set of answers. She had such an upbeat attitude and such a caring demeanor that I thought she probably helped the patients just by being there. When my rebellious stomach, angry at being ignored, let out a particularly loud rumble, she smiled and opened her desk drawer. "I'll bet you're a lunch skipper, like me," she said. She pulled out a can of liquid diet food. "Not the greatest tasting stuff, but it does appease the appetite. You want it?"

"Guess I'd better. I'm going to be here until eight." I took it and stuck it in my briefcase. We finished up the interview and I went back to our newly decorated office to wait for Lisa. She came dragging in a few minutes later and caught me drinking DietPro.

"Now I've seen everything," she said. "I think I'm offended. You've got the best figure of anyone I know, you never eat, and now you're dieting?"

"Someone gave it to me because my stomach kept rumbling. Can't interview with a noisy stomach. I was going to feed it a candy bar, but the woman I was interviewing gave me this instead. Ever tried it?"

"You're kidding. That stuff's all chemicals. Well, I did try it once, but it tasted like chalk. Hard enough to diet anyway, without making yourself eat chalk. Have a good day?"

"Fine. Spoke to some real people this afternoon. I think tomorrow afternoon we should go to the office, evaluate this stuff, then see if we can meet with Cliff and map out a strategy for the next phase. What do you think?"

She sat down, kicked off her shoes, and put her feet up on the table. "I think we should take a vacation and move on to the next phase next week. My feet hurt and my head is pounding. Whatever made me think I wanted to get back to work?"

"Reentry difficulties?" She did look tired.

"Sleep deprivation. That's what does it. I think I could work and mother if only I had enough sleep. You know what not getting enough sleep does to the brain?"

I did know, of course, since another of my bad habits, right up there with not eating properly, was working too hard and not getting enough sleep. "Impairs its function," I said.

"Right. I'm practically brain dead. I don't know what I've written down on these interview sheets. Probably my grocery list." There was a crash as the door flew open, knocking over one of the broken chairs. Someone stuck his head in, pulled it back quickly, and slammed the door. "What was that?" Lisa asked, taking her feet off the table. "A runaway patient?"

"Who knows. I didn't get a good look, did you?"

"No. Don't know who it was and I don't care. I'm going to go get Charlotte and take her for a nice long walk." She shoved her feet back into her shoes, grabbed her stuff, and left. "See you in the morning. You want a croissant or a bagel tomorrow?"

"Croissant. Chocolate, if you can get it."

"No problem, mon," she said, in perfect imitation of our Jamaican janitor. "Catch you later." She made her fist into a little handgun, aimed it at me, and fired.

I read the list of ingredients I'd just consumed and considered sticking my finger down my throat, but there wasn't time. I pitched the can across the room, using the wall as a backboard, and scored a three pointer. Basketball is one thing tall girls do well. My heavy hair was pulling loose from the pins, and I was tired of looking like Heidi anyway, so I pulled out the rest of the pins, unbraided it, and set it free. Then I consulted my interview list. I hadn't noticed it before, but Cliff had put himself down for the last appointment of the day. My briefcase was so full of papers it looked like a short snake that had just swallowed a pillow and it was heavy. Two and a half more hours seemed like a long time.

Time flies when you're having fun, but the opposite is also true. Time crawls when you aren't having fun. When you're tired, and the people you are interviewing are just as tired as you are, and don't have your professional reasons not to be cranky, simple little structured chats like the ones I was conducting can be grueling. At 7:30, I headed for Cliff's office with a headache worthy of the Jolly Green Giant. Even my feet were sore. When you look at a beautiful campus with widely spaced buildings, it looks very nice. When you hike from building to building in high-heel shoes—shoes designed by sadists frustrated because they can no longer bind women's feet—carrying an overstuffed briefcase, you realize how impractical such a design can be.

I wasn't disappointed to find the outer office empty. Sharing space with Roddy gave me the creeps. Cliff's door was closed, and when I raised my hand to knock, I heard voices inside. I was about to knock anyway when his voice suddenly got louder. "I don't understand why you did that." A softer, female voice responded with words I couldn't make out. Then Cliff's voice again, still loud, ". . . could have been thinking. She's not the kind to . . ." and then it died out again, and anyway, my ears were blocked by a prodigious yawn. Time to call it a day. Maybe I'd hunt around and see if I could find some coffee, and come back when Cliff was done with his interview. As I turned away, his voice rose again, ". . . can't make a habit of it, just because you don't like the way people are behaving." And then the woman's voice, ". . . do what's necessary." The voice sounded vaguely familiar. Probably one of the women I'd interviewed today. I felt a little sorry for her. When someone who rarely raises his voice finally does, the effect can be devastating.

I met Rowan Ansel in the hall and he didn't look happy to see me. I asked him if there was any place I could get some coffee while I waited for Cliff. He shrugged. "Cliff usually has some in his office. Otherwise, I doubt it. I have a machine, but I'm out of coffee. Have to pick some up on the way home. I think the kitchen is locked. If you want me to get you some, I will. He won't mind if I disturb him."

I didn't like asking him favors, but he wanted to show off his connection to Cliff anyway, so I let him. I asked him to tell Cliff that I'd be waiting in my office. Since I'm never one to waste time, I got out the interview sheets and started making notes on the responses. A few minutes later the door opened. I looked up, expecting to see Dr. Ansel, and found Roddy. He thrust a cup of coffee at me ungraciously. "Dr. Paris asked me to give you this. He's just finishing something and then he'll come and get you." Some of it slopped onto my papers.

"Thanks." I took a sip of the coffee. It had so much sugar in it it was almost like syrup but I needed the caffeine so I drank it.

It seemed like a long time before Cliff came to get me. I tried to work, but I was sleepy enough so I couldn't concentrate and the coffee didn't seem to be helping at all. He finally came to get me, and I followed him back to his office, but though we both made an effort, I couldn't seem to keep up my end of the conversation. I kept losing my place on the questionnaire and having to ask him to repeat answers. He wasn't much better. He didn't seem to be paying attention and kept fiddling nervously with things on his desk. It was like the day he'd fallen asleep on me in reverse.

"I'm sorry. I don't think we're going to get anywhere tonight," I told him. "I can't seem to keep my eyes open."

"I've noticed," he said. "You should have another cup of coffee before you go out on the road. Have you been having trouble sleeping?"

"No. I haven't. I've been sleeping well. Maybe I've been getting too much fresh air, if there can be such a thing."

He poured me some coffee. "Cream or sugar?"

"Both, please." The coffee was too hot but I gulped it down anyway. I waited for the expected reviving effect, making small talk with Cliff and setting up our next meeting, but nothing seemed to be happening.

In the end, I dragged my failing body out of his office. Eve was sitting on the edge of Roddy's desk, swinging her legs. "Surprise," she said. "I was supposed to meet Cliff for dinner. He said he needed a few minutes with you first."

"We're finished."

She watched me curiously but she didn't say anything. Maybe hanging up on her had finally gotten my point across. Not likely, though, knowing Eve. She was probably just planning out what to say. She was dressed for her dinner out in something my mother might have worn to gym class in college, a kind of a one-piece romper with very full shorts on the bottom and a camp-shirt top. It was white with a black-and-red print and she had funny little black sandals with all sorts of crisscrossed straps. Her toenails were painted gold.

"Well," she said rudely, "do I pass inspection?"

"You look nice." I hesitated. "I thought you were mad at Cliff."

"I don't think my relationship with my father is any of your business."

"Sunday you were quite sure it was my business."

"That was Sunday," she said. She jumped off the desk and

flounced into his office. Her outfit was perfect for flouncing.

I trudged down to my car, wondering if this could be a chemical reaction to the diet drink or the onset of some terrible illness. It wasn't flu season but that's how I felt. Spacey. Disoriented. As though my limbs weren't quite connected.

The glory of the day was reluctantly releasing its hold on the world as the last of the sun faded from the sky, leaving only a streaky blue-pink memory. The city below had a warm, pink glow. Even the smokestacks out by the Charlestown bridge looked pretty. A jet taking off from Logan Airport gleamed like a silver bullet in the sky. It was all an ironic tease to me as I blundered down the path almost too weary to move. I felt like my brain had been sucked out by a vacuum cleaner.

Across the parking lot, I could just see the bobbing back of someone bending down behind my car. A flash of adrenaline restored me enough to reach in my briefcase and bring out the alarm. I rushed around the car and pressed the button.

Roddy Stokes, looking like he'd just been set on fire, reared up away from my tire and whirled to face me, knife in hand. Leaving the alarm wailing, I pulled out the STUN, pointed it at him, and squeezed. He dropped the knife and went down like I'd used dynamite, rolling on the ground, yelling and rubbing his eyes. It was a revolting sight, the flopping, bloated body and beet red face. Ignoring him, I bent and checked my tires. They seemed to be all right.

I started the car and backed up slowly so I wouldn't run over Roddy. Not that I would have minded much after what he'd tried to do. If he'd succeeded in slashing my tires, I would have been alone in an almost empty parking lot with a disabled car. Open-minded as I tried to be, I couldn't pretend it wasn't scary to be on the deserted campus of a mental hospital at night. I was grateful for Andre's gifts.

Probably no sensible person would have come up and challenged a vandal the way I had, but he knew that I could be hot tempered and impulsive. Not that I felt very hot tempered now.

The oppressive sense of heaviness and lethargy, sent reeling briefly by my encounter with Roddy, had returned more strongly than before. There was probably a mountain of stuff waiting for me at the office, but I was going straight home to bed.

Maybe I was coming down with some kind of a fast-acting flu. My arms and legs were weak, my hands were trembling so violently I could barely grip the steering wheel. My eyelids felt like they were holding up gigantic cinder blocks and were threatening to give up the fight. I crept carefully down the hill, trying to master my body. Trying to keep my eyes on the road. Trying to keep the car on the road. I crept through the gate and turned onto the street. An oncoming car charged at me, horn blaring. I swung back into my own lane, swung too far, felt the tires bite gravel and the car shift sideways. I fought with the wheel, pulling it back onto the road.

There was a strange ringing in my head and my ears felt hot. The rest of me was experiencing an odd, almost euphoric lassitude. The combination was unpleasant and vaguely familiar, like the only time I'd taken Valium. It had been prescribed by a well-meaning doctor at the hospital after David died. All I'd been doing was trying to personally dismember the cop who had kept me from seeing him. A perfectly reasonable response under the circumstances, but the doc had found my behavior unseemly and offered a tranquilizer. Perhaps offered isn't the right word, since as I remembered the circumstances, two burly cops held me as the doc jabbed a needle into my arm, while the third cop stood there fingering the scratches on his face and called me a bitch. Bitch is such a tiresome word. But if it was bitchy to be angry at someone who kept you from sharing your husband's last minutes of life then I was definitely a bitch.

My head dropped forward onto my chest and my eyes closed. I forced it up, forced them open, but I knew I wasn't going to make it home in this condition. Not even the chilling realization that someone *must* have drugged my coffee brought an energetic response. I was losing the battle of mind over body and I had to get off the road before I hurt myself or someone else. Just ahead a sign announced the Wheeler Brook Conservation Land. I put on my blinker and turned down the rutty dirt road. The road, showing the effects of the rainy spring we'd had, was like a minefield. I finally bumped to a stop in a small parking area surrounded by trees. I got out, limbs shaking, and leaned against the car, my lungs dragging in the evening air in a desperate attempt to revive myself. My body swayed and trembled like an old chair with loose legs.

I stuck my fingers down my throat, trying to make myself throw up in case there was still more of the stuff in my stomach. It didn't work. I was too listless to try hard. Gradually my knees gave way until I was sitting on the ground beside the car. My eyes closed and I fell into a kind of stupor.

Through my eyelids I sensed more than saw the headlights bumping along toward me. I wanted to get up, to not be found here collapsed beside my car, but I couldn't get my body to cooperate. I heard a door shut, then footsteps crunching toward me. I tipped my head back, forcing my eyes open like one of those old-fashioned baby dolls that closes it eyes when you lay it down and opens them when it sits up. I instantly wished I hadn't. The figure coming toward me was dressed all in doctors' whites, including plastic gloves and a surgical mask. It raised a hand and shined a flashlight into my face. I put up my hands to shut out the beam and lowered my head until I saw only its feet.

"You'll get cold out here. Let's get you back in the car." A gruff, muffled voice. Two strong hands grabbed my arm, pulled me to my feet and pushed me into the car. "There, that's better. Don't go away. I'll be right back."

I fumbled with the ignition key, trying to start the car. The flashlight came down hard on my arm. "Don't do that." My arms and legs felt limp as overcooked spaghetti and my mind wasn't much better. I couldn't summon the energy for another try. I was helpless as a newborn confronting someone who definitely meant me harm. The pounding of my heart was so loud it drowned out all other sounds. If I could have run, fought back, done anything, it wouldn't have been so terrifying, but my fear was compounded by my helplessness. Like poor Pauline tied to the railroad tracks, like a cornered mouse facing a grinning cat, I knew this person was here to kill me and there was nothing I could do.

A gloved hand, unreal, bloated and yellow-white, reached in and switched off the dome light. Then both hands grabbed my arm, roughly shoved up my sleeve and I saw the gleam of a knife blade. "This will only hurt for a minute," in the same gruff voice, faintly amused. One hand held my arm down while the other, with a quick slash, cut my wrist. The pain was instantaneous, intense and terrible. A voice I recognized as my own cried out. The hands grabbed my other arm. I made a feeble attempt to pull it back. "Just one more minute and we'll be all finished." Doctor's office clichés. Meant to be reassuring. A gruesome, sadistic choice of words. The knife moved again, bit down and tore through my arm. This time I screamed.

A bloody hand tossed the knife into my lap. "Sweet dreams, McKusick." The door closed with a heavy thud. Warm sticky blood was soaking my lap and the seat underneath me. I could smell its faintly coppery tang. Was this the end? I was going to die here all alone in my car? I felt a small tongue of anger fighting the lassitude. I was not going to just sit here and let someone kill me without a struggle.

It was a pretty pathetic struggle. I gradually inched my way forward until I could reach the car phone, forcing my wounded hands to reach, to grasp. Oh God. The pain. Just play through, Thea, play through the pain. Keep going. Don't quit now. I coached myself. Pushed the right buttons. Got it on. And almost gave up. My bloody fingers kept slipping off the buttons. Too weak to push. I remembered one of the numbers I'd stored was Dom's. Pushed four. Someone answered. Rosie.

I tried to talk to her. My voice was barely a whisper. I inched closer to the phone. "Don't hang up, Rosie," I yelled. My yell wouldn't have frightened a mouse.

"Who is it?" she said. "Is someone there?"

"It's Thea. I need Dom." Speaking slowly, forcing the words out. Trying not to mumble.

"He's not here . . . no . . . wait, he's just coming now." I could hear the change in her voice. "Hold on, Thea. He's coming." She dropped the phone with a clatter and I could hear her calling, "Dominic, hurry! Thea's in trouble."

He picked up the phone, breathing heavily as if he'd come from far away. "Thea, what's wrong?"

"They've killed me, Dom."

"Where are you?"

"In my car. Help me." I was almost out of words. Out of breath. Out of everything.

"Where are you?" Dom the Controlled, sounding frantic.

"Conservation land. Near Bartlett Hill. Come get me. I'm bleeding."

"Don't talk any more," he said. "I'm on my way. I'll come get you."

"Don't let them fool you," I said, "I didn't kill myself. Rescue the Viking. God, I'm a bloody mess here. Stop the killing, Dom." I was losing it, floating away, babbling nonsense. The receiver slipped out of my hand and I couldn't be bothered to pick it up. I lay there slumped on the seat, listening to it buzz, to the odd series of noises phones make to themselves. It seemed very cold in the car. I pushed myself more upright. Crossed my arms on my chest, trying to keep my wrists up to reduce the bleeding. Holding back the red tide. Red sea. Seeing red. Brief disjointed thoughts came to me, like someone was channel surfing with my brain. Mrs. Merriam would be depressed if she knew what had become of the nice clothes she'd helped me pick out. I was just one of those girls who are hard on their clothes. Always bleeding all over them.

My mother would never forgive me if I died and she had to bury two daughters in one year. They'd never get a white coffin for me like they had for Carrie. I was the black sheep. Too big anyway. They'd probably just throw me in an old trunk. Michael and Sonia would sneer and blame my death on my incompetence. Damn them. I'd live just to show them.

And it would spoil Suzanne's honeymoon. My poor friend. She'd feel she had to come back for my funeral. I hadn't left any instructions, either. How would they know what I wanted? Painfully, awkwardly, I fumbled with the tape recorder in my briefcase and I started talking, outlining, in my ancient, feeble voice, what I did and did not want. Told them what had happened. The last thing I managed to say, before my energy ran out like sand through an hourglass, was "tell Andre I love him." Sappy but true. He'd probably prefer a sappy message to none at all.

Where was Dom? I was cold as ice and running out of blood. I fell into a sort of trance, mesmerized by the buzzing and whirling in my head. The buzzing went from electric yellow to red and blue and then someone was bending over me, calling my name. I tried to open my eyes, but they were glued shut. Held down by rocks. The light came on and I tried again. It wasn't Dom but his partner, Steve Meagher. He tore his handkerchief in half. I heard the sharp sound of ripping cloth and then he wrapped it around my wrists and lifted me out of the car. Easily. All that weight lifting was good for something. Set me in his car.

"You're going to ruin your seats." My mother's daughter to the end.

"Don't worry about it."

"Am I going to die?"

"Tough girl like you? No way. You're going to be fine," he said, his voice calm and soothing. "I'm taking you to the hospital."

"I don't like hospitals," I said, irrationally. "Briefcase." He probably thought I was out of my mind. "Bring it."

"I've got it," he said. He wrapped me in a blanket and in seconds we were bouncing back up the road. I heard him talking into his radio but didn't focus on the words. I'd zoned out again. I opened my eyes once or twice on the way, and maybe everything was distorted by the drugs and the pain, but I had the impression we were traveling as fast as I'd ever been in my life. We pulled up at the hospital in true cop style, siren blasting, and he was out of the car and opening my door before the car even stopped rocking.

Then I was on a gurney and they were wheeling me inside. I looked back at him standing on the curb. The front of his white shirt was covered with blood. I realized he was wearing a suit and tie, too, and wondered where he'd been, what sort of evening had been interrupted to come and rescue me. He hesitated a minute, then turned off the car, left it where it was and followed me inside. "I didn't like you," I murmured.

"I won't hold it against you," he said.

"Where's Dom?"

"Trying to get out of his driveway. I wouldn't want to be the asshole who parked his car there."

"Excuse me," a man in green with a stethoscope around his neck leaned over me and spoke to Steve, "you her husband?"

"Detective Stephen Meagher, Anson police," Meagher said.

"What've we got here? Attempted suicide?"

"Attempted murder, doc," he said.

Disbelief was writ large on the doctor's face but he didn't say anything, just went to work in a cool, impersonal way, still without speaking to me, treating me like a bothersome piece of meat. Ordinarily that would have brought me right up off the mattress, but I was too tired and too dizzy to put up any sort of a fight. They were sticking needles into me, taking my temperature and blood pressure. Establishing for the record that I was alive, at least when I arrived. Weren't they supposed to pump my stomach? I tried to tell Steve but he wasn't there so I tried to tell the doctor. He told me to lie still and be quiet. For the second time I felt completely helpless. Unable to stop the person who did this to me and now unable to get the help I needed.

Suddenly Dom was there, his warm hands on my shoulders, leaning down to talk to me. "How could they do this to you, Thea? What happened?"

"It was the coffee. Put something in my coffee. Couldn't stay awake." My voice was weak but I was articulate. I could get out about every third word. "Must have followed me." I wanted to hold his hand, but they were doing something to my hands and I couldn't. I was awfully sleepy but I was afraid if I went to sleep I'd never wake up. "I'm cold. Am I going to die?"

"You're too tough to die. Who was it?"

"Don't know. All in white. Gloves, mask like a doctor. Thought it was funny. Talking like in a doctor's office . . . you know . . . this will only hurt for a minute . . . it still hurts. I . . ." I struggled to tell him before I went into the soft darkness that beckoned to me. ". . . couldn't fight back. Drug made me weak. Helpless. You know how I hated it." Trying to organize my words was like trying to collect thistle down. They floated away whenever I got close. "Make him pump. Doctor. Stomach," I said.

"Any idea what sort of drug they gave her?" he asked the doctor.

"Drug?"

"Of course drug," Dom said, "you don't think she just sat there and let someone do this to her, do you? She was drugged and then her wrists were cut."

The doctor shrugged. "I just assumed . . ."

Dom went ballistic. I felt it through his hands the way they gripped my shoulders. "Assumed! You could be assuming this girl right into a grave!" There was a steely anger in his voice that made the doc pay attention. "Someone tried to kill her tonight. What are you trying to do, help out?"

"Get a grip on yourself, Detective," the doc said, shifting uncomfortably, "or I'll have to ask you to leave."

"You and whose army?" Dom said, and I loved him for it. "What are you going to do? Call the police?"

"Give him hell, Florio," I whispered.

Ignoring both of us, the doctor said something to one of the nurses. She disappeared and came back with something in a cup. The doctor waved it at Florio with a sort of malicious pleasure on his face. As I'd discovered in my recent, unpleasant journeys through hospitals, doctors and nurses hate having their authority questioned. They like you passive and grateful. Well, I was passive enough, and I'd be very grateful if I came out of this alive, but I couldn't help resenting them for making incorrect assumptions and I couldn't help being grateful to Dom for being my champion. "You want to help out, Officer, why don't you prop her up so she can drink this?"

"Detective," Dom said. He lifted me up—I was just like a rag doll—and a nurse held something to my lips. It was nasty going down and didn't stay there very long. When it came back it tried to bring my stomach with it, an effort it sustained for fifteen or twenty minutes. He held me the whole time, resting my limp body against his shoulder. Holding the bowl while my body was wracked with nausea and gently wiping my face afterwards. Finally the nurse announced that I was probably done and he could put me down. He eased me back onto the table. I lay there, reamed, hollow, shivering, and waited for the next torture.

A tall, graying man with a hawkish face and deep-set dark eyes came in, examined my wrists gently with warm fingers and spoke to me. His voice was calm and kind. "Mrs. Kozak, I'm Dr. Danczyk. I'm a plastic surgeon. I'm going to try my best to repair your wrists while minimizing the scarring. I know you've had a very frightening night and I'm sure you're very tired. I'll try not to hurt you but you will feel things—pricks and pressure and tugging. Sometimes it's easier to handle if you know what's happening. If you can do it, the best thing would be to go to sleep."

They had wheeled up a small table alongside the gurney and the nurse took my arm and started to pull it onto the table. The image of other gloved hands pulling on my hand and the knife gleaming in the darkness flashed across my mind. Panicked, I tried to pull my arm back, struggled to get up, get off the table, get away. "No! Don't touch me," I screamed. "Don't touch me. Leave me alone. Please, Dom, help me! Don't let them cut me."

Hands were grabbing at me, pushing me back down on the table. Someone was trying to tie me down and I was struggling against them.

"Hold it! Don't do that," Dom said. "Don't tie her down. You're scaring her to death."

"What do you suggest?" Dr. Danczyk asked. "We can't sedate her."

"Let me talk to her." All their eyes went to Danczyk, who nodded. The hands that had been grabbing at me went away, all except Dom's which stayed on my shoulders. He lowered his head and spoke to me softly. "Thea. Listen to me. I know it scares you, but they have to handle your arm in order to fix it. They aren't trying to hurt you." He kept his words slow and distinct. I tried to shut out the others who hovered nervously around him. Tried to relax. I was so scared I could hardly breathe. As he spoke, Dom was massaging my shoulders in a steady rhythm that matched his voice.

"Close your eyes," he said. He waited. I closed them. The warm hands began to move again. "Good girl . . . uh . . . woman. I won't let anyone hurt you, but you've got to calm down and coop-erate. Can you do that?" The warm hands stayed with me, calm, steady, reassuring. "I promise you I'll be right here. I won't leave you."

I nodded. "Okay. Do it."

"Take your time," he said. "Let us know when you're ready."

"I'm cold."

There was a mumble of voices and then Dr. Danczyk spoke again. "We're going to get you some blankets. Then we need to get to work."

"Go ahead." Dom kept his word and stayed by my head, hands on my shoulders. Someone put a warm blanket over me. They took my arm and held it down. I fought a wave of black terror, concentrated on Dom's steady voice. Steady hands. I let myself drift.

CHAPTER 28

I HOVERED IN a half world, suspended between asleep and awake, not daring to go either way. Awake I felt a stifling terror at being forced to lie there letting them manipulate my arm, knowing that if I truly woke up fear would impel me to get off the table and run. Asleep I was afraid of the images that might come, unbidden, controlled by the director of my dreams. I stayed there in my nowhere land, waiting for the stitching to stop, that painless but still frightening process, wanting them to go away and leave me alone.

During the attack, the drugs had made me limp and passive, helpless to defend myself. Now I lay rigid with fear waiting for more pain, for the next bad thing to happen, once again helpless and at the mercy of others. The only thing that kept me on the table instead of cowering in the corner was Dom. He stayed with me, a calming, steady presence, keeping up a constant murmur of reassurance. As long as he kept his hands on my shoulders, I could handle this.

As they were working on my second wrist, he took his hands away and others took their place. Different hands that massaged my shoulders in a familiar rhythm. Andre brought his face next to mine, his familiar voice in my ear. "You're stiff as a board. Relax and let go, Thea. Just relax and let go. No one is going to hurt you anymore. You can trust us. You're safe. We'll be right here, I promise." He repeated his reassurances over and over in his rich, deep voice, his big hands gently kneading the stiff muscles in my shoulders until I began to relax.

"I thought I'd never see you again." Then, absurdly, "What took you so long?"

"Long?" he said. "I never drove so fast in my life. You'll have to do more than this to get away from me."

"Wasn't trying to get away from you. Just tryin' to go home and get some sleep."

"You can go to sleep anytime you want. You don't have to stay awake for us."

"How did you know?"

"Dom called me. Said you were up to your usual tricks. At least you didn't run into a tree this time." The words were his familiar gentle teasing but his voice was ragged from pain and worry.

"Never did run into a tree." I was finally beginning to feel safe. Bit by bit, I began to let go of my defenses, to relax the rigid self-control I'd imposed on myself to try and stay alive and coherent. All my wariness and tension seemed to be being drawn out through his warm fingers. It was as though I'd been holding my breath for hours and now, finally, I could exhale. Maybe I could go to sleep, as long as Andre stayed with me.

"Thea, will you please go to sleep now?" He must have read my mind.

"I was scared. I thought I was going to die."

"You were right to be. If you weren't so tough and sensible, you could have."

"You like your women tough and sensible?"

"Only you," he said. "I like you tough and sensible. Now go to sleep. I'll be right here. I won't let anything happen to you."

"Promise?"

"I promise. I'll be right here beside you. I'll chase the dreams away."

He knew me so well. Well enough to know why I was afraid to go to sleep. I closed my eyes and let myself go. As I was drifting away, I heard Dr. Danczyk say, "Forgive me my curiosity, but are you all detectives investigating the case or is one of you romantically involved with this young lady?"

"This is Snow White, Doctor," Dom said, "and we be the three dwarves. The other four are out tracking down the bad guys. What do you think?"

"I vote for the big guy who looks like he almost lost his best friend. And I think I'm going to go home, have a couple of drinks and try not to wonder what the world is coming to. What did she do to deserve this?"

"She didn't deserve it," Andre said.

"Stepped on the wrong toes," Dom added. I left them to their discussion of the causes of crime and went to sleep.

I woke up with a drug hangover, screaming pain in my wrists, and a stomachache, feeling as weak as a kitten. As they had promised, I was not alone. My room was full of the groggiest looking people I'd ever seen, one of whom was sleeping beside me on the bed. "Is this what they mean by police protection?" I croaked.

The room came slowly to life, a seedy, decrepit form of life. In the far corner, still wearing the bloody shirt, his suit rumpled from being slept in, was Steve Meagher. Dom and Rosie were snoozing in chairs by the door, heads together, holding hands. Andre was beside me on the bed, taking up more than his share, one arm wrapped protectively around me. "Why aren't you all out catching bad guys?"

"Didn't want to miss your sleep-over party," Meagher said. "How do you feel today?"

"Down a few quarts." Beside me, Andre stirred, tightened his arm around me, and tried to pull me closer, trapping my wrist between our bodies. "Stop it," I yelled. My yell had all the punch of a newborn's fist. I had no voice and no volume today, but he heard me, let go, and sat up with a jerk, bursting with apologies. He looked a little gray today, the smile lines around his eyes changed to worry lines. Once he was reassured that I was alive, he got right down to business.

"Tell me everything that happened last night."

Before I could begin, a nurse came in. She halted midway across the room and surveyed my entourage. "Would you all mind giving me about five minutes alone with the patient?"

Everyone obediently got up and started out. Everyone except Andre. He inspected the name on her badge, then pushed the call button and waited until a second nurse appeared. "Can you confirm that Ms. Guyette is a staff nurse at this hospital and assigned to this floor?" he asked. Flustered, the second nurse confirmed that my nurse was genuine. "Thank you," he said. "You understand why we have to be careful."

"Of course, Officer," she said, stepping timidly out of the room.

His precautions had made Nurse Guyette a little huffy. "Is there anything else you'd like to check, Officer?"

"I'd rather be too careful and risk annoying you than be careless and let Thea get killed. I'm sure you can understand that," he said, and left.

She established for the record that I had a pulse and blood pressure and asked if I felt like getting up to visit the bathroom. It sounded like a good idea, but by the time I reached the edge of the bed I was trembling, and when I stood up, the edges of the room got fuzzy and began to move. "Forget it," I said, and coped with the indignity of the bedpan. By the time they came back, I was brushed, both tooth and hair, and my hands and face were clean. My mother would have approved.

"Did you call my parents?" I asked Andre as soon as he came through the door.

He shook his head. "I thought I'd let you decide about that." He got right back to business. "Who is Erik? And what did you mean when you said, 'the Vikings are next'?"

"I said that? When?"

"In your sleep. Last night."

"I don't know. Did I say anything else?"

"Something about golden slippers."

I considered that, but it made no more sense to me than warning Erik. I didn't know anyone named Erik. "I'm coming up empty, Andre. I don't know what I was talking about."

"How about fires and the sweet smell of success?"

"I said that? That doesn't ring any bells either."

"Don't worry about it. Maybe it will come back to you. You ready to do the cop thing now? Tell us everything that happened last night?"

"Only if you wrap your arms around me and hold me."

"Oh, man," Meagher said, "this is gonna be some weird interview."

"I thought you did all your interrogations this way, Steve," Dom prodded.

"Only the women. Men I interview from a distance."

The three of them, razor sharp even after their uncomfortable night, took me back through the whole thing, their questions fitting together like puzzle pieces. It was every bit as unpleasant as I'd anticipated. When they were finished, I was as limp as a dishrag. "Well, guess it's time to round up the usual suspects," Dom announced. "We've got at least three people who handled the coffee. It must have been one of them."

They were all impatient with me because I couldn't tell them more about my assailant. Even Andre. "Come on, Thea," he said, "think again. How tall was the person? Taller than you? Shorter? What kind of car was it?"

Finally I couldn't take it anymore. "Damn it, Lemieux. I was halfway to never-never land. I can only tell you a few things. Whoever it was had strong hands, was mean and enjoyed hurting me. Or at least didn't care about hurting me. And wasn't tall."

That didn't stop them. Not three of the best, intent on plying their trade. They went on asking questions until I was in tears and begging them to stop. Rosie had disappeared or I would have asked her for help.

She finally returned to rescue me. She fed me cereal and tea and gave me one of her own nightgowns. Then she sat by the bed in her wheelchair and read to me until I fell asleep.

In my dream I was sitting in the car. The dark figure had finished cutting me and was waving the knife in front of my face. "Maybe a little cut here and here." The knife lightly touched my cheek. I lowered my eyes to avoid seeing the blade, watching the ground instead. A steady stream of my own blood gushed into my lap. "Sweet dreams, McKusick," the figure said, closed the door and backed away.

"Did you notice the shoes?" I looked up in surprise. Carrie was sitting beside me, staring curiously at my gory wrists. "Don't let them kill you, Thea. It's a real bummer, being dead, believe me." She smiled sadly, brushing ineffectually at the streak of blood across her face. "Did you notice the shoes?"

"What about them?"

She shook her head. "I can't tell you, Thea. I'm dead. I just hope you can remember." She opened the door and vanished into the night.

"Wait, Carrie," I called, "don't go yet. Tell me what you meant. . . ."

It was time for another nap. Maybe Carrie would come back and tell me what she meant, but first I needed a drink. I looked around for Rosie to help me, but she'd fallen asleep in her chair. The plastic pitcher of ice water beside my bed was too heavy. It hurt to lift it. I ended up sticking my straw into the spout and drinking that way. Inelegant but effective. Dealing with my thirst left me depleted, like a spent battery. Last night it had been drugs that made me physically inert. Today it was exhaustion and loss of blood. My body had undergone a savage assault and a major shock. If I was patient, I'd recover, but right now I was weak and helpless and I couldn't fight it. I settled back against the pillow, closed my eyes and dozed.

A sharp click woke me. An unfamiliar nurse with frosted blond hair and tinted black-framed glasses was watching me. She laughed at my confusion, tugged off the wig and glasses, and locked the door. Then Eve Paris stood back, smiling maliciously. Under her white coat she was wearing a black pantsuit over a crisp white shirt, and the same strappy shoes. My eyes stopped on her gold toenails. Golden slippers. The answer to Carrie's question. Now I'd noticed her feet. Now that it was too late my mind flashed back quite clearly to those same feet, those same shoes, standing on the gravel beside my car as I looked helplessly away from the knife that was descending toward my wrist. To her familiar parting line, "Sweet dreams, McKusick." I reached for the call button but she took it from me and tossed it away. I looked for Rosie but she was gone.

"You're a bit slow today, aren't you," she said. "I wonder why? Looking for your pal on wheels I'll bet. Too bad. She went to get some food. I said I'd stay with you until she got back. People are so trusting, aren't they?" She came and sat down beside me on the bed, fingering the bandages on my wrist. "You just won't do what I want you to do, will you, Thea?"

"What do you mean?"

She shook her head. "You were such a loyal friend you wouldn't help us out. You were supposed to help me point the finger at Cliff, who would, of course, turn out to be perfectly innocent, leaving the police with a mysterious list of suspects and nothing they could prove. But you wouldn't play, even though I'd cast you perfectly. Who better than you to manage Florio and Meagher. Meagher because he'll follow any hot crotch that crossed his path, but you had to go and pick a fight with him, and Florio because he's a male menopause type who needs to prove he's still attractive and he's married to a cripple. But no. You're out there—the female equivalent of Honest Abe—trying to be so fair that every time you accuse Cliff, you accuse me as well. You wouldn't even die when you were supposed to. Oh well," she fumbled in her purse, "better late than never."

"You killed your mother?" I still couldn't quite grasp it, even now, even knowing that she'd tried to kill me. "Why?"

She stared at me in disbelief. "You can't mean you didn't figure it out? Come on, you're the detective. You tell me."

I struggled to organize my thoughts. I don't think very clearly when I'm panicked. What had I seen in her apartment that made her think I'd figured it out? "I never was a detective, Eve. You know it. I was just trying to make things right."

She nodded. "Thea the Fixer. Can you believe it? My parents wanted me to be like you. . . ."

I thought I had it. "The poem, right?" I said. "You killed her because you knew she'd slept with Padraig. And the catalogues where you bought the knife."

Her smile made my skin crawl. "You're getting warmer."

I thought about what Martha Coffey had told me. Of Eve sitting in her car. So she had been watching her mother. Following her. "Because she was sleeping with Waldemar?"

"Bingo. Score one for Thea." Her face crumpled up like a little girl about to cry. "Every time I got a boyfriend, she had to sleep with him. Not because she cared about any of them. Just to prove she could do it. To prove she was still more attractive."

I'd figured that out, too, I just hadn't realized it. That was what I'd been trying to tell Andre. Warn the Viking. Erik the Viking. Eve's Viking. Because he was bound to be next. "That was you I heard talking with Cliff last night, wasn't it."

She plucked a piece of lint off her sleeve and watched it float away. "Was it? I was afraid you might have heard that. Another one of the things that made this business necessary. You're slow, but you're smart."

"Did Cliff know?"

"About Helene? Before last night? No, but he had his suspicions, once he got over his fear that his beloved Rowan might have done it. He must have known I was going to kill you, though, when I told him about Helene and Padraig. He gave me the pills.

Gave back, that is. The ones he took from my apartment. They were too strong for me, he said."

"Padraig?"

"Well, I couldn't let him treat me that way and get away with it. You have no idea how much I loved him. How much it hurt me when he slept with her. Such a tragic thing, that accident. He really did have talent."

"What good do you think killing me will do? The police already suspect you. . . ."

"Suspicions are all they've got. Without you, they've got nothing," she said angrily. "No witnesses, no fingerprints, nothing! That's why I had Roddy bring you the coffee."

While she talked I was studying the room for something to use as a weapon. There was the IV pole, but I was too weak to swing it effectively. And the water pitcher, which presented the same problem. "Was it you who broke into my apartment and set the fire?"

She seemed genuinely surprised. "No. That wasn't me. Sorry to disappoint you. Guess you must have more than one enemy. I'm not surprised, the way you piss people off."

Maybe I could throw a Gideon's Bible at her and effect a miraculous transformation. She was digging around in her bag again, looking for whatever it was she needed to kill me. Even if I had to crawl, I wasn't going to wait around and make it easy for her. While her head was bent, I pulled the IV needle out of my arm and jerked on the tube so the whole apparatus fell on her. As it fell, I rolled out the other side of the bed and staggered to the door, fumbling with the lock, heard it click, and grabbed the doorknob.

"Stop or I'll shoot."

"Go ahead and shoot." I grabbed the handle and opened the door. A bullet smashed into the door frame beside my head, showering me with splinters. I crouched down and threw myself into the corridor, running into Andre. "Get down," I said, "she's got a gun." Dom and Steve, just behind him, went for their guns. Andre swung me into his arms and carried me down the corridor.

"Someday, Kozak, I am going to figure something out before you do."

"Just a knack for being in the right place at the right time, Trooper. Where the hell were you, anyway?"

He plopped me down in an empty wheelchair beside the nurses' station. "I'll be right back. . . ."

I grabbed his hand and held on with all my remaining strength. "No way, Andre. Let the other kids play cowboys and Indians. You said you wouldn't leave. That you'd keep me safe. Don't leave." My fingers were slipping off. I couldn't hold him if he wanted to go. There was blood seeping through the bandages on my wrists, and I could feel blood on my face. If he left me now, I'd never speak to him again. I stood up, using the counter of the nurses' station to support me, and got ready for my big scene. He was staring longingly down the corridor, where the action was.

"It's a simple matter of making choices, Andre. If you have to be a cop, and you can't resist going down there and joining the other guys, go ahead. And don't bother to come back. I'm a very understanding woman. Truly I am. But right now I need you more than they do." I concluded by pitching forward onto my face in a graceful Victorian faint and he was thoughtful enough to catch me, a nurse told me later, before I hit the floor and broke my nose. A good thing, since I am especially averse to breaking my nose. Once was enough.

After that I slept for a long time, a bottomless, immeasurable sleep, dreamless and untroubled. Sometimes I would come up, like a fish from the deep, and float just below the surface, never opening my eyes, listening to the sounds around me before plunging back down into the depths again. From my hiding place I heard Dom and Rosie come and go, checking on me, checking on Andre. I always knew when Rosie was there. She had an aura of strength and tranquillity. Once she sat beside me for a while and talked to me. She knew I was hiding out and she understood why.

Andre was always there. I could feel him. Sometimes lying beside me, sometimes sitting in a chair or talking on the phone. Once he sat and read to me for an hour, a wonderful funny story—I listened to it all—but even then I didn't wake up. My body needed the down time. I could almost feel it healing, making new blood, restoring itself. I wanted to know what had happened with Eve and I wanted to know who the intruder in my apartment had been, but both things could wait. Had to wait. For once I wasn't impatient. I was rushing nowhere. Just lying in the bed, letting my body sink down into the mattress, hugging my covers, glad to be warm, grateful to be alive. Somehow my friends kept the nurses from bothering me. Sure, they gathered vital signs, but at least they didn't wake me up to discuss my condition.

I understood, as I never could have before, the meaning of "scared to death." I had been. Once I woke up and started functioning again, I'd jump right back into the rat race—I knew myself well enough to be sure of that—this was the only chance I'd get to recover, reflect and heal.

They finally coerced me into waking up by preying on my weakness—hunger. The whole gang of them stood around and pressed delicious things under my nose. It was the bacon and coffee that finally teased me out. I opened my eyes and caught them all standing there, grinning like they were posing for a dumb family picture. "I'd like mine with cream, two sugars," I said, my voice odd and creaky, like a long-abandoned tool.

"I told you it would work," Dom said. "Welcome to the world of the living. We've missed you."

"You catch all the bad guys?"

"We've been waiting for you. You're the one with all the answers, you know. Actually," he said, "you told us a lot while you were sleeping. I think we know just about everything now. We just need to confirm it with a real live, conscious human being."

I raised my arms and held them out in front of me, assuming a zombielike trance. "Thea Kozak knows nothing. It is the Spirit. The Spirit speaks through me." My arms were too wobbly. I dropped them.

"Look, Spirit," Dom said, "let's get down to brass tacks here. We're all a bit impatient out in the real world."

"The spirit world is the real world, unbeliever. Only the spirits know for sure."

"I thought that was her hairdresser." Meagher said.

"Spirits don't have hairdressers. Are you ready for the answer?"

"Hold on, I'm lost," Rosie said, "what is the question?"

Andre answered. "The question is, what are the names and occupations of the two bad guys who attacked Thea Kozak during the month of May?"

"It sounds stupid when you put it that way," I said. "You do have them locked up, I hope."

"You mean there was more than one?" Rosie asked.

"Two. Eve and Valeria," I answered. "Do you?"

"Do I what?" Dom said.

"You mean the bad guys were both women?" Rosie said.

"That's right," Dom told her. "And yes, we have them."

"But you guys said Valeria couldn't have done it," I reminded him. "Though I never quite believed that. She was such an accomplished liar I wouldn't have believed anyone who said she was at home. What made you change your minds?"

"Her roommate had an attack of conscience when she heard the full story of what had happened," Dom explained. "Does this mean you finally remembered what it was you noticed that night? Harris will be tickled pink."

"I have had some time to think," I said, amused by the image of Officer Harris turned bright pink.

"Think?" Andre looked at me dubiously. "I thought you were sleeping. I've never seen anyone sleep like that."

"Sleeping is one of the things I do best."

"And sleep-related things . . ." He arched his eyebrows in that sexy, sardonic way I find so irresistible.

"Cut it out, you two. We're trying to get the facts here," Dom said, "and I don't mean the facts of life."

"Excuse me," Rosie said, "but what was it you remembered?"

"Perfume. She used to wear too much of it. Some awful thing she blended herself. She was very proud of it. Musk and gardenia. It smelled like a cheap bathroom cleaner. She called it 'Success.' It always made me sneeze. The person who hit me, who set the fire, wore that same scent."

"So that's what you meant by the sweet smell of success," Dom said. "Hell of a lot easier than trying to track down a perp identified only by the fact that he wore Old Spice."

"There's a business for you, Thea," Andre suggested. "Signature scents for the classy criminal."

"I already have a business, thank you very much." Which reminded me of the ambiguities surrounding my current contract. "What about Cliff? How much was he involved in all of this?"

Dom answered that, sounding bitter. "He says not at all. She says the same, and we've got nothing to tie him in. Only I don't believe him."

From what Eve had told me, I could fill in the missing lines from the conversation I'd overheard. Now it went something like this:

Eve: I got Thea involved to confuse things by casting suspicion on you.

Cliff: I don't understand why you did that.

Eve: She was supposed to get everyone thinking that it was you, but there isn't a thing anyone can use to connect you, and with things so stirred up, and Thea helping me, the poor, distraught daughter, no one would suspect me.

Cliff: So it was you. I don't know what you could have been thinking, involving Thea. She's not the kind to just adopt the party line. She's going to hear too much, and think about things. You know she searched your apartment.

Eve: So I'll just kill her, too. No big deal.

Cliff: You can't make a habit of it, Eve. Killing people just because you don't like the way they're behaving.

Eve: I do what's necessary. To protect myself. To protect you.

"Earth to Thea, come in please. What were you thinking?" Dom asked.

"He knew. That she planned to kill me at least, if not the details. Eve told him. Maybe not about the others until she told him, though I'm sure he suspected. That's why he was there to search the apartment just like I was. I guess I'm hopelessly naive. I was trying to protect him . . . for him . . . for both of them . . . so they could come out of this with a chance for a healed relationship. I thought she was off-the-wall, wrongheaded, but I never suspected . . . how could I be so loyal to him while he could listen calmly to her announcement that she was going to kill me and then let her go and do it? Without a word. Without any effort to warn me, or save me. Like I was as disposable as a used tissue. It makes me feel like such a fool. I had so much loyalty to them and they had none to me."

"Maybe he didn't know what she'd done," Dom suggested.

"But he saw me. He had to know I was drugged."

"He was used to seeing drugged people. Maybe it didn't register," Meagher said.

"Don't make excuses for him," I began, feeling a sort of resigned despair as another hero crumbled, "he may not have played an active part, but he at least failed to help me when he could have. It might not be a legal crime but it's a moral crime. . . ."

Rosie shook her head. "But Eve was all he had left."

"Don't you dare take his side," I said.

"Believe me, I'm not. I'm horrified at what they did to you. I'm just trying to understand."

"I still feel like a fool," I said again, "a trusting fool." I collapsed back against the pillows. "What about Eve's boyfriend?"

"He's okay," Andre said. "Guess she hadn't gotten around to him yet."

"But she killed Padraig. She told me so. When I was trying to figure out Helene, everyone I talked to gave me such a different picture that it was like looking in a funhouse mirror. It must have been even stranger for Eve, seeing everything distorted through the prism of her own anger and self-involvement. To her, we were all the bad guys and she was just trying to make things right."

Suzanne had come in while I was talking and stood by the door, listening quietly. When I finished, she said, "Valeria was the same way. So sure all her problems were someone else's fault. Maybe you didn't see through Eve but you saw through her. You aren't a fool, you know, you're just a good person and you assume the people you know and care about are good people, too."

It didn't cheer me up very much. Despite the rest and the support of my friends, I felt like a retread that was shedding. All achy and tired and useless. "Tell me again. You did arrest them? They are in jail? Because otherwise I'm going to Tahiti. I can't go around watching my back all the time. I couldn't live that way."

"Don't worry," Dom said, "they are both off the streets."

"Maybe I'll go to Tahiti anyway. I'm not doing much good around here. If there's something like the reverse Midas touch, I've got it," I said. "Everything I touch I spoil. Now I've spoiled your honeymoon, too."

"Not at all," she said. "I couldn't stay away and neither could Paul. Too many interesting things to do here. Like going to the doctor."

"And if I believe that, you've got a bridge to sell me, right? I've spent a fair amount of time around doctors myself and I wouldn't cross the street to see one if I didn't have to. I sure wouldn't come back from Bermuda for the pleasure." Then it hit me that maybe this wasn't something casual. "You aren't . . . I mean, there isn't . . . I mean, are you all right?"

She gave me this enormous, playful, exasperating grin. "Well, it's pretty serious. I'm pregnant."

"Pregnant? You just got married on Saturday!" The others were watching us with amusement.

She shook her head and rolled her eyes. "Maybe I shouldn't tell you this, sweet naive thing that you are, but I was not a virgin bride."

I nestled down into my pillow, blinking back absurd, sentimental tears. Paul, who had gone down the hall to find some cups, came in waving a bottle of champagne.

"None for me, thanks," Suzanne said, "I want junior or junioress here born with all its fingers and toes." The cork exploded with a satisfying pop.

And we all lifted our cups and drank to life.

BOSTON PUBLIC LIBRARY

3 9999 02793 391 8

m

10/95

MYS

FLORA, K

WITHDRAWN
No longer the property of the
Boston Public Library.
Sale of this material benefits the Library